"I wanted to know what passion was like," Caro said. "I had read about coupling in medical texts and . . . I was curious."

"Did I satisfy your curiosity?"

"I suppose so." Which was a masterful understatement. Passion was so much more devastating than she had ever expected. At least passion with this man was.

Max put his finger to her lips. "I had never experienced anything like that night. And pray don't tell me it was the island's magical spell. It was far more than that."

"What do you mean?"

"You have no idea, do you?" Reaching up, he gently pushed a tendril of hair back from her forehead. "Let's just say you helped me face returning to the war."

She was taken aback by the look in his eyes. It was almost . . . sensual. No man had ever looked at her that way, with desire. Except for Max. Except for that night.

"You have haunted me ever since," he said simply, his voice no more than a whisper.

He had haunted her as well. . . .

Also by Nicole Jordan:

THE LOVER

Notorious Series:
THE SEDUCTION
THE PASSION
DESIRE
ECSTASY
THE PRINCE OF PLEASURE

MASTER of TEMPTATION

NICOLE JORDAN

BALLANTINE BOOKS • NEW YORK

This book contains an excerpt from the forthcoming edition of *Lord of Seduction* by Nicole Jordan. This excerpt has been set for this edition only and may not reflect the final content of the forthcoming edition.

A Ballantine Book
Published by The Random House Publishing Group

www.ballantinebooks.com

ISBN 0-8041-1981-3

Manufactured in the United States of America

First Edition: May 2004

OPM 10 9 8 7 6 5 4 3 2 1

This book is dedicated to
veterans of all our wars,
my late father and my brother included,
with thanks for their courage and sacrifice.

Ancient Myth or Enduring Truth?

Around myriad hearth fires, tales are recounted of a time long vanished—songs of romance and passion and glory, of a legendary leader who wielded his sword for right. Legend holds that he perished but that his legacy lives on, his sword harbored by an enchanted isle, enduring to safeguard and protect humankind.

Most believe the world is kept safe by powerful rulers and mighty armies. Only a select few guess at the truth. For a millennium, the Guardians of the Sword have stood against evil. Operating in secret, they use an arsenal of guile and skill to champion justice and defend right with might.

Prologue

The Isle of Cyrene,
August 1813

The ruins seemed enchanted in the moonlight. Silver pools rippled luminously in the night shadows, fed by a hot spring that cascaded gently down terraced stairs of granite, the last vestiges of a Roman bath. Yet the spellbinding sight failed to soothe Caro Evers as usual. Her restless tension only heightened as she rode closer.

Halting at the foot of the terrace, Caro slid from the aging mare's back. Beyond the cliff's eastern edge stretched the shimmering Mediterranean, calm and serene beneath the brilliant disk of the moon. This was a spectacular place, even on an island known for its uncanny beauty, but tonight the serenity seemed a stark contrast to her disquietude.

She felt as nervous as a girl meeting her secret lover.

Which was absurd. The major wasn't her lover, no matter what foolish fantasies her mind insisted on conjuring. She wasn't even certain he would come.

In agitation Caro bent to pluck a delicate white orchid, then left her horse to graze on the wild grass and ferns that grew among the crevices as she made her way toward the baths. A fresh salt breeze ruffled her muslin skirts, scented by honeysuckle that twined among the ancient stones and with pine from Cyrene's wooded mountain slopes. Although night had long fallen, the rock beneath her bare feet still held warmth from the summer sun as she climbed the carved steps that had been trod for more than a millennium.

When she passed beneath an arched portal, her heart leapt. A man stood at the parapet wall above her, gazing out at the vast, moonlit sea.

Major Maxwell Leighton.

She recognized him at once, even though they had met only three days ago. Few of the islanders possessed such a tall form, such powerfully set shoulders, such authoritative bearing. And no one else could make her pulse quicken with a mere glance from his compelling blue eyes, as he could.

Since the major's arrival on a mission of mercy, she'd spent nearly the entire time with him, locked in a desperate battle, fighting for a dying man's life.

You came tonight, Caro reflected with relief. He obviously intended to bathe. He had already removed his boots and the short blue jacket of his Hussars uniform, and wore merely breeches and a white shirt.

When he glanced over his shoulder at her, she suddenly became conscious of her own disheveled appearance: the skirts of her oldest gown swirling around her bare feet, her curling brown hair unpinned, spilling in even wilder disarray than usual. She tried to control her self-conscious flush.

He spoke in a low voice. "Are you certain you want me invading your haven?"

No, I'm not certain. She came frequently to the Roman ruins to bathe in the pools, usually when she was physically spent and aching after a hard bout of fencing practice. Rarely did she allow anyone to intrude on her solitude here. But after the strain of the past few days, the major needed the peace and beauty of the ruins to allay his exhaustion. Needed the soothing effects of the silken waters. They both did.

"I don't consider your presence an invasion," she replied honestly. "I asked you to come."

Climbing, Caro moved to stand beside him at the crumbling stone wall, her heart beating faster simply at his nearness.

It was startling how her body responded to him. She had never felt such a primal reaction to any man. The island of Cyrene was said to have a mythical ability to seduce the senses, but until now she'd always thought herself immune to the spell. True, Maxwell Leighton was one of the most strikingly handsome men she had ever met, with his deep blue eyes, lean features, and raven hair. But she had known stunning men before. Quite a number of them, in fact, for Cyrene had more than its fair share.

She rarely had felt such powerful feminine feelings, though. For three days now she had tried to repress her fierce attraction to Major Leighton, as well as the missish emotions that were so uncharacteristic of her.

Most disturbing was the heat and intensity in those eyes; when he looked at her, he aroused a wild yearning in her blood, making her feel as if she couldn't take a deep breath.

Willing herself to calm, Caro focused on the glimmering vista of the sea. She could hear the soft whisper of the waves below as they swelled in a gentle, timeless rhythm.

"Is Yates still sleeping quietly?" she asked, breaking the hush.

"Yes, thank God," the major responded. "For the first time in weeks he has found a semblance of peace."

Lieutenant John Yates had lost a leg in Spain during the most recent grueling battle against Napoleon's forces, and the wound had refused to heal. When he'd grown weaker and more feverish by the day, he had begged his commanding officer to take him home to his island, but the raw wound had turned septic during the voyage.

Unwilling to abandon the dying man, Major Leighton had remained on Cyrene, waiting for the end that had never come. Miraculously the young lieutenant's condition had turned around early this morning; his fever had broken, and he was expected to survive.

"I am immeasurably grateful to you," the major murmured. "You saved Yates's life."

"It was not just I," Caro demurred. "Dr. Allenby has the true medical skill. I merely helped."

"No, you were the one who stayed by his side hour after hour."

True, she had nursed the lieutenant constantly because the island doctor had other patients to tend. But Major Leighton had played a vital role as well—keeping vigil between his agitated pacing, obediently performing whatever tasks were needed without complaint, holding the delirious lieutenant down while she poulticed the terrible injury and poured noxious-tasting medicines down his throat and applied cold compresses to his burning body.

"Yates is alive," Leighton insisted, "because you refused to let him die. I think it was your sheer willpower that saved him."

Caro felt absurdly warmed by his praise. "Well, I am known for my stubbornness."

That drew a fleeting smile from him. She had never seen him smile, and the charm of it made her breath falter. Still, it had been Leighton's concern for his wounded subordinate, rather than his potent masculine appeal, that had drawn her to him from the first.

They had grown closer during the long, dark hours of their ordeal. They were no longer mere strangers, not after sharing such a turmoil of emotions: fear, despair, hope, and finally, profound elation. In winning their victory, they had formed a bond that was almost tangible.

She found herself fiercely regretting that he would be leaving on the morrow.

"I think you give me too much credit," Caro said. "According to John, you were the one who saved his life by warding off a saber attack."

"Yet he would never have been wounded in the first place if he hadn't leapt directly in the path of a cavalry charge in order to shield me. I am greatly indebted to him. As I am to you."

At the fervency of his tone, Caro turned her head and saw the major gazing down at her in intense contemplation. When she met his dark-lashed eyes, an unexpected heat washed over her, starkly primitive and unmistakably sexual.

Caro looked away. It was foolish to feel such yearnings. She doubted she held much sexual appeal for this beautiful man. Her looks were comely enough, but she suspected he found her femininity wanting after observing her for the past few days.

She couldn't blame him. Ladies of genteel station did not deal with blood and gore and dying men by choice, assisting the island doctor with patient surgeries and the injuries of unrelated men.

Nor did they engage in dangerous missions across much of Europe, wielding weapons in defense of a valiant cause—to root out evil and tyranny.

She was not like most other women. Her natural gift for healing set her apart from her peers, but her clandestine vocation separated her even further. She was a Guardian, a member of a secret society of protectors sworn to uphold the ancient ideals once championed by a legendary leader.

But her unconventional career was *not* a subject she could discuss with an outsider. Certainly not Major Leighton, who would leave Cyrene tomorrow, likely never to return.

The thought of his leaving sent a pang of distress welling within Caro. One thing was certain: She would never forget him. Although she fervently wished she could.

Maxwell Leighton made her long for things she'd convinced herself she didn't want or need. At the ripe age of twenty-four, she had forgone the things most women considered important—marriage, children, husband . . . even lovers.

Lovers. Caro felt an ache constrict her chest.

In her wildest fantasies she might have wondered what it would be like to experience this man's lovemaking, but he was unlikely to choose her as his lover. After battling beside her for the lieutenant's life, she imagined he regarded her more as a comrade in arms than an object of desire.

"You will continue to care for Yates?" he asked, his voice dark with concern.

"Of course," she replied with a sigh. "I don't think you need worry, Major. He is past the danger now. He will heal eventually."

"But he will be forever maimed." Leighton shut his eyes, while his body gave a faint shudder.

She thought she understood his despair. He felt responsible for his lieutenant's sacrifice. And he himself was clearly suffering from the terrible stresses of war.

The major hadn't been wounded in battle as his subordinate had been, but after serving as a cavalry officer for eight years, he had invisible wounds that were just as raw. His emotional pain was palpable. Through their dark hours together, she'd seen the torment in his eyes that hinted at the inner demons he was fighting. A battle-weary soldier sick to his soul of death and destruction.

She wanted to help him, to bring him comfort somehow, but she felt at a loss. His wasn't a physical wound that could be healed by potions and poultices.

"The lieutenant says you are a hero," she said finally.

Leighton's response was a faint scoffing sound. "If you only knew." He looked at his hands, as if seeing them still stained with blood. "You are a healer, but I take lives. And I am not even considering the countless men who have died under my command. Or the . . . friends I've lost."

"But think of the countless others you have saved."

His reply was filled with bleakness. "That's the hell of it. I couldn't save them."

Her heart ached for him. She didn't need him to explain his feelings. He felt the guilt of surviving when he wasn't able to save others.

As a healer, she had fought similar battles herself, attempting to defy the Grim Reaper. And too many times she had lost.

"You cannot hold yourself to blame for the madness of war, Major," Caro said quietly. "You can only keep striving." She placed a gentle hand on his arm. "It takes remarkable courage to confront death as you do, day after day. But I—and all our countrymen—am supremely grateful to you and the other brave men like you who are willing to keep trying."

For a long moment he didn't answer. He simply stared down at her, searching her face, his eyes dark and fathomless as the night.

"An angel of mercy," he said finally. "Are you always this comforting?"

Caro felt a flush rise in her cheeks. "I try. As you said, I am a healer. And I don't like to see anyone in pain."

"And you think I am in pain?"

"Are you not?" she asked softly.

He gave a harsh whisper of a laugh. "You're too damned perceptive."

Eager to shift the focus of his intense contemplation, she responded with another question. "Must you return tomorrow? Perhaps you could remain on Cyrene a while longer."

"It's tempting, I admit." He glanced to his left toward where France lay north of the island, then farther west, toward Spain, where the bloody Peninsular War was being fought. "I'm not eager to return to the slaughter. I have little stomach for watching my men become cannon fodder." The major shook his head. "But they need me. I can't forsake them."

"Even a few days would do you good. With the lieutenant in such a critical state, you had no chance to enjoy the peace of our little island. I assure you, it can prove a balm for the soul."

"Are you saying your island possesses some peculiar magic?"

"No magic, but the sun and fresh air and the sea are healing. And legend holds that Apollo cast a spell here to create a lovers' paradise."

"I've never been one to believe in such things as spells."

"Nor I," Caro agreed.

But spell or no, Cyrene was a haven of beauty with its azure seas, sun-splashed slopes, and golden valleys. It had the power to soothe raw, ravaged nerves, bitter wounds of the spirit, even the deepest grief. Which was why she had asked the major to come here tonight.

He glanced behind him at the moonlit ruin with its shining, terraced pools. "There does seem to be an enchantment about this place."

His unsettling gaze focused on her again, and a long silence followed.

Then slowly he reached up to slide his hand beneath her hair, capturing her nape in a gentle vise, half turning her to face him. Caro drew a shallow breath as he stared down at her mouth, his lids half-lowered, fringed by black lashes.

Her heart began to pound. No man had ever looked at her this way, with something very much like desire. Was it possible he felt desire for her?

"Major Leighton . . ."

"My name is Max."

She thought perhaps he intended to kiss her, but instead his other hand closed over hers, where unwittingly she had crushed the orchid between her fingers.

He took the bloom from her and lifted it to her cheek, running the delicate petals over her lips.

Helpless to move, she could only stare up at him.

"I need healing, sweet Caro. Can you heal me?"

Her heart lurched crazily at the question. He seemed to be asking for more than simple comfort. And she wanted to give it to him. . . .

Suddenly he gave a start, as if waking from a daze, and took a step back, distancing himself with a muttered oath. "Forgive me. I didn't come here to seduce you."

Caro felt oddly bereft. That simple contact had left her shaken—yet his curse had filled her with hope. Perhaps he truly had wanted to kiss her but remembered that he was an officer and a gentleman. An honorable man would be reluctant to take advantage of their isolation.

But what if I want to be seduced? The unbidden thought caught her off guard.

"My coming here was a mistake," he said in a low voice, starting to turn away.

A feeling of panic swept through Caro. "No! Please don't go." She couldn't bear to see him leave. "You haven't tried the bath. And I promised to show you the techniques of massage."

"I don't want to put you to such trouble."

"It is no trouble, truly. And you need it, Major. You know you do."

He must have heard the plea in her voice, for he stood there in indecision. "This isn't wise."

Striving for calm, Caro adopted a mock sternness in her tone. "I have far more medical expertise than you do, Major. You should heed my advice."

The shadows in his eyes softened slightly with a faint hint of amusement. "Or what? Will you bully me into doing your bidding the way you did Yates?"

"Indeed. I have a variety of methods to deal with recalcitrant patients, which I won't hesitate to use if necessary."

"Your threat sounds ominous. Very well."

Stripping off his shirt, he tossed the garment down beside the stone wall. Immediately Caro felt her pulse leap at the sight of his powerful torso, rippling with muscle.

"Which pool should I use?"

"The middle one is the deepest—and the warmest. You'll find it more appealing, despite the warmth of the night."

"Do you intend to join me?"

She hesitated for a heartbeat. "Yes. A massage will be more effective in concert with the heat of the water."

He gave a deliberate shrug, circling his shoulders as if trying to relieve the ache. "I would give a year off my life if you could give me some respite from the pain."

Turning, he made his way across to the middle pool. "You told me your Dr. Allenby sometimes employs the Eastern arts here on Cyrene. Is massage part of the Eastern philosophy? You were constantly working Yates's limbs to keep the blood flowing and to ease the pain."

"Yes," Caro said. "Eastern medicine puts great faith in the healing power of touch."

She watched then as the major silently shed his breeches.

She had studied human anatomy before. And she had seen unclothed men countless times. But they were all cadavers or patients who were ill or injured. There was nothing frail or infirm about this man. He looked more like a Greek god, long-limbed and perfectly sculpted. There was a wild, primitive beauty to his body. The silvery light accentuated every hard muscle in his wide shoulders, his powerful back, which tapered to narrow hips, his taut buttocks, his sinewy horseman's thighs. . . .

The brazen sight of him took her breath away, while his casual nudity flustered her. But then, he evidently didn't suspect she was sexually inexperienced. With her unconventional vocation, he would likely assume she knew about men and lovemaking. In the army, the only female medical orderlies to attend wounded soldiers were camp followers.

He eased himself into the pool. The lower side sloped much like the head of a chaise lounge, and he lay back, reclining so that the surface level came halfway to his chest. Shutting his eyes momentarily, he gave a harsh sigh of contentment as the heated water washed over him.

"You were right," he murmured at last. "This is paradise."

The silence that ensued, however, had the opposite effect on Caro. Her tension had returned with a vengeance.

She knew now that she couldn't remain professional and indifferent with Max Leighton, as if he were any other patient. How had she ever thought she could?

"Are you coming in?" He was waiting for her, she realized. Watching.

It struck her then that she also had been lying to herself. She'd thought she had persuaded him to come here tonight out of simple compassion. Because he was hurting and she had never been able to turn away from anyone in pain.

But had she secretly hoped for something more?

She could hear her heartbeat vying with the low hum of the cicadas in the warm night and wondered if her inner turmoil showed.

Was this her chance to indulge her wild yearnings? Her feverish imaginings? She had controlled her restless longings for years, content to live her life without passion, on the shelf by choice. Yet tonight that could change. . . .

"Caro?"

When he called to her again, she obeyed, as if lured by some irresistible force. She halted at the edge of the pool, and after a moment's hesitation, let her gown drop to the ground.

When she lowered herself into the bath, her cambric shift floated around her hips. The warmth of the water caressed her body as she waded toward him, but it was the heat in Max Leighton's eyes that made her feel flushed and feverish. His intense glance set her quivering.

By the time she reached him, she felt clumsy with nerves, yet she tried to keep her tone even. "Give me your back."

He eased away from the wall and turned so that his back was to her. Kneeling behind him, Caro raised her hands and gently curved her fingers over his shoulders. At first contact she could feel the rigid tightness of the muscles.

"Close your eyes," she ordered softly.

With a light pressure, she began massaging, making small circles with the tips of her fingers. The flesh beneath his skin felt as hard as wood, the tendons in his neck as taut as bow strings. His body was one massive knot, no doubt from both physical exertion and keeping his dark emotions bottled inside for so long.

"Just try to relax and feel my touch," Caro murmured. "Let the water's warmth soothe you."

She heard him exhale as he surrendered to her ministrations, and she earnestly set about her task, using her fingers to work the strained, tight muscles in his shoulders, her thumbs pressing more deeply into the worst knots. When she struck a particularly painful spot, he arched in protest but made no sound.

Eventually she shifted lower, moving over the slick wet skin of his upper back. She faltered when her thumb found a long ridge near his right shoulder blade. "What is this?"

"A bullet graze."

The answer disturbed her, reminding her of the dangerous life a military officer led, but she moved on, slowly kneading down his back with her fingers, pressing with the heels of her hands.

She covered every inch of skin, feeling the texture

marred by other scars of war. At last the hard muscles seemed to be softening, even though the tension in his body was not relaxing as she'd hoped. Worse, an unmistakable tension was rising within her own body. The sleek flesh beneath her fingers seemed suddenly hot.

Abruptly leaving off, she moved up to his neck again. He gave a faint groan of mingled pleasure and pain as her fingers gently dug into the tendons there. After a moment, she lifted her hands to his ebony hair. It felt soft and satiny to the touch as she began massaging his scalp. She heard him sigh in pure pleasure this time, a sound that filled her with pleasure as well.

Caro drew an uneven breath, aware of the erotic sensations flowing through her. The rippling warmth of the water was somehow seductive, the silver hush of the night as unreal as a dream.

Was he feeling any of the same primitive feelings that were claiming her?

Slowly she let her hands slide down his back again, her palms molding to the warm skin, the sculpted muscles. He must have sensed the difference in her touch, for she felt a sharpened tautness in his body at her unintentional caresses.

And yet she couldn't stop herself. Of its own volition, her thumb returned to the bullet scar. She let her fingers linger there, brushing the grooved ridge, wishing she could have prevented his pain. With a murmur of sympathy, she bent to press her lips against the scarred flesh.

She felt him stiffen, felt his long hesitation before he slowly turned to lean back against the sloping wall once more.

Her heart beat an erratic pulse in her throat as he

looked at her. She was no longer a healer now; she was a woman. And the molten heat in his gaze only heightened the wild urges rioting within her.

He lifted his hand to touch her cheek, holding her gaze with his passionate intensity. "You must be some kind of dream . . . a lovely figment of my imagination. But if I am dreaming, I don't want to wake."

"Nor do I," she said, her voice scarcely a whisper.

He drew her down to him to lie fully against his hard length while his arms came around her. Only the wet fabric of her shift lay between their naked skin.

Caro felt her stomach flutter violently.

His mouth almost touching hers, he brought her even closer, pressing her lower body against the rigid, swelling flesh at his groin, letting her feel his arousal.

She had seen animals mating, so she understood in principle the act of lovemaking. And her dearest friend, Isabella, had shared risqué tales of her various lovers. But nothing had prepared Caro for the reality of this man, for the feel of him, so swollen with male need. Or for the hot, shameless sensation that washed over her helpless body.

His warm breath caressed her lips when he spoke. "I want you."

The fierce declaration took her aback. No man had ever said those words to her. His desire for her couldn't be more clear. Yet she thought she understood: he wanted her for physical solace. He wanted to feel *life*, not death—and passion was a most profound expression of life. No doubt Max Leighton would respond this way to most any warm female body.

Even so, Caro couldn't deny the responsive desire his words stirred in her.

His mouth covered hers then. His kiss was hard and fervent, demanding and desperate at the same time. She could feel the dark need in him as his tongue slid urgently into her mouth, stealing her breath completely.

An aching sound came from her throat, and her fingers clutched reflexively at the taut muscles of his shoulders. She had never experienced anything like Max's dark, almost savage kiss.

Long moments later he broke off with a groan. Shutting his eyes, he rested his forehead against hers, as if struggling for control.

"You should stop me before this goes too far," he urged, his voice undeniably hoarse.

Bewildered and more than a little dazed, Caro shook her head. "I . . . don't want you to stop," she said shakily.

For a dozen heartbeats he didn't respond. Then he drew back, his eyes searching. "What *do* you want, angel? Tell me." His hands came up to cup her breasts, his palms pressing against her nipples, which pebbled beneath the cambric bodice.

A streak of fire shot through her, and Caro had to fight to suppress an instinctive whimper. What she truly wanted was scandalous. She wanted *him*. To hold her. To touch her. To show her what pleasure was.

What if she was to give her body to him? an insistent voice asked. She never expected to see Max Leighton again after tonight. Once he returned to the war, he was unlikely to have any other reason for coming again to the island. And he could be killed. . . .

The thought of this strong, vital man dying wrenched at her heart. But it only made her internal argument stronger. This could be his last night for passion.

And hers.

She couldn't deny her yearning to be fully a woman. And now it was like a fire burning deep in her heart.

For once in her life she wanted to experience a man's lovemaking. One moment to last her a lifetime.

Absurdly, though, she couldn't bring herself to declare her need so boldly. In her role as a Guardian she had faced danger and intrigue countless times, but now she felt ridiculously awkward and shy. She could only answer indirectly and hope he understood.

"I . . . am not as experienced as you think me."

He went very still. "Have you never been with a man?"

"Truthfully . . . no."

A new silence lay between them. Moonlight played over his chiseled features while she waited for his response. Water lapped at her breasts and eddied between her legs, further sensitizing her feminine flesh, awakening long dormant desires, making her keenly aware of the hollow ache inside her.

"You had better go, then." His voice was raw, almost harsh.

"I want to stay." Her own voice dropped to a nearly inaudible whisper. "Please . . . I want to know what passion is. Will you show me?"

His hesitation drew out for an eternity. "I should be shot for even considering what you're suggesting."

"Please, Max?"

A tenderness stole over his expression. "Are you certain?"

She had never been more certain of anything in her life.

Tonight she would finally understand the mysteries

between a man and woman. She could surrender to her most secret desires. She could be as wild and needy and womanly as she wished.

She had little doubt this man's lovemaking would leave her breathless. She had no doubt whatsoever she would cherish this memory for as long as she lived.

In answer, she reached up to touch his lean cheek. "I know sometimes there is pain, so please . . . be gentle."

"You needn't even ask."

He *was* gentle. Incredibly so. She could feel his determined control as he brushed kisses soft as butterflies' wings against her lips, along her jaw, the skin of her throat. Still nuzzling, he lifted her up and eased her legs on either side of his hard thighs.

With long fingers, he lowered the bodice of her shift so that her bare, trembling breasts spilled out.

Caro tensed, wondering if he would be disappointed at her physical attributes, but the heat of his gaze never faltered as he surveyed her wet, glistening flesh. His brazen scrutiny made her cheeks flame. And when his hands molded to the swelling curves, they seemed warmer than the water.

He took his time, massaging gently, rhythmically, and she forgot her apprehension. He drew out his caresses, as if determined to arouse her the way she had unwittingly done to him.

The slow, languid motion was unbelievably sensual. Yet Caro was unprepared for the rush of feeling when he bent to capture a peaked nipple with his mouth. Her breath fled as he suckled her. Heat flooded through her, while a nearly unbearable ache curled low in the pit of her stomach and between her thighs.

For long minutes his lips and tongue aroused her. It was tantalizing, intoxicating, sending thrills of sensation to every nerve in her body. With the same languor his hands began to stroke down her back, tracing the curve of her hips, her buttocks, making slow, kneading circles.

Her head fell back, and she sighed at the sweet pleasure of his seduction. Finally his lips left her breasts and traced a blazing path back up her throat. His breath was hot in her ear when he asked, "Do you need this?"

Not waiting for a reply, he caught the hem of her shift and drew the dripping garment over her head, baring her fully to his gaze.

His eyes grew darker if that was possible. He seemed enthralled and fascinated by the sight of her.

It was the night magic, she knew. No doubt the island's seductive sensuality was intensifying his hunger. But she didn't care what the reason. She felt the same hunger. She felt beautiful when he looked at her.

A drugged, dreamy languor filled her as his hands slid down her body again, sensuously caressing. Slowly his palm moved over her thigh to her belly, then lower to the curls at the juncture of her thighs. When he found the most tender, vibrant part of her body, Caro shivered.

He cupped her, stroking. Then one finger slid slowly into her, making her gasp aloud.

Ignoring her instinctive protest, he went on exploring, arousing, his teasing fingers gliding inside her . . . lingering . . . withdrawing . . . only to begin all over again.

At his rhythmic assault, desire swelled dizzily within

her, along with a wanton excitement. Caro arched against him, her aching breasts seeking closer contact with his naked chest.

"Easy," he murmured, but the husky rasp of his voice held satisfaction.

Drawing back, he guided her hand to his loins, to the male member that swelled so rigidly erect against her abdomen. Even in the silken water, it felt hot, throbbing to the touch.

He gave her the choice, waiting. But there was no longer any choice for Caro. Foolish or wise, she wanted this. Wanted him.

"Yes," she whispered, replying to his silent query.

His eyes burned as his hands went to her hips and lifted her up, centering her over the engorged crest of his phallus, only to gently lower her again.

His entry was infinitely slow and careful; her body was slick with feminine need. But even so, the invasion felt overwhelming. She went very still with the shock of it.

There was no real pain, but she felt stretched and penetrated almost to the breaking point.

His warm lips touched her fluttering eyelids, her cheeks, her lips, until her panting breaths began to lessen.

"Better now?"

"Yes . . ."

The dull ache had subsided, yet she was afraid to move with the huge, pulsing shaft so deep inside her. But then his hands closed over her hips, and he drew her the slightest degree nearer.

A spark of pleasure kindled inside her that made her shudder. When she felt his hard, masculine flesh press deeper, filling her, she realized her body had begun to accept and even welcome his impalement.

His mouth went from earlobe to throat, sliding down to her bare collarbone, then farther. He was suckling her breasts again, this time more strongly, his tongue rasping and licking, setting off a hot, urgent clamoring inside her.

Whimpering, Caro melted helplessly against him, pushing her quivering flesh hard against his searing mouth. She was trembling with sensations so vibrant, she thought she might burst into flame.

Then his wonderful hands slid down once more between their bodies, his thumb finding the slick bud hidden within her feminine folds.

"No . . ." She said the word instinctively in a raw, shaking voice as she tried to pull back from the frightening intensity.

"Yes," Max insisted, not allowing her to escape.

One hand clamped on her hip while his other fingers stroked her sexual center. He kissed her again, his tongue thrusting deep into her mouth, just as his rampant arousal was doing to her body.

The dark waves of pleasure built relentlessly until the ache was almost intolerable. Caro writhed with the wild sensuality of it.

A moment later a panicky, anguished sound escaped her. Her fingers bit into the corded muscles of his arms as molten fire engulfed her.

She clung to him, shaking helplessly, her cries shattering the night as the inferno continued . . . so powerful, so devastating, it left her senses reeling.

Dazed and depleted, she collapsed on his chest, her heartbeat loud in her ears as he cradled her in his arms.

"I never knew," she murmured long moments later, her voice hoarse with passion. "I suppose that is why they call it 'the little death.' "

"That is exactly why." She heard the smile in his voice, felt his lips press against the damp hair curling at her temple. "But there is more, sweetheart."

"*More?*" She gave a husky, disbelieving laugh.

"Much more." He moved his hips slightly, so that she could feel his still-thick arousal thrusting deeper.

Breathless once more, Caro drew back to gaze into his dark eyes. "Will you teach me?"

"It will be my honor—and my pleasure."

His hands cupped her buttocks once more, and he began to rock her gently against him.

His eyes squeezed shut as he surged slowly into her. He was just as careful this time, but she sensed his effort at control. His face grew taut, his jaw rigid, while his breathing became as tortured as hers had been.

She felt his desperate need when his mouth blindly sought hers, heard it in his voice as he whispered against her lips, "Heal me, fierce angel."

At his plea, she was lost. His dark desire filled her with tenderness, with the ardent longing to soothe his war-ravaged soul.

Her arms came around him tightly, and she returned his fervent kiss with all the yearning she'd kept hidden for years.

For tonight she belonged to this magnificent man. Whatever he wanted, she would do. And what he clearly wanted, *needed,* was to surrender to the night, to the moonlight, to the island's passionate enchantment.

To her.

Chapter One

London,
September 1814

Partially shielded from view by a potted palm, Max Leighton leaned against a marble column and surveyed the crowded ballroom without enthusiasm. After enduring so many years of war, he had returned to England resolved to banish his grim memories by losing himself in the mundane pleasures of civilian life.

But this was not what he had in mind—pursued by countless matchmaking mamas and their nubile young daughters, eager to ensnare him in their nets. In the current craze of victory celebrations, a wealthy, decorated war veteran made an extremely eligible matrimonial prize, Max had learned to his chagrin.

His mouth curled in a wry grimace. He had little appetite for fighting on the battlefield of love, especially when he had no interest in settling down in marriage. But even the more seasoned beauties of the ton were vying for his attention now. Needing a respite from his popularity, he'd escaped the ballroom floor moments ago and sought refuge behind the palm.

If only his cavalry regiment could see him now, Max thought, amused in spite of himself.

But few of his men would be sympathetic to his

plight: nestled in the lap of luxury, courted and feted by so many eager females.

What had happened to him? Before his army days, he hadn't considered balls and soirees and garden parties so trivial. But perhaps the genteel challenges of the Beau Monde simply couldn't match the satisfaction of saving Europe from the bloody machinations of a despot.

Or perhaps it was the women themselves who aroused his dissatisfaction. None of them had the honest charms of one woman he'd found impossible to forget.

His gaze narrowing, Max let his mind drift back, as it had countless times since his mission of mercy more than a year ago.

He had never expected to discover a Mediterranean island paradise, or experience an enchanting night of passion with an innocent temptress. He hadn't been able to forget that night on Cyrene or the bewitching woman who had offered him solace.

He'd fought the growing urge to return to the island and seek out Caro Evers simply to see if the magic he'd felt with her was real or the result of the extraordinary circumstances. If, during the long months of war, he had built her up in his memory into an impossible ideal.

He had no real excuse to make such a journey. By all reports Lieutenant Yates had recovered well enough from his injuries to lead a satisfactory life. Yates had found gainful employment as a secretary to an elderly noblemen on the island, and his cheerful letters showed no hint of bitterness at becoming a cripple.

But even so, Max told himself, he could use the pretext of checking on his former subordinate—

"Don't tell me you are in hiding?" an amused male voice broke into his reflections. "Do you realize how many belles you are disappointing?"

Christopher, Viscount Thorne, stood before him, surveying him with wry understanding. They had met the previous year on Cyrene during Max's brief visit there, and in recent months had become friends—quite against Max's better judgment. He wanted no more close friends while he was still so raw from losing so many others.

"Here, perhaps this will help," Thorne said, offering him a snifter of what looked to be brandy. "I thought you would prefer a more potent libation to my aunt's insipid punch."

Max accepted the brandy gladly and took a long swallow, letting the fire burn down his throat.

Thorne was the rakehell son of a duke—tall, fair-haired, and athletic. It was Thorne who had introduced Max to many of the notorious pleasures London had to offer. And Thorne who had coerced him into attending the ball this evening.

Max raised his glass of brandy. "This helps," he said, "but you are still bloody well indebted to me."

Thorne flashed a grin. "I am indeed." He was primarily in London for the fall Season because he'd reluctantly promised his aunt, Lady Hennessy, that he would squire around his young debutante cousin, who was trying to acquire some social polish in preparation for her come-out next spring. He had asked Max to attend tonight so he didn't have to endure Lady Hennessy's ball all alone.

He gave Max a friendly cuff on the back. "It must be a severe plague, being hounded so mercilessly by so many women who love you."

"It isn't my person they love. It's the size of my income and my prospective title that draws them." As the only living male relative of an elderly uncle, Max was the heir presumptive to a viscountcy.

"Along with your charm and looks," Thorne interjected. "And the fact that you're a celebrated war hero. Have you any notion how many men would kill to be in your shoes?"

Max returned a pained smile. "I would rather be anywhere else than here. Back on your island, for example."

Thorne shook his head. "I'm not certain that would be an improvement. Cyrene has more than its share of marriage-minded debutantes. There are some three dozen British families who lead society there. They have their own little ton and can be quite as ruthless as London's Upper Ten Thousand."

"I would be willing to risk it just for a little peace."

Thorne gave him a scrutinizing glance. "Ah, I fancy I know what your problem is. You were infected."

"Infected?"

"By Cyrene's spell. It gets in your blood."

Taking another swallow of brandy, Max shook his head. "I heard something about a mythical spell, but I don't believe in such things."

"Even so, the island affects some people strangely. It has seductive qualities that can be downright dangerous."

That much was true, Max agreed silently. He had found it enchanting, seductive, beguiling. . . .

"Is that why you settled there?" he asked his friend. "You were seduced by the island?"

To his surprise, Thorne gave an enigmatic smile. "In part. But Cyrene has other appealing traits that aren't apparent at first glance."

Reportedly, Thorne had been exiled to Cyrene years ago by his infuriated noble father. But even though he'd eventually reformed enough to appease his sire, he still chose to make his home on the tiny island in the western Mediterranean, between Spain and Sardinia. Max had never quite understood why; he wouldn't have thought such serene allure could attract a man of Thorne's reckless nature.

"Perhaps you should pay another visit there," Thorne added. "The tranquillity might do you good."

Indeed it might, Max reflected, remembering the peace he'd found so briefly. Warm, golden sun. Sparkling aquamarine seas. Mountain peaks wooded with pine and holm oak. Rich valleys lush with vineyards and orange orchards and olive groves. Ancient ruins. Spellbinding, moonlit nights . . .

Paradise.

The thought was so tempting. Though he loathed admitting it, he still hadn't completely recovered from the years of war. The long conflict had been over since Napoleon's abdication in April, yet Max was still plagued by the nightmare. By his own private hell. He had returned alive, when other, more deserving men had not. In the darkest hours of night, it was only by determinedly dreaming of his ministering angel that he could keep the guilt and grief at bay.

Just then his attention was diverted by a familiar curvaceous figure beyond the potted palm, and he let out an oath, barely quelling the urge to shrink farther behind the column.

"I certainly haven't found tranquillity here," Max muttered, eyeing the blond-haired widow who was scanning the ballroom, doubtless in search of him.

"Then come home with me at Christmas," Thorne said. "My obligations will keep me in London until then, but I plan to spend the holiday on Cyrene and would be delighted to have you join me."

"I could easily be persuaded. I'm eager to see for myself that Yates has recovered." *And to meet a certain tempting angel again . . .*

He knew better than to bring up the subject, but the question seemed to be dragged out of him. "What do you hear about Miss Evers?"

"Caro?" Thorne's eyebrows rose with curiosity. "Ah, yes, you met her when she nursed Yates." He smiled slowly, as if recalling a fond memory. "Why, she's as singular as ever. Caro tends to set the blue-blooded denizens of Cyrene on their ears with regularity."

"She did strike me as rather unconventional."

"She is that indeed," Thorne said with a low laugh that suddenly faltered. "What in blazes . . . ?" His eyes narrowed. "Speak of the devil."

Following his gaze through the palm fronds, Max glanced past the throngs of dancers, toward the main entrance to the ballroom. A woman stood there, looking starkly out of place among the begowned, bejeweled, befeathered ladies. She wore plain dark traveling clothes, and she was searching the crowd impatiently.

Max felt every muscle in his body tense. He recognized her from his dreams. The proud carriage of her slender body. The delicate strength in the set of her jaw. The compassion in her healing touch . . .

Wondering if he was again dreaming, Max blinked rapidly, just as Thorne said in a suddenly terse tone, "Excuse me. Caro may be looking for me. I need to discover what brought her here."

As his friend strode away, Max stood momentarily rooted, feeling slightly stunned. Like Thorne, he had no idea what had brought Caro Evers here to London, specifically to Lady Hennessy's ballroom.

Yet he had no doubt whatsoever why his life had suddenly brightened.

Relief flooded Caro when she spied Thorne approaching. At least she wouldn't have to search further for him.

When he reached her, she forced herself to return his smile of welcome, knowing that she was the object of countless curious stares. The notoriety didn't bother her—she was fully accustomed to it by now. And in the five years since her horrible Season in London, she had conquered the sick, hollow feeling of being an outcast. But no one needed to suspect that she and Christopher, Lord Thorne, were anything more than longtime acquaintances and neighbors, or that she had come here to fetch him for an urgent mission.

"Did you just arrive in London?" he murmured as he bent gallantly over her hand.

"Yes. I called at your house but was told I could find you here. Thorne, it is Isabella. We think she has been taken captive."

His pleasant smile never wavered, although a spark of dark emotion flared in his eyes. "I am delighted to see you again, Miss Evers. Come, you can give me all the news from home."

Tucking her arm in his, he ushered her from the ballroom and along the elegant corridor to a large library.

Caro shivered as he closed the door behind them. A fire had been lit in the grate, but it was still far colder here than home on her beautiful island.

"So tell me what happened," Thorne said brusquely, all business now that the need for pretense was over.

"Five weeks ago Isabella was returning home after visiting Spain, but her ship never arrived on Cyrene. In all likelihood it was overrun by Barbary pirates and she was enslaved."

Caro heard the note of fear in her voice, saw the dismay in Thorne's frown as well. There was always danger in sailing the Mediterranean. Now that Napoleon had been vanquished, the French fleet no longer threatened merchant vessels. But for centuries corsairs from the Barbary Coast of North Africa had menaced the waters, practicing the lucrative business of seizing ships and selling their captives as slaves. In fact, a decade ago the American navy had fought a war with Tripoli over that kingdom's enslavement of its citizens.

"Sit down and start from the beginning," he suggested as she began to pace.

"I couldn't possibly sit. I have been doing nothing but sitting on board a schooner for two weeks now. I wish it didn't take so blasted long to reach London!"

"Well, you won't do Isabella any good by wearing out my aunt's carpet," Thorne replied. "Would you care for some sherry?"

"Yes . . . thank you."

His pragmatic tone had a calming effect. Taking a deep breath, Caro moved over to the hearth and held out her gloved hands to the fire while Thorne went to a table and poured her a glass of sherry.

Memories rushed through her mind as she stared at the flames. Lady Isabella Wilde was her dearest friend—a beautiful Spanish noblewoman who had outlived three husbands and now frequently traveled the globe, living life as she pleased. The adventuresome Isabella had been like a mother to her, ever since Caro's own mother died when she was a girl. Isabella was also a role model of independent thinking and had encouraged her in countless ways to pursue her dreams.

Caro was fiercely determined to save her friend from captivity—and so were all the other Guardians. This was not just a personal mission for them. As the daughter of an exiled Spanish statesman, Isabella had been granted sanctuary on Cyrene many years ago. And the capture of someone under the Guardians' protection struck at the heart of their order. Their leader, Sir Gawain Olwen, considered their very honor to be at stake. There was no question they would mount a rescue if necessary. Caro had come directly to London to give Thorne his orders.

He handed her a full wineglass, then settled himself on a sofa while she explained the facts they had pieced together after Isabella went missing—facts that suggested she'd been taken captive by Barbary corsairs.

"We actually had little information to go on. When Isabella's ship never arrived, we sent out inquiries. There had been no storms that week, or any other reason to suggest it might have sunk. And then we learned that a vessel flying an Algerian flag had been sighted in the packet's wake."

"And there has been no word of Bella since? No demands for ransom?"

"None. Sir Gawain sent two agents to Tripoli just in case our intelligence was mistaken, but the odds are greater that she was taken to Algiers."

"And Sir Gawain wants me to go directly to Algiers to search for her?"

"Yes."

"Doubtless he understands the difficulty of locating her there."

Caro nodded. From what she'd heard, Algiers was a large, crowded city with dwellings crammed together like rabbit warrens. And the country itself—the Kingdom of Algiers—was a vast expanse of rugged mountain and hostile desert.

Her sherry remaining untouched, Caro set her glass on the mantel to reach into her reticule. Drawing out a thin sheaf of folded papers, she handed them to Thorne.

"All the particulars are here," she said. "Everything we have planned thus far . . . each of our assignments, including yours."

Thorne perused the details quickly, not questioning why Caro had come personally to deliver his orders. The Guardians often communicated by mail dispatches and carrier pigeon, but this assignment was too important to risk being lost.

Caro shuddered to think of what might have happened to her friend. It was hoped that Isabella's dark beauty and elegant manners would have spared her the fate of many slaves—a terrible life of toil and beatings—and landed her instead in some wealthy lord's harem. The Kingdom of Algiers was ruled by a Turkish dey, who governed from a massive castle. If Isabella was imprisoned there, breaking her out might be next to impossible.

Yet first they had to find her. A half-dozen Guardians were in Barbary now, seeking information, while several others had been recalled to Cyrene in the event they had to mount a rescue.

Thorne looked up from studying his orders. "Hawk is leading the search in Algiers," he verified, "and I am to link up with him there."

"Exactly. And I don't need to tell you how imperative it is that you proceed quickly."

He nodded. "I'll leave tomorrow morning, as soon as I arrange a few details to put my current assignment on hold."

The light of anticipation in Thorne's eyes greatly encouraged Caro. For the first time in weeks, she felt her taut nerves relax the slightest measure. She was infinitely glad to have Christopher Thorne on their side.

She had known he would be eager to participate in the mission, since he loved the thrill of danger. A rebel at heart, Thorne was the hotheaded, reckless member of the group. And of all the Guardians besides Caro, he was closest to Isabella, so he understood perfectly her anxiety for her friend.

Thorne rose from the sofa and crossed to her, taking her gloved hands in his larger, stronger ones. "We'll find her, never doubt it."

Caro smiled faintly. She was far more troubled about this mission than any previous one, doubtless because she had such a high personal stake in the outcome. "It is just so frustrating to be this helpless. I cannot stop seeing Isabella at the mercy of some cruel master. She is all alone, Thorne—"

"Have you considered another possibility? That Bella may look upon her captivity as an adventure rather than a tragedy?"

He was trying to reassure her, Caro realized, yet he did have a point. Most women would be terrified at being enslaved by Barbary pirates, but the spirited Isabella was far more resourceful and enterprising than any average woman. If anyone was a survivor, it was she.

But still, it distressed Caro immeasurably that they couldn't even begin to make detailed plans until they discovered if and where Isabella was being held captive, which could take weeks or even months.

"You are right, of course," she murmured. "But I shall go mad with nothing to do but wait."

Thorne chucked her under the chin. "Oh, no, my girl, you won't get off so easily. At the moment I have the perfect task for you. You may make my excuses to my aunt. She won't be eager to free me from my promise to squire my cousin around London."

"Why me?"

"Because Aunt Hennessy likes you. And she will be more willing to forgive me if you ask it of her."

Lady Hennessy had sponsored Caro's disastrous London Season years before and held her in high affection, despite the scandal she'd inadvertently caused.

"Just tell her that Bella has gone missing," Thorne added, "and that I'm needed to rescue her." He led Caro to the library door and opened it. "Go attempt to wind her around your thumb, love. Meanwhile I'll fetch some dispatches for you to carry to Sir Gawain tomorrow. I should return in an hour or so. Do you mean to stay here tonight?"

"If Lady Hennessy will permit me."

"I have no doubt she will—*if* you promise not to cause a scene at her ball. She is still trying to live down your Season."

Color rose in her cheeks at his wicked teasing. "Of course I won't cause a scene. I intend to make myself scarce as soon as I speak to her."

"She will be grateful, I'm sure." Thorne turned to go, then glanced back over his shoulder. "Oh, and Caro? One other thing you may do for me. . . . Extend my apologies to Max Leighton."

Caro felt every nerve in her body tighten. "Major Leighton is here?" she asked, her voice a bit too high and breathless.

"*Mr.* Leighton. He's a civilian now. But you should know that. He is in all the society pages."

She did know. Sir Gawain had the British newspapers shipped to Cyrene with his weekly reports so he could keep up with current events in both the world and in the Beau Monde.

"Why must you apologize to him?" Caro asked, trying to appear casual.

"Because I dragged him to this ball so he could keep me company. It was a supreme sacrifice on his part, considering how persistently the ladies are hounding him. I regret having to abandon him to their sweet mercies. Tell Max that I am sorry and that my invitation to him to visit Cyrene at Christmas still stands."

Caro lowered her gaze to hide her dismay. "If I see

him," she answered reluctantly, "I will give him your message."

"That isn't good enough, love. Promise me you will seek Max out after I leave. Otherwise I will have to delay long enough to do it myself."

"Very well . . . I promise."

"No doubt he will be pleased to see you. He was just asking about you earlier tonight."

She gave Thorne a startled glance. "He was?"

"Yes. You evidently made quite an impression on him during his brief visit to the island last year. Now go find my aunt. I will return as soon as possible."

As Thorne strode away, Caro stared dazedly after him, wanting to curse. The last person she wanted to see was Maxwell Leighton, but it didn't seem as if she would have much choice.

Caro returned to the ballroom with grave reluctance. She wasn't a coward—ordinarily. But the thought of encountering Max Leighton again was unnerving.

It astonished her that Leighton had asked after her. *You evidently made quite an impression on him.* Heat rose to her cheeks. She could only imagine what he thought of her behavior that night. Acting like a perfect wanton. Pleading with him to make love to her. Practically seducing him. Even now her face burned at the memory. Even now the memory of his touch filled her with a sweet, aching longing.

Did he have similar remembrances of their night of passion? After all the women he had likely been with, Caro doubted their tryst had meant anything special to him.

She certainly would never forget it, though. That

magical night had shown her so clearly what she was missing in her life. And Max's wonderful lovemaking had only increased her yearnings. . . .

It had been a profound mistake to surrender to her wanton urges, but still she cherished the memory. So much so that she didn't want it spoiled by cold reality, or the disappointment of encountering him now in the light of day. She had read numerous newspaper accounts of Max Leighton over the past months—the titillating gossip about his amorous affairs and the predictions regarding the race to secure his hand in marriage.

Lamentably, however, she saw him the moment she entered the ballroom. The crowd had parted slightly, revealing his tall, commanding form a short distance away. Rather than the dashing uniform of the 7th Hussars, he wore an exquisitely tailored blue coat that molded his muscular shoulders to perfection and no doubt reflected the striking color of his eyes.

He was surrounded by a half-dozen beauties, as she'd expected. Determinedly Caro tried to repress the hollowness in her chest. She had often wondered if Max was still the wounded warrior, or if he had somehow managed to heal after the terrible conflict with Napoleon had ended. He certainly did not look as if he was suffering now, she reflected wryly.

She was infinitely glad that he had come through the war safely. And he deserved happiness, certainly. Considering the horrors he must have endured, the mind-numbing pleasures that London offered a battle-weary soldier would go a long way toward helping him to forget. But still, it had disillusioned her to learn that he had turned into such a rake. More damningly, it hurt to see him with so many beautiful women.

Just then he turned and met her gaze across the ballroom. Her heart seemed to stop completely. He was still the same unforgettable man she saw so frequently in her dreams. Those were the same striking features. The same compelling blue eyes fringed by black lashes. He still possessed the same powerful, potent masculinity.

She could feel herself flushing with warmth as his glance hotly connected with hers.

Chastising herself, Caro managed to swallow past her dry throat. If she was required to speak to him, she would do her utmost not to let her tumultuous feelings show. And if, heaven forbid, he happened to mention that long-ago night between them, she would brazen it out, pretend to be as sophisticated as all the worldly beauties who presently flocked around him, vying for his attention.

For now, however, she needed to find Thorne's aunt.

Dragging her gaze away with effort, she spied Lady Hennessy along one wall, sitting with the other dowagers. Grateful for the distraction, Caro threaded her way through the crowds.

The portly, silver-haired lady looked up with surprise, her expression first breaking into a smile of delight, then fading to one of concern. "My dear girl, whatever are you doing here? Sir Gawain? Is something amiss?"

Caro bent to kiss the soft cheek that was presented to her. "Sir Gawain is well, my lady. But I fear I have some other regretful news—as well as a request regarding your nephew. May I have a private word with you?"

Lady Hennessy's friends on either side of her took the hint and vacated their chairs, allowing her to draw Caro down to sit beside her.

"Very well," the elderly lady said, narrowing her sharp eyes. "Tell me what daring deeds my scapegrace nephew is involved with this time."

"You seem to be taking an extraordinary interest in Miss Evers, Mr. Leighton," a plaintive female voice murmured. "Surely you realize that she is merely trying to draw attention to herself."

"Yes," another young lady complained. "It is just like her to create a scene by appearing at a ball in all her travel dirt."

Forcing his attention back to his companions, Max raised an eyebrow. "You think she is here merely to create a scene?"

A half-dozen ladies responded, all eager to regale him with tales of Caro Evers, it seemed.

"My come-out was the same year," one remarked. "She was old for a deb even then."

"I remember her as a silent, awkward creature. No social skills to speak of."

"She would not even dance."

"But it was the scandal she caused that was the final straw."

"Indeed, Lady Hennessy was mortified."

The trills of laughter became a chorus as they all seemed to share a common memory.

"What sort of scandal?" Max asked curiously.

"Miss Evers dressed up as a man to attend medical lectures."

"She was caught studying naked bodies!"

"Worse, she examined the entrails!"

Several of the ladies shuddered. The tall blonde who had hunted Max earlier added with malicious glee, "And for that, she was banished from the ton in disgrace."

His eyes narrowing, Max fixed the widow with a cool frown. She evidently noticed his disapproval, and fell silent—but one of her conspirators did not.

"It was quite absurd, her pretending to be a man, although she certainly could be one, her complexion is so coarse and brown."

Feeling a rush of protectiveness for the woman they were so eagerly demeaning, Max found it an effort not to clench his teeth. Caro Evers's golden-hued skin was not the pasty, milk-white ideal favored by English beauties, but he found it immeasurably more attractive. "Her complexion is no more tanned than usual for someone who lives on a Mediterranean island."

"Do you know her, Mr. Leighton?"

Smiling faintly, he again came to Caro's defense. "I had the distinct pleasure of meeting Miss Evers last year when she saved the life of one of my lieutenants. In fact, I consider her to be one of the most remarkable women of my acquaintance."

His response put an abrupt pall over the conversation. "Now if you ladies will please excuse me," he added with a wicked smile, "I must go pay my compliments to Miss Evers."

Ignoring the looks of dismay on their faces, as well as the blond widow's indignation, Max turned sharply and made his way across the ballroom toward where Caro Evers was deep in conversation with Lady Hennessy.

It was obvious that some urgent business had brought her to London, and he was highly curious to know what it was. He was even more interested to see if any remnant of the fire that had once blazed between them still existed.

He kept his gaze fixed on her and was gratified to see how she froze when she looked up and saw him.

Her gray eyes were as large and lustrous as he remembered, like silver smoke, while her features had the stamp of character and intelligence. Not stunningly beautiful perhaps, but with an inviting appeal all the same.

Max bowed to his hostess, Lady Hennessy, but it was Caro he addressed. "Good evening, Miss Evers. I wasn't certain I would ever have the good fortune of meeting you again."

She frowned, as if searching her memory. "Do I know you, sir? Oh, yes . . . Major Leighton, is it not?"

His eyebrow shot up in surprise. Max studied her, wondering if she truly had difficulty remembering his name, or if she was just dissembling for the sake of their audience.

He feigned a wince. "You wound me, Miss Evers, if you cannot even recall my name."

She pursed her lips. "Oh, I recall it quite well, Mr. Leighton. How could I not, when the gossip columns are full of your amorous adventures?"

Lady Hennessy made a sound that was suspiciously like a chuckle, but Max ignored her. With deliberate gallantry he took Caro's hand and bent over it, pressing his lips to her gloved fingers, interested to see how she responded.

Not only did she give a start, but when her eyes locked with his, something warm and primitive arced between them. Her gaze then flickered lower, over his mouth, and Max knew for certain that Caro Evers had not forgotten him.

A sharp surge of male satisfaction rippled through him, even though she withdrew her hand coolly.

"Actually, I was on my way to find you," she said. "Thorne asked me to convey his apologies to you. He was called away on sudden business. He regretted"—she glanced pointedly toward the gathering of ladies Max had just abandoned—"having to leave you to the tender mercies of your gaggle of admirers."

She rose then. "I hope you won't mind if I excuse myself, Mr. Leighton. I have had a long journey, and I have another long one ahead of me tomorrow."

Bending, she kissed Lady Hennessy's cheek. "Thank you, my lady. Thorne will be grateful that you have released him from his promise."

The dowager shook her head with mock sternness. "You can't fool me, my girl. I can see right through him. He wasn't brave enough to face me, and so he coerced you into pleading his case."

Caro smiled. "True, but you must admit, you are quite formidable when you get in a high dudgeon."

She turned to Max, her gaze flickering over him before she nodded toward the cluster of ladies who were still watching him. "Perhaps you should return to your devotees. It is obvious they anxiously await you. Good night, Mr. Leighton."

Max remained where he stood, staring after her. He had just been dismissed, he realized.

It was a novel experience for him, to be spurned by the only woman he longed to be near. And his dismissal had a decided effect on him—arousing the primitive male urge to chase fleeing prey and stirring even deeper instincts of possessiveness.

He had a claim on Caro Evers, whether she realized it or not.

Watching him, Lady Hennessy let out a deep chuckle. "Perhaps you have already discovered that Caro is not like any other conventional young lady."

"Indeed," Max said wryly.

"She despises balls and all the other trappings of society. I doubt she will come down again this evening. Most likely she will hide herself away reading one of those infernal medical tomes." The lady's eyes took on a calculating gleam. "But she is staying upstairs in her former rooms. If you wish to speak with her, Mr. Leighton, I suspect you will have to go after her."

Max curved his mouth in an amused, calculating line of his own. "Thank you, my lady. I have every intention of doing just that."

Chapter Two

It was absurd how flustered Maxwell Leighton made her, Caro thought as she escaped the ballroom. She felt his gaze locked on her back, hot as flame, which only served to further kindle her overheated senses.

When finally she reached her bedchamber, Caro closed the door and leaned against it while she waited for her wits to stop whirling, for her heart to stop pounding. She had hoped he wouldn't be as devastating as she recollected, but her wish had been futile.

How could he have such an affect on her?

How could he not? a logical voice responded.

Not only was he the kind of hero maidens dreamed of, he had been her first and only lover. He'd helped her to fully become a woman. To experience passion. Surely it was only reasonable that she would see him in a different light from any other man. That she would remember him more vividly. That a simple glance from his startling blue eyes could set her heart leaping and her stomach fluttering like an army of butterflies had taken residence there.

Had he noticed her reaction? She had tried to feign indifference but wasn't certain that she'd succeeded. Especially since she couldn't refrain from sniping about the admiring beauties who were pursuing him, which had made her sound like a jealous witch.

How could she possibly feel jealousy? Caro scolded herself. She had no right. She had no place in Max Leighton's life. He likely wouldn't *want* her in his life. If not for the special circumstances of that long-ago night, he wouldn't have given her a second glance.

Tonight he had seen her as she really was, without the benefit of moonlight, without the island's spellbinding enchantment. He wouldn't feel the same fiery attraction that she still felt for him. True, for a moment he had stared at her as if absorbing the sight of her. But she'd obviously been indulging in fanciful dreams, mistaking his look for the fierce ardor she'd imagined in her most secret fantasies.

With a sigh of self-disgust, Caro took off her pelisse. A fire had been lit in the grate, and a light supper awaited her on a small table near the hearth, but she was too agitated to eat.

Her valise had been delivered by a footman, and she debated whether to change into her nightdress. But then she recalled Thorne was supposed to return shortly. Moreover, the ball would probably go on for hours—she could hear the faint strains of music below—and being undressed would make her feel too defenseless when the house was filled with so many lovely ladies wearing splendid ballgowns.

Caro paced restlessly for a moment, then forced herself to stop when she caught sight of herself in the cheval glass. Her dark brown hair was wild and untidy, with dozens of curls escaping from their pins. No wonder all those haughty beauties had stared at her. That *he* had stared at her. But it was only one more mark against her in a social ledger that was full of black marks.

She brushed out her hair, then poured herself a cup of tea and settled in the wing chair before the fire to read a recently published medical treatise, although she comprehended perhaps only one word in three. Her mind kept returning to Max Leighton, to the incredible night she had spent in his arms.

Perhaps half an hour had passed when she heard a soft rap on her door. Expecting Thorne, Caro rose and opened it.

She felt herself go cold, then hot, when she saw who stood there.

"You escaped before I could make a single inquiry," Max said lightly as he sauntered into the room without so much as a by-your-leave. "I wanted to ask you how Lieutenant Yates is faring."

Caro snapped her gaping jaw shut. She would *not* let him fluster her again, even if he *had* invaded her bedchamber uninvited. Thank heaven she had kept on her clothing.

"Surely you know his status, Mr. Leighton. John told me that he writes to you regularly, just as you requested him to do."

"I want to hear your account. How else can I trust that he's being truthful when he claims to be recovering?"

The defensive set of Caro's shoulders relaxed somewhat when she understood the reason for Max's visit; he needed to know about his former lieutenant to set his mind at ease.

She swung the door almost closed, allowing them privacy, but leaving it open a crack for propriety's sake. "John Yates actually is doing quite well. His spirits are far higher than I ever would have expected."

Max roughly ran a hand though his hair. "I'm glad he isn't merely trying to spare me."

For a moment he stared down at the carpet, as if caught in some dark memory. Then he looked up at her, his glance once again setting her heart scampering. "And you? How are you faring?"

She clasped her hands in front of her to steady them. "Well enough, thank you," she answered, preferring not to open the subject of her missing friend.

"From your haste in departing the ballroom, I wondered if I had offended you in some manner."

Caro felt fresh color stain her cheeks. "No, you didn't offend me."

He took in the length of her . . . her mouth, her breasts, her hips, as if remembering. All the nerves in her body seemed to flare with heat. "I am not accustomed to women running from me."

"No, I would expect not." Her lips pursed in unwilling humor. "They are much more likely to be chasing you. By all accounts you are the marriage prize of the decade."

His own mouth curled in a wry grimace. "Are you quoting the gossip columns again?"

"Indeed. We read newspapers on our island, Mr. Leighton. They are weeks old, but we still get them. Your name has been linked to any number of heiresses and titled ladies eager to become your bride. Last month it was a European princess, was it not? The predictions are that a match will be announced very soon."

"The predictions are wrong. I have no interest in

marriage." He gave her a speculative glance. "Are you interested in marriage, Miss Evers?"

Caro returned a startled look at the strange question. "No, not in the least."

"Good. That greatly relieves my mind."

"I don't know why it should."

Instead of replying, he strolled over to the window, pushing aside the heavy drapery to peer out at the dark night. "I trust you won't object if I take refuge here for a while?"

She hesitated a moment. "It would hardly be proper. This is my bedchamber."

Turning, he propped a shoulder against the window frame. He remained silent, merely studying her with a raised eyebrow, his expression seeming to say, *I have been in a much more intimate setting with you than your bedchamber.*

"Are you so concerned with propriety?" he asked. "Judging from the rumors, you thumb your nose at decorum every chance you get."

It was Caro's turn to deplore the gossips. "Not *every* chance. I imagine you heard the shocking details of my London Season," she said stiffly.

"I wasn't overly shocked. It seems that your chief offense was inspecting human entrails. And I saw enough of those bloody things during the war to become inured."

"But I am a *female*," Caro retorted, unable to keep a tart edge from her tone. "To the ton, it is a crime for me to do anything more than ply a sick patient with calves' foot jelly."

"You are criminal indeed," he murmured in amusement.

Shrugging off her longtime disaffection, she managed a smile. "Why don't you return to the ballroom and your admirers? I'm certain they can regale you with tales about me that would curdle your blood."

Max shook his head. "I'd wager they know almost nothing about the real Miss Caro Evers. They wouldn't know, for example, that you like to bathe in the moonlight."

Caro felt her breath falter. "You really shouldn't be here, Mr. Leighton."

"Why not?"

When she made no answer, he slowly crossed the room to stand before her. His nearness made Caro retreat a step. A mistake, she realized, since her back pressed against the door, shutting it with a loud click.

"Are you afraid of me?" Max asked, his hushed voice somehow more intimate than his bare hands on her skin.

"Of course not. But it seems that for some reason you are trying to intimidate me."

He smiled at that. "It would be futile of me to try. You are obviously not a woman to be easily intimidated."

"I'm not. But I still would prefer that you leave."

"You weren't concerned about propriety that night."

"What night?"

"Are you again claiming you don't remember?" His gaze searching her face, he took a step closer and reached up to touch her lower lip with the pad of his thumb.

Caro drew a sharp breath. Of course she remembered. He had filled her dreams for months afterward. Even now she still sometimes dreamed of him. . . .

"I think you haven't forgotten about that night," he murmured. "I certainly haven't."

She couldn't lie so brazenly, but she could at least prevaricate. "No, I haven't forgotten. It was . . . interesting."

"Merely interesting?"

Determined to resist her ridiculous attraction to him, Caro moved across the room to the table where her valise lay and busied herself folding a shawl. "You are asking a great deal of probing questions," she observed.

"Just answer this one question, then. Why did you give yourself to me that night, a stranger?"

The intimacy of his question flustered her, but she stuck to her pretense. "I took pity on you. Merely that."

His eyebrow shot up. "Pity?"

"You were in pain. You needed comforting."

"So you made a virginal sacrifice?" His voice held a wry edge. "Do you comfort every stranger like that?"

"Obviously not," she said unevenly.

"No, obviously not. I was your first lover. Some men would feel damned guilty for taking your innocence."

"You have no reason to feel guilty," Caro pointed out. "You weren't responsible for what happened between us. It was my fault entirely. I was the one who . . . insisted."

"I believe I went along," Max said dryly. "What I don't understand is *why* you insisted. Because you're a healer and you wanted to heal me?"

"Not only that." She looked away, unable to meet his intense gaze. "I told you then, I wanted to know what passion was like. I had read about coupling in medical texts and . . . I was curious." To prove her point, she withdrew a heavy leather-bound volume from her valise and held it up for him to see.

Yet Max ignored the book and moved toward her again. It took all of Caro's willpower to stand her ground.

"Did I satisfy your curiosity?" His voice was suddenly husky.

"I suppose so." Which was a masterful understatement. Passion was so much more devastating than she had ever expected. At least passion with this man was.

He seemed to echo her thoughts when he said softly, "I have never experienced anything like that night." When she started to speak, he put a finger to her lips. "And pray don't tell me it was the island's magical spell. It was far more than that."

"Perhaps it was," she said carefully. "You had seen too much of death, and you needed just the opposite. Physical passion is a way to defy death, to know you are alive. And intimacy is a natural means of seeking comfort. You needed comfort that night. A few moments of warmth and closeness to another human being."

"How did you grow to be so wise?"

She stirred uneasily at the amused admiration in his eyes. "I am not wise, merely pragmatic. And I want you to know . . . I may be unconventional, but I am not normally the kind of woman who gives herself to strangers."

"Clearly not. Otherwise you wouldn't have been a virgin."

He was teasing her this time, she reflected, feeling flaming color spread over her cheeks.

Max studied her for a moment before nodding sagely. "I think I begin to see the problem."

His oblique comment confused her. "What problem?"

"You are embarrassed by what happened. You needn't be. You saved my life that night, angel."

"What are you talking about?"

"You have no idea, do you?" Reaching up, he gently pushed a tendril of hair back from her forehead. "Let's just say you helped me face returning to war."

She was taken aback by the look in his eyes. It was almost . . . sensual. No man had ever looked at her that way, with desire. Except for Max. Except for that night.

"You have haunted me ever since," he said simply, his voice no more than a whisper.

You have haunted me as well.

Caro tried to swallow, but she failed. When she remained speechless, his thumb slowly rubbed over her cheekbone as his glance slid down her body to linger on her abdomen. "There was no child?"

"N-no," she managed to reply.

"I wondered."

He took a step closer, until his body was almost touching hers.

Dear God, he was dangerous, with his beautiful face, his dark-lashed blue eyes, his sensual mouth.

A shudder running through her, Caro shut her own eyes. His nearness made her dizzy. She could feel the warmth of his body, could remember what it felt like to have him kiss her, to touch her, to make love to her. She could still feel him moving between her thighs. . . .

Sweet heaven, she couldn't dwell on those sensual memories.

With a murmur of protest, Caro pressed her palms against Max's chest, pushing him back a step.

Breathless, she moved to stand near the hearth, away from the threat of his embrace, putting the wing chair firmly between them.

Max watched her in silence, wondering at her skittishness. Surely she didn't think he would harm her? No, more likely her unease was simply due to self-consciousness at meeting him again. He strongly suspected Caro Evers wouldn't like exposing her defenses to him as she had that night. He'd recognized the hint of shyness in her lustrous gray eyes just now. Of vulnerability.

Yet he felt vulnerable as well. His relationship with her was unlike any he'd ever had with a woman.

He couldn't remember ever being this damned intrigued by a woman, either. It was refreshing to find one he had to chase rather than the usual beauties who saw him as prey, but that didn't wholly explain his fierce attraction to her. His desire for Caro hadn't dissipated since that night; if anything, it was stronger.

Perhaps it was madness, Max admitted to himself. He'd known her for a few brief days, over a year ago, but his strongest drive now was to claim ownership. And now that he had found her again, he wasn't about to let her go.

He had no intention of showing his hand, however.

"You mentioned that you have a long journey ahead of you tomorrow. Isn't that rather sudden, when you just arrived?"

She looked relieved by the change of subject. "I accomplished what I came for."

"And what is that?"

Her hesitation was curiously noticeable. "Actually I came to fetch Thorne. A very dear friend of mine is in grave trouble."

"And he can help?"

"I hope so."

"Thorne works for the Foreign Office, I understand."

Caro looked at Max in surprise. "How did you know?"

"He told me."

She frowned, wondering why Thorne had disclosed even that much about himself. That was the tale all the Guardians used to protect their identities and to explain their clandestine activities. In fact, Lady Hennessy believed her nephew to be one of Sir Gawain Olwen's chief representatives in London.

It wasn't precisely a lie. In theory the Guardians of the Sword reported to the British Foreign Office.

Publicly Sir Gawain was thought to head a select branch of the Foreign Office, and his work was considered a sanctioned government service. But few people realized the considerable number of agents he had under his command. Fewer still were privy to the secrets behind how the order had been established, or how deeply the Guardians permeated present British and European society.

There was a good reason for secrecy, since it provided a major advantage to their successful operations.

Caro started to reply, but her response was interrupted by another rap on the door.

"That should be Thorne now," she murmured as she went to admit him.

He entered, carrying a leather pouch, which she knew contained dispatches for Sir Gawain. He handed the pouch to her, but before he could speak, she called his attention to her other visitor.

Thorne halted abruptly when he spied Max, arching an eyebrow in surprise.

"Mr. Leighton was just leaving," Caro announced.

"Loath as I am to contradict a lady, I wasn't," Max refuted genially. "I was waiting to learn about the grave trouble her friend is in, and why you are being summoned to help."

Thorne hesitated a long moment, looking from one to the other of them. "Lady Isabella Wilde," he said finally. "Do you know her?"

"I've heard of her, certainly, although she was away when I visited Cyrene last year. An eccentric, wealthy widow."

"She isn't truly eccentric," Caro said in her friend's defense. "She is merely fond of exploration and less chained by convention than most women. Her father was the Count of Aranda, one of Spain's greatest ministers."

"But Bella's adventures have been known to land her in scrapes before now," Thorne added. "And this one is more serious than most. Her ship was likely seized by Barbary corsairs. . . ."

He proceeded to tell Max much of what Caro had told him, including their suspicions that Isabella had been sold into slavery.

Thorne's divulgences surprised Caro. She saw no reason to share any of the details with Max, since Isabella's disappearance was none of his concern.

She couldn't understand, either, why Max was still here in her bedchamber. Any gentleman would have acknowledged her requests and politely taken his leave. But Max Leighton was obviously not any typical gentleman. Rather, he was accustomed to command and to being obeyed. And unlike her, his consequence was exalted enough that he could choose to ignore the rules of polite society without causing a scandal and being shunned in disgrace.

"So you intend to search for Lady Isabella?" Max asked Thorne at the conclusion.

"Yes. I leave first thing tomorrow for Algiers. Meanwhile, several other of Isabella's friends have been summoned to Cyrene to be available in the event we must plot her rescue. It may take a few weeks for them all to gather there, but by then I hope to have some tangible information as to her whereabouts."

"Perhaps I could be of help," Max said slowly.

"You are volunteering to aid us?" Thorne asked.

Max nodded. "At least a half-dozen times during my military career, I orchestrated the liberation of captured British soldiers. I would be happy to offer you the benefit of my experience."

"You shouldn't have to make such a sacrifice, Mr. Leighton," Caro replied swiftly. "You only recently returned from years of war, and it would be asking too much of you to embroil yourself in further conflict."

Max's glance focused on her. "You saved my lieutenant. I could begin to repay that debt if I could help you save your friend."

"He has a point, love," Thorne said. "And Max is said to be a brilliant military tactician. He could be of significant value in any rescue attempt."

She gave Thorne a puzzled frown, surprised by his obtuseness. To maintain their effectiveness, the Guardians needed anonymity. If Max became involved in a rescue attempt, it would be difficult to keep the order a secret from him. And only Sir Gawain made the decisions about whom to invite into their confidence.

"I think you are forgetting Sir Gawain's dislike of involving outsiders," Caro said pointedly.

Thorne grinned. "In this instance I'm certain Sir Gawain will forgive me. Max isn't considered a war hero for no reason. In countless battles he succeeded against overwhelming odds when he was outmanned and outgunned. His efforts made the war come to an end that much sooner. We could use someone with his skills and keen intelligence."

Caro raised an eyebrow at Thorne, silently trying to convey her concern. "Might I have a word with you in private?"

"There is no need for privacy, love. We can speak freely in front of Max. He doesn't need to be employed by the Foreign Office to participate. I have no doubt Sir Gawain will eventually want to recruit him, but for now he can simply join us as a civilian."

Perhaps it was true, Caro admitted reluctantly. Max wouldn't need to be told about the Guardians, just that Isabella had a group of protectors who were determined to rescue her. And any newcomer would have to prove himself before being extended an invitation to join the order. Clearly Thorne saw this as an opportunity for Max to prove himself as a future Guardian.

She highly doubted that Max Leighton would want to commit his life to their endeavors, but she could hardly debate the matter when he was standing right here, attending their interchange with avid curiosity.

"It is quite simple," Thorne said. "Max can accompany you back to Cyrene tomorrow, and he can billet at my house there until we recover Isabella."

Caro hesitated, all her instincts urging her to resist. No doubt Max *would* be a highly valuable asset. And she shouldn't let her own personal reservations interfere with far more important goals.

Yet she much preferred to have no further involvement with Max at all. She wasn't prepared to deal with the complications of his returning to Cyrene with her. He would prove too great a distraction, she was certain. Already whenever he came near her, his potent effect made her so flustered and self-conscious, she could scarcely keep her wits about her. If he accompanied her on the journey, her nerves would be in a constant state of chaos.

Moreover, she didn't want to risk repeating her brazen, foolish seduction of him. Or the inexplicable sense of loss she'd felt after he had gone.

She couldn't possibly admit her reasons to him, though.

"I still don't think it a good idea for him to become involved," Caro murmured.

"Why not?" Max asked curiously.

"For one thing, I could never forgive myself if you were to be hurt helping us."

"I doubt the danger will be anywhere near the magnitude of the recent war."

"If we mount a rescue in Barbary, it won't be a mere lark, Mr. Leighton. You could risk serious injury or even death."

"I am willing to chance it. And while I'm not particularly eager for the thrill of adventure, I could use the diversion. All these months of soft civilian life are beginning to wear on my nerves."

"You find it tedious and dull, you mean?" Caro asked sweetly.

"Something of the sort." His tone was dry.

"Then you don't want to come to our little island, I assure you. Our community is highly rural and extremely slow compared to anything in London. You will find few of the amenities you are accustomed to, and certainly not much of the social life. You will come to miss civilization as you know it. And the ranks of admiring ladies eager to worship you will be exceedingly thin."

His slow smile was quite devastating. "That, frankly, is a point in favor of my going. There are countless matchmaking mamas sharpening their knives for me here. Participating in your venture would provide me a good reason to escape all the ardent young misses who are looking to snag me as a marriage prize."

"Exactly," Thorne agreed with a chuckle. "And I'm sure Max will appreciate the chance to enjoy some peace and quiet. Furthermore"—Thorne fixed Caro with a stern look—"you, my sweet hoyden, could use the diversion yourself. Having Max around for company will help take your mind off Bella's fate. It might even help pry you out of your shell."

Caro's eyes narrowed at his deliberate provocation. "I don't have a shell."

"You do, love. And I'll wager it's only grown thicker without me there to poke and prod you. You need someone like Max to challenge you and keep you sharp in my absence."

"Your absence has been a pleasant respite, I must say!" Caro retorted.

Max watched their lively sparring, watched her gray eyes flashing, and felt a renewed surge of fascination—along with a more inexplicable craving.

His reaction confounded him. He had spent the final, hellish year of the war dreaming about this woman, but he'd considered her his guardian angel, not merely an object of desire. He hadn't expected his response now to be so . . . carnal. Hadn't expected his hunger for her to rekindle with such intensity.

When earlier he'd moved close enough to touch her, he'd felt the overpowering need to kiss her, to taste her, to drive himself deep within her sheltering warmth. Even now his loins were half-hard.

It had stung when Caro claimed their lovemaking had been nothing more than a curiosity for her, although Max suspected that night had meant more to her than she was willing to admit.

It also stung to see her evident close friendship with Thorne, Max acknowledged. He'd never felt this savage slash of jealousy over any other woman.

His eagerness to accompany her to Cyrene amazed him as well. The last thing he wanted was to be reminded of the war by becoming involved in another rescue mission. But he owed Caro a great deal—not only for saving his lieutenant, but for virtually saving his own sanity this past year.

An artillery barrage could not have kept him away now.

He could lie to himself and offer any number of excuses to justify his reasoning. Quite possibly a sojourn in the golden serenity of the island could help him find the peace that had eluded him since the war ended.

But he knew his true reason for wanting to return to the island was much more profound: this was his chance to discover if the enchantment he had felt with Caro Evers that night was real or simply a spell cast by the island's beauty—one that wouldn't survive a deeper acquaintance in the harsh light of day.

He'd spent countless months haunted by her image. If he let her go now, he would forever wonder if he'd made a vital mistake.

He had to return, if only to prove to himself that her strange hold over him could be broken. That the vaunted power of the island was no more than myth.

Surely then he would be able to drive Caro out of his thoughts, his dreams, and he could move on with his life.

It remained to convince her to accept him, though, Max knew. She obviously didn't want to capitulate.

His gaze locked with hers. "I thought you said you aren't afraid of me, Miss Evers."

The spirited flash of defiance in her eyes told him he had struck a nerve.

"I am *not* afraid of you!"

"Then I don't understand your objection."

"Very well," she said, not hiding her exasperation. "You may come if you wish. In truth, I would use the devil himself if he could help find Isabella."

Max couldn't help but smile. "Are you putting me in the same league as the devil?"

"I'm beginning to think you belong there," she snapped. Her hands went to her hips. "Of course I will be grateful for any assistance you can give us, but pray don't blame me if you go mad from boredom."

"I suspect boredom will be the least of my worries," Max murmured half under his breath, hiding his exhilaration at Caro's surrender.

"Then it's settled," Thorne declared with satisfaction. "The two of you sail for Cyrene tomorrow."

At that pronouncement, Max felt the muscles of his belly clench. He recognized the sensation; he'd felt it before every battle: his entire body taut with tension, nerves alert with anticipation, with excitement, with fear.

The thrill of danger. The dread of defeat.

He held Caro's gaze, relishing the lively sparks in her eyes. Yet he recognized the challenge ahead of him. And he had a strange suspicion that this battle would be more important than any he had ever fought—one it was imperative for him to win.

Chapter Three

The ship voyage home proved every bit as unsettling as Caro expected. The enforced intimacy with Max Leighton made her vividly recall his former visit to her island: The three intense days they'd spent together fighting for a man's life. Their ardent, enchanting night of passion. The bittersweet ache she'd felt for so long afterward, once Max was gone from her life.

To her dismay, her dreams of him returned in full force, sensual fantasies that left her breathless and hungering and more restless than ever. Worse, the voyage gave him too many opportunities to probe her secrets—and for her to unwittingly learn some of his.

Certainly he was impossible to ignore, in part because they were the only passengers on board the private schooner. They shared meals in the captain's cabin with the crew's officers, but although she was never alone with Max, Caro found his powerful presence disquieting in such tight quarters.

Initially she tried taking refuge in her small cabin, but by mid-afternoon of the second day, restlessness drove her above decks to brave a chill sea wind and the possibility of encountering Max. She spied him at once, standing at the port railing, braced against the rhythmic dip and sway of the ship as it sliced through the gray waves. The image had a deplorable effect on her heart, flooding her with memories of their night at the ruins, when Max had stared out at the moonlit sea. Then he turned and met her gaze across the deck, and she felt a thrill that was sharp and hot and intense.

Cursing her lamentable attraction, Caro sought out the captain and demanded employment of some kind, hoping that occupation would distract her from the striking, raven-haired man she would much rather forget, as well as keep her from despairing about Isabella's fate.

The ruddy-cheeked elderly sea master, Captain Biddick, had been a Guardian for decades and had executed numerous missions with Caro. Thus, he not only put her to work on the never-ending tasks that faced a ship's crew, he continued her instruction in sailing the ship and navigating by the stars.

That night when she was practicing using a sextant, Caro saw Max pacing the stern of the schooner. It surprised her that he seemed as restless as she herself was.

She managed to avoid any private conversation with him, however, until the third day. The afternoon was blustery and overcast, so Caro found a spot in the lee of a bulkhead, protected from the wind, and sat down to mend a sail.

In only a few moments she heard a strange, muted thud to her right. When it happened several more times, she abandoned her mending and went to investigate, wending her way across the deck, avoiding lines and cargo in her path.

She halted when she spied Max beyond the mizzenmast, her eyes narrowing in surprise at the glint of steel in his hand as he raised his arm.

The knife blade flashed as it hurtled through the air

to land with a thud in the barrel lying some ten yards distant.

He was throwing the weapon at a target, she realized. The cask must have been empty, since no liquid spilled out, even though with each throw he buried the blade deeply enough to create a gash.

Riveted, Caro stood watching as Max strode over to the cask, withdrew the blade from the wood, returned to his post, and then hurled the knife again. He kept up the rhythmic cycle, never seeming to aim, but his deadly precision earned her unwilling admiration.

It was several moments more before he became aware of her presence. Arresting his next throw, he turned and gave her a piercing look.

"Is the captain aware you are putting holes in his brandy cask?" Caro asked as she came out of the shadows.

"This is my brandy cask, actually. I won it from Biddick at cards."

"Quite a feat, since he is a veritable sharp."

Max's mouth twisted in a smile, making her heart give another painful flutter. "Ah, but I became quite a sharp myself during the endless Peninsula campaign."

"As a way to stave off boredom?"

"In part."

"You seem to be quite skilled with that blade."

Max glanced down at his knife. "This is merely a . . . hobby."

"You throw knives as a hobby?"

"It helps pass the time," he said indifferently.

"I warned you that you would find the journey tedious."

"As have you." His gaze narrowed on her. "I've

watched you these past few days, angel. You've been restless as a cat in a thunderstorm."

"Because I am worried about my friend Isabella."

His eyebrow lifted. "Is that the only reason? Is it my imagination, or have you been avoiding me ever since we left England?"

Forcing a smile, Caro prevaricated. "I'm sure I don't know what you mean, Mr. Leighton."

"Max. And you have no cause to treat me as if I were a total stranger."

"But you *are* a stranger."

"We were lovers once. I think that puts us on a more intimate footing than mere acquaintances."

The reminder made her pulse falter. Caro found herself staring at Max's full, sensuous mouth, remembering the damp heat of it laving her breasts. A sharp, sweet sensation shot to her loins.

She drew a steadying breath. "That night was a mistake, obviously."

"From my point of view it was nothing of the kind." Casually Max slipped the knife into his coat pocket. Then upturning two barrels to make seats, he settled on one, leaning back against the stern bulkhead. "Tell me about Lady Isabella."

Caro hesitated a long moment before joining him. Surprisingly, she found herself wanting to explain to Max why she was so determined to save her friend and how their relationship had come about in the first place.

"My mother died when I was eight, and Bella was our nearest neighbor. She took control of raising me, even though she claimed to be lacking in maternal instincts, because my father was away a great deal of the time. It was only after her second husband died that Isabella began to travel the world in search of adventure."

"Have you always lived on Cyrene, then?" Max asked.

"Not always. My parents moved there when I was a child. My mother suffered an affliction of the lungs, and the doctors thought a warm climate would benefit her. It helped, but not enough." Caro smiled sadly. "In fact, my mother's debilitating illness was the main reason I became so interested in learning to heal."

"And your father supported your interest?"

"Completely. He was thankful I had something to occupy me while he was gone."

"What took him away so much?"

"Various diplomatic duties for the Foreign Office," she replied, offering the same tale that the world knew. "He grieved so keenly at my mother's death that he threw himself into his work. And then he was killed when I was sixteen—"

Caro broke off suddenly. Her father had been killed in France during a mission for the Guardians, which had led to her taking his place in the order. But she shouldn't be skirting the truth this closely, for Max was too clever for her to blithely share such confidences.

When she remained silent, he asked another probing question. "Yet you lived with Thorne's aunt for your Season. How did that come about?"

He had chosen a safe subject, at least. And she could look back on those days now without the misery she'd felt then; she could even laugh at herself now for entertaining such naive desires of fitting into that haughty, disdainful society. Their acceptance seemed so insignificant to her now, doubtless because she had far more meaningful ways to occupy her time.

"Oddly enough, Lady Hennessy and I became friends when she visited Thorne on the island. Her own daughters were grown by then, and I think perhaps she was appalled to find me so . . . provincial and lacking in social graces." Caro couldn't suppress a wry smile. "You're aware that Lady Hennessy is one of the leaders of the ton?"

"Yes," Max said.

"Well, she firmly believes that every young lady should have a Season. She took me on as her special project and offered to sponsor me. But it was Isabella who convinced me to go to England. Bella never cared a fig for British society, but she persuaded me that I needed to broaden my horizons before deciding on my future. To see more of the world before burying myself on the island. She contended that if I was exposed to more of life, I would make better choices." *Such as not becoming a Guardian,* Caro thought. "It *is* common for all the island's young ladies to have a Season. So five years ago I set out for London, along with two other debutantes and their families. To put it succinctly, I didn't 'take.' "

"Because of your unconventional interest in medicine."

Caro wrinkled her nose while giving him a pert glance. "Precisely. And as you may have observed, I am not sedate or proper or missish."

She could see a glimmer of amusement in Max's eyes even before he responded. "No, sedate and proper are not qualities I would attribute to you."

"Nor was I willing to master the feminine arts to

ensnare a husband. So to spare Lady Hennessy any further embarrassment, I cut short my London stay. But I didn't mind in the least having to return home to Cyrene to work with Dr. Allenby." Her smile took on a hint of defiance. "I happily settled down to live out my days as a spinster. And I've made a very fulfilling life for myself."

She had indeed, Caro added silently. Going on missions for the Guardians whenever a woman or a medic was needed. Assisting the aging island doctor . . . although at first she'd had to fight the prejudice of the male islanders especially.

Yet once more Max was looking at her with that odd expression in his eyes, as if he couldn't quite make up his mind what to believe about her.

"And you have willingly remained unwed all this time?" he asked.

"Yes." There were numerous reasons she had refused to wed. Her strongest was her concern that a husband would demand she give up both her unusual vocations.

She gazed up at Max, her mouth curving with dry humor. "In my experience, few respectable gentlemen want a wife who deals daily with blood and gore and naked bodies."

"You have a point," Max acknowledged, his eyes glinting in response. "But surely not all men would object to your medical pursuits."

Perhaps not, Caro thought, but they would hardly countenance her dangerous career as a Guardian. Nor would she risk exposing the order to an outsider by indulging in a normal courtship. She had long ago accepted that she would never lead an ordinary life.

"Most of the eligible bachelors on our island are not quite so open-minded," she said, striving for a light tone. "And I would never want to leave Cyrene to live in England."

There were other reasons as well for her remaining single, beyond the fact that most gentlemen wanted a proper wife. The men themselves.

Rising restlessly to her feet, Caro looked out over the railing at the gray waters of the Atlantic. All the men she admired and respected enough to marry were other Guardians: men she thought of as brothers rather than prospective bridegrooms. And idealistically, she had always envied the deep, abiding love her parents had known. If she couldn't have love, then she had no desire to marry.

Furthermore, she was now no longer a virgin, and gentlemen usually preferred innocence in their brides.

Feeling herself flush, Caro focused her gaze on the choppy sea below. In the past few days, she'd been reminded of yet another reason she intended to remain single. Max himself.

He'd given her an incredible night of enchantment, and more . . . a tantalizing, compelling glimpse of something profound and powerful between a man and a woman.

The truth was that ever since she had experienced this man's passion, she hadn't wanted to settle for anything less.

She stole a glance at him, her gaze lingering on the beautiful, sculpted features of his face. The fierce tenderness of his lovemaking had changed her. Since their night together, she'd found it much harder to feel content with her life. Max had awakened instincts in her that had lain dormant. Intensified feminine desires she had striven to deny. She'd even found herself wondering what it would be like to have a husband, perhaps a family . . . children.

Her solution had been to throw herself into her duties, but sometimes she wasn't entirely successful.

Nor was she able to dismiss Max now. When he rose to stand beside her at the rail, she could feel the heat of his powerful magnetism. His very nearness brought all her senses alive, made her blood sing. Filled her with need, with a wild yearning she had known only once before . . .

She fought the sudden rush of feeling that assailed her, yet his next casual comment still caught her off guard.

"I find it hard to believe no man ever tried to claim you as his lover. Are all the men on Cyrene blind?"

Somehow Caro managed a calm reply. "Not in the least. They simply find me intimidating. Moreover, most men prefer a certain kind of beauty in a woman. I hardly fill their ideal. I'm not pale or fragile or helpless, nor am I statuesque or voluptuous. Many gentlemen prefer ample bosoms, I've found."

"I think your sun-kissed skin lovely. And I can attest that you have an exquisite body."

Caro sent him an arch glance. "There is no need to shower me with empty flattery, Mr. Leighton."

"It is hardly empty. I find you immensely desirable."

Her brows drew together in skepticism.

Max was surprised by her response. Caro Evers was oblivious to her own beauty, he realized.

It was true, he thought, surveying her; she didn't fit the ideal mold of womanliness or femininity. Her outspoken frankness alone set her apart, as did her lack of artifice. Her figure was lithe and slim, more boyish than the accepted fashion, her body firm and lightly muscled, he knew from experience. And she did nothing to enhance her features, favoring dark, practical gowns and wearing her unruly hair scraped back in a stern knot. Her hands, although gentle, were strong and capable rather than dainty and ladylike.

If he was honest, she was very different from the soft, voluptuous women he'd found appealing in the past. Yet to his surprise, he did consider Caro beautiful. And wholly remarkable.

Beneath her restrained surface lurked something unexpected, something fierce and passionate and unbelievably sensuous.

The enchantress he'd known that night on Cyrene had possessed more sensuality than any woman he'd ever encountered. Her innocent, eager response to his lovemaking had turned him inside out. Even now Max felt a rush of heat whenever he remembered.

And she was courageous and intrepid—many of the qualities he had thought primarily the prerogative of men. From the first he had been struck by her keen intelligence.

Most importantly, she cared ardently about the things that really mattered. About saving lives, about rescuing her captive friend. He suspected Caro would never do anything by half measures. Thorne had been right when he'd dubbed her singular.

The thought of Thorne, however, rekindled the spark of jealousy lingering in Max's breast.

"So what is your relationship to Christopher Thorne?" he asked. "You aren't lovers?"

She blinked at his unexpected change of subject, then gave a soft laugh. "Good heavens, no. He thinks of me as a sister."

"So there is no other man in your life?"

She eyed him with puzzlement. "Why would you ask?"

"I'm possessive enough to want to be your only lover," Max admitted.

He could hear her sharp intake of breath, could see surprise flit across her face.

A moment later, though, her chin lifted. "If you think to use me merely to pass the time and relieve your boredom, you can abandon that notion at once."

Max shook his head. "Dealing with boredom has never been a problem for me. During the war I grew accustomed to long hours of waiting between battles and learned to develop vast reserves of patience."

"Then what are you about?" Her eyes narrowed. "Are you trying to provoke me as Thorne suggested? He was entirely wrong about my needing a diversion. I don't require a seduction to distract me from dwelling on Isabella's fate, I assure you."

"Provoking you wasn't my design, but I want very much to be your lover again."

"Why?" Her tone was challenging.

"Because ever since a certain moonlit night," Max replied honestly, "I've been obsessed with a ministering angel. I need to know if what I felt for her was real or merely a fantasy."

For a long moment Caro remained silent while she struggled with disbelief. "I told you, you were suffering from the stresses of war that night."

"Perhaps so. But my mind doesn't seem to respond

to logical arguments. Nor does my body." His gaze dropped to her breasts. "Does yours?"

No, certainly not. She had little control over her body's sensual reaction to him.

Lifting his gaze, he smiled in satisfaction, as if guessing her thoughts.

After a searching glance, she shook her head. "I understand your problem, Mr. Leighton. It *was* merely a fantasy that night. You were affected by Cyrene's spell. That is why you found me desirable then—and why your imagination is playing tricks on you now."

Max leaned an elbow against the railing. "You claimed Apollo created your enchanted isle, but it's pure myth, of course."

"Probably, but the legend is one I have always found appealing. Cyrene was a water nymph and princess who relished the hunt and enjoyed wrestling lions—"

"Lions?" Max sounded faintly amused. "She must have been rather unique."

"She was. Apollo saw her and fell in love, but when she spurned him, he cast a spell over a secluded isle to create a lovers' paradise and then kept her captive there until she came to love him in return. Even now the island has an inexplicable effect on all who come there."

"It affects mere mortals, you mean."

"It makes them feel passion. *That* is why you think you wish to become my lover again."

Taking her elbow, Max turned Caro to face him. "Did you feel passion that night, angel?"

She flushed. "Well . . . yes . . . but I was affected by the same spell."

His gaze examined her face intently. "I think what

we both felt that night had little to do with any spell." He took a step closer. "And I don't believe you are as sanguine as you pretend now."

He reached up to stroke her cheek in a gentle caress, making Caro feel a sudden heat. She drew back abruptly.

"It burns, doesn't it, my touch?" he murmured.

Yes, it burns. Caro had a momentary flash of strong, bronzed fingers cupping her pale breasts in the silver moonlight.

He lowered his voice to a hush. "Do you remember the feel of me, moving between your thighs?"

At the question she was assaulted by a sizzling memory of Max's hard male flesh lodged deep within her, and her breath faltered.

Refusing to admit her weakness, though, Caro managed a light reply. "I remember everything about that night, and I am not eager to repeat the experience. I don't relish letting my senses be carried away again by the enchantment of the moment."

The slow, knowing smile he gave her made her pulse race. "I think you are deceiving yourself."

"And I think you vastly overestimate your appeal."

Max's eyes darkened as he studied her for a long moment. "I promise you, I don't intend to let you forget what it was like between us that night."

Their gazes locked. The air was suddenly charged with a heated current, and Caro found it difficult to breathe.

The hot attraction sizzling between them grew stronger, more intense. Then Max raised his hand again, letting his thumb brush her lower lip.

His touch was as searing as a bolt of lightning. The

warmth spread through Caro, feeding her nerves little shocks of desire. It left her skin tingling with raw, sexual awareness—

Alarmed, she took a step back . . . and then stopped herself, tilting her chin up instead.

"Don't worry," Max murmured, a smile flickering over his mouth. "I'm not about to ravish you here and now."

"I would advise you not to try."

Yet her warning would have little impact, Caro realized. It was clear Max had no idea of the kind of dangerous skills she possessed. Thus far he'd seen only the healer side of her—the gentle talents a soldier would doubtless find appealing. If he knew the masculine side of her, she suspected he wouldn't be so eager to renew their lovemaking or profess to find her desirable.

Caro held out her hand. "Pray, give me your knife."

Her order gave him pause, made him lift an eyebrow. But he complied, retrieving his knife from his jacket pocket.

"Allow me to show you precisely why gentlemen find me intimidating," Caro said sweetly.

Turning, she took careful aim at the cask Max had been using for a target, then drew back her arm and let the knife fly. The blade landed point down in the wood, vibrating, perhaps two inches to the right of center.

"My aim is a bit rusty," she complained, "since I am out of practice. I can do better, I assure you. But for the moment I must return to the tasks Captain Biddick gave me." She gave Max a deliberately provoking smile. "If you tire of playing with your knife and seek other diversions, you can make yourself useful by mending sails."

With that dig, she spun on her heel. But as she

walked away, she thought she heard Max's low, husky chuckle follow her.

Caro put little stock in his admission that he wanted to become her lover again. Most likely, she conjectured, he was merely attempting to relieve his boredom with a seduction because she was the only woman available, or trying to divert her as a favor to Thorne, even though he had denied both.

Nor could she take seriously his other startling claim—that he'd become obsessed with her after their passionate night together. To her mind, Max had undoubtedly been entranced by the magic of that enchanted night. And because of his memories, he might still view her as an object of desire. Yet she was certain his professed obsession wouldn't last upon deeper acquaintance.

Even so, Caro regretted they still had the major part of their two-week journey remaining. The sooner they reached the island, the sooner she would no longer have to deal with Max in such close quarters.

She was also anxious to arrive home and discover if there had been any word of Isabella. The schooner had been specifically commissioned by Sir Gawain and designed for speed, and thus was remarkably swift compared to other sailing vessels. But the voyage still took far longer than she had any patience for.

When they rounded Gibraltar and the gray Atlantic gave way to the welcoming blue brilliance of the Mediterranean, Caro felt comforted by her more familiar surroundings and the much warmer climate, yet her mood remained dark. On clear days she could make out the Barbary Coast to the south, where Isabella was presumably being held captive. And when she thought of Bella being lost in such a vast expanse, she nearly despaired.

Surprisingly, however, Max's mood seemed even darker than her own. By early in their second week, his restless pacing had grown obviously more agitated. And sometimes at night, she saw him prowling the decks with the slow, angry gait of a caged animal. He looked bedeviled by something.

Her concern prompted her to approach him one afternoon as he again stood at the railing.

"I would be happy to prescribe a sleeping draught," Caro offered, "if you think it would help."

He turned a grim gaze on her. "What makes you think I need a sleeping draught?"

"Perhaps the way you are wearing a hole in Captain Biddick's deck?" She smiled, but his expression only shuttered further.

"I don't care for the aftereffects of laudanum."

"There are several herbals that don't result in the same bad dreams as laudanum."

"You needn't try to cure me, angel."

His terse reply irked Caro, yet she didn't want to just walk away when he was clearly suffering. "Does sailing bother you?"

Max hesitated such a long while that she doubted he would answer, but then he shook his head. "No, but this voyage brings back memories of when I went off so blithely to war. Although the transport ships that carried us to the Peninsula had far less luxurious accommodations than this vessel."

Caro waited, hoping he would say more. But he remained silent.

"Well . . ." She put a hand on his sleeve and felt the tension vibrating in him. "If I can be of any help, you need only ask."

His jaw flexed as if biting back a response. Then he eased his arm from beneath her fingers. "I will be fine."

Realizing he would brook no further discussion, Caro took her leave. Yet she couldn't stop thinking of the bleak expression in Max's blue eyes, or wondering what dark memories had caused it.

. . . exploding ground . . . a horse's scream . . . falling . . . crashing to the wet earth . . . chest pain . . . shot?

Must move . . . mired . . . struggling to rise . . . ahead, Philip wheeling his horse . . . hurts . . . can't stand . . .

Philip returning . . . leaping off . . .

"Philip . . . get the hell away . . . save yourself."

His grim smile . . . "You're bloody mad to think I would leave you. . . ."

His hand reaching down . . . a sharp crack of rifle fire . . . his head . . . his face . . . the blood.

Philip sinking to his knees.

God, Philip, no. No! Please, God, no . . .

"Max, wake up. It is only a bad dream."

Her soft voice. Her soothing hand on his brow . . .

Max woke drenched in sweat. It was the nightmare again, squeezing the breath from his lungs.

Chest heaving, he glanced wildly about him, seeing only darkness. Yet the rhythmic pitch of the ship made him recall where he was. His cabin on board the schooner.

He lay back, struggling for air.

The nightmare had been worse of late. More vivid, more debilitating. He always knew what to expect, and he could never stop it. He could only try to fight it.

He shut his eyes, conjuring up Caro's face. His guardian angel. She could calm him with her soothing voice and gentle hands. Her gray eyes, so soft and luminous and understanding.

She couldn't make him forget his guilt, though.

Flinging off the disheveled covers, Max swung his legs over the side of the bunk and dragged his hands roughly over his face. He still felt the searing pain as sharply as if it were yesterday, instead of five years ago. That moment of doomed courage when his closest friend had returned to save him and been killed right before his eyes.

God . . . he was still shaking from the vision.

Max drew a rasping breath into his lungs, wishing he had better control over himself. He didn't want to forget entirely. He only wanted respite from the pain.

During the day, he knew how to numb himself. On dry land, he would go on long rides, driving himself to the limits of his endurance, making himself weary enough so that sleep would come. But he had no horse at the moment, or at any moment since this damned, endless voyage had begun. In London he would have gone directly to Jackson's boxing salon, so he could take out his bitter frustrations in physical violence, using his bare fists. But there was no one to spar with on board the schooner, certainly not at this late hour of the night when most of the crew was asleep.

Rising from the bunk, Max strode across the dark cabin. He didn't need light to find the knife. Rifling through his belongings from memory, he withdrew a leather sheath that protected the three-inch steel blade set in a carved wooden handle.

Philip's knife. Philip had used it to occupy himself during the interminable hours before battle, whittling objects out of wood—roughly detailed figures of men, soldiers, horses. Not as intricate as the toy soldiers they'd played with as boys, yet somehow more real. Philip had carried the knife with him always, including that final, terrible day.

And Max had kept it so he would never forget his friend's sacrifice.

In the intervening years, he'd developed a strange habit that helped soothe him when he couldn't sleep. Throwing the knife repetitiously, over and over again. The monotony sometimes gave him respite from his bleak thoughts.

Silently, Max dressed in the darkness. Then unsheathing the knife, he left the cabin to go above deck, where he could breathe.

Chapter Four

Caro awakened slowly from her restless dream, wondering what had disturbed her. The hushed closing of a cabin door? The quieter sound of footsteps in the corridor?

She lay there a moment, listening to the wind in the sails, comforted by the usual creaking sway of the ship. The fiery ache aroused by her dream of Max still lingered, yet she couldn't shake the sense that something was wrong.

Climbing out of the narrow bunk, she fumbled for her half boots, then flung a cloak over her nightdress before slipping from her cabin.

The corridor was dark, as was the ladder leading above decks. But when she ascended into the open air, a crescent moon cast a silvery light over the schooner, making the billowing sails appear stark white overhead.

Caro paused to let her eyes adjust and heard a familiar muted thud to her right. Turning, she saw a man near the stern of the ship, silhouetted against the night sky.

The powerful set of his shoulders told her clearly his identity. She had clung to those same hard-muscled shoulders in her erotic dreams a few moments ago. She knew the masculine contours of his body; every line and plane of flesh and sinew had etched itself into her memory more than a year ago.

When she heard another quiet thud coming from his direction, she moved closer, drawn by an inexorable force.

She paused in the shadows to watch Max hurl his knife, but then he suddenly halted his throw, his head sharply turning in her direction, as if he sensed her presence.

"Max, it's Caro," she identified herself, not wanting to become his target should he mistake her for a threat.

Even in the dim light she could see his fingers flex on the knife handle.

"I didn't mean to disturb you," Caro added. "I thought something might be wrong. I will leave you now—"

"You needn't go."

She felt his gaze rake over her, taking in her disheveled appearance, her hair spilling down around her shoulders, and heard him draw a steadying breath. "I would like your company."

She hesitated, glancing at the knife he held.

Max seemed to force a smile as he lowered the blade. "I'm not dangerous."

Are you not? Caro thought to herself. She considered this man supremely dangerous. She should know better than to be alone with him on a moonlit night. He didn't look in the mood for company, either; a dark stubble shadowed his jaw, and his raven hair was wild, as if he'd raked his hand through it countless times.

And yet he had asked her to stay.

He gestured politely toward the cask that he'd been using as a target. "Come, join me."

Crossing the deck, she settled gingerly on the cask. To her surprise, Max moved a slight distance away, as if he thought her dangerous as well.

Yet his tone was genial enough when he spoke. "So what lured you from your nice, hard bunk, sweeting?"

Determined to keep their conversation light, Caro answered in the same vein. "My nice, hard bunk, no doubt. And you? Were you having trouble sleeping again? If it is insomnia, Max, there are medical remedies."

His expression was inscrutable, but she sensed his grimness. "There is no cure for my kind of sleeplessness."

She frowned at his reply, wondering what he wasn't saying, wondering just how serious his suffering was. In London she hadn't thought Max in pain. Certainly nothing like the torment of a year ago. Yet his emotional wounds might have cut so deeply, they'd only had time to scar over on the surface. Perhaps his torment, while diminished, hadn't subsided altogether. She had heard of cases where soldiers recovering from battle took years to resume normalcy.

Perhaps she should leave him alone, Caro told herself, but the words seemed to be dredged from her. "Why can't you sleep, Max? Because of your memories of war?"

He laughed softly. "You might say that." She could hear his anger, his frustration. Shoving the knife in his pocket, he raised his head to stare out at the dark sea. "Does a soldier ever forget what he's seen?"

She could only imagine what he had seen. The horrors that went beyond the soul's ability to understand.

Her heart went out to him, just as it had more than a year ago. The stark, haunting beauty of his face, too, reminded her of that night.

"I wish I could help," she said softly.

He turned to look at her, his voice low when he replied. "You did help, angel. More than you know. That night at the ruins . . ." He took a shuddering breath but held her gaze intently. "My memories of you sustained me through that final grueling year of the war. If not for you, I'm not certain I could have gone on."

Her eyes widening, Caro could only regard him with incomprehension.

His lips curved in a faint smile. "It's true. You gave me the strength to carry on the battle. I have little doubt you are the reason I returned from the war alive."

Perhaps she had contributed in part to restoring his fortitude, Caro conceded. Max had been seasoned in hell, and for a brief while she might have made him forget his demons. Yet she found it hard to credit that she had saved his life.

He seemed entirely serious, though, as his gaze delved into hers. "From that night on I began to think of you as my guardian angel."

Astonished by his revelations, she regarded him mutely, her thoughts an unwieldy jumble of emotion.

Max had called her his guardian angel, yet he couldn't know she truly was a *Guardian*. Still, his admission undermined all her defenses. It was strangely seductive to be told she had meant so much to him. Enticing to think she had held that much importance in his life.

As she returned his intense gaze, yearning sprang up in her, so sudden and sharp, it frightened her.

Her feelings, however, were far less important just now than his. Perhaps getting him to talk about his memories would ease his burden further. After a moment, she asked another question. "Was it very terrible, what you experienced?"

She had struck a raw nerve, she could tell at once. For a score of heartbeats Caro watched the emotions war on his face. She could see the desperation and the desolation there, a torment in his eyes that wrenched her heart.

"There is one nightmare that won't end," he said in a hoarse voice.

"What nightmare?"

"My closest friend—" He broke off, shutting his eyes.

Caro couldn't bear to see him like this. She longed to make that terrible shadow go away.

"I want to help," she said again softly.

He drew another steadying breath, clearly struggling for control. "There is nothing you can do."

But perhaps there was.

She sat there a moment longer, battling the feelings that fought and tangled inside her—her own desire, her fierce need to comfort him.

Rising slowly then, she went to him, knowing she would do anything to take that look of anguish from his eyes. Reaching up, she set her hand against Max's cheek, flush against his warm skin.

"Caro . . ." The word was rough, a warning.

She saw heat and deep hunger in his eyes, felt the hard pressure of his fingers as they clutched her upper arms, yet she could see the battle he was waging with himself.

His hands moved to her hair then, twisting in the unruly tresses.

Staring down at her upturned face, at her skin bathed in moonlight, Max struggled against his deepest urges. He wanted nothing more than to take what Caro offered, yet he couldn't trust himself when he was this raw, this vulnerable. If he let his mouth cover hers, he knew he wouldn't stop until he was buried deep within her body. He would haul her into his arms and carry her to his cabin where he would sate his primal desire for the rest of the night.

Max clenched his jaw, striving to rein in his savage need. If Caro's surrender was all he wanted, he knew he would succeed. He recognized the desire in her eyes, the unmistakable yearning. She was his for the taking.

But he wanted more than her seduction. More than her compassion. He wanted her *passion*, complete and unequivocal. Not just her comforting solace as she tried to heal him.

He fought down the urge to take her right now.

"You need to go," his ground out, his voice gruff. Abruptly he gripped her shoulders to set her away from him.

Caro remained staring at him, searching his face in confusion.

Max retreated a half-dozen steps, shuttering his expression. "I don't want your comfort, sweetheart. I don't need it."

That was entirely debatable, Caro thought darkly, torn between humiliation at his brusque dismissal and mounting anger. But she didn't intend to stand there arguing with him.

"Very well. I will leave you to your own scintillating company."

Stiffening her spine, she turned sharply and made her way across the deck and through the hatch to the ladder.

By the time she negotiated the dark corridor and reached her cabin, Caro was furious at herself. She had practically thrown herself at Max again! And this time he had rebuffed her in no uncertain terms.

Caro flung herself on her bunk facedown, cursing herself and him both. In another instant, she drew back her fist and punched her pillow violently. How could she have behaved like such a witless fool again?

She was *glad* Max hadn't wanted her comfort. Glad she hadn't made the same idiotic mistake she'd made a year ago—giving him her body in an effort to heal him. She should have learned her lesson the first time.

From now on, however, she intended to crush every soft, feminine feeling she'd ever felt for Max. Every ounce of compassion. Every trace of desire. Every fragment of lust.

Ruthlessly.

She would conquer her damnable attraction for him or die trying.

Max stood at the ship's railing in the brilliant light of day, remembering his regrettable encounter with Caro last night. Despite his harshness in sending her away, his intent at least had been laudable. It would have been indefensible to take advantage of her compassion for wounded creatures. He'd wanted her more than his next breath—but not on those terms.

He hadn't wanted her probing his secrets, either.

Didn't want her knowing how many nights he woke in a cold sweat, fighting a clawing sense of suffocation, shaking with recollections of Philip's death. As it was, Max reflected, he'd said too damned much last night. Revealed too much of himself.

Still, just a taste of Caro's tenderness had banished some of the chill that gripped him.

It wasn't the first time. Since making love to her at the ruins, he'd felt an invisible bond between them. She was his guardian angel, the loving spirit who stood watch over him.

He'd lost count of the many times she had coaxed him through the darkest hours of night. Sometimes she called his name softly, waking him from the nightmare. Sometimes she sang his name, soothing him into sleep. Sometimes he even had long imaginary conversations with her.

Always he deliberately conjured her lovely image in his mind, purposely dreaming of her to keep the visions at bay.

That last year he might have gone mad if not for her.

Perhaps he was still a little mad. He couldn't forget what had happened on that battlefield at Talavera. Couldn't forgive himself.

How can you live with yourself when your best friend sacrificed his life for you?

Max stared out at the brilliant sea as golden-bright sunlight glinted off blue water. If not for him, Philip would never even have entered the army. Philip Hurst had been heir to an earldom, and eldest sons of the nobility weren't destined for use as cannon fodder. But he'd needed little persuasion to follow Max off to war.

They had both been so eager then, so bloody idealistic. They'd shipped out for the Peninsula, laughing and jesting about how many Frogs they would rout. They'd learned soon enough the gruesome realities of war.

Max's jaw tightened at the memory. He'd always refused to speak of his friend's death to anyone. Even now he couldn't bring himself to bare his grief, his guilt. Not even to Caro. But he could have been more gentle in his rebuff of her.

He did want her comfort. Needed it. There was something profoundly healing in her touch. But even more, he wanted her passion.

Squinting against the glare, Max turned and braced his back against the railing. He'd positioned himself so he would know the moment Caro emerged from belowdecks.

He wanted her badly. The fire they'd kindled at the ruins still blazed between them—merely touching her was proof enough of that. But after last night he would have to convince Caro of his desire.

He had deliberately driven her away then, but now he intended to remedy his mistake.

He meant to make very clear that his anguish over his friend's death had nothing to do with his feelings for her.

She saw Max the moment she came up on deck. Caro's step faltered, a flush suffusing her face when she recalled her brazenness last night. Even after a restless sleep, she still felt the sting of his rejection.

When he made his way across the deck toward her, she squared her shoulders and stood her ground. His raven hair was windblown, though, and an errant lock had fallen onto his forehead, making him look younger and a bit vulnerable. She fisted her fingers to prevent them from reaching up and smoothing it back from his face.

Before she could say a word, Max held up a hand to forestall her. "I owe you an apology, angel. I know you only meant to help last night."

She regarded him warily. "Yes, I did."

"I don't like to talk about my nightmares."

"I could tell," Caro said dryly. "But you should have no fear that I will repeat my mistake. I won't try to comfort you again."

"I would regret that immensely. Last night I wanted like blazes to do much more than kiss you. But I knew if I started, I would never stop."

The dark, intent look in his eyes suggested he was telling the truth.

"Well, it doesn't matter now in the least," Caro replied with a shrug.

"It matters a great deal," Max countered.

Taking a step closer, he slipped a hand behind her nape and brought his mouth down on hers. His kiss was hard, sensual, compelling . . . deliberately arousing.

Beyond her gasp of surprise, Caro was too startled to struggle. How could a single kiss resonate in every inch of her body, filling her with such dizzying waves of sensation? At the delicious taste of his mouth, all her senses came to instant, vivid life, while scalding heat flared inside her, pooling low in her middle.

His kiss was all too brief, though. Just as abruptly, Max released her.

Caro stood there, dazed and momentarily speechless, while his searching gaze raked her face. He must have been pleased by what he saw, for a gleam of male satisfaction lit the blue depths of his eyes.

"I thought so," Max said, his voice low and slightly husky. "You can't pretend indifference any more than I can."

Lifting her chin, Caro speared him with an accusatory glance. "What the devil do you mean, kissing me right here where anyone in the crew could see?"

"Next time I will be certain to ensure our privacy."

"There won't be a next time!"

"Of course there will. You just proved my point."

"What point?"

"That I want you, sweet angel. And that you want me almost as badly."

That was indisputably true, Caro admitted to herself. She did want him—intensely. But she didn't mean to give Max the satisfaction of knowing it.

Cursing her deplorable reaction, she inhaled a steadying breath and fumbled for the knife in the pocket of her cloak. When she drew it out, showing Max the sharp, four-inch steel blade, his eyes abruptly narrowed.

"As you can see," she declared, "I have my own knife."

It was Max's turn to look wary.

"Don't worry, I promise not to hurt you," Caro said with an indulgent smile of her own. "I thought we might hold a competition."

"A competition?"

"A knife-throwing contest. Something to distract us both. To help work off our restlessness. I intended to make the suggestion before you so unceremoniously assaulted me. What?" Caro asked when Max's gaze continued to measure her. "Are you afraid I will best you?"

His mouth curved in a grudging—and unmistakably amused—smile. "Perhaps I *should* be afraid. I'm beginning to realize it is unwise to underestimate you."

"It is indeed. But our competition will have to wait until this afternoon. I told Captain Biddick I would review the ship's ledgers this morning, since he has so little fondness for tallying. Shall we say three o'clock?"

"Very well, angel. Three o'clock it is."

They met at the appointed time and set the rules and conditions of their competition, agreeing on the best of ten throws for each target, with ten different targets to make a game, three games to a match.

"You may very well win for now since I am out of practice," Caro acknowledged as they placed casks at varying heights and distances and marked bull's-eyes, "but I am a swift learner."

"I remember," Max said, a glint in his eyes.

At his pointed reminder of their night of lovemaking, color rose in her cheeks, but it was Max's next remark that flustered her.

"If I win, I intend to claim you as my prize."

"Certainly not! We will play for pennies."

When she took her first practice throw and came only inches from the bull's-eye, Max nodded in appreciation.

"Who taught you to wield a knife?"

"My father."

"He evidently had some unique ideas regarding a daughter's upbringing."

You don't know the half of it, Caro thought. "True. But our island is much more accepting of unconventional females. We also have a great many intriguing male characters. I once knew a pirate who liked to throw knives at live targets."

"That was his idea of entertainment?"

"Yes, but he encountered a fellow pirate who preferred sabers, and so lost his head."

"A bloodthirsty lot on your island."

Caro smiled enigmatically. "Not at all, but we do have more than our share of adventurers."

The afternoon sun was warm enough that Max took off his coat. Seeing the play of muscle beneath the fine cambric of his shirt, Caro told herself it was only the exhilaration of the competition that made her heart pump faster, but she knew she lied.

They both quieted when the match began, for winning required concentration. Watching Max, Caro knew at once she was dealing with a master. His throws seemed effortless yet so controlled they landed with lethal precision. And unlike her, he knew how to make allowances for the roll of the ship.

It irked her that Max was so skilled, since it had taken her years to perfect her own talents.

It annoyed Caro more that she couldn't repress her admiration for him. He was every bit as good as the Guardians who had taught her. The distressing truth was, she reacted very differently to Max than she did to her fellow Guardians. She couldn't possibly look at him as a brother. The raw sexuality that hummed around him was impossible to ignore, as was his vital strength. Even more profound was the almost tangible sense of fortitude she recognized in him.

He was a warrior, every inch of him, and it spoke to the warrior in her.

That was what made him so dangerous to her, Caro realized.

It was also during their match that she acknowledged her miscalculation. She had meant to prove to Max how misplaced his desire was by showing off her masculine skills, but he seemed to find her unconventionality highly intriguing rather than worthy of disdain.

She almost regretted suggesting their competition. And yet she had only to see the fierce gleam in Max's eyes to know he was taking great pleasure in their contest.

When the match concluded, Caro had lost, but by a respectable margin. She owed him six shillings but told Max she would wait to pay her debt.

"For tomorrow I intend to beat you," she announced with a defiant toss of her head.

A lazy smile flickered across his mouth. "Did I ever tell you, my fair witch, how much I relish a challenge?"

She had the distinct feeling Max wasn't simply talking about their game with knives.

"So do I," she retorted.

His blue eyes narrowed, appraising her. His look was provocative and sensual enough to make her heart skitter. "Then we are well matched, I would say."

A shiver of anticipation ran down Caro's spine. She would say the same thing—they *were* well matched. Yet she knew she would require not only all her skill but all her willpower to hold her own with Max.

Although she never quite won, Caro did come to relish her rivalry with him, for their contests not only helped ease her restlessness during the final days of the voyage, but provided her a distraction from the despairing thoughts that had haunted her ever since learning of Isabella's disappearance.

It was only, however, when they passed Ibiza and the other Balearic Islands, Mallorca and Menorca, that the knots in Caro's stomach began to lessen. Soon she would be home. She would be able to act, to do something toward helping find her dear friend, instead of merely enduring this interminable waiting.

She wanted to reach Cyrene for Max's sake as well, knowing the serenity of the island would benefit him. His own restlessness seemed to have diminished—he was a fierce competitor and seemed to find their rivalry as stimulating as she did. But she knew he still sometimes woke in the dark hours of night to pace the decks.

And finally, she wanted to be home for her own sake, on her own familiar ground where she could have better control of herself. She still hadn't conquered her damnable attraction for Max, especially in moonlight.

On the final night of their voyage, they dined with the captain and first mate. When afterward Caro accepted Captain Biddick's invitation for a stroll, Max joined them. Then a short while later, the captain was called away on a matter involving a crew member's discipline—much to her dismay.

Left alone with Max, Caro felt an abrupt return of the tension that had plagued her during the first part of their journey. The waxing moon was only half-full, but brilliant enough to turn the sea to a shimmering, rippling mirror, reminding her of their moonlit tryst when she had made love to him.

And when Max turned his head to gaze at her, she

knew he was remembering as well. The intensity of his expression made her heart race, sent heat lancing through her body.

"Whenever I see a moon this bright," he murmured, "I think of you."

Caro couldn't trust herself to reply. Her nerves suddenly felt on a razor's edge, her senses sharply heightened.

Then Max moved to stand behind her.

If he meant to remind her of the passion they had shared, he was succeeding. He didn't even have to touch her—he aroused her just by his nearness. Her body reacted with sexual need; her heart leapt and her skin ignited with searing warmth.

She reached out to grip the railing to steady herself, gazing helplessly out at the vast, silver sea.

Behind her, Max remained silent. They might have been in their own secret world, their own dream, just like at the ruins.

But if this were a dream, Caro thought, dazed, he would take down her hair and twine his fingers through it, stroking and arousing her. If this were a dream, he would bare her breasts to the moonlight and lower his mouth to suckle her. If this were a dream . . .

Caro squeezed her eyes closed. She didn't want this moment to be a dream. She wanted it to be real. She felt so alive when she was near Max, felt reckless and wild. He was temptation incarnate.

She dragged in a breath. It was alarming how badly she wanted him to touch her.

As if granting her wish, he brought his hands up to lightly clasp her arms and pressed his lips against her hair.

Every muscle in her body tightened. Then he bent lower, his lips hovering at the nape of her neck, his hot breath fanning her skin, assaulting her senses. He was intentionally tormenting her, she suspected.

Her breathing sharpened painfully, blood pounded in her ears. She could feel her nipples suddenly ache with longing, could feel moisture gathering between her thighs. She wanted to feel Max glide sleek and hot inside her. . . .

When his lips touched her nape in the lightest of kisses, she arched against the exquisite pressure. The physical attraction assailing her was as powerful, as overwhelming as her first time with him, perhaps even more so. Desire flared in her, wild yearning roaring again with life, with hunger.

Heaven help her, this was dangerous, Caro's conscience screamed silently. Max was dangerous. He made her feel too much. He made her *crave* too much.

A craving she *had* to conquer before she foolishly succumbed to his temptation again . . .

Pulling away from him abruptly, Caro stepped aside on shaking limbs. "I intend to retire now," she said unsteadily, "since I want to be well rested when we arrive tomorrow."

He didn't try to stop her, but she felt his gaze follow her as she made her escape and took refuge in her own cabin. She could feel her heart still thudding, her body thrumming with awareness.

Forcing herself to let out the breath she had been holding, Caro went to the porthole window and opened it, letting the night breeze flood her tiny cabin and cool her fevered pulse.

It was deplorable how she lost control of her senses

whenever she encountered that man in moonlight. She was a Guardian, as close to a warrior as a female could get. She had faced challenges that would daunt the bravest of souls.

Yet she was clearly unable to deal with Max.

Swearing under her breath, Caro curled her fingers into fists. She couldn't let this continue. She would have to find some way to take the offensive.

It was either that or allow Max to slowly drive her mad.

Caro spent a restless night tossing and turning, but by the following morning she had settled on a plan. The moment they arrived on Cyrene, she intended to find someone else to capture Max's interest. Another woman, a ravishing beauty to attract and fascinate and comfort him. She had two excellent candidates in mind, both far more alluring than she was.

Perhaps then she could turn his unwanted attention away from her.

Once she resolved to fight back, Caro felt more in control of herself. After breakfast, she went above decks to watch for signs of land.

A shout from the lookout in the rigging alerted her that Cyrene had been sighted. A short while later, Caro finally spied a dark speck on the horizon. And at length, the speck grew until she could make out the outline of Cyrene's two forested mountain peaks.

Her heart lightened at the sight of her beloved home. Even from a distance, the island seemed to possess an enchantment that never failed to stir her soul. The very air shimmered with brighter clarity here, the sky gleamed a deeper blue, the sea dazzled with vibrant jeweled colors—sapphire and turquoise and aquamarine.

Already the magic was having a soothing effect on her restless nerves. She turned her face up to the sun, drinking in the nourishing warmth.

She sensed Max's presence even before he spoke from behind her. "You look as if you're paying homage to the sun god."

Caro smiled, knowing her expression showed pleasure, if not actual awe. "That isn't as far-fetched as it sounds. Apollo has long been revered on our island."

"I take it you are eager to be home?" Max asked as he joined her at the railing.

She nodded fervently. "There is nowhere I would rather be." She gave him a curious glance. "Don't you prefer your home to anywhere else?"

"I'm not particularly attached to my home, no. Possibly because I have spent little time there since I entered the army. My estates are in Yorkshire. The land there has a sort of rugged beauty, but nothing like your island." Max paused before adding, "Why don't you tell me about Cyrene? On my last visit I was too preoccupied with Yates's critical state to notice much about it. But I understand that several thousand people of different nationalities live there."

"Yes," Caro replied. "The population is largely Spanish, but also British, French, Italian, and even Greek."

"Thorne told me the prominent families are English. How did that come about?"

Her mouth pursed as she debated how much to say. The remarkable history of how the island had come to be settled centuries ago by the first Guardians of the Sword was a well-kept secret.

"I suppose you could say wars have been the main cause. The first Britons came here long ago, even before the Moors took control of the western Mediterranean. And scores of British exiles settled here over the centuries as the result of various political and military upheavals. Cyrene eventually became a Spanish possession, and then was ceded to Britain nearly a hundred years ago."

"With the Treaty of Utrecht."

"Yes, along with Menorca and Gibraltar. The English population increased significantly after that, and the Spaniards began to copy our English customs as well. Menorca ultimately reverted back to Spain, but we remained a British protectorate, with our own rule and our own lieutenant governor. We've always been rather independent-minded."

"How did you manage to keep from being swallowed up by all the different conquering forces over the years?"

"We were wise enough to pay tribute to the ruling powers for protection," Caro said dryly. "It's also fortunate that we are somewhat isolated and have our own natural defenses. Do you see the cliffs there?" She pointed to the jagged, soaring cliffs that rimmed the western edge of the isle. "Much of the island is difficult to scale. We also have three fortresses and dozens of watchtowers overlooking the more vulnerable coves and bays. And note the whitecaps there below."

Caro lowered her hand to the sea, indicating where the brilliant blue waters gave way to shallower green flecked with white. "Those are rock reefs, and around them swirl dangerous currents. Captain Biddick knows all the navigable channels around the island, but to the uninformed, the currents can be treacherous."

"So Cyrene generally escaped the bloody history of many other Mediterranean isles."

"Thankfully," Caro said. "The biggest threat has always been pirate raids. There are numerous incidents of pirates pillaging and carrying off slaves. But any larger invasions were never successful. When the Moors tried to attack Cyrene nine hundred years ago, a great storm sank half their fleet. And a decade ago, when the French gathered for an assault, a strange fog enveloped their ships for days and sent several of them crashing into the reefs."

Max looked skeptical.

"Those are historically documented facts, not legends," Caro insisted.

He was afforded a good view of Cyrene as they sailed around the southern tip. Caro hadn't exaggerated about the natural defenses that protected the island, Max saw. The towering cliffs, the rocky reefs, the wicked currents, all would have been significant deterrents to invasion over the centuries.

Additionally, during their approach, he counted no fewer than eight watchtowers, along with an imposing fortress guarding the rugged western coastline. Plus another castle stronghold at the southern end of the island, where the hills were the lowest and most vulnerable to attack.

"Sir Gawain Olwen lives there," Caro informed him, pointing to the latter. "Olwen Castle has been in his family for centuries."

"The man who heads the Mediterranean branch of the Foreign Office? Thorne's superior?"

"Yes."

Another massive fortress fortified with cannon overlooked the seaport to the southeast, Max noted as they sailed closer. Simply to access the small harbor, they would be required to navigate a narrow strait formed by two jutting rock promontories.

Significant defenses indeed.

When the schooner changed course to approach the strait, Caro pointed to the bluffs on her right. "Thorne's villa, where you will be staying, lies a few miles up the coast. The house overlooks a secluded cove and has a magnificent view of the sea."

"What about the ruins? I remember they face east, but where exactly are they?"

Caro felt herself blush at what she suspected was his deliberate reminder. "Another seven or eight miles directly north of Thorne's estate."

"I intend to visit there again with you."

Her heart skipped a beat. She rarely visited the ruins anymore, since there were just too many emotional memories for her there. Certainly she would never go there again with Max. She was far too likely to lose command of her senses there with him.

"I will be happy to draw you a map," Caro said, "so you may visit on your own."

"I never expected you to be so fainthearted."

Her eyes narrowed. "I am not fainthearted. I simply don't wish to be your lover."

"Why not?"

Because nothing can come of it. Because I won't

make myself so vulnerable to you again, for you will only leave me. . . .

"Because you will only be on Cyrene for a brief time," Caro replied.

"Time enough for us to become better acquainted. There is so much more to lovemaking that I never showed you."

Her heart somersaulted wildly, but with effort she summoned a nonchalant smile. "Pray let me repeat myself, Mr. Leighton. I am not interested."

"Forgive me if I don't believe you." Max raised a hand to trace his thumb along her lower lip to the corner of her mouth—and smiled when Caro drew back sharply. "See? You can't deny you felt that."

She couldn't make any such denial. Max had only to touch her and fire leapt between them.

"You can't pretend I don't affect you," he murmured. "I recognized all the signs of an aroused woman last evening—your shallow breath, your rapid pulse, your flushed skin."

She cleared her throat. "Perhaps. But according to medical journals, arousal is a common phenomenon in nature."

"Is that why your body felt so tight?"

How did he know how her body had felt? Had he been aware of the hot tingling inside her? How her nipples had contracted into taut buds that throbbed with a pleasurable ache . . .

Averting her gaze, Caro pretended to study the bluffs overhead. "A natural phenomenon," she insisted more hoarsely than she intended. "Simply a spontaneous physical reaction to an . . . attractive man. Just as your condition is natural and predictable."

She sent Max a provocative glance. "The male of a species is readily stricken by lust. That is your trouble, Mr. Leighton, I'm certain. You are suffering from simple lust." Caro let her lips spread in a smile. "And I know the perfect cure. Another woman to capture your interest. I know several beauties who would welcome your attentions. Two in particular you will find far more appealing than you find me. I will introduce you at the first opportunity."

Max stood looking at her with veiled amusement. "I am not interested in any woman but you, sweeting."

It was true, he thought with conviction. He still desired Caro—keenly. The passing days had made no difference to his strange obsession for her, in fact had only sparked his craving.

Caro stirred his blood like no woman ever had. Against his will her spirited challenges had pierced the protective shell he'd formed around himself, making him slowly begin to come alive again. And for the first time since the tragedy, his dark memories of Philip had diminished.

Oh, yes, he wanted Caro. Even more so during the past week. His dreams had quieted since he'd told her about his nightmares. The trouble was, they had also become more erotic . . . and featured Caro prominently, despite his effort to keep them tame. Simply looking at her now made him recall vividly what it felt like to lose himself in the magic of her sweet body. Made him want to plunge deep inside her and feel her velvet heat close around him . . .

"We will be lovers again, I have no doubt," Max observed with unwavering assurance.

Arching an eyebrow, Caro managed a laugh. "You are very arrogant."

"Merely confident."

"Your confidence is misplaced. I have no intention of succumbing to any seduction."

"Shall we put it to the test?" Max asked.

Her brows snapped together. "What do you mean?"

"I thought we should hold a competition. To see how long you can resist me. I wager it will only be a matter of days."

She regarded him warily, obviously debating with herself, Max saw. He'd deliberately provoked her, but he doubted she could stop herself from taking up his challenge. Caro Evers was not the kind of woman to back down.

He was right.

"I would require certain terms," she said. "If I succeed, my prize will be that you cease to plague me. Agreed?"

"Yes, since I have little concern you will succeed. As for length . . . say, until the next new moon?"

"That is more than a fortnight from now."

"Crying craven so soon?"

She gave him a defiant look, then tossed her head. "Very well. If you want a competition, I will gladly give you one. But you are sure to lose."

Max had to work hard to control his smile of triumph. Caro obviously wouldn't consider the possibility of defeat, but neither would he. He was prepared to employ whatever tactics necessary in order to win her.

Turning away, Max focused his gaze on the approaching harbor. The vista held an enchanting charm characteristic of the Mediterranean, he thought, listening to the cries of gulls and terns that swooped down to greet them.

Above, bathed in golden warmth, a bustling town perched precariously on the hillside, its whitewashed houses gleaming in the sun, colorfully accented by splashes of blue trim and roofs of red tile, shaded by tall palms and draped with bougainvillea. A steep cobblestone lane zigzagged down the steep face to the water.

The harbor itself smelled of brine and fish and tar but appeared spotlessly clean. Along with dozens of fishing vessels, Max saw two ships lying at anchor. Caro seemed to recognize them, and appeared relieved.

Max would have asked her about them, but just then the schooner began to slow as the captain shouted orders to lower sails. And Caro spoke first, informing him of her plan.

"Once we dock, Captain Biddick will have someone show you to Thorne's villa. It isn't too long a drive from town."

"You won't be accompanying me?"

She flashed him a pert glance, reminding him of the competition they had just declared. "You hardly need me. And I must meet with Sir Gawain as soon as possible to discover what he has learned of Isabella in my absence. I have dispatches to give him as well."

"Shouldn't we discuss my participation?"

"That can wait. He will need time to read the letter of introduction Thorne wrote for you and to decide how he wishes to use you, if at all."

Max's mouth curved. "You weren't in favor of my joining you. Can I trust you not to thwart my cause, angel?"

"If you are as skilled as Thorne says, then I will welcome your help. And regardless of my opinion, Sir Gawain will make up his own mind about you. He is an excellent judge of character."

Max might have made a reply in defense of his character, but Caro's attention was riveted on the quay.

"It is possible someone will meet me," she murmured, her gaze anxiously scanning the crowd that had gathered there. "Ah, there is Señor Verra."

She seemed to be acknowledging a tall, swarthy man who stood beside a cart drawn by two mules. And when she lifted her hand to wave, the man responded in kind.

"I hope you will forgive me for abandoning you," Caro said sweetly to Max, suggesting an obvious desire to be rid of him.

"Of course," he replied, keeping his tone easy. "Your friend Lady Isabella comes first. Will I see you tomorrow?"

"Perhaps the day after. Dr. Allenby may need me tomorrow since he has been without an assistant all the weeks I've been gone. But I will arrange to have some of our island gentry call upon you first thing tomorrow morning so you will feel welcome."

Clutching the leather pouch Thorne had given her, she crossed to the quarterdeck, where the captain stood. They conferred for a moment, with Captain Biddick nodding several times, before he escorted her to the railing.

Despite her skirts, Caro scurried agilely over the side and down a rope ladder into a small skiff, which rowed her to the docks.

Max felt oddly bereft at her departure. Moments

later he suffered a decided pang of jealousy as Caro spoke animatedly with Señor Verra. He watched as she allowed Verra to assist her into the cart, feeling a surge of pure male possessiveness, and continued watching as they began the long climb up the hill.

Max was almost startled when the captain spoke at his elbow.

"Welcome to Cyrene, Mr. Leighton. I trust you will enjoy your stay on our beautiful island."

His mouth curled wryly as he watched the retreating cart. Caro had won this round, he conceded. He had no idea when he would even see her next. And considering the fact that she had just driven off with another man, his campaign to win her had just suffered a decided setback.

But he had always relished a challenge, Max reminded himself. If he had any say about it, he would definitely enjoy his stay on Cyrene.

Chapter Five

Brandy in hand, Max moved restlessly across the study to the French doors, which looked out upon the vast Mediterranean. Thorne's luxurious villa sat high on a bluff above a secluded cove and offered every possible comfort. Like many Spanish-style manors, it boasted four galleried wings built around an open central courtyard. But it was the magnificent night view of the sea that called to Max.

He opened the doors to let in the gentle, salt-tinged breezes. In England autumn would be ripening, but here summer seemed still to linger, with a swollen half-moon casting a silver light over the endless, shimmering stretch of water.

Beholding such scenic splendor, he found it easy to believe in mystical spells. To accept that Cyrene was an isle of bliss with the ability to seduce the senses and arouse wild, primal urges in its inhabitants. He did indeed feel a strange, beguiling power. He attributed it, however, to the island's extraordinary beauty. Here was a genuine paradise, with a serenity he'd found nowhere else in the world.

He shouldn't feel so restless, then. Since his arrival this afternoon, he'd taken a long swim in the cove and enjoyed an excellent dinner served by Thorne's capable staff, then strolled in the terrace gardens and perused several rare volumes of history in Thorne's well-stocked library until it was time to retire to bed. But peace had eluded Max.

As usual he resisted sleeping so as to keep his dark visions at bay.

Fingering the knife in his pocket, Max took a slow swallow of brandy. For a time after Philip's death, he had tried to drink his nightmares into oblivion, but sotting himself hadn't helped.

After his visit to Cyrene last year, however, he'd had his guardian angel beside him, keeping him company, giving him strength.

It comforted him simply to think of her. Her image alone could often banish the chimeras that plagued him.

He closed his eyes now and let his mind fill with vivid memories of Caro. The pulse of her throat under his fingertips when she arched in pleasure against him. The taste of her warm lips as she opened to him. The fiery ecstasy as her sleek heat clenched around his aching shaft . . .

Perhaps he was under Caro's spell, not the island's, Max reflected. And he might never be free of the haunting power she held over him. Might never be able to get her out of his mind, his blood—

Max tensed suddenly, unable to shake the feeling of being watched. He caught the pungent odor of a cheroot at the same moment he saw the red glow of ashes in the darkness.

A figure stood in the shadows of a carob tree, within striking distance.

Needles of alarm pricked Max's spine, making him reflexively reach for his sabre. Finding no weapon hanging at his side, he withdrew the knife from his coat pocket. Just then the stranger ground out the cheroot beneath his heel and strode forward, into the light from the study.

He was followed closely by a shorter, bulkier man.

"I see," the first gentleman said easily as he sauntered past Max into the room, "that you have made yourself at home with Thorne's brandy." When Max's eyebrow shot up at his temerity, the stranger introduced himself. "I am Alex Ryder. And this is Santos Verra."

Verra was the man Caro had driven off with this afternoon, Max recalled.

"*Buenas noches,* Señor Leighton," the Spaniard said, flashing a grin that made his teeth gleam white in his swarthy face.

Ryder had dark hair and eyes as well, but his tanned skin was the result of bronzing by the sun rather than the olive complexion of many of the Mediterranean peoples. And his accent was pure, blue-blooded British. Verra, Max surmised, looked to be about ten years older than himself; Ryder near his own age of thirty-two.

Meeting Ryder's gaze, Max knew instantly that he was dealing with a worthy adversary; those keen, dark eyes held the alert, measuring intensity of a man who would give no quarter in battle or otherwise.

Ryder didn't offer to shake hands but helped himself to a generous glass of the aforementioned brandy and offered his Spanish friend one as well.

When Max's mouth curled dryly, the Spaniard flashed another grin. "Señor Thorne will not object, I assure you. We are compadres."

"Do *you* object?" Ryder asked Max coolly as he settled himself in a stuffed leather chair.

"If I did?"

Ryder returned a dangerous smile as he eyed the knife Max held. "I would take your lack of hospitality into consideration."

"If you expect me to be hospitable, you might explain why you've been watching me."

"Sir Gawain Olwen sent us to welcome you—and to ask you a few questions."

"Ah," Max said, relaxing for the first time. He did understand. "You're here to see if I pass muster."

That brought the first gleam of approval to Ryder's eyes. "Something like that."

Restoring the knife to his pocket, Max settled in an opposing chair and regarded his unexpected visitors. Of the two, Ryder seemed far less forthcoming than the jovial Verra. Max thought he would do better to address the Spaniard if he hoped to learn anything while they conducted their own investigation of him.

"Captain Biddick told me something about you, Señor Verra. You own the local tavern."

"*Si,* señor. I have the finest wines and liquors on the island. I supply Thorne with all his vintages. You should try the Madeira."

"I have—and found it most excellent. Biddick never mentioned you, though," Max said to Ryder.

"I only arrived yesterday. I have been in Spain."

Remembering the two ships lying at anchor in the harbor, Max nodded. "I take it you both work for the Foreign Office?"

"For Sir Gawain, yes."

"Any new developments regarding Lady Isabella Wilde?"

"Only one thus far. We're certain now that her ship

was taken to Algiers, but her trail went cold after that. Regrettably, we are still searching for her." Ryder's dark eyes narrowed measuringly. "Now it is my turn to ask the questions."

"By all means, ask."

"I hear you have volunteered to be part of a rescue mission if we mount one. Why?"

His tone held both skepticism and challenge, but Max answered easily. "Because Miss Evers was instrumental in saving my lieutenant's life, and I would like to repay the favor."

"Thorne has vouched for you," Ryder admitted. "And we have John Yates's testimony. Yates thinks you a candidate for sainthood, by the way. And Sir Gawain is impressed with your credentials. You're obviously brave and intrepid and a good commanding officer, but I am not convinced that you are what we need."

"And you base this opinion on . . . ?"

"You're a professional soldier, Leighton. Accustomed to certain rules and conventions of warfare. But any rescue attempt we conduct will be nothing like a military offensive. We won't use an army outfitted with artillery."

"Of course not," Max replied. "Instead you'll rely on stealth, lightning strikes, night raids."

"Some army men might think a frontal assault is the only honorable means of conducting a war."

"A frontal assault has strategic value when you have superior forces, but not when your objective is to liberate a hostage. If Lady Isabella is being held captive under guard, a direct attack could be the surest way to get her killed."

"Exactly," Ryder said, sipping his brandy. "And our organization has few rules for a reason. We're more interested in success than adhering to convention."

"Let me guess. You operate in highly select units—small but effective. Your customary tasks involve spying, espionage, clandestine missions . . . in short, a guerrilla operation."

"*Now* you begin to impress me," Ryder acknowledged, his smile grudging.

Max glanced at Señor Verra. "In Spain I became acquainted with a number of Resistance fighters. You have that look about you, señor."

"I have a cousin who was in the Resistance, but my skills run to smuggling." Verra grinned broadly. "I was a smuggler before I came to be employed by Sir Gawain. I am the wily one."

"We each bring various specialties to the organization," Ryder said.

"And what is yours?"

"Munitions. Ordnance. Explosives."

The dangerous one, Max thought. "And Thorne?"

Ryder smiled with real amusement this time. "Thorne is the daredevil. Nerves of steel."

"I presume Sir Gawain is your master strategist?"

"Yes. He gives the initial orders—but even those are not sacrosanct. He expects us to use our intellect and instincts as well as our skills in the field. We plan for contingencies, but events don't always go as expected or planned. In such cases, we're free to break the rules of honor and convention if need warrants."

Such freedom held a vast appeal for Max, who more than once had questioned the orders of his superior officers, even the great Wellington.

"We could use an expert tactician," Ryder added. "It's possible you could fill that role." He paused, although his intense gaze never wavered. "But I will be frank with you, Leighton. Most of us have worked together for years, and we don't welcome outsiders readily."

Max understood what Ryder wasn't saying. They were more than a band of adventurers and rebels who'd joined together to do daring deeds; they were a close-knit group of friends who risked danger and death together. "A brotherhood of sorts," he murmured.

"Yes. We would die for one another and for our cause."

"And just what is your cause?"

The mocking gleam in Ryder's eyes grew enigmatic. "I will leave that for Sir Gawain to explain. He would like you to call on him day after tomorrow to discuss your role. . . . Presuming you are still interested in joining us on those terms—risking injury and death for your fellow compatriots."

Averting his gaze, Max stared down into his brandy, flashes of war passing before his mind's eye. He'd known enough blood and gore to last a lifetime and beyond. But the possibility of dying wasn't what terrified him; it was having his friends die for him that made his gut wrench.

Could he stomach that horror again?

"If I do join you," Max said finally, his voice low, "I promise to give you no cause to find me wanting."

Ryder nodded with apparent satisfaction. "That is what Caro said of you, and I tend to trust her judgment."

The mention of Caro made Max raise an eyebrow. "What would she know of risking death?"

The corner of Ryder's mouth curved. "Caro is one of us, didn't you know?"

"*She* works for the Foreign Office?"

"Yes, and she will be accompanying us on any rescue."

"You are jesting," Max said skeptically.

"Not at all. We couldn't stop her if we tried. Nor would we wish to. Have no fear, Leighton, Caro will pull her own weight. I know few men who are a better shot or who possess her expertise with a rapier, not to mention her skill as a medic. And there are times when only a woman can accomplish our designated mission. That alone makes her invaluable."

Max found himself shaking his head. He had known Caro was unconventional, but not to that extent. He found it difficult to reconcile her two personas—a guerrilla agent employed by the British Foreign Office and the enchanting woman he knew as his guardian angel and healer. Evidently she was even more remarkable than he'd realized. This new divulgence, however, made him wonder what else Caro hadn't told him, what other secrets she might be keeping from him.

Realizing his thoughts had wandered, Max returned his attention to his unexpected guests. "So what is your verdict of me?" he asked Ryder. "Have I swayed your opinion in the least?"

"It's early yet," Ryder drawled, his eyes glinting. "Another glass of Thorne's superb brandy might go a ways toward persuading me."

With a wry smile, Max waved his hand toward the

decanter. "Pray, help yourself. I'm certain Thorne will understand if we deplete his stock for a commendable purpose."

He studied her silently as he undressed her, his jeweled eyes hidden by a fall of thick, dark lashes. Yet she saw his hard, virile face tighten when he bared her breasts to his gaze. His strong hands cupped the swells, his thumbs coaxing, making the sensitive tips engorge painfully under his light touch.

A heated tremor eddied deep in the pit of her stomach.

For a time he went on stroking the hard points of her nipples to aching peaks before he bent closer to kiss her throat where her pulse hammered wildly. Then his mouth lowered to suckle one breast, closing hot and moist over the taut bud.

Fire plummeted to her yielding, throbbing center.

He nuzzled softly, his lips roughly tender, his tongue tracing burning caresses around her fullness. Unable to bear the torment any longer, Caro molded herself against his powerful body, opening to him, clutching the hard muscles of his shoulders.

At her urgency, his hands skimmed down her back and lifted her up. Her breath splintered at the first thrust of his rigid flesh parting the slick folds of her body. She felt impaled, stretched taut. . . .

"Take me deeper, sweetheart." Raw desire darkened his husky voice, and she heard her own breathy plea in response.

His fingers clenching on her bare buttocks, he swelled inside her, thick and full, surging, igniting a scorching heat deep within her.

"Yes, be on fire for me."

Her body surrendered, overwhelmed by blind desire as he swept her to a dark place of searing pleasure—

"Señor Leighton to see you, señorita."

Caro gave a start as Max was shown into the courtyard where she had just finished breakfasting.

Her cheeks flamed as she unwillingly met his gaze. He had caught her daydreaming about him. Could he tell? Did he know what foolish, erotic visions she had been entertaining just now, or the passionate dreams that had haunted her sleep last night and so many other nights? Could he discern by simply looking at her that she was still aroused?

He greeted her casually, but she felt sure he noticed her flushed face. When his eyes finally broke contact, Caro breathed a sigh of relief.

Max glanced around him with evident approval. The interior courtyard was a place of beauty, one her mother had taken great pride in. A profusion of flowers and vines—bougainvillea, hibiscus, oleander, geraniums—sweetened the air, while a soothing marble fountain whispered a quiet melody.

"So this is your home," Max said when she had dismissed the Spanish footman. "It's charming."

"It seems so to me." The rural estate she'd inherited from her late parents was not as grand as Thorne's luxurious villa, but the manor was graceful and comfortable, and the farms provided a generous income that allowed her complete financial independence.

"You live here alone?"

"A friend keeps me company. After my father's passing, Señora Padilla came to stay with me as my duenna to chaperone me and lend me respectability.

But now that I'm well into the age of spinsterhood, she is merely my companion. She hasn't risen yet, since it is still early."

"I expected you to be an early riser and risked intruding on you," Max remarked, offering her a smile that immediately put Caro on the defensive; it was the kind of sensual male smile that made sensible women do foolish things.

"Why are you here?" she asked to hide her flustered warmth. "You are supposed to be at home to callers this morning."

"I try never to do the expected. In battle, the element of surprise is a prime advantage."

Her eyebrow lifted. "I wasn't aware we are engaged in a battle."

"A skirmish, at the very least. And to make our competition fair, you must give me a fighting chance." Max's heated gaze lowered to linger provocatively on the bottom curve of her mouth. "Besides, I look to you to play hostess while I'm here on your island."

Caro winced, wishing she'd never let herself be goaded into accepting his challenge. "I planned to show you some of the island tomorrow, but I must visit Dr. Allenby this morning. In fact, I was just leaving."

"I should like to accompany you, if I may. I want to thank Allenby for his part in saving John Yates."

She drew a sharp breath at the dismaying thought of sharing the morning with Max. His unexpected arrival had given her no time to prepare herself. At the moment she couldn't even look at him without remembering the way he'd touched her in her dreams, the way his lips had caressed her, the beguiling things he had whispered in her ear. Her gaze fixed on the sensual lines of his mouth. . . .

Abruptly recollecting herself, Caro set down her coffee cup and stood. "I may be gone all day. Most likely I will make Dr. Allenby's rounds for him today."

"Is that your usual duty, making his rounds?"

"Upon occasion. He is getting old, and his rheumatism frequently bothers him. And I need to keep busy."

"Lady Isabella," Max said sympathetically.

Caro nodded. In her absence, the search had been narrowed to Algiers, but there was still no real word of Isabella's whereabouts. Yesterday Caro had met at length with Sir Gawain and Alex Ryder and carefully studied Hawk's report written from Algiers two weeks ago. But her frustration was obvious enough that Sir Gawain had reminded her gently that life must go on. A score of other Guardians were gathering on Cyrene, but there was nothing more to be done at the moment.

Caro had gritted her teeth and acknowledged his wisdom. Meanwhile, she was determined to throw herself into her work to keep from fretting about her friend.

Realizing that Max was still waiting for her answer, she stifled another sigh of frustration. She had no choice; she knew that if she refused, he would accuse her again of being craven.

"You are welcome to come with me this morning," Caro said, wondering if she was making a mistake.

She led the way outside to the stable yard, where her horse and gig awaited along with Max's mount. She expected Max to ride alongside the gig, but when after handing her up he joined her on the narrow seat, she had no choice but to give orders to the groom to unsaddle and stable Mr. Leighton's horse until they returned.

Her intense awareness of Max flustered her so much that she snapped the reins with unnecessary force and sent the bay gelding into a startled trot. She couldn't get her dreams out of her mind. Couldn't forget the beauty of his naked body, his potent masculinity, his gentle possessiveness when he'd touched her, caressed her, filled her. . . .

Cursing herself silently, Caro vowed to get her wayward thoughts under control. But Max's next remark unsettled her nearly as much as his nearness.

"I keep discovering new and surprising things about you. You never told me that you worked for Sir Gawain."

She cast a wary sideways glance at him. "Why would you think I do?"

"I had some interesting visitors last night. Alex Ryder and your Señor Verra. They told me some curious things about you. It must be quite a story, how you came to be involved in such a masculine pursuit."

Caro managed a shrug. "My father worked for the Foreign Office. I merely took his place after he died."

"Ryder also mentioned your expertise with a rapier and said you were a crack shot."

"And I ride and sail and read Latin," she said lightly. "And I can saw off a leg if I must. I told you I possessed few feminine qualities."

"I happen to think your qualities quite remarkable."

Caro eyed him with skepticism, knowing she shouldn't allow herself to listen to Max's admittedly appealing flattery. He was simply being gallant when he called her male pursuits remarkable. Perhaps her uniqueness intrigued him for the moment, but she was a curiosity for him, nothing more.

"Obviously I shall have to speak to Ryder about his loose tongue," she said reprovingly.

"I confess I encouraged him to talk, and not just to discover your secrets. I wanted to know more about him as well. I have the impression he once sold his services as a mercenary."

"He did. Ryder is from Cyrene, but before he returned here to work for Sir Gawain, he was employed by a number of foreign governments."

Her spirits had been buoyed to hear of Alex Ryder's arrival, for he was one of the most deadly of all the Guardians. In every mission there was the possibility that someone of Ryder's skills would be needed.

"He's seems rather enamored of you," Max observed.

"Ryder? Of *me*?"

"He was singing your praises last evening. Is *he* my competition?"

She couldn't help smiling at the thought of Ryder being her lover, when he was like a protective older brother to her. "Like Thorne, Ryder is merely a good friend."

"And Santos Verra? When I saw Verra carry you off yesterday, I naturally was jealous."

Caro rolled her eyes. "You have no cause for jealousy. Verra is happily married, with four young children."

"That relieves my mind."

"Tell me," she said to change the subject, "why did Ryder and Verra visit you last night?"

"They came for the purpose of looking me over before reporting to Sir Gawain. I had the feeling Ryder thinks I may be too fainthearted to join your group."

"He doesn't question your courage, I'm certain. He is merely concerned about your conviction. Ryder doubts that anyone who isn't committed to our organization would truly want to risk dying for strangers."

"I am not afraid of dying. I'm not even particularly afraid of killing the enemy."

She caught the dark note in his voice. "What is it that troubles you, then?"

"Truthfully? It's having my friends' blood on my hands. I don't think I could stand anyone else making sacrifices for me."

The way John Yates had done, Caro reflected. And Max had spoken of a nightmare, she remembered.

"You can still withdraw your offer," she said softly. "If we organize a rescue, you needn't accompany us."

"No, I want to participate. Like you, I believe taking action is the best way to keep from dwelling on problems. Besides, I owe you a great debt for saving Yates, angel. And I know what it's like to lose a cherished friend. I would spare you that, if I possibly can."

His eyes had grown dark, Caro realized, with that hint of bleakness she'd seen during their voyage. She felt a disastrous weakening in the heart she was trying to steel against him.

"Well," she said, trying to lighten the mood, "you have time to make up your mind. I am to take you to meet Sir Gawain tomorrow afternoon, did Ryder tell you?"

"Yes. I gather I'm to be interviewed." Max's mouth curved. "And there is always the possibility that Sir Gawain may not want me along."

"I don't believe there will be any question of your being welcomed," Caro assured him.

Shaking his head to banish his dark thoughts, Max settled back to enjoy the moment. He wasn't accustomed to having a woman drive, but Caro's gloved hands were sure and gentle on the reins—those same gentle hands that had soothed his fevered brow in his dreams so many times. The memory made him want to reach out and lace his fingers with hers, just for the pleasure of touching her.

The peace of the morning was like a balm to his soul. It was impossible to think of war in this sun-drenched valley ripe with olive groves and orange orchards and vineyards. In the distance to the north, he could see Cyrene's two forested mountain peaks, and to the south, a lower ridge of rugged hills. The valleys in the interior of the island were carefully cultivated, but the higher slopes possessed a wild beauty that called to him.

Caro seemed to follow his gaze. "Our mountains protect us from the dry winds that blow from the north and help to catch rain. The Romans brought us irrigation, but drought is our biggest worry. There is a lake at the base of our western peak that has a splendid waterfall. According to legend, Apollo created it for Cyrene as her bath. I know," Caro said when she saw his mouth twist in amusement. "You don't believe in legends."

"Your island does resemble a paradise," Max admitted.

"It is not very large. You can ride across Cyrene in an hour, and traverse its length in three. But it is a very special place," she murmured with obvious pride.

Dr. Allenby lived near the edge of town in a small whitewashed cottage. Caro lamented the size as they walked to the front door. "His house has only one room to perform surgeries and to examine patients, but someday we hope to have a real hospital."

They were greeted by the doctor's Spanish housekeeper, who looked relieved to see Caro. "Señorita Evers, it is good you are here. I can do nothing with him. He had no sleep last night . . . not since the baby came."

"Señora Tompkins's baby?"

"No, it was Señora Garcia."

"I did not know her time was so near."

"It was not. But the little one, he came early. The doctor is in the infirmary."

Seeming unsurprised to find Dr. Allenby slumped over his desk, Caro gently shook him awake. When he started upright, Max recognized the portly, balding man as the brilliant physician whose novel methods reportedly had saved countless lives.

"You are back at last," Allenby said, scowling at Caro.

"As you see."

Fumbling for his spectacles, he peered up at Max. "Do I know you?"

"You remember Major Leighton," Caro replied. "He brought John Yates home last summer."

The doctor grunted a welcome and brushed off Max's attempt to express gratitude for his efforts last year. He was even more irascible now than during their previous meeting, Max decided, but his banter with Caro showed a mutual fondness as she chided him about his work habits.

"You have to take better care of yourself. You have been driving yourself to the point of exhaustion."

"And whose fault is that? If you had stayed here instead of flitting off to England—"

"It could not be helped."

"You were gone long enough."

"Regrettably the voyage takes time."

"It would have been entirely unnecessary if not for that damned Isabella getting herself captured."

"You don't mean to blame her," Caro replied.

"I do! She should stay safely at home instead of gallivanting all over the globe—and so should you. You are needed here. I have been putting off several surgeries until you returned . . . blast my damn eyes." Plucking off his spectacles, he rubbed the offending orbs.

"My eyesight is better than his," Caro murmured to Max, "so I have been performing some of his surgeries under his direction."

"And I must order supplies," the doctor said gruffly.

"That can wait. For now you need to go to bed and get some sleep."

"I have no time to pamper myself. I have rounds to see to—"

"I will make your rounds today. Maria is already making out a list of patients. Now come. I am not leaving until you are in bed."

Taking his arm and helping him to rise, Caro bullied and teased him as if he were a recalcitrant patient and finally persuaded him to lie down on the cot in the infirmary.

After covering the weary doctor with a blanket, Caro quietly led Max from the room and accepted the list that the smiling housekeeper gave her, along with a black leather satchel. It appeared to Max that they had performed this routine frequently.

"If you like," Caro told him once they were settled in the gig, "I can drop you at Thorne's villa before I make my first call."

"I want to accompany you. Perhaps I might even be of use."

Glancing down at his gleaming boots, she arched an amused eyebrow. "I warn you, you aren't dressed for some of the places we will visit. Your bootmaker would be horrified if you were to ruin those, and you didn't bring your valet from England."

"Thorne's servants are more than adequate to the task of caring for my boots," Max replied blandly.

"Very well, then. You are welcome to come."

For the better part of the day, Max accompanied Caro on her rounds, watching as she dispensed jellies, herbs, and medicines and checked on the progress of injuries and illnesses.

Dr. Allenby's patients were scattered across the island and were mostly Spanish and English, he realized—easily differentiated by their attire. The Spanish women were garbed in black like much of the female population in the Mediterranean, while the English wore simple but more colorful attire.

Most of the islanders welcomed Caro warmly.

"They seem very fond of you," Max remarked after visiting the first half-dozen patients.

"They are even more fond of Dr. Allenby," Caro said. "He is beloved on Cyrene, despite his gruff bedside manner. There is scarcely a family whose lives he hasn't touched. But he is getting old. I don't know what we will do when he is no longer able to serve his patients."

"Can the islanders not rely on you?"

"I am not qualified to be a surgeon. And I don't wish to be a physician full-time."

"Why not?"

"Because working for Sir Gawain interests me more."

"But you obviously have a natural gift for healing."

"It seems so. I've always had a desire to help creatures in pain. From the time I was a child, the islanders brought their wounded and ailing animals to me to tend. Becoming Dr. Allenby's assistant, however, was much more challenging. Even after ten years, some of the men here still don't trust me, I suppose because they feel threatened. A few even consider me a witch."

Max raised an eyebrow. "Superstitious, are they?"

"Highly." Her mouth curved wryly. "During the Inquisition I would have been burned at the stake. But at least here I am accepted. In England I would never be permitted to practice any form of medicine. The typical British citizen would have to be on his deathbed to suffer care from a woman. Instead they prefer the services of quacks and charlatans."

He heard the hint of scorn in her voice and had to sympathize, even when Caro turned an arch look upon him.

"Admit it, Max, you yourself had reservations last year when Dr. Allenby gave me the nursing of John Yates."

"But you quickly proved yourself," Max said, "and your gender ceased to matter to me. Believe me, I've seen enough men die of minor wounds to appreciate good medical care."

And he had watched her deal with difficult patients all morning. She was unfailingly kind and patient, and employed the same gentle teasing she had used on Yates and the doctor to get her way. The islanders obviously respected and even adored her.

Caro clearly appreciated them in return. When she and Max shared a simple midday meal with a large family of peasants—their only means of paying for medical services for two of their young children—Caro showed them as much deference as she would have wealthy aristocrats, and probably far more fondness.

The next patient, though, received her with outright hostility—a bedridden farmer whose foot had been severely gashed by a plow. The wound had grown so putrid and painful, he could no longer bear to put any weight on it. He allowed Caro to treat and bandage the injury only because his wife stood over him, threatening mayhem if he didn't behave.

Caro made light of his animosity once she and Max were settled in the gig. "*He* is one of the ones who considers me a witch," she jested.

But she *was* a witch, Max silently agreed, feeling a sudden arousal when the jolting gig caused his thigh to press intimately against hers. A bewitching temptress who made him feel a fierce heat, despite her unconventionality and her masculine occupations.

By late afternoon they were driving in the foothills, through a wild scrubland that Caro had called "maquis." Max recognized various shrubs and mountain plants—low-growing clumps of rosemary and broom, taller thickets of laurel and myrtle and evergreen junipers. And all around them, a sweet, fresh scent filled the golden air.

The effect on his senses reminded him of Caro, Max realized. Sweet, a little untamed, and thoroughly compelling.

"This island setting becomes you," he said honestly. "You're in your natural element here."

Caro merely raised one eyebrow and smiled. "I suggest you ply your charm on more gullible females, Max."

"I don't know any other females here besides you."

"Cyrene has plenty to offer. I told you I mean to introduce you to our island's beauties. Doubtless you will find many of them to your liking."

"I'm not averse to meeting Cyrene's beauties. Just make certain you don't burden me with any innocent young debs who only have marriage in mind. I have no desire to be tied in a parson's noose." He sent her an appraising glance. "*That* is one of your prime attractions, my lovely Caro. You aren't set on landing a husband."

"No, I am not. But I am curious why you have such an aversion to marriage."

He answered her truthfully. "Because of the complications a wife or family would present."

"Complications?"

"I don't want to risk losing anyone else I care for. For the first time in nine years I have no close ties to anyone, and I mean to keep it that way."

He saw compassion immediately darken her eyes. Realizing he had grown too grim then, Max flashed her a grin. "Celibacy, however, is not a condition I relish."

A responsive smile curved her lips. "I can always concoct a potion to cool your lust."

"A potion won't have any effect. I want you, Miss Evers."

"Well, you cannot have me. You will just have to content yourself with someone else."

"Tell me," Max prodded, "why you are so resistant to our becoming intimate again."

Her smile faded. "For one thing, I have too much else to occupy my time just now, seeing to Dr. Allenby's patients."

"But you will need an occasional respite, surely."

"Perhaps. But I don't think it wise to become intimately involved with gentlemen I work with."

"We aren't working together yet. And if I do wind up joining your organization, it will only be for this one mission."

She hesitated, as if wanting to say more, but then merely replied, "It is better if we just remain friends, Max."

"Very well, we can be friends for now," he said.

Caro sent him a look that said she didn't quite trust him. "I assure you, you will be far more satisfied with some sophisticated beauty who will gladly indulge your carnal needs. Mrs. Julia Trant is a ravishing widow. She would be happy to entertain you in a discreet liaison. Or if your taste runs to the more exotic, Señora Blanca Herrera de Ramos is reputedly between lovers."

Max appraised her with sardonic amusement, not bothering to refute her. Even at the end of the long day, Caro Evers was still more appealing to him than all the sophisticated beauties who had ever indulged his carnal needs.

True, she looked the worse for wear at the moment. Her somber gown was marred by various stains of her profession, while curling tendrils of dark hair escaped from the severe knot she wore. Yet he could remember those silken tresses falling loose around her naked shoulders so that her nipples peeked out from between the wet strands—

Max felt the hard clutch of desire at the memory. Not for the first time today he found himself craving to free her glorious hair from its imprisonment, to bury his hands in the lustrous, springy mass, just as he wanted to bury himself in her supple, slender body.

He silently muttered an oath. All day he'd determinedly ignored the slow burn of his own body. Caro brought out the most primitive instincts in him. She made him feel dangerous and male, both predator and protector, carnal and tender at the same time. It was all he could do to keep from reaching for her when she pushed her rebellious hair out of her eyes. Yet just now they were approaching another farmhouse for her next call.

An hour later Caro climbed into the gig for the final time and gathered up the reins. She was tired, Max could tell from the slight drooping of her shoulders. And she didn't object when he confiscated the reins from her.

"Allow me," Max said. "You've run yourself ragged today, and I have done nothing to help. Home?" he asked.

"Yes, home. But I have one last patient to see there."

It took them nearly half an hour to return to Caro's estate in the south-central part of the island, and by then dusk had begun to fall. Her two-story, galleried manor house was built in the Spanish style, but the stables seemed properly English to Max. The cobblestone yard had a long row of spacious box stalls, as well as a large barn, a carriage house, and living quarters for the grooms and stable hands.

When they came to a halt in the yard, a groom appeared at once, still chewing on a crust of bread. Seizing the gig's reins, the young man looked expectantly to Caro for his orders.

"When you finish unharnessing the gig, Humberto, will you saddle Mr. Leighton's horse? Then you may return to your supper."

"*Si,* señorita."

The moment Caro had spoken, several equine heads emerged through the open upper half doors of the stalls. With Max following, she went down the row, greeting each horse fondly, stroking faces and muzzles until she reached the last stall, which held an aging chestnut mare.

The mare whickered softly as Caro reached up to scratch between its dark, liquid eyes. "This is my most special patient," she murmured. "This sweet lady belonged to my mother."

From a grooming box on the wall, Caro retrieved a brush and cloth and then entered the stall. Max followed her inside, closing the lower door behind them.

"Like Dr. Allenby, she is getting very old," Caro explained as she began to brush the chestnut coat that was sprinkled with gray. "She has trouble chewing, and her eyesight is failing, but I ride her occasionally because she likes to feel appreciated. And she has an old injury to her shoulder. I try to massage it regularly to keep it limber."

"Lucky horse," Max murmured.

Leaning against the stall wall, he watched while Caro groomed the mare and then began massaging the animal's left shoulder.

Beside him, a three-legged cat sprang up on the ledge of the half door, sniffed at Max, then despite its obvious handicap, agilely leapt down into the straw. Meowing, it rubbed against Caro's skirts until she picked it up and administered a generous dose of affection.

"He lost his rear leg in a fight with a dog, but he is an excellent mouser," Caro explained. "I think he missed me while I was away."

Clearly the cat agreed. Purring loudly, it sprawled contently in her arms—until the mare turned and pushed her muzzle against Caro's neck, demanding the same attention.

They all wanted to be the recipient of Caro's tenderness, it seemed. Max could sympathize, for he shared the sentiment.

Just then the groom appeared at the stall door. "I have done as you asked, señorita. Is there more that you require?"

"Thank you, Humberto. That will be all. Go and finish your supper."

With a quick grin and a tug of his forelock, the groom disappeared again.

Setting the cat down in the straw, Caro returned to massaging the mare's injured shoulder. The old horse closed its eyes and snuffled in obvious bliss.

Silence reigned for a time. In the deepening shadows, Max watched Caro stroke the horse, her fingers pressing gently into the tight muscles, kneading, easing the stiffness and pain away. It made him recall the feel of her hands on him that long-ago night.

Arousal stirred in him, sharp and insistent.

As the moments passed, the feeling grew stronger, more urgent, until a low oath escaped him.

"What is wrong?" Caro asked immediately, glancing over her shoulder.

"I was remembering that night. The way you touched me."

For a long moment she said nothing. "You were in pain that night."

"I am in pain now after watching you work your magic." His mouth quirked. "I would willingly become one of your patients. I could curl up in your lap and have you pet and caress me. . . ."

"You can fend for yourself," Caro countered with a smile. "These animals cannot."

"What about you? Who massages your shoulders after a long day such as this?"

"No one."

"I would be happy to volunteer."

"I am touched by your solicitude," she said firmly, "but I will make do with a hot bath."

"At the ruins?"

At his provoking question, she returned a quelling glance. "No, here at home. In *private*."

Max went on watching her as the heavy ache of desire pulled at his groin. And as twilight settled over them, a deeper ache unfurled inside him—the need to touch her. He found himself drawing nearer to her, as if lured helplessly by a spell.

"You have remarkable hands," his said quietly.

"Not so remarkable, really."

"They are. I can't forget the incredible feel of them."

Her hands faltered in their task. When slowly she turned her head, Max allowed the heat of his gaze to travel from her lush mouth to her eyes and back to her mouth. . . .

Caro felt all her muscles tense at the brilliant sapphire of his gaze. Not daring to risk any further intimacy, she gave the mare's shoulder one last pat and turned to leave the stall. But when she tried to move past him, Max closed his fingers around her wrist to stay her.

Just that simple heated touch made her shiver.

"I remember everything about that night. Vividly." His low, husky voice echoed through her like the memory of a caress. "I remember what your skin tastes like, angel. I remember the feel of you when I thrust into your wet silk. The husky cries you make when you shatter in my arms . . ."

Her mouth went dry, leaving her unable to speak.

"I want very much to experience that passion again, Caro. I want to make love to you."

His voice was a sensual murmur, hot and deep and riveting.

Steeling herself, Caro shut her eyes as brazen images formed in her mind, sensual thoughts of flesh pressed to naked flesh, remembered from her dreams and from reality.

She wanted Max as well—urgently. But she wouldn't allow herself to indulge her hunger. It had taken her too long to get over him the first time; in truth, she had never quite managed it. She'd spent countless months afterward missing Max. She didn't want to endure that misery again.

"No," she managed to reply, her voice a hoarse rasp.

Turning her, Max gently guided her till her back came up against the wall. "Are you certain?"

His teeth grazed her ear, and she shivered. How tempting he was, how impossibly tempting. She shook her head, fighting the erotic memories of their bodies joined, fighting the pulsing need he was arousing in her.

Then the backs of his fingers brushed against her bodice, and her nipples instantly peaked, making her shudder with longing.

His breath warmed her lips as he whispered her name. And when he pressed his body fully against hers, the pulsing moved lower and deeper within her, centering between her thighs.

"Max . . ."

His arms came around her then, the vibrant heat of his body spearing her through her clothing. When he engulfed her mouth in a possessive kiss, desire flared hot and bright inside her. He was both rough and gentle, and she clung, helplessly aware of her surrender, of the wild, welling hunger he incited.

In only a moment his kiss became more fervent, as if he couldn't control his own hunger, his tongue plunging rhythmically, searing her with fiery demand, burning away her willpower. The sensations were so riotously hot, they made Caro feel as if she were dying of need.

She needed Max, craved him. She had dreamed about him, longed for him, ached for him for so long. . . .

Far too long . . .

It required a herculean effort, but she brought her hands up to push against his chest as she tore her mouth away. "Please stop!"

Max heard her rasped plea but couldn't make himself obey. He bent again, his mouth urgently seeking hers—and not finding it.

She caught him off guard.

Somehow her leg became tangled up with his, and to his bewilderment, Max found himself flat on his back in the straw, with Caro sprawled on top of him, her forearm lying dangerously across his throat.

Dazed, he stared up at her in the dim light, his breath ragged.

She offered him a shaky smile. "Perhaps you aren't aware, but my knee is poised in a strategic position. Were I to use it, you would find the result exceedingly painful . . . although not deadly, as my arm would be if I were to increase the pressure against your throat."

Suddenly he knew: she had tripped him deliberately.

"I warned you," Caro said in an unsteady tone, "I have an unusual education for a female. This is one of my skills, knowing how to defend myself when assaulted."

"I was hardly assaulting you," he rasped, his own voice still hoarse with desire.

"Perhaps not, but I saw an urgent need to protect my virtue."

She pushed herself off him and struggled to her feet. Then pulling open the stall door, she disappeared into the stable yard.

Max lay there a moment, trying to absorb what had just happened. He *had* nearly assaulted Caro. When he'd kissed her, all he could think about was drawing her long, slender limbs around his waist and plunging hot and deep inside her. His desire had been so fierce, he could have taken her in a stable, for God's sake.

Hell and the devil. He had no excuse for his lack of control. True, his desire was fueled by pent-up sexual frustration after weeks of abstinence. Weeks of being alluringly near her but unable to touch.

Just then he felt a soft, warm breath against his cheek. Max flinched in startlement and swore a low oath as he stared up at a graying equine muzzle. To add insult to injury, the old mare was nuzzling his face—whether out of sympathy or curiosity he wasn't certain.

Torn between laughing and groaning, Max rolled to his feet, and immediately winced at the painful state of his erection. This was hardly the outcome he'd hoped for when he'd surrendered to his fierce need to kiss Caro.

He was determined to carry on the battle, but perhaps a tactical retreat was in order so that he could marshal his forces.

Chapter Six

Since Caro had pledged to arrange his welcome into society, Max wasn't surprised when he had a considerable number of callers the following morning.

Gentlemen from all over the island, primarily British and Spanish and a few French, came to make his acquaintance, either singly or in groups of two or three. His visitors extended numerous invitations for the ensuing week, to shoot, to ride, to foxhunt, to dine, and especially to meet their families.

It was only when Max realized how many of the gentlemen had daughters of marriageable age that he began to suspect Caro's hand at work. She was attempting, evidently, to divert his attention from her by initiating a campaign to make him the toast of the island's unwed females. And getting their proud papas to meet him was the first step.

That afternoon when Caro drove him to his interview with Sir Gawain Olwen, Max remarked on her deviousness.

"I never would have suspected you capable of such underhanded tactics, angel."

"Whatever do you mean?" she said with provocative innocence.

"It's hardly a coincidence that this lavish display of hospitality comes from fathers eager to foist their daughters off on me. You aren't by chance scheming to exhibit me as a matrimonial prize?"

Her smile was noncommittal. "I simply want you to feel welcome on our island. You cannot blame me if the fathers here—or their unwed daughters—are eager to make your acquaintance."

"I certainly can blame you. You know very well I came to Cyrene in part to avoid all the snares set for me."

Her smile broadened. "I have no doubt the distraction of being pursued by our young ladies will do you good. You needn't actually *wed* any of them."

Max let out a low curse.

"Would you care to cry pax?" she asked sweetly.

"Not on your life."

"I didn't think so. But truly, I have little to do with your popularity. The simple fact is, our citizens wish to give you the homage due a war hero."

"I wager you've gone to great pains to exaggerate my heroics."

"Not at all. I never had to say a word. It so happens that everyone on Cyrene knows of you. John Yates has been singing your praises for months now. Which reminds me, John is eager to see you."

Max's expression turned sober. "That surprises me."

"Why? You saved his life by bringing him home to Cyrene."

He grimaced. "On the contrary. Yates is the one who saved my life on a battlefield. And he cannot have forgotten I was the cause of him losing his leg."

"He doesn't hold you responsible. In any event, you are likely to encounter him at the castle this afternoon, since he is Sir Gawain's secretary."

"I know," Max said tersely, his long-held guilt returning.

He focused his attention on the castle ahead, trying to ignore his mounting tension.

On their approach to the island by ship, Max had viewed Sir Gawain's stronghold from a distance, but up close it was even more impressive than he remembered. The massive walls were thick enough to withstand a pounding, while the battlements bristled with enough cannon to repel an assault by even the most determined enemy.

The interior was less warlike, Max noted as they were shown into the great hall. Fine tapestries and carpets and gleaming furnishings graced the huge room, tempering the cold stone. Yet he saw so many artifacts of a bygone era scattered about—armor and weapons, swords and maces and shields—that Max could almost imagine himself swept back in time.

The knights of a chivalric order would feel quite at home here, he had no doubt.

But then his attention was claimed by the young man hobbling toward them on a wooden leg. John Yates was thinner than when he had served under Max's command, but unlike then, his face now glowed with good health and his grin was lively.

He pushed a shock of blond hair from his eyes before pumping Max's hand. "You cannot know how elated I am to see you again, sir. I never properly thanked you for saving my life."

Max felt his tension ease a measure. He could detect no signs of bitterness in the man who would have to endure life as a cripple.

"But you did thank me, my friend," Max replied seriously. "Countless times during your delirium. And I can never begin to even the score, since I would now be lying in a Spanish grave if not for you."

Yates flushed at the praise. Turning, he greeted Caro by fondly bussing her cheek, then addressed Max again. "If you will follow me, Major, Sir Gawain is eager to meet you."

He led them through the great hall and along a stone corridor to a large, comfortable chamber that evidently served as the baronet's study. Papers and maps were strewn over every surface, including the massive desk, where an elderly gentleman sat hard at work scribbling.

Sir Gawain rose immediately at their entrance. Tall and lean and gravely serious, he had penetrating, light blue eyes that seemed to miss nothing. His lined face looked strained, as if he carried a great burden on his shoulders. He also limped slightly, Max noted.

Sir Gawain's greeting was cordial and genuinely welcoming. "I apologize for neglecting to receive you before this, Mr. Leighton, but we had a situation in France that required my attention."

Yates withdrew then, while Sir Gawain offered his guests seats.

"I formed an interest in you after you brought John home," Sir Gawain observed, "and I have been following your military career avidly ever since. You are considered a brilliant leader—an expert if unconventional tactician, with a reputation for winning. And Christopher Thorne's letter of introduction has nothing but the highest praise."

"Thorne no doubt exaggerated my exploits," Max

said with what Caro thought was undue modesty. She watched as Sir Gawain eyed Max keenly.

"That is arguable. At any rate," the baronet continued, "I was delighted to hear you have offered your services as adviser should we need to rescue Lady Isabella. Let me say at once that I would readily welcome your help. I understand you have experience liberating captured soldiers."

"A fair amount."

"Can you plan our mission for us?"

"I will give it my best effort," Max replied. "The key to success will be accurate intelligence, adequate resources, careful preparation. If you can see to the first two, then I should be able to devise a plan that has a strong chance of succeeding."

"We are doing our utmost to gather intelligence as we speak. And I will make certain you have adequate resources. I assure you, Mr. Leighton, I intend to bring Lady Isabella home safely. Her father was a dear friend of mine, and when he was forced into exile, I promised him sanctuary. That vow extends to his family."

"I will certainly do my best, Sir Gawain."

"I know you will." The elderly man hesitated. "To be frank, we could use a man of your talents permanently in our organization."

"Permanently?" Max repeated, sounding cautious.

"I would like very much for you to join us."

"You are offering me a position working for the Foreign Office?"

Sir Gawain nodded. "You would not necessarily have to remain on Cyrene. We are situated here because this location gives us rapid access to Europe, where crises tend to develop with alarming frequency. But we have positions in England as well."

"From Alex Ryder I was given the impression your operation is rather powerful."

"We are well connected and well financed, if that is what you are asking."

"I gather you function something like a modern force of mercenaries."

Sir Gawain's smile was enigmatic. "We like to think we have a higher calling. Protecting the weak, the vulnerable, the deserving. Fighting tyranny. Working for the good of mankind."

There was so much more Sir Gawain wasn't saying, Caro reflected as she watched Max. The Guardians of the Sword had been formed more than a thousand years ago by a handful of Britain's most legendary warriors—outcasts who had found exile here. Now the order was run by their descendants and operated mainly across Europe, although the British Foreign Office had a nominal say in what missions the Guardians undertook.

It was a long moment before Max replied. "I am flattered by your offer, Sir Gawain, but perhaps you will understand why I simply want to remain a civilian. After nine years of war, the thought of more fighting and bloodshed holds little appeal for me."

"Only a madman relishes bloodshed, Mr. Leighton, but regrettably there are times when it becomes necessary. Yet I can certainly understand why you wouldn't be eager to return to conflict. You have served your country valiantly, and you need a respite. Perhaps you will find it here on our beautiful island. And if you do take part in a mission to rescue Lady Isabella, you will have a better knowledge of how we function. I have high hopes that you can be persuaded to join us."

Max appeared reluctant to answer, Caro realized. During their discussion, she had carefully observed his reaction. Although unaware of it, he was being interviewed for a permanent role in the Guardians, but their extraordinary secrets would remain concealed unless Max committed to joining the Foreign Office.

Clearly Sir Gawain was eager to recruit him. Yet she very much doubted Max would accept. She understood his aversion. He was loath not only to kill, but to be the cause of any more crippled or dead lieutenants.

"But you will at least consider my offer?" Sir Gawain pressed.

"I won't refuse outright, Sir Gawain."

"Then I will have to be satisfied with that. And perhaps Caro will have better luck at convincing you. Meanwhile, I wish to make you feel welcome on our island. I am planning to hold a ball next week in your honor, Mr. Leighton. I have set John to work on arranging it. John?" Sir Gawain called over his shoulder.

John Yates must have been waiting outside the door, for he immediately hobbled into the room, followed by a butler and two footmen bearing tea and other refreshments. At Sir Gawain's invitation, the former lieutenant joined them for tea.

Max waited until they had been served and the servants dismissed before addressing his host. "There is no need to trouble yourself with a ball on my account, Sir Gawain."

"There is every need." Caro spoke for the first time. "You must meet all our neighbors, Mr. Leighton. It is our duty to advance your introduction to society."

"And everyone on Cyrene," Yates interjected, "is always delighted to have an excuse for a ball. The ladies are especially eager to try the new dance imported here from the continent. They have kept our one dancing master hopping, learning the waltz. Except Caro, of course. She refuses to learn."

"Because I dislike dancing," Caro said lightly. "But perhaps you should arrange for Mr. Leighton to take lessons."

"I know the waltz," Max said.

"Dancing," Yates explained to her, "was one of our diversions on the Peninsula." He returned his attention to Max. "Even I will be waltzing, sir. I am not as spry as I once was, but I can still hold my own on a ballroom floor."

"John is eager to impress his sweetheart," Sir Gawain observed dryly.

Yates grinned. "At first I feared she might be put off by my loss of limb, but my infirmity hasn't concerned her."

Sir Gawain tactfully changed the subject then, and they spoke about numerous other things until it was time for Max and Caro to take their leave.

"Yates does seem genuinely happy," Max remarked to her as they drove away from the castle.

"I truly believe he is. He enjoys working for Sir Gawain—he says because it gives him a laudable purpose in life. And he is courting a lady . . . Miss Danielle Newham. Miss Newham and her brother came to our island this past spring for a visit and decided to stay."

Max felt himself frowning as the name pricked at his memory. "What does this Miss Newham look like?"

"She is quite beautiful, with auburn hair and a statuesque figure. I confess it surprised me a little that she encouraged John's attentions, since she appears to be a few years older and is far more sophisticated than he is. But she seems to be good for him."

Max had once known a sophisticated, auburn-haired beauty by that name, and he suspected it was not mere coincidence. "I would like to meet her."

"I'm certain you will have the opportunity at Sir Gawain's ball."

"You actually mean to attend?" he asked. "Even with your aversion to balls?"

"Yes, I do," Caro retorted. "Genteel society here on Cyrene is much more agreeable than in London. And Isabella would be the first to scold me were I to stay at home. Moreover"—a serene smile curved her lips—"I am eager for you to find some other woman to make the target of your lust."

"How many times must I tell you, sweeting, I have no intention of lusting after anyone but you?"

When a flush suffused her cheeks, he flashed her a slow, sensual smile that took her breath away.

Caro clenched her fingers on the reins, regretting her deplorable reaction. She didn't want Max to dazzle her with a smile. Didn't want to feel the tingling, alarming surge of heat in her body. Didn't want to remember the seductive power of his caresses.

Their competition was only a game to him, Caro reminded herself. And to end it, she needed to introduce him to Julia Trant and Blanca Herrera. With their ravishing beauty, they would instantly capture his interest, she had little doubt.

Caro tried to ignore the pang of distress that

thought caused, and instead considered how to contrive a meeting. Sir Gawain's ball would provide a prime opportunity, unless she asked Ryder to arrange it beforehand. Yet such a blatant request would earn Ryder's curiosity and incite questions she wouldn't care to answer. . . .

No, Caro decided, she would handle the introductions herself.

She couldn't deny that she wanted Max, but she wouldn't give in to her foolish urges the way she had once done. The less she entangled herself in his life, the more easily she could bear his leaving this time.

She would do her best to see him established in society, with a woman who could prove a match for his remarkable passion. And then their competition would end, and she could finally conquer the irrational, deplorable, undeniable attraction she still felt for him.

To his regret, Max saw nothing of Caro over the next several days. She was busy assisting the doctor and caring for the island's patients, of course, but he suspected she was purposely avoiding him.

He missed her keenly, although admittedly he had plenty to occupy his time. He swam regularly in the cove beneath Thorne's villa and rode frequently, exploring the rugged splendor of the mountains and the wilder coastlines. Yet not even those pleasant physical activities diminished his restless craving for Caro.

He thought of her often—her smile, the taste of her mouth, the silken texture of her skin beneath his hands. He saw her in his dreams.

He also found himself itching to wring her neck.

She was clearly set on winning their competition.

His social calendar grew daily. The invitations continued to pour in, brought in person by eager callers, so that his days quickly filled with sporting pastimes and his evenings with dinners and soirees and musicales. And he couldn't go into town without being accosted by a dozen strangers asking to meet him and requesting to introduce their daughters. He was being courted and feted and fawned over, just as he had in London.

Then three days before the ball, Caro had the audacity to send him a list of the eligible females on the island, with extensive descriptions by each name, along with remarks offering advice on how best to attach their interest. She had starred two of the candidates, praising their beauty and their allure.

I trust you will give this careful study, her accompanying note read. *Perhaps then you will cease to pester me.*

Her jab brought an unwilling smile to Max's lips. He could have told her that no amount of scheming could make him stop wanting her, or cure his irrational hunger for her. But he pledged to throttle Caro when he next saw her—which would likely be at Sir Gawain's ball.

He had no real desire to attend a ball held in his honor. When he'd returned to London as a civilian after so many years of campaigning, he'd found mindless social pursuits appealing and the regard flattering. Now he simply wanted to spend his time with one particular woman, who was set on throwing him to the wolves.

Feeling somewhat like prey on the afternoon of the ball, Max escaped into Santos Verra's tavern, hoping to find respite from all the unwanted female attention in favor of simple male camaraderie, perhaps Alex Ryder or some of Ryder's bachelor friends.

The public room boasted a sizable crowd, many of them fishermen enjoying pints of ale after a long day at the nets. But there was no sign of Ryder or any of Max's other new acquaintances. No doubt they were all preparing for the evening's festivities, he thought darkly.

Señor Verra came over to join his table, bringing a fine bottle of Madeira. The Spaniard seemed to sympathize with Max's expressed aversion to attending the ball, but then something else caught their attention: A gentleman with reddish brown hair and a well-tailored coat had sauntered into the public room, yet the moment he spied Max, he gave a start and spun around, making quickly for the door.

Verra raised a heavy eyebrow. "Mr. Newham seems particularly anxious to avoid you. Did you offend him in some manner?"

Max's lip curled. "I expect he's not eager to become reacquainted. The last time I saw him, a friend of mine died under suspicious circumstances, and Mr. Peter Newham and his sister left town under a cloud."

"You know the sister as well? Danielle Newham?"

"Not by choice. I found her a bit too lethal for my taste."

Verra nodded. "A wise man does not turn his back on a woman like that."

"I understand John Yates is courting her."

"He is indeed, which I think very curious. I wonder what she sees in young Yates."

"I wonder what she is doing on Cyrene at all," Max replied. "Miss Newham and her brother seemed far too fond of elegant society to willingly immure themselves on your isolated island since spring."

"An intriguing question," Verra remarked. "Perhaps you might attempt to determine the answer."

Max frowned thoughtfully. He would indeed be interested to discover what the Newhams' ulterior motives were for being on Cyrene. At the very least he intended to warn Caro that the Newhams had once been suspected of being traitors. And the puzzle might serve to gain her attention when other methods had failed.

"Perhaps I will," he said, draining the final swallow of wine from his glass and asking for more.

He looked for Caro the moment he entered the castle's great hall, but saw nothing of her among the milling crowd beyond the doors. Instead his eye was caught by the auburn-haired beauty in the receiving line—the only woman so honored. Danielle Newham.

Sir Gawain welcomed him warmly, as did John Yates. Yates stood bracing his weight on a crutch, no doubt in anticipation of a long evening. Beside him, Miss Newham appeared as elegant and beautiful as Max remembered, gowned in bronze silk with a filmy overskirt shot with gold threads. Of her brother there was no immediate sign.

When Max bent over the lady's hand, her green eyes flickered with recognition. She didn't seem dismayed to see him. Rather, she seemed a woman confident of her own power.

"Did your brother accompany you, Miss Newham?" Max asked, prodding.

She returned a calculating smile. "Alas, Peter is indisposed this evening."

"I am sorry to hear it. I hoped we might reminisce over old times."

Her smile froze on her lips, while John Yates gave Max a curious frown. "Do you know each other?"

"We are old acquaintances," Max said blandly. "Someday I will tell you how I met Miss Newham and her brother."

Her eyes flashed, just as Max heard his name hailed by someone else. He turned away, but he could feel the lady glaring daggers into his back.

The great hall already teemed with guests, and several of them pounced as soon as they discovered Max's arrival, which prevented him from searching for Caro. But she was indeed present; he finally saw her near the far wall, speaking with a group of gentlemen that included Ryder.

Max felt his heart jolt hard in his chest. It was the first time he'd ever seen Caro garbed in anything resembling fashionable attire. Tonight she wore an empire-waisted gown of pale blue lustring that displayed a modest amount of bosom but showed her slim figure to advantage. Max, however, was very aware of the instantaneous reaction of his body. He wanted to divest Caro of that gown and explore the sensual charms he remembered so vividly.

He wanted even more to drag her away from the men who, judging from their convivial laughter, seemed to be enjoying her company all too well.

Then Caro looked up, and their gazes locked across the room. Max wondered if the intensity of his expression unsettled her, for her cheeks flushed and she turned away abruptly.

After what seemed an interminable time, she made her way toward him with two young ladies in tow.

Both were obviously debutantes, for they blushed and simpered prettily as they gazed up at Max in awe.

Caro smiled as she introduced him to Miss Emily Smythe and Miss Phoebe Crawford. "They have been longing to meet you, Mr. Leighton. And they are both delightful dancers. I assured Miss Smythe you would ask her to stand up with you for the first set. And then you may claim Miss Crawford for the second."

Narrowing his eyes at Caro, Max silently sent her a message that promised a fitting retribution.

Her cool, keen gray eyes merely looked amused.

She took her leave as the beautiful but vapid Miss Smythe began to gush, "Miss Evers has told us *all* about you, Mr. Leighton. . . ."

Max sighed, preparing to endure an endless evening.

The first two hours did indeed seem unending, for he was hard-pressed to find a moment's peace. As the celebrated guest of honor, he was expected to dance frequently and to spend much of his time conversing with the dignitaries and notable members of the company.

He met many of the island's prominent families, as well as the lieutenant governor of Cyrene. Thorne had warned him that the structure and manners of society here resembled those of the London ton, and Max found it true, except for the Spanish influence. Fully a quarter of the assembled guests were Spanish, as were nearly half the elder chaperons and duennas.

When he managed between dances to approach Caro, she introduced him to her companion, Señora

Padillo, a stout, elderly Spanish widow who seemed to have little energy. Garbed entirely in black, the señora habitually sighed and fanned herself, as if she might faint at any moment.

Just then he caught a glimpse of Danielle Newham gazing seductively into John Yates's dazed eyes as they awkwardly negotiated a waltz. Begging the duenna's pardon, Max firmly took Caro by the arm and drew her away.

"I told you, I do not dance," she said in protest, coming to a halt.

"Then we will sit out the next set," Max retorted. "I have something to say to you."

Their gazes locked in a contest of wills, and Caro was the first to concede. He led her toward a far corner of the great hall, where several chairs remained unoccupied, but their progress was interrupted no fewer than three times by young ladies wanting to attract his notice.

When they finally settled in the chairs, Max muttered an oath under his breath and gave Caro a scowl. "I hold you fully to blame, you know."

She had the temerity to return an innocent look. "Whatever do you mean?"

"You know exactly what I mean. Your campaign to throw me to the wolves."

"I am not the only one seeking to introduce you to our island's eligible young ladies. Sir Gawain and John Yates have made an effort as well." Caro essayed a provoking smile. "Did you study the list I sent you? I thought surely you would find it helpful in finding a new target for your desire."

"Wretch," he murmured, finding it hard not to respond to the laughing gleam in her eyes.

"Truly, I took great pains to include some beauties other than marriage-minded debutantes. Julia Trant is here tonight, and so is Señora Herrera. You really must meet them."

"I'm not the least interested in your damned list," Max said. "I have another matter altogether to discuss with you. I thought you should be aware that Yates's sweetheart is not all she seems."

Caro frowned, her mirth fading. Holding her rapt attention, Max proceeded to tell her about his former acquaintance with Danielle Newham and her brother, Peter.

"Three years ago I was in London on leave when a university friend of mine killed himself after becoming embroiled in a scandal. He had worked for the War Office—logistics—and was in charge of sending reinforcements to the Peninsula. When an entire battalion of infantry was annihilated by the French shortly after landing, his loyalties were called into question. He was courting Danielle Newham at the time—or perhaps I should say she was wooing him. She left town directly after word of the massacre reached England.

"Nothing was ever substantiated," Max concluded, "but she was suspected of copying dispatches detailing troop movements and selling them to the French. And shortly after Miss Newham's disappearance from London, her lover put a pistol to his temple."

Max's grim tone held a smoldering anger, his eyes a dangerous glitter that made Caro shiver unconsciously; she would not want this man for an enemy.

Disturbed by his revelations, she searched his face. "And you think she may be a spy?"

"At the very least she has a pattern of preying on gullible young men. Yates won't stand a chance once she has her claws in him. I advise you to try and steer him away from her if you can. And if you have any secrets that need guarding, I would keep them under lock and key."

"I will," Caro replied, knowing the island had significant secrets that required guarding.

Just then she spied Señora Blanca Herrera standing a short distance away. Although her heart wasn't in it, Caro beckoned to the beautiful jet-haired Spanish lady and, rising, introduced her to Max.

Exquisitely dressed in black and crimson lace, the strikingly lovely señora slowly fluttered her fan while giving Max a sensual appraisal from her dark sloe eyes. "It is a pleasure to meet you at last, señor," she murmured in her husky voice as he bowed over her hand.

"The pleasure is all mine, señora, I assure you. I have been eager to make your acquaintance."

Hearing the admiration and male interest in Max's tone, Caro felt a sharp arrow of jealousy spear though her. Suddenly she regretted making the introductions. Her fingers clenched reflexively into fists, which was a mistake, since Max noted her response.

He sent her a fleeting—perhaps taunting?—glance of amusement, as if he knew very well that having to watch his flirtation with another woman nettled and even unsettled her. After gallantly asking Señora Herrera to dance the upcoming waltz with him, he offered his arm to escort the lady to where the dancers were taking their places.

Resuming her seat, Caro watched them leave, appalled by her savage impulse. Normally she was very fond of Señora Herrera; never before had she wanted to do damage to the beauty's lovely face.

Caro shook her head, silently scolding herself. Wasn't this precisely what she had wanted, to divert Max's interest from her? To crush her own obsessive desire for him?

She had missed him dreadfully this past week, despite her fierce resolve not to. And when she'd first spied him tonight, looking so incredibly striking in his black superfine coat and pristine white cravat and white satin breeches, her heart had suddenly fluttered violently in her chest. She was certain he could see the yearning on her face.

Just as she was certain he'd seen her deplorable reaction a moment ago. She had no business feeling such rampant jealousy—and no time for it, either.

She had to take his warning about Danielle Newham seriously, for the Guardians had secrets that could be in jeopardy. Perhaps there was nothing sinister about Miss Newham, but to be safe, she would advise her colleagues to keep an eye on both Newhams.

No sooner had the thought crossed Caro's mind than she glimpsed Miss Newham at the far end of the great hall. The lady sent a swift, almost surreptitious glance over her shoulder, before making her way from the chamber.

For an instant, Caro sat frozen. Then, after one last, longing glance at Max, she marshaled her scattered thoughts and followed.

Chapter Seven

Caro's heart rate escalated to an angry rhythm as she watched Danielle Newham slip into Sir Gawain's study. Miss Newham had been a guest at the castle on several occasions and certainly knew where the baronet conducted his business. If she was indeed searching for secrets, this would be a prime place to start.

Pausing outside in the corridor, Caro debated whether or not to interrupt just yet. On the one hand, knowing what a possible spy might be looking for would be valuable in formulating an effective defense. Yet she couldn't risk Miss Newham discovering knowledge that might endanger the Guardians.

Quietly Caro opened the door.

The auburn-haired woman was indeed at Sir Gawain's desk, searching through the stacks of papers that littered the surface.

"May I be of some assistance, Miss Newham?" Caro asked, keeping her voice innocent.

Danielle froze . . . but then quickly recovered. Setting down the papers, she offered a wan smile as she picked up a quill pen. "Perhaps so, Miss Evers. I was feeling a bit faint, so I decided to seek out the ladies' withdrawing room. But then I realized a burnt feather might be just the restorative I needed. Alas, I couldn't find any feathers but this one, and I doubt Sir Gawain would care to sacrifice his writing implements."

An inventive excuse, Caro thought with reluctant admiration.

"I will be happy to show you to the withdrawing room," she offered. "I believe you will find a supply of vinaigrettes and feathers there."

"Thank you," Miss Newham said with a meekness that was certainly counterfeit.

Caro accompanied her to the bedchamber set aside for female guests and waited while Danielle made a show of burning a feather and sniffing the acrid scent until she could claim her sensibilities were fully restored.

Then together they returned to the great hall and joined John Yates. Smiling brightly, Danielle told her suitor how helpful Miss Evers had been.

A performance worthy of the London stage, Caro thought wryly. But the incident was indeed alarming. If Danielle Newham was a spy, she would have to be watched closely.

After delaying a polite interval, Caro excused herself and wandered casually through the crowd of guests, pausing to speak to various friends. Eventually she came upon Alex Ryder.

Taking his arm, she pretended to laugh and jest with him as they strolled to the refreshment table, but in truth she was warning him about what had happened and enlisting his aid to observe the Newham woman.

"If she is engaged in spying," Alex said at the conclusion, "her brother is likely neck deep as well."

"No doubt. Do you think I should tell Sir Gawain?" Caro asked.

"I see no need to disturb him just now. I'll inform him after the ball. Meanwhile, I'll alert everyone else here."

She smiled in relief. In short order all the Guardians on Cyrene would be on notice.

"Yates will have to be told," Ryder added, his tone turning grim.

"I know," Caro agreed with regret. "But I would prefer to do it myself. The news will surely distress him, he is so fond of her."

When Ryder left her, Caro shifted her attention to the ballroom floor, her gaze unconsciously seeking out Max.

He was partnering another woman this time—Mrs. Julia Trant, the widow she had plotted for him to meet. Mrs. Trant's beauty was as striking and elegant as Señora Herrera's, but she had the opposite coloring, with pale, delicate features, golden blond hair, and cerulean blue eyes.

Caro experienced another irrational urge to do damage to a rival, even as she admired Max whirling the lady across the floor. He was obviously an expert at the waltz; indeed, he danced amazingly well, just as he seemed to do everything else.

It had taken so little effort to make him the center of attention. The female population of the entire island had flocked around him like eager butterflies, drawn to his raw, masculine appeal. Even when he wasn't trying, the force of his charm was irresistible.

Watching him gaze down at the beautiful blonde in his arms, Caro felt her heart twist painfully. She wondered if Max had any notion just how devastating that sensual half smile of his was.

When Julia Trant, however, returned a dazzling smile of her own, Caro swore a very unladylike oath.

She had known that two such beautiful, alluring people would be attracted to each other. She should be delighted her efforts were so successful. But still, observing Max now gave her cold comfort. It *hurt* to see him holding the glamorous, graceful beauty so closely.

Julia was a former London actress and the closest thing to a demimondaine that Cyrene had to offer. And from the wanton way she was looking at Max, she clearly was eager to have him in her bed. No doubt he would be there soon, perhaps even tonight.

Feeling a fierce ache, Caro turned away abruptly. She could never compete with such feminine perfection. She had little of the dash or flair or elegance that men like Max seemed to admire. She didn't belong at a ball, either. Her gown, although well tailored, was five seasons out of date. But then, she had never placed much emphasis on her appearance, for she'd always had far more pressing matters that required her attention. She was a practical, *sensible* woman, Caro scolded herself, without much vanity.

So why did she suddenly have this rash longing to be exquisitely beautiful? Why this fervent wish for Max to look at her as if she were, the way he'd looked at her that night at the ruins? Why did she want him to hold her as he was holding Julia Trant? Why did she feel so damnably hot and restless?

Determined to conquer her pathetic feelings, Caro skirted the crowd and headed toward the stone stairway at the far end of the great hall. She intended to make her way outside the castle, where she could enjoy the spectacular view from the parapet walls.

Perhaps in the cool peacefulness of the night she could find a cure for her foolish yearnings.

"Your lack of attention is hardly flattering, darling," Julia Trant murmured, a hint of petulance in her tone.

Max dragged his gaze back to the woman waltzing in his arms. He had been following Caro's progress from the hall instead of concentrating on his dance partner. A tactless lapse on his part.

"Miss Evers is certainly amicable, but I frankly cannot comprehend why the gentlemen are so fond of her," Julia complained with genuine puzzlement. "She has only a small claim to beauty, and she has such extremely odd interests for a female."

Max could have told her why gentlemen were partial to Caro Evers: because she was accepted as one of them. She had been admitted into their fraternity, where bonds of friendship were nearly as meaningful as honor.

Yet Max could understand why that rare camaraderie would be a source of jealousy for ladies such as Julia Trant; they felt resentful of the rapport they couldn't share, as well as challenged by Caro's uniqueness. Caro was not only a healer, she was a warrior.

Yet she had fire and passion in her veins, Max knew firsthand.

Unlike the blond beauty in his arms, he suspected.

He gave Julia Trant a charming smile and a reply that flattered her wounded vanity, but he made his escape as soon as the dance ended.

Standing at the parapet, Caro stared out at the shimmering sea. The waning moon was nearly full, bathing the night in beauty, while a fragrant breeze caressed her flushed skin.

It was times like this that her loneliness was most acute. When she felt a discontent that was palpable. She relished her life, yet she still felt as if something was missing.

Max was greatly to blame, she knew. Only since coming to know him had she even been aware of her loneliness, or realized how deep the ache ran.

But she herself was even more to blame, a prodding voice insisted. *She* had chosen this life, no one else. She alone had denied herself the comfort of male companionship for fear of hampering her dual vocations. She had turned ignoring her womanly needs into a practiced skill.

Yet none of her determined reminders could soothe the yearning inside her. No amount of brutal honesty could make her view the empty future with eagerness.

It startled her when she heard a familiar male voice lightly chiding her. "So this is where you have hidden yourself."

Glancing over her shoulder, Caro found Max moving toward her. "You should not have left the ball," she replied, forcing a smile. "You will disappoint all your admirers."

"Damn my admirers," he said devoutly. "And damn you for abandoning me. I needed you to protect my virtue, and yet you disappear at the first opportunity."

She couldn't repress her unwilling amusement. "I imagine you lost your virtue long ago."

"Very well, then, let me be blunt. I would far rather be with you than suffer the attentions of all those fawning females."

The corner of her mouth curved. "If you don't return, you will miss the best part of the ball. A late supper is to be offered shortly."

"I know. The feast they are laying out would have fed Wellington's army for a month. But my appetite has failed me after my efforts to dodge your scheming. I thought I might persuade you to waltz with me instead."

Her smile faded. "I told you, Max, I don't dance."

"What do you have against dancing?"

Embarrassment flushing her face, Caro ducked her head as she admitted in a low voice, "I feel foolish when I attempt it. I have felt awkward at every ball I have ever attended. In London I was a total—" Suddenly she shook her head and managed a short laugh. "I didn't mean to sound so self-pitying. But you must see what a misfit I am."

Max leaned casually against the parapet. He himself considered her remarkable, yet he was beginning to comprehend how little faith Caro had in her own allure. It surprised him to see her discomfort in a social setting. In her own world she was assertive and confident and outspoken, but here among the Beau Monde her insecurities were more obvious. She seemed actually intimidated by her lack of feminine graces.

Max felt a surge of protectiveness at her unexpected vulnerability.

He could have told Caro how enchanting he found her, but he doubted she would believe him. No, Max reflected tenderly. He would have to show her instead.

"Come here," he said, holding out his arms.

"Why?" was her wary response.

"Because I want to dance with you." One hand

swept wide, indicating the stone floor of the parapet. "We have our own private ballroom, with only the moon and the stars and the night sky for an audience."

Caro studied him for a long moment before giving a brief laugh. "If this is your idea of retribution for my plotting, I wish you would think of some other punishment."

"I am vexed enough with you to want retribution, witch, but I promise you this will not be punishment."

Still Caro hesitated. "Even if I knew how to waltz, you would not want me for your partner, I assure you. I would be hopeless."

"If Yates can dance with his wooden leg, so can you."

"But John Yates has always relished dancing. I have not."

"You know how to fence, didn't you tell me?"

"What does that matter?"

"Dancing is no more difficult than facing an opponent with a rapier. Indeed, most people would consider it a far less dangerous pastime. Now come here. I mean to teach you to waltz."

"Aren't you concerned that I might throw you to the ground again?" Caro asked, a smile in her voice.

Her dismissive humor was her shield, Max realized, her means of defense. He found it endearing. "Not at all, for I will be on my guard this time. Pray now, pay attention and follow my lead."

Lightly grasping both her hands, he showed her the steps and the rhythm. They could hear the faint strains of a waltz coming from the great hall, and Caro found herself emulating Max with surprising ease as he counted time . . . one-two-three . . . one-two-three . . .

coaching her now and then, murmuring soft words of encouragement.

Finally, though, he drew her into his arms. "Now close your eyes, angel, and simply feel."

She obeyed, matching his effortless rhythm, letting the lilting music flow through her. In only moments they were moving together as one.

She could scarcely believe it. Yet as she gave herself over to his embrace, Caro was filled with a strange tangle of emotions, exhilaration and joy and gratitude. She had always wanted to feel graceful, to dance as she saw other women dancing, and somehow Max had managed to turn her into a swan.

An uneven breath escaped her. For the second time in her life, this man was making her feel beautiful. Making her feel desirable.

She felt as if she were moving in a sensual dream.

A long while later she became vaguely aware that Max had slowed their steps. He drew back, his eyes half closed, surveying her.

Their dance dwindled to a full stop, and suddenly the night was alive with sound and sensation.

His eyes locked with hers, molten sapphire. "I intend to kiss you," he warned, his voice deep and hushed.

Her breath caught like warm liquid in her lungs. His gaze hypnotized her as he held her in the light protective circle of his arms. She felt the heat of his body, felt her breasts swell and tighten. Against all wisdom, she hungered to be kissed.

With beguiling tenderness his hands spread possessively over her back, molding her to him. The heavy arousal at his loins was obvious, and Caro felt a sudden sweet ache between her thighs that she was helpless to control.

His hands moved up to cradle her neck with exquisite possessiveness, making her recall another magical night, the silver moonlight, the whisper of the ocean waves below, the incredible sensuality of this man. . . .

Then Max curved his fingers on either side of her face, tilting it upward, his touch lingering and provocative. Caro stared back at him, trembling at the knowledge that she was the target of his desire.

His beautiful face filled her entire vision now, and then his mouth settled over hers, soft flesh to soft flesh.

She expelled a pent-up sigh. She had no thought of resistance; she had no thought at all, only feelings.

His kiss was a slow, intimate knowing of her mouth. She could feel the treacherous heat of desire build in her, of craving.

A whimper of protest escaped her, though, when she realized where this was leading. She was too needy, too yearning, too hungry. Max stirred the wildness in her blood.

She dragged in a raw breath and tried to draw back, but he captured her face and held her still.

"What are you afraid of?" he demanded, his voice ragged. "That I might touch you like this?" Deliberately his hand cupped the curve of her breast. "Might taste you like this . . ."

Caro nearly moaned as his lips found the hot, flushed skin of her jawline.

Fierce sensations shuddered through her as he stroked her with his fingers, nuzzled her with his lips.

"All I can think of is being inside you," he whispered.

It was all she could think of as well. Her body had

come to life. Powerful urges swept through her, carnal feelings that set her nipples throbbing, that left her already weak limbs even more limp.

This time when she pushed against his chest, she managed to free herself. Shakily Caro reached out for the parapet wall for support, keeping her gaze averted as she fought the tide of arousal flooding her.

She wanted to deny this wild hunger in herself. Max could so easily make her tremble, make her lose control. He was so dangerous . . . and oh so wonderful. The sweet tenderness of his kiss had filled the deep, long-hidden need she had striven so long to quell.

She made the mistake of looking up at him then. His gaze seemed to hold her captive to his will.

"What is it you want from me?" she whispered, her voice hoarse.

"Everything you have to give," he answered just as hoarsely.

When she made no response, his searing fingers lifted to brush the column of her throat. "You want it as well, but for some inexplicable reason, you are set on denying your own needs."

Caro leaned against the stone wall, feeling as if she were balanced on an emotional precipice. A dozen arguments tumbled over and over again in her mind.

She knew better than to become more intimately involved with Max, knew that she needed to maintain a safe distance.

Yet did she really want to stand by while he turned to some other woman? Made love to a beautiful rival when she wanted him to choose her?

And what harm would there be in indulging in a

liaison? Isabella would have been the first to encourage her to live her life to the fullest.

Was it so wrong to want Max? To fulfill her yearning to feel cherished and womanly and feminine again? To end her loneliness for a time? To know his lovemaking once more?

She hungered for physical warmth. His warmth. And he was offering it to her.

More critically, this could be her last chance to experience true passion. She would have the memories to sustain her for the cold, barren years ahead.

There was only one answer she could give, Caro knew.

Yet they couldn't just brazenly indulge their passions at a ball.

"Not here," she murmured, gazing up at him. "Not now."

"Where, then? When?" His mouth twisted in a wry line. "I would prefer a real bed this time, rather than the hard stone of the ruins."

She rubbed her temple, her thoughts searching. She could meet him somewhere, but no good choice came to mind.

And in any case, she would have to return home from the ball with her companion, Señora Padilla. But the señora was a heavy sleeper. And Caro's small staff of servants would long ago have retired. They wouldn't be surprised to hear any nocturnal noises from her quarters, for she regularly came and went at odd hours of the night.

If Max came to her there, she would be able to conceal his presence from prying eyes, as long as he left before first light.

"My house," Caro said in a low voice. "After the ball. At the southeast corner, you will find a stairway leading to the gallery outside my bedchamber. I will leave the doors unlocked."

Chapter Eight

The moon-drenched night held the promise of passion.

Nerves raw with anticipation, Caro sat at her dressing table, trying to calm her excitement by slowly brushing her hair. She had never expected to be in this situation, waiting for her lover to come to her.

She'd put out all the lamps but left the draperies open. The room was white with moonlight, and so hushed she could hear the beating of her heart.

Was this how a bride felt on her wedding night?

Caro glanced over at the bed she had slept in since she was a child. White gossamer sheers hung from the tall posts, bathed in silver radiance, while the sheets were turned down in invitation—seductive and innocent at the same time.

An odd sense of wistfulness tempered her agitation. This was likely the closest she would ever come to a true wedding night, and she wanted it to be perfect.

She had no doubt it would be unforgettable. Max would make it so with the fierce tenderness of his lovemaking.

His approach was so silent, she wasn't aware he had entered her room until she saw him standing there a short distance away.

All her senses leapt.

Dropping the brush from her nerveless fingers, Caro rose on shaking limbs. Now was the time to let common sense and self-preservation reassert themselves, but she couldn't seem to think.

Max was watching her, his compelling eyes dark and intent. And when he spoke, his voice was a low, throaty command. "Come here."

Hesitantly, she obeyed. When she reached him, Max drew her against him in a light embrace. Caro held herself rigidly as the heat of his body seared through their clothing. She could feel her breasts swell painfully against his powerful chest, feel the hard contour of his manhood, but it was his gaze that riveted her, that held her enthralled.

It alarmed and thrilled her to be the sole, intense focus of this beautiful man's attention. One look from his sapphire eyes could make her pulse go wild. He had simply to touch her and her breath fled—as it did now.

His thumbs flickered over the tight buds outlined by her cambric nightdress, sending a ripple of desire shivering through her. Until Max, she had never realized how sensitive her breasts could be.

Then he loosened the ribbons of her bodice to expose the rounded globes. The knot clenching her stomach seemed to tighten as she realized he meant to undress her.

Reflexively she raised her arms to cover her bosom, reacting with a woman's private fear of looking foolish.

"I am hardly the kind of lover you are accustomed to," she whispered.

His expression softened, holding a tenderness that made her heart flutter. "You are the only lover I want, sweet Caro. See how desirable I find you?" Drawing her close again, he let her feel the bold evidence of his desire.

As she stared up at him, his smile was gentle and starkly masculine, his eyes caressing. "If you think I become this acutely aroused for just any woman, you haven't nearly the intelligence I credited you with."

He was teasing her misgivings away, she realized with gratitude.

"You are incredibly lovely," he insisted, bending closer. His lips grazed her ear, sending waves of fiery chills throughout her. "And your body is perfectly suited for making love. It fits mine superbly. See?"

He held her against him, letting her feel how their bodies matched. After a moment, his hands rose to her hair, his fingers slowly sliding through the curling tresses, stroking.

Caro shut her eyes at the sensual feel of it.

"Every night for the past year," Max said quietly, "I've lain awake thinking about you. I've wanted this moment to come. Wanted to make love to you again."

Caro felt her tension ease a measure. She couldn't maintain her defenses in the face of his beguiling avowal. She couldn't sustain her panic, either.

Max had once initiated her into the mysteries of love, had given her the most riveting kind of pleasure. She had nothing to fear from him now.

His lips covered hers then in a featherlight kiss, and a sigh of longing escaped her. She made no protest as he slipped her nightdress down over her shoulders, exposing her breasts to his warm breath.

Her nipples contracted into tight, aching buds at his acutely masculine appraisal. With excruciating slowness, his warm hands cupped the swells, while his lips brushed the taut crests. His touch was deliberate, knowing, making fierce, restless feminine need whisper though her body.

"Let me show you how much I want you," he whispered, seeking her lips this time.

The night trembled around them as he explored her mouth with his tongue. He kissed her so softly, so deeply that a silky fire flowed between them, fanning downward to pool in a molten well between her thighs.

Caro was dazed and quivering when Max finally broke off. His fingers nudged her nightdress lower, letting it fall to the floor. Then he stepped back and drank his fill of her, his blue gaze touching her everywhere.

"Your body is even more beautiful than in my memories," he said almost reverently, making her want to believe.

He moved away to undress then, leaving an aching awareness in all the places where his gaze had caressed.

He had changed his clothing from the ball, she saw. He wore no jacket or cravat or waistcoat, merely a white shirt and dark breeches and boots. He sat in a wing chair to remove his boots, then shed his other garments and stood nude before her. When he moved toward her in the silver light, the graceful motion of his body took her breath away.

Would the impact of his presence ever lessen?

His muscles were coiled with a vital, dangerous energy she could feel even from a distance. She was smotheringly aware of his magnificent body, scaldingly aware of his nakedness as her gaze locked on his loins. . . .

Rising there from swirls of dark hair was that hard,

pulsing maleness she'd felt burning through their clothing. His rigid phallus arched nearly to his navel. She thought of how that swollen arousal felt entering her, filling her, and an urgent need began to throb in every part of her body.

Max felt the same throbbing ache as he stood before Caro. Her eyes were clear and huge, touched with a shy yearning—a guileless, vulnerable confession of innocence. The thought of bringing her to passion interfered with his breathing and made his loins burn.

How many times had he dreamed of this? How many times had he imagined her beneath him, writhing in the throes of desire that he'd awakened? It seemed he had waited for this moment forever.

She was even lovelier than he remembered. Freed from its customary strict knot, her curling brown hair rippled wildly over her shoulders and down her back; her skin was creamy, its satin texture pearlized by moonlight. He wanted to make love to her slowly, kissing every hollow and pulse of her slender form. He wanted to take her fiercely, till neither one of them could think.

His body felt molten with desire. The need that had gripped him in its talons for weeks now tightened its hold ruthlessly. The need to feel her softness spread and filled by his man's heat. The desperate need to touch her, to taste her, to feel her quicksilver responsiveness. To hold her and not let go.

He lowered his head again. Her lips had the texture of newness. His kiss stroked her mouth, relearning the shape, the unique contours, the sweet, dark recesses.

After a long moment he lifted Caro in his arms. The

moon sent a wash of gleaming light over the bed as he lay her down and sat beside her.

With both hands, Max set about arousing her. His fingertips made a languid, circular motion around the peak of each breast, then drifted lower, roaming with slow thoroughness over her body. He watched the movement of his hands against the pale, shivering flesh of her abdomen, then the dusky hair curling at her thighs.

It was then that she grasped his arm lightly, staying him. "Max?" she murmured, uncertainty lacing her tone.

Reaching beside the bed, she retrieved a small leather pouch from the table there.

"I would like to make use of these," she stated. Opening the pouch, she showed him several small sponges with strings attached, along with a vial of amber-colored liquid.

"A sponge soaked in vinegar?"

"Yes," Caro replied. "Some of our island women rely on these to prevent conceiving more children, and I think it wise that I do the same. Would you object?"

"No." His solemn gaze swept across her face. "I think I told you," he said in a low voice, "I'm not anxious to sire any children. Nor do I want you risking the scandal of being with child out of wedlock."

She hesitated before asking another embarrassing question. "Would you . . . happen to know how to use these? I know in principle what to do, and Isabella explained it to me once, but if you are experienced . . ."

His mouth curved in a tender smile. "I can show you how, angel. But not just now. I have something else in mind for the moment."

Setting aside the pouch, he stretched out beside her. Then bracing himself on one elbow, he resumed his earlier caresses, letting his hand sweep over her abdomen to her thighs.

Instantly Caro felt renewed desire shiver through her. When he brushed the tight nest of curls there, she gave a soft whimper. Her femininity throbbed with a hot and heavy urgency that made her eager for his searching fingers.

His touch was profoundly tantalizing, burningly tender, as he explored the slick velvet bared to his fingers. Pleasure flared wherever he stroked. Then he cupped her between her legs, and one bold finger thrust deep, making Caro draw a sharp breath. She could scarcely bear the brazen heat that uncoiled inside her.

Hungrily, she reached for Max, and he obliged by easing his weight over her. She could feel the press of his male hardness against her swollen folds as he kissed her lips lightly, yet he didn't enter her. Instead his mouth traced downward to her breasts, then lower, burning a path to the juncture of her thighs.

She felt the silken probe of his tongue parting her, and her breath splintered at the pure sensuality of the act. When she felt his arousing, inflaming tongue lapping her, she tried to repress a strangled moan.

Max paused to gaze up at her. "No, don't hold back. I want to hear every sweet, husky gasp."

She forced herself to remain still as his tongue found her again. Like dark fire, it flickered and teased, determinedly arousing. In only moments, her hips were restlessly straining against the velvet torment.

The shameful pleasure built until all Caro could

think about was what his scandalous caresses were doing to her. She was so feverish beneath him, her body was no longer hers.

When a tremor shook her, she tried to ease away from the scalding heat, but his fingers spread and clasped her hips, giving her no opportunity to evade him. The sensation of being held still while he pleasured her was almost paralyzing.

A shudder rocked her when his tongue dipped inside her, and she made a soft sound, a wild sound.

"Yes, let me hear you cry for me," Max urged in a husky whisper.

She could do nothing else. By now she was writhing under a lash of sensation so exquisite and unbearable, she thought she might ignite. Then he gave her one last arousing kiss, delving deep, setting off a firestorm within her.

Stunned, she arched upward, straining with frenzy as she plunged into a raw pleasure so intense it seared.

When her dazed senses finally returned, she realized Max was suckling her rigid nipples, intensifying the slow-ebbing bliss.

Unable to move, she lay panting, her eyes closed, her tongue wetting her dry lips. Then he shifted his position again, and she could feel his kisses moving upon her flushed face, could sense his satisfaction at giving her such a shattering release.

After another long moment, he reached for the pouch beside the bed. When he had made use of the vial, he parted her thighs and slid a soaked sponge deep within her body.

To her surprise, then, he lay down beside her, easing onto his back. When he made no move to kiss her,

Caro realized Max was letting her take the lead. Raising herself up, she let her gaze drift over his nude body, admiring the rippling play of sleek muscles in his bronzed arms and chest. Filled with the searing impulse to touch him, she let her hand follow suit. His skin felt like raw silk, his flesh vibrant and alive under her palm.

She leaned closer, smelling his warm, musky scent. His throbbing manhood lay arched against his belly, and she reached down. When her fingers gently traced the pulsing length, he shuddered, seizing a raw breath.

Satisfaction flooded her. For the second time in her life, Caro felt a true sense of feminine power.

Yet when she tried to stroke him, Max grasped her hand, stilling her caresses. "Do you know what it's like to have you touch me?" he asked hoarsely.

She suspected it was very much like what she felt when he touched her—like kindling ready to burst into flame. He felt that way now, Caro was certain. She could sense the pulsing urgency in his body, the coiling tension, as he drew her down so that she stretched against him full length.

Heat leapt between them, shocking and primal, as she felt the throbbing maleness of him against her loins.

"Max, please . . ."

He didn't need to be asked again. Immediately he rolled over, easing her beneath him. His weight felt wonderful, the strong, virile power of his body making her feel fragile and feminine and sweetly helpless. The heated look on his face took her breath away.

Holding her gaze, he levered his knee between hers

and spread her thighs, his member intimately knowing the cradle of her womanhood.

When her eyelids fell shut, he murmured a soft command. "No, look at me. Let me see your eyes."

Probing her slick folds with his hardness, he tightened his buttocks and slowly began to enter her. When her breath faltered, he halted partway inside her, which only made Caro crave to possess all of him.

Deliberately she raised her hips, urging Max to complete his penetration. With no further encouragement, he pressed deeper, until her hot, moist flesh tightly sheathed him.

He held himself still then, giving her body time to grow accustomed to his penetration. Caro lay still as well while her body adapted to the sweet shock of Max filling her so powerfully.

She could see fire and tenderness in his eyes as she stared up at the dark beauty of his face.

When he finally began to move, he kept his strokes slow and long and deliberately drawn out. His chest chafed her peaked nipples, while his heavy thighs pressed hers wider so that he could penetrate her to the hilt. And shortly the blaze that had so blindly consumed her earlier began to lick at her senses again. The next time he withdrew, her inner muscles instinctively clenched at the wonderful, hard length of him.

She could feel Max shudder against her as he struggled to control his reaction. But he murmured soft encouragement as he showed her how to move, matching each silken thrust to her rasping breaths. His surging rhythm became hers. Soon she was whimpering with the burgeoning pleasure.

His eyes were burning as he bent his head to kiss

her. Her lips parted to accept his hot, thrusting tongue, and she returned his kiss fervently, seeking and wanting, overwhelmed by his touch and scent and taste. The fever of his possession, the urgency in his lips, were ecstasy to her.

His mouth never ceased its drugging torment as he drove her to greater heights. Her body pulsed with a craving need so great that she hurt from it. He made her feel delirious with need. Wild, elemental, consumed by heat.

Yet Max's desire was as great as her own. He delighted in her moans, reveled in her helpless response. His body throbbed with the need to pound hard and deep, and after a time he could no longer hold back.

He rocked against her, the rawness of his male hunger shattering the last pretense of gentleness between them. His voice as tight as his arms, he took her ruthlessly, but Caro clawed at his back, meeting his violence with her own as they strained together.

When she cried out, he captured the sound, kissing her fiercely, his lips drinking her keening moans. Then his back arched as his body spasmed. A fierce sound welled in his throat. His teeth bared in an almost agonized expression, he surged into her one final time.

Climax, savage and blinding, ripped through them both in a white-hot eruption. Their bodies shook with the rapture of it.

In the aftermath, Max collapsed upon her, his breath a raw whisper as he rasped her name. He could hear her heart beating in a frenzied echo of his own, feel her skin dewy from the heat and violence of his possession, her body flushed with erotic warmth.

"You make me feel so wild," she murmured.

Wild was exactly what he felt when he was inside her, out of control, beyond the reach of reason.

At last finding the strength to ease his weight from her, he bent to kiss her brow beneath her riotous hair, then gathered her against him.

He lay there, marveling at the searing pleasure of their joining. He had felt an explosion of passion he hadn't felt in years, maybe never. He'd mindlessly lost himself in Caro, in a way he never had with any other woman.

He wanted to lose himself inside her again. He knew he had to temper his demands on her inexperienced body, but already his shaft had started to fill and throb once more. He wanted her now, more fiercely than before.

At the same time, he wanted simply to hold her. To savor this moment—the warmth of her body pressing against his, her glorious hair spilling across his chest.

He tightened his hold, knowing he couldn't let her go after just this one night.

"I used to dream of this," he said after a time, his voice still jagged from the relentless ecstasy they had shared.

Beside him, Caro sighed, lost in a thick daze of pleasure. She had dreamed of Max, too. Countless times. But the reality was far better than her dreams.

"When I couldn't sleep," he murmured, "I would think of you." He was playing with a strand of her hair, letting a curl entwine around his fingers. "In my imagination, you would stroke my brow to help me fall asleep."

Rousing herself from her lovely daze, Caro rose up

on one elbow and brushed a lock of raven hair from his forehead.

"Like this?" she asked, smoothing her fingers gently across his brow.

His eyes fell shut and he made a soft sound of assent, something between a sigh and a moan. "Exactly like that."

Caro gazed down at him, puzzled and admittedly a bit wounded as well. "Max? Do you truly want to sleep just now?"

Giving a low laugh, he opened his eyes. "No, I was trying to be considerate of your inexperience."

"I am hardier than I look."

"That you are."

He drew her down to him but made no move to do anything more sexual—merely pressed his lips against her hair.

"I won't be satisfied with a single night," he said finally. "One night won't be enough for me. Or for you, either, I expect."

Caro stilled. "I concede you won our competition. I couldn't resist you after all."

His fingers tightened on her arm. "This is no contest between us now, Caro. Nothing to do with any game. And I don't intend to give you up."

She stirred restlessly against him, assailed by a return of the conflicting emotions that had fought and tangled inside her all evening.

"Can you honestly say you don't want us to be lovers after tonight?" Max asked in a rough whisper.

She knew what her answer should be. What common sense dictated. But then his warm palm covered her breast, sending a shock of desire coursing through her.

At the heated rush of feeling, Caro squeezed her eyes shut. She couldn't think when Max was touching her this way, assaulting her senses with his potent male vitality. All she could think of were his magical hands and burning lips and lithe, magnificent body.

"You were an innocent when you gave yourself to me," he continued softly. "Wouldn't you like to know more about lovemaking?"

Yes, she would like it very much. Max could teach her. He would show her the kind of passion that she had once only dreamed of. He was a man who enjoyed giving pleasure as much as taking it, and he would see to it that she experienced all the blissful secrets between a man and a woman.

"What are you suggesting?" she asked finally.

"Simply that we enjoy whatever time we have together."

When she didn't reply, his thumb caressed her hardened nipple, shooting sparks to all her nerve endings and between her thighs. "Can you deny you want me?"

"No." Of course she couldn't deny it. Max *made* her want him.

And tonight, at least, she had done the same to him. The memory of his male body saying so openly and truthfully that he wanted her filled her with a sweet sense of triumph.

Yet Max would leave her again, Caro reminded herself. Once they brought Isabella home safely, he would have no reason to stay on Cyrene.

And he only wanted her body, while she wanted . . . what?

Longing, as strong and desperate as the need to breathe, rippled through her. She wanted Max, any way she could have him. She wanted his passion, his caresses, for the short remainder of his time on the island.

Yet she would have to protect herself somehow, she knew. He wouldn't hurt her, not on purpose. The danger would be in becoming too emotionally involved with him. She would have to guard against coming to care for him too deeply. It was imperative that she maintain a certain dispassion, Caro warned herself.

"We will have to keep our relationship purely physical," she said slowly. "Nothing more intimate."

His breath was a warm shiver against her neck as his lips nuzzled her skin. "Nothing?"

"No, nothing. That is all I want, Max—an affair based entirely on pleasure."

"Very well, if that is what you want," he responded in that same sensual, arousing voice she'd heard whispering endearments and bold persuasions in her ear a short while ago.

She felt his maleness rigid and hot against her thigh, reminding her of his hunger.

Her breath caught in her chest, while all the primal womanly instincts she possessed sprang to life. Perhaps she was foolish, but it thrilled her to be wanted so fiercely by this man.

She knew she should say no to his proposal, but she couldn't summon the strength. Max had stolen her willpower, one caress at a time.

Just as he was doing now. His teeth tasted the softness of her skin with ravishing delicacy, flooding her raw nerves with a warm bath of sensation. Her newly sensitized body thrummed with desire, feverish for his touch.

Then he rolled over, easing between her thighs.

Caro stared up at him, the moonlight dancing over his beautiful features. She was agonizingly aware of how hard and huge he was against her swollen sex, how sweet the ache of her breasts was inside his gentle grip, how molten his gaze.

"Only physical gratification," she repeated, reminding herself more than him.

"As you say."

His eyes were hot and held dark promise as he slid into her. Instantly all fires swept to life, white-hot. Her body shimmered with fierce response.

Releasing a breathless sigh, she arched beneath him, her arms helplessly reaching up to encircle his neck.

He smiled, a slow, sexual smile that burned right through her.

Caro made a soft whimpering sound of need as she raised her lips for his kiss. Max obliged, taking her mouth with an urgency that made her ache.

Throwing away every last sense of caution then, she returned his fervent embrace, surrendering herself to him, to his passion, to the night.

Chapter Nine

Max left before the dawn. Caro lay in bed for a long while, cherishing the lingering warmth of his passion.

After a second enchanting bout of lovemaking had left them both gasping, she had persuaded Max to close his eyes and stroked his brow until he fell into a healing sleep. Yet as she'd listened to the sound of his deep, even breathing, to his heart beating quietly beneath her cheek, she renewed her vow to keep her emotional distance.

Reminding herself again now, Caro pushed away the bedcovers that still carried Max's scent and rose to bathe and dress. She couldn't let herself think about him, for she needed to focus her attention on business.

Normally she met Alex Ryder on Thursday mornings at the castle for a regularly scheduled bout of fencing practice, but she intended to ride over early and catch John Yates at his work—in order to inform him about Danielle Newham.

She wasn't eager to tell John that the woman who had captured his heart might not be what she seemed. Yet it was her duty to warn him that they had a possible traitor in their midst. Danielle and her brother, Peter, could not be allowed to carry out whatever nefarious acts they had planned.

Dreading her upcoming interview with John, Caro

found she had little appetite, so she merely ate some fruit while her riding mount was saddled. Then she struck out south for Olwen Castle.

She had asked Max to meet her there. She thought it best to speak to John alone but to have his former commander available to support her story, in case John either didn't believe the allegations or had questions.

She encountered Max at the castle stables, for apparently he'd arrived moments before her.

Her pulse leapt the instant she saw him.

"Good morning, Miss Evers," he said mildly as she slid down from her sidesaddle and surrendered her mount to a groom. His tone was casual, but his eyes were searing in their intensity.

When she met the flare of heat in the blue depths, the hot, sweet memory of the past hours poured through her.

Caro managed a response to his slow smile of greeting, but she feared she sounded too flustered. It was difficult to pretend she hadn't just spent a magical night in his arms.

"I trust," Max added as he escorted her from the stables, "that you enjoyed pleasant dreams last night."

"Quite pleasant."

"Mine certainly were," he admitted in a low, husky voice that started a deep throb burning through her body.

As they made their way to the great hall, Caro kept remembering how Max's lips and hands had felt on her skin, how he felt moving within her. And when his fingers pressed the small of her back to usher her through the huge wooden entrance doors, she shivered at the responsive ache between her thighs.

She had to discipline herself in order to greet John Yates solemnly and ask for a private word with him.

Leaving Max in the great hall to peruse the medieval artifacts there, she accompanied John to his office—a small antechamber off Sir Gawain's study. As dispassionately as possible Caro told him about Max's former knowledge of the Newhams, and recounted finding Miss Newham rifling through Sir Gawain's desk papers the previous night.

John stared down at the floor during the entire recitation. To her surprise, he didn't offer any protests or disclaimers, or even try to defend his sweetheart as Caro had expected.

When he remained mute, she squeezed his arm in sympathy. "If you find my concerns hard to credit, then you should talk to Mr. Leighton yourself."

"I believe you." The anguish in his voice was mirrored in his eyes when he looked up. "She has played me for a fool, hasn't she?"

Caro let her silence speak for itself.

"I knew it was too good to be true," John whispered, "that a beautiful woman like Danielle would show such avid interest in a cripple like me." It was the first time he had ever admitted grief to Caro at the loss of his leg, but she imagined he found this blow even more devastating than his maiming had been.

"I am very sorry, John," she murmured, feeling inadequate to console him, yet knowing she needed to focus his attention on the future. "We will have to keep a watchful eye on Danielle, though, and try to discover what she is after."

His jaw clenched. "You are right. And we cannot let her know we suspect her."

"Agreed. It would be best if we could set a trap for her. She may be trying to thwart one of our missions. If she were to expose any of our members . . ."

"I know. Their lives could be at stake." The sheen of wetness in his eyes wrenched at Caro's heart. "But she is my responsibility. I will deal with her, Caro, I promise you."

"If you are certain . . ."

"I am certain. May I be alone now?" he asked, his voice unsteady.

Understanding his desire to deal with his despair in private, Caro kissed his cheek and then quietly left him. Her own sorrow was mixed with a growing anger at the heartless jade who had almost certainly used John Yates to further her own sinister ends.

And this coming on top of an already simmering frustration over Isabella made Caro yearn to strike out at something. It had been nine days since she'd returned to Cyrene and still there was no word of her friend's whereabouts.

Caro knew her anger must have shown when she found Max, for he raised an eyebrow. "He didn't take it well?"

"He is heartbroken."

She glanced around the hall. "Where the devil is Ryder? He was supposed to meet me here for our fencing practice."

"If you need a partner, I would be happy to oblige."

Pressing her lips together, Caro gave him a dark look. She would very much like to fence with an opponent so worthy as Max. As a cavalry officer, he would doubtless possess superb swordsmanship, and beating him with foils would be a true challenge. Yet as irritable as she felt, she would hardly be at her best this morning.

"This will be your chance to show me what you can do," he prodded when she hesitated. "You've boasted of your skills often enough."

"Boasted!" He was trying to provoke her, she suspected. "Very well," Caro retorted, "but I warn you, I am in no mood to be lenient."

She led him into the depths of the castle, to a long gallery. The chamber was generously lit from sunlight streaming in the high windows, and equipped with any manner of weapons. She gave Max his choice of foils, which all had buttoned tips.

"I'm surprised you hold your practices here at the castle," he said as he tested the weight and flexibility of one blade.

"I can hardly pay regular visits to a bachelor's establishment," Caro snapped. "Nor do I wish to flaunt my unusual interest in a masculine sport. Here there is no one to censure what I do. All the servants are totally loyal to Sir Gawain."

Max's brows narrowed at her sharp tone. "Do you intend to take your frustration out on me?"

She took a calming breath. "No. I know better than to let my emotions rule me when I am facing an opponent."

"Good, since if you can't control your temper, you give me an immediate advantage."

Caro chose a gleaming rapier and made a few experimental slashes of her own before moving to the center of the stone floor. Knowing she needed to shrug off her anger in order to concentrate, she stood patiently waiting while Max stripped off his coat.

"There is the matter of the victor's prize to discuss before we begin," he said as he joined her. "If I win, I get to claim a kiss."

"And if I win?"

"You get to claim a kiss."

She smiled wryly. "There is hardly any point in competing, then, if we will only wind up kissing each other."

"Oh, no. I mean to hold my victory over your head when I make love to you."

She had a sudden vision of his hard body stretched full-length above hers, moving sensuously between her thighs, and her cheeks warmed. Now she *knew* Max was provoking her. Especially when his eyes roved lazily over her, lingering on her breasts before moving down her body.

"You fence encumbered by skirts? Isn't that rather hazardous?"

His hot gaze burned through the fabric of her gown, but she wouldn't give him the satisfaction of knowing he could fluster her. "It is only practical. Whenever I find myself in a dangerous situation, I am usually wearing skirts, so it is best to practice under the same conditions."

"They will likely put you at a disadvantage."

"Are you already making excuses in case you lose, Mr. Leighton?"

He grinned. "Perhaps. I would find it disconcerting to be beaten by a woman."

"I will try not to embarrass you too severely."

When he took his place opposite her, Caro raised her foil. An instant later their rapiers came together in a clash of steel, and the match got under way.

From the first engagement Max realized he was facing a formidable opponent. Caro fought with surprising quickness and a determined concentration that immediately forced him to keep alert.

After a swift pass, she lunged deftly and nearly slipped through his guard. When he recovered and claimed the offensive, he had to admire the adroit manner in which she fended off his attack.

There was a brief moment of silence while they circled each other as in a dance.

"I don't think I would care to meet you on a dueling field," Max remarked. "You are quite good."

"So are you."

"But I learned at Angelo's *salle* in London, from one of the premier swordsmen in Europe. Who taught you?"

"Ryder, in part. And one of our American friends whom you haven't met yet—Brandon Deverill."

Their blades crackled again.

"Do you have any weaknesses?" Max queried.

She parried his next thrust with ease and leapt nimbly aside. "If I did, I would not admit it to you," she retorted with a taunting smile.

Then she made a quick feint and advanced with agile steps, executing a series of neat slashes as he retreated.

After a few moments, Caro disengaged abruptly, giving Max a dark glare. "You aren't trying your best, are you?" she demanded.

"Not entirely," Max conceded. "I admit it goes against all my chivalrous instincts to fight a woman."

Her eyes turned the gray of storm clouds. "If you intend to continue this match, then stop insulting me by holding back. I don't want you handing me the victory out of chivalry."

"I stand corrected," Max said with all sincerity, raising his foil.

He put all his effort into winning this time, but their battle went on for several long minutes.

Caro was no hobbyist playing at a man's sport, Max acknowledged. She was a warrior who fought with extreme finesse and a skill that was superior to most men's. And she fenced the way she made love—with intensity and passion. In fact, her face was lightly flushed and held a sheen of sweat from the exertion, and her breath came in soft pants, as if she was nearing climax. . . .

Max felt himself harden at the image, and his mouth curved in an ironic smile. This was a hell of an inappropriate time to become aroused.

"Something amuses you?" Caro challenged as she executed an expert riposte.

"I just realized," he drawled, "that you spar as passionately as you make love."

She faltered at his wicked pronouncement. Off balance, she tripped on the hem of her skirt and fell backward, landing hard on her posterior.

Ruthlessly, Max followed her movement with his foil and brought the buttoned point to her throat. A cool smile of triumph touched his lips as he stood over her.

Breathing raggedly, Caro gave him a look that was both frustrated and sheepish. "That was hardly fair." Yet an unwilling smile tugged at her mouth.

"It wasn't fair at all, but it was effective in making you lower your guard. Let that be a lesson, my sweet witch."

"My lesson was realizing how devious you are—that you will do anything to win. But I will try to be gracious in defeat."

Max extended a hand and helped her to her feet. "You shouldn't feel discouraged. There are few men who can prove a match for me. You were a valiant opponent."

Caro couldn't help but feel warmed by his praise. She was indeed pleased that she'd held her own with Max till the very end.

"I suppose you are expecting flattery in return," she replied. "Very well—you are the devil of a swordsman. I have never seen anyone better."

It was true, Caro thought, eyeing Max as he stood at ease before her. His abilities were exceptional. The strength and skill and agility he displayed were those of a master. He would make an admirable Guardian—

"Now to claim my prize," Max said, interrupting her thoughts. "Come here, witch."

"But we aren't finished yet!" Caro protested.

"No, but I need sustenance if I'm to continue."

When she moved toward him warily, Max slipped his hand behind her nape, his gaze heating to molten sapphire as it lingered on her mouth.

This was swordplay of the sexual kind, Caro realized. But she could play this game. When he bent to capture her mouth, she returned his kiss ardently, her tongue darting between his lips, luring his into a contest of thrust and parry.

Max made a low sound in his throat, and his kiss turned carnal, possessive, stealing her breath away.

She wouldn't be the victor this time, either, Caro

realized after a heated moment; when he finally released her, she felt dazed.

"You are being devious again," she muttered as she stepped back and positioned herself, prepared to engage foils once more.

Just then their bout was interrupted by the appearance of a somber footman, who cleared his throat.

Flushing, Caro abruptly turned, pushing some unruly strands of hair off her face. "Yes, what is it?"

"Sir Gawain requests your immediate attendance, Miss Evers. And Mr. Leighton's also. Mr. Ryder has brought news."

Hope and fear both suffused her. She didn't even pause long enough to put down her rapier as she hastily exited the gallery, leaving Max to follow.

She found both Sir Gawain and John Yates in the baronet's study, gathered around a table, listening avidly to whatever Alex Ryder was saying.

"Have you news about Isabella?" Caro demanded as she joined them.

"Yes," Ryder answered, his gaze flicking to Max, who had moved to stand beside her. "Thorne's message just arrived. As we feared, Isabella was sold into captivity as a slave, but it was at a private auction rather than the public market. That, in fact, was why her trail was so difficult to follow. But at least now we have a good notion where she was taken."

"Where?"

"There." He pointed to a place on the map of Barbary that was spread on the table. "In the mountains southwest of Algiers, beyond a stretch of desert. She was bought by a Berber chieftain for his harem and fetched an enormous price. Anyone who paid that much is likely to take good care of his purchase. The difficulty is, the Berbers are warriors, much more fierce than Arabs, and this man is head of his tribe, more warlord than sheik. And his fortress is in a remote mountain area. If Bella is being held there, rescuing her will not be simple or easy."

Caro's right hand clenched her rapier while her left balled in a fist of despair. This news coming on the heels of John's heartbreak made her want to scream and weep at the same time. "So what is our plan?" she asked Ryder.

"We must first be certain Isabella is at the fortress. Hawk has headed there to scout it out. Hawk," Ryder said for Max's benefit, "is the Earl of Hawkhurst. He owns a renowned breeding stable here on Cyrene and makes regular trips to Barbary to buy Barb and Arabian stock."

"And he works for the Foreign Office as well?"

"Yes," Sir Gawain answered. "Hawkhurst is one of us."

Again pointing to the map, Ryder continued. "When Thorne arrived in Algiers, Hawk had already determined which corsairs had captured Isabella's ship. But it took some time to bribe them to reveal her purchaser. Hawk is traveling there with a few servants on the pretext of searching for breeding stock, while Thorne remains in Algiers, arranging for horses and weapons for a full expedition into the interior."

"We need to develop a rescue plan at once," Caro interjected. "We should sail for Algiers tomorrow."

"Thorne has advised us to wait until Hawk returns," Ryder said. "We need solid proof of Isabella's location before we head off on a wild-goose chase. It may take a week or two more, but the delay will likely not matter."

"It could certainly matter to Isabella!" Caro exclaimed. "If we are already in Algiers, we could set out for the fortress the moment we hear from Hawk."

"Yet we don't want to show our hand precipitously," Sir Gawain said calmly. "If we land a significant force in Algiers with no destination in mind, we could not only arouse the suspicions of the local authorities, but lose the element of surprise. And if Lady Isabella is not at the fortress, we will have to start over trying to locate her. Furthermore, not all our resources have arrived on Cyrene. You heard Mr. Leighton, my dear. It is imperative to have adequate intelligence and resources and prepare carefully in order to mount a successful operation."

Caro shot an obdurate glance at Max.

"No," Sir Gawain declared, "before acting, we will wait for confirmation that Lady Isabella is being held in this chieftain's fortress. I promise you, my dear, we will conference the moment we have enough intelligence to form a detailed plan."

Caro clamped her lips shut, Max saw, but while she didn't argue, her frustration was apparent.

Sir Gawain turned to Max. "Mr. Leighton, I would like you to take charge of the planning. I presume there are initial considerations to be weighed?"

"Quite a number of them," he replied. "If we're to trek across a desert in order to breach a mountain fortress, we'll need to decide on our exact roles, what diversionary tactics to employ, the possible contingencies to allow for. Most importantly, what damages we are willing to sustain—what we're willing to risk.

There often comes a point in any operation when the cost could be counted as too high."

"The cost could indeed be high in this case," Ryder agreed, frowning. "Getting there is one problem. Getting Isabella safely out, then across harsh mountain terrain and a hundred miles of arid desert is entirely another. Especially since I doubt a warlord will easily give her up. We may have to fight our way out of the fortress and back to the coast."

Max also found himself frowning as he pictured Caro fighting in hand-to-hand combat.

"You aren't seriously thinking about participating?" he asked her. "There's no reason to risk your life in what will doubtless be a dangerous expedition."

Without warning Caro raised her foil and slashed the blade in a hissing arc before letting the tip come to rest at Max's throat.

"My life is my own," she said tightly, "and there is no one I would rather risk it for than Isabella."

The men watching her went still with startlement, while Max froze. He didn't honestly believe himself in danger, but he could see the fury and frustration in her eyes.

"Caro, my dear," Sir Gawain murmured. "I am certain Mr. Leighton is not fully aware of your credentials, or the depth of your friendship with Lady Isabella. You needn't take his head off for it."

She ground her teeth visibly and spat out a terse apology before tossing the rapier down on the table. "There should be no doubt that I am going to Barbary. When you finally decide to plan our course of action, *pray* let me know."

Spinning on her heel then, she stalked from the room.

At length, Ryder cleared his throat, breaking the tension. He met Max's eyes, a glint of humor shining in his own. "You would be unwise to underestimate Caro's skills simply because she is a woman, my friend. Or to challenge her to her face, even if it is out of concern for her safety. You will learn that she detests being coddled."

Max's wry smile was self-deprecating. "I can see that. If you will excuse me, gentlemen, I think I will try to make amends for my mistake."

By the time he reached the stables, Caro had already mounted and spurred her horse across the cobbled yard. As she galloped past him and through the castle gates, Max flung himself upon his own mount and rode after her.

He kept her in sight as she headed north toward the island's two mountain peaks. She eventually slowed—out of concern for her winded mount, he suspected. Max followed at a discreet distance, even though he felt certain Caro knew he was on her trail.

After nearly twenty minutes she allowed him to catch up to her. Max started to speak, but Caro shook her head sharply, refusing even to look at him. They passed another few miles of cultivated fields and silver-gray olive groves and well-tended vineyards before the terrain became steeper and they began to climb.

He judged that they had ridden more than half the length of the island when the terrain suddenly became wilder. When Caro turned left off the road onto an overgrown path, Max could smell the scents of juniper and pine and hear a faint rush of water in the distance—a sound that gradually muffled the rhythmic clop of their horses' hooves.

After a while they emerged from a glade of holm oak and Aleppo pines into an open clearing and a scene of incredible beauty. Centered between the two forested slopes lay a small blue lake, glimmering in the sunlight like a brilliant sapphire. A narrow, silver-white waterfall cascaded off the western mountainside into the blue depths, throwing up a delicate mist that settled over the thickets of myrtle and wild oleander adorning the banks. In every shaded crevice, orchids grew in abundance, vying with rock roses and cyclamen and ferns for supremacy.

The quiet splendor rivaled every sight Max had thus far seen on this island paradise.

Caro halted her mount and gazed about her reverently for a moment, then dropped to the ground. "Come, I want to show you something."

Crossing to a ferny bank on her right, she climbed up and pushed through a tangle of shrubs and bramble before apparently disappearing into the mountainside. Max swung down from his horse and followed her.

Behind the screen of greenery, he realized, was an entrance to a grotto. The dim-shadowed interior was cool and lovely, but he had no trouble seeing, since on the far side, a gap in the rock roof let in a measure of sunlight.

The grotto was perhaps the size of his own library at home, and to his surprise, it was furnished similarly, with a stone shelf of books gracing one rock wall. At the rear, golden light spangled down through a canopy of overhanging oak leaves, illuminating the simple furnishings—two hand-hewn wooden chairs, a small table, several wooden chests, a brazier, and a straw pallet for sleeping.

"I like to think this was Cyrene's home," Caro murmured softly, "where she welcomed Apollo. Isabella gave this to me."

"This is your hideaway," Max said with a sudden flash of insight.

"Yes. My secret place. Isabella thought I needed somewhere of my own, a quiet retreat where I could study my medical journals without interruption or fear of censure."

He glanced around the tranquil little grotto with its rippling sunlight. The splash of the waterfall was merely an echo here, giving it the feel of a protective haven.

Under normal circumstances, one could find peace and solace here, Max had no doubt. But at the moment Caro was too wrapped up in her anger and frustration to allow herself to be soothed.

Her voice was tight when she went on. "I told you Isabella was like a mother to me, but she was even more than that. She is the reason I was able to study medicine. Isabella made Dr. Allenby take me on as his apprentice."

Max nodded. Everything he'd learned about Isabella suggested she had been the prime instigator in encouraging Caro to forge an independent path for herself.

"I owe her so much." Caro's hands clenched into fists. "I won't let her remain a captive, even if it means risking my life. I have to set her free, can't you understand that?"

He did understand. "You intend to rescue her, no matter the cost."

"Yes! And I want to do it *now*, not weeks from now.

This waiting is killing me! I can't bear to think of what might have become of her." Abruptly Caro gave a fierce shake of her head, squeezing her eyes shut.

"We will find her," Max said quietly, knowing he would do anything in his power to make that vow come true, anything to erase the bleakness on her face.

Her voice caught on a sob, and she bent her head, burying her face in her hands.

Max had never seen Caro give in to despair, and a surge of tenderness swept through him. He took a step toward her, intending to pull her into his arms . . . but then instinctively stopped himself.

Caro didn't need soothing. What she needed was a focus for her anger. A challenge. She responded best to challenges.

"So you mean to weep about it?" he drawled, infusing an edge of sarcasm into his tone. "What good will that do your friend?"

Caro stiffened, as if not quite believing what she was hearing.

"I never would have taken you for a watering pot," he added deliberately. "Or a weakling who gives up at the first obstacle."

Dropping her hands, she raised her tear-bright eyes to glare at him. "You think me a weakling?"

"I think you are letting your emotions rule you."

She took a step toward him, her fingers balling into fists again. "I wish I still had my foil."

"So do I. It would help you release some of your anger."

Closing the distance between them, Max reached behind her neck to curl his hand around her nape. She tried to jerk away, but he tightened his grasp, holding her immobile.

"What the devil are you doing?" Caro demanded.

"Obliging you. Now keep quiet." He lowered his head to cover her lips with an intentional fierceness.

The sudden, dark seizure of his kiss caught her off guard.

She fought him at first. Futilely Caro shoved her hands against his chest, a startled sound of rage coming from her throat. But Max smothered her mouth with his, forcing her lips open, robbing her of breath.

Desire scorched his body at their first contact, and he hardened instantly. Since leaving her bed early this morning, he had wanted this. And judging from the way Caro arched against him in unmistakable arousal, he knew the same brutal rush of feeling had caught her in its power.

She made another incoherent sound of protest as his thrusting tongue plunged into her mouth repeatedly, stoking her hunger, and after only a few heartbeats he could sense her responding. Her arms twined around his waist, and she opened to his plundering caresses.

The battle subtly shifted between them. Caro was still trembling with angry need but no longer resisting him, instead meeting his assault in a heated duel of tongues. When his mouth attacked hers with bruising force, she sank her hands into his hair. And when he gripped her yielding buttocks and ground against her, he felt her immediate reaction: she trembled and moaned sharply.

Unable to wait, Max pressed her backward till he pinned her against the rock wall, imprisoning her against his hard length. Lifting his head briefly, he saw that her eyes had kindled, sparking yet darkening with sensuality.

At the desire in her gaze, blood pooled hot and thick at his groin, enough to drive his throbbing manhood against his breeches.

"Max . . . this isn't wise," she said in a shaking voice.

"I am not inviting debate."

He captured her hands in one of his and held them high over her head as he raised her skirts.

"No," she declared weakly.

When he said simply, unequivocally, *"Yes,"* her eyes fluttered shut.

He dipped his fingers into the spirals of dusky hair between her thighs, making her limbs go rigid with tension. When he slid his middle finger into her slick folds, it came away drenched with her moisture.

"You're already wet for me," he uttered with satisfaction.

Gritting his teeth against the surge of heat shafting through his own loins, he thrust his fingers inside her moist cleft, withdrew, and invaded again, his thumb stroking the nub of her sex.

A shudder rocked Caro as he deliberately explored, and she found herself grinding her hips against his arousing hand, blindly seeking more of this fevered pleasure. His erotic touch was shooting almost painful arrows of excitement deep between her thighs at the same time he held her powerless to move. The sense of being at his mercy was not so much frightening as thrilling. The intensity made her ache with wild longing.

When her hips began writhing, Max broke off to

tear at the buttons of his breeches, freeing his rigid phallus; it sprang to attention, thick and hot and throbbing.

Grasping her hips, he lifted Caro to meet his full, swollen length and pressed open her quivering thighs.

She tried not to gasp at the searing jolt when his flesh parted her aching, feminine folds. And somehow she managed to accommodate all of him. The muscles in her entire lower body tightened and clamped down around him, swelling around his large possession.

His blue eyes holding a molten brilliance, he arched up into her, his shaft spearing her until he was sheathed completely inside her. Caro bit back a low, delirious moan at the sensations crowding sweet and tumultuous in her blood.

She heard Max whispering roughly in her ear, telling her how hot and tight it felt to be deep inside her, and she responded feverishly, wrapping her legs around him, her heels digging into his muscled thighs, urging him even closer as he began to move with tender violence.

It was a primal mating, with no pretense of finesse or politeness. His hand tangled in her hair in a hard fist of control as he drove himself into her, big and hard, his powerful body slamming against hers. Caro thought she might burst into flame at the brutal heat of it. His urgent thrusts were twisting her into knots of desire.

She clutched at his shoulders, her flesh shivering under the pounding force of his loins as he took her against the wall, ravishing her again and again.

Her breaths came in gasps now, her body bucking and straining.

"Yes, be wanton for me, be wild and reckless. . . ."

His dark words only inflamed her more, until she was so shameless and needful of release that she was frantically shuddering near the brink. When she pleaded with Max to end it, his fierce, driving rhythm quickened.

She bit his shoulder through his jacket. Max growled in frustration and buried himself to the hilt, as if he couldn't absorb the feel of her into him deeply enough.

It made her wild. She was beyond words now, beyond thought, overwhelmed by his heat and sexuality, trapped in the dark grip of passion.

Caro strained madly against him. She was on fire, her senses reeling. When her climax came, Max ground his mouth against hers, catching her high, keening sounds as he hurled her into ecstasy.

He held her convulsing body still for his thrusts, his lips drinking in her wild moans. She was still heaving in his arms when at the last instant he withdrew and twisted slightly. His body contracted fiercely, repeatedly, emptying his seed, not within her, but shooting against the rock wall.

When it was over, he sagged against her. His breath beat raggedly against her ear while his body leaned heavily against hers.

Slowly, very slowly, Caro's senses returned. Even more slowly her body stopped its trembling.

She could scarcely believe what had just happened. Their coupling had been hot and urgent and rawly carnal, unlike the tenderness of last night. They had both been almost frantic with the sheer, overpowering need to mate. Or she had been, at any event. Max at least had had the presence of mind to withdraw from her, she remembered, so he wouldn't run the risk of impregnating her.

Sated and aching, Caro buried her face in his shoulder. She had gone wild in this man's arms, yet she didn't regret it at all. She felt cleansed of her anger, warm and intensely alive. And Max felt intensely vital against her, his body gloriously strong and virile.

"You did that on purpose . . . made love in order to distract me."

He smiled into her hair. "Yes. You needed a target for your anger, and I merely obliged."

"I suppose I will contrive to forgive you," she conceded.

With a groaned chuckle, he lifted her higher and carried her to the pallet, then followed her down, briefly kissing her lips, which were still dampened and reddened from his mouth.

When he propped himself up on one elbow, gazing down at her, she studied him seriously. "You may have succeeded in your aims this time, but don't presume too far, Max. Don't dare try to tell me that I shouldn't involve myself in Isabella's rescue because it might be dangerous. I refuse to be coddled, by you or any other man."

At her challenge, a flicker of something dangerously, sinfully warm shone in his eyes. "Very well, I promise not to coddle you. But you might do well to take some advice."

"Advice?"

"Your desire to save your friend is admirable, but you need to learn patience. I understand your frustration at not being able to rescue her at once, but railing about it won't help. Believe me, I know."

"I realize that," Caro retorted.

"Then you also realize that weeping about her fate will do no good. You can't develop a rational plan when your emotions are overwrought. To strategize successfully you have to be cool and dispassionate."

Caro returned a stubborn frown. "I suppose you mean to tell me that I must mind my temper."

"No. There's nothing wrong with anger, as long as you control it and focus it in a constructive fashion." He flashed a quick, enchanting smile. "Nearly skewering me, however, is *not* constructive. For a moment there I feared you might slit my gullet."

"I am sorry, Max," she said, a trifle ruefully. "I would never have truly hurt you." She let her lips curve in a provocative smile. "Not mortally, at any rate."

Her qualification made him laugh. "You relieve my mind."

His expression became thoughtful then, while his thumb absently stroked her jawline. "What if I suggest to Sir Gawain that we do some preliminary planning in the next few days, based on the assumption Isabella is at the fortress? It will allow me to meet some of your other agents, and we can be ready to leave for Algiers at a moment's notice, as soon as we receive confirmation."

Her smile turned brilliant. "That is precisely what I wanted."

Max bent to kiss the tip of her nose, then glanced over his shoulder at the grotto. "At least this solves our problem of privacy. I didn't relish the thought of creeping up to your bedchamber like a thief to steal a few hours with you. That is, if you mean to share your haven with me."

Caro pursed her lips thoughtfully as she pretended to debate the issue. "I could be convinced. As you said, I need to learn patience, and you could perhaps teach me. I have frequently been told that I am an excellent pupil."

A slow smile, irresistible in its male charm, crawled across his mouth as he bent his head. "Well then, angel, if you insist . . ."

Chapter Ten

"You say Apollo created this lake for Cyrene's bath?" Max murmured lazily three afternoons later. They were lying naked on a rock ledge near the cascading waterfall, drenched in sunlight, Max on his back, Caro half dozing on her stomach beside him, her cheek pillowed on her arms.

At the skeptical amusement in his tone, Caro returned a sleepy smile. "So legend holds. More logically, forces of nature formed the lake. Rain collects here in this little vale along with the flow from several hot springs that originate higher up. Our two mountains were once volcanos and still generate heat—which is what the Romans harnessed to build their baths."

"The Romans had the right idea," he observed, shutting his eyes with a contented sigh. "But I'm glad they didn't spoil this place."

The setting had much to do with his enchantment, Max acknowledged. Caro's hideaway was unbelievably beautiful, splendorous and wild, truly a seductive paradise. But it was a haven as well. He could feel the healing effect as he lay letting the golden warmth touch his body, the peace seep into his soul.

Yet Caro herself had proved a more profound remedy

than even the tranquillity. She had stilled the restlessness of his mind, if not his body.

In turn he had tried to calm *her* restlessness. They had met here at her secret grotto each of the past three days, spending long hours in sensual exploration, indulging in the wildness and desire of new lovers. Their passion was alternately urgent and tender, and, for Caro, an exercise in learning patience. Max could tell she still chafed at the delay of rescuing her captive friend, but she was making a visible effort to quell her anxiety.

Opening his eyes, Max turned his head to gaze at her. The sun beamed down richly, bathing her creamy skin in golden light—and once again rousing his craving for her.

He reached out to touch her shining hair, forcing the clawing rawness of desire to mute.

Just then a sharp hoot sounded above the rush of the falls, coming from the oak branches directly overhanging their ledge. Max jolted upright as if he'd heard a pistol shot. "What the devil . . . ?"

"There is no need for alarm," Caro said in a soothing voice. Rising to her knees, she peered up through the leaves. "Hello, George."

Max caught sight of a fluffy brown ball that was nearly concealed by the foliage. An owl, by the looks of it.

With a puffing of feathers, the bird let out another plaintive hoot—"Tyoo!"—and moved along the limb, closer to Caro.

"This is George," she murmured, smiling. "A scops owl. I found him here with a broken wing two years ago."

George seemed small for an owl, Max thought, but he had huge eyes that stared piercingly at the strange interloper.

"So you nursed George back to health?"

"Yes, and it took weeks. I fashioned a splint and kept him tethered and fed until he was healed. But even after I gave him his freedom, he chose to stay here. He usually comes out only at night, though. He must have been curious about you." She glanced at Max. "I am sorry he startled you."

He ran a hand raggedly down his face. "Loud noises still tend to do that."

Caro nodded in sympathy. "It is a common affliction with veterans of war." She paused. "Will you talk about it? I'm usually credited with being a good listener. And it is said that if you can face your worst memories, then you can face most anything."

Max felt a shudder run through him. Did he want to tell her about the nightmare? About the vivid images that still haunted him? His regiment in the midst of a battle, charging a French artillery position, fighting through the blind chaos of smoke and blood. The thunder of cannon, the ground exploding beneath him. The scream of his falling horse. Philip returning for him, reaching a hand down to save him . . .

"No," he said, shuttering his gaze and looking away. "I don't want to talk about it."

Caro's heart wrenched at the anguish she'd seen flicker in his eyes. It was a pain she would have given anything to ease, a pain she would have borne herself if she could have. The cost of war was so terrible, but Max had paid a higher price than most.

She reached out to touch his arm, wanting to offer

him comfort. "After the night we were together," she said softly, "when you had left Cyrene, I always lit candles for you here, praying you would be safe."

"Your prayers must have worked," he replied, his voice tight, "for I managed to survive when others didn't."

She wasn't so certain her prayers had worked; certainly Max still lived with the horror.

She had seen his troubled sleep for herself. Two days ago when he'd dozed off after an exhaustive bout of lovemaking in her grotto, she had watched him as he lay on the pallet, admiring his beautiful features, the curve of his lowered lashes like ebony silk, his chiseled mouth. . . . His sudden cry had startled her. When his head began twisting on the pillow, his body shuddering, she had pressed her fingers to his brow, stroking gently. Her touch had instantly soothed him, and he'd fallen back to sleep, murmuring her name.

Yet Max still needed healing, to be made whole again, she knew.

She also knew she couldn't force him to speak of his nightmares, even though unburdening himself would help.

Rising, Caro scooped up the leather flagon of wine they had brought with their bread-and-cheese lunch and picked her way along the rock ledge, closer to the waterfall. Barely a foot from the cascade, she sat down on the damp edge, her legs dangling over the side. After drinking deeply, she turned her face up to the sun and waited, hoping Max was like so many other wounded creatures she'd tended who had learned to trust her.

In a few moments Max reluctantly followed, joining her on the ledge.

A gentle mist swirled around her, he noted as he settled beside her. When she offered him the flagon, he took it.

The wine was sweet and potent on his tongue. The mist cooling, the sun warm and nourishing. A long silence reigned, broken only by the musical sound of the waterfall.

Max looked out over the sapphire lake and found himself speaking words he had kept buried inside him for five years.

"I lost a good friend in the war," he said quietly. "He was like a brother to me."

Caro turned her gaze to him, her gray eyes searching his. Yet she didn't press him the way he expected. "Do you have any brothers? Any other family?"

Max felt grateful she hadn't probed his deepest wounds. "Only an elderly uncle. My parents both died of illnesses while I was in the Peninsula."

"I'm sorry."

"So am I, although we were never very close. And I didn't see much of them after I joined the army. My father's way of showing his disapproval of my choice."

"He didn't want you going to war?" She sounded more curious than surprised.

"No. In part because he didn't want to lose his only son." Max's mouth curved in a grimace. "But in his opinion, the sons of wealthy gentry weren't supposed to shed blood for their country."

"So why did you join the army? Surely an heir to a viscount needn't put himself at such risk."

Max shifted back against the rock ledge, remembering his adamant arguments with his father. "It wasn't necessary at all. But I wanted adventure and glory, and a greater purpose for my life as well. To make a difference in Napoleon's rush to conquer the known world. When Boney attempted to invade England a second time, I decided I had to act." *And Philip had followed.*

His throat tightening, Max gazed down at the lake whose near surface frothed and rippled with the plunging waterfall. His life had been much like the lake until he'd left England and home for the turmoil of battle. "The hell of it is, my friend would never even have gone to war if not for me. And then four years later . . . Philip was killed. Trying to save me." Max squeezed his eyes shut. "I wish to God it had been me."

Caro's voice was soft in response. "That was why you went to such lengths to help John Yates when he was dying. Because he had tried to save you."

Max swallowed hard, finally nodding.

"And after you lost your friend? You remained in the army when you could have sold out?"

"I stayed to make Philip's death mean something. I intended to defeat the French or die trying."

"You must miss him greatly."

He missed Philip like blazes. As boys they had been inseparable. As young men they had attended Oxford together. They'd sown their wild oats together, laughed and sported and played pranks together, pursued the same lightskirts . . . fought side by side. They'd saved each other's lives more than once. Until the last time.

"I imagine your life is very different now," Caro murmured when Max was silent. "If I had commanded hundreds of men for so many years as you did, I think I would find myself lonely now at times."

His fingers clenched the flagon. He *was* lonely at times. He'd lost the most important things in his life—his family, his closest friends. After Philip died, he'd deliberately cut himself off from his fellow officers. He no longer felt any joy. Oh, yes, he had lost a great deal.

Drawing a ragged breath, Max put a halt to his morose thoughts, realizing how indefensible they were. Others had lost far more than he had, like lives and limbs. Others had sacrificed far more than he had.

And the loneliness was his burden to bear. His punishment for Philip's death.

He tilted the flagon to his lips and drank.

"I've heard tell," Caro said finally, "that soldiers in war form a bond that can be closer than most brothers. Is that true?"

Seeing the image of Philip's laughing face in his mind, Max tried to shrug off his bleak mood. "It's true. You do form a bond when you endure so much together . . . all the hardships and miseries of numerous campaigns. I miss that camaraderie—"

He cut himself off and slanted a glance at Caro, frowning. "Are you trying to pry all my secrets from me?"

"No, of course not," she replied, although her quiet smile said otherwise.

Max felt the dark tension easing inside him. The swirling mist had formed a rainbow prism around Caro's face and set tendrils of dark hair curling at her temples. He couldn't remember ever seeing anything quite so lovely.

Reaching up, he tucked an errant curl behind her ear. "Then why the devil do I wind up telling you things I've never told a soul?"

"Possibly because you can let down your guard here." She swept a hand toward the lake. "This island is special. This place is special."

No, *she* was special, Max reflected, with her healing touch, her tenderness. And her lips were wet with wine.

His gaze locked on her mouth.

Caro had willingly given him her body, but his need for her went far deeper than mere carnal hunger. If he simply wanted to ease the ache in his loins, he could have taken care of himself, as he'd done countless times when campaigning. Or he could have enjoyed the charms of a half-dozen island beauties who'd cast out lures to him since his arrival. If it was only a female body he craved, he could have sated himself with Caro and been done with it. But he wanted, needed, much more.

Only Caro could ease the ache in his soul. Only she could drive away the darkness.

When she looked up at him, desire lanced through his body. Needing to touch her, Max reached up and gently framed her face in his palms. And when she raised her lips to his, he gave a soft groan and kissed her fervently, needing to drink in every ounce of her comfort, accepting her hot, sweet solace as a cherished gift.

Caro felt torn when Max escorted her home at nearly three in the morning, a waning moon lighting their way. The serene beauty of the night, coupled with Max's passion, had filled her with a sense of tranquillity. Yet that was her chief problem, she admitted. She was failing her promise to herself.

She had thought she would be safe at her grotto. That was why she'd chosen to bring Max there rather than the ruins. Both were enchanting, healing places in their own right, but in her own private domain, she'd thought she would have much better control of herself.

Her plan to keep their relationship purely physical and impersonal, however, was suffering gravely.

Max was largely to blame for her weakness, Caro knew. He made her feel beautiful. He made her feel desirable and womanly, drawing from her the deep sensuality that she had always repressed in herself. For the first time in her life she had begun to feel her feminine power. It was enthralling to discover she could make such a powerful male creature as Max respond wildly to her touch.

And his tender solace made it easier for her to repress her anxiety over her missing friend. Max understood her urgency and had arranged a meeting for the day after tomorrow to begin planning their expedition to Barbary.

And then there was his pain and her instinctive yearning to banish the shadows from his eyes.

Abruptly Caro's warring thoughts faded when through the darkness she spied a horseman ahead on the road, riding toward them. To her surprise she recognized John Yates. And since they were near her house, she guessed that he had come to summon her.

John spurred his horse faster, halting when he reached them.

"Your suspicions were correct," he said to Caro in a low voice. "I have proof."

"Proof of what?"

"That my lovely Danielle is not what she seems." His tone was bleak. "After you warned me, I set a trap for her, just as you suggested. This evening I . . . let her seduce me, then pretended to sleep. I had left a journal where she could find it."

"And did she take the bait?"

John nodded sadly. "She poured over the journal, taking copious notes. There was no incriminating evidence for her to find, of course, for I had falsified all the entries."

"Do you have any notion what she was seeking?"

"From the probing questions she's asked me over the last few days, the little comments she let slip . . . I'm almost certain she wants to know the identities of all the Guardians."

It was a measure of his agitation, Caro knew, that he had used the term for the members of their order. She shot a glance at Max, hoping he hadn't noticed, but he seemed focused on John's tale.

"If so," John continued grimly, "she now has a list of false names. She will be looking for a dozen agents who don't exist. Except for you, sir." He looked at Max. "I added your name to one of the entries. I thought it would seem more credible if she recognized at least one of the names on the list."

"You led her to believe I am one of your Foreign Office agents?"

"Yes."

Caro interrupted to steer the subject back to Danielle Newham. "She cannot be working solely on her own. We need to discover who employed her."

"I know. She must be apprehended and questioned."

"Where is she now?"

"I'm not certain. She slipped away while she thought I still slept. I suspect she returned to town, to the lodgings she shares with her brother . . . possibly in order to pack."

"You think she means to leave the island?"

"I fear so," John said dismally. "From her furtiveness, I wouldn't be surprised if she tries to make her escape tonight. That is why I came to find you. I cannot stop them alone."

"What about Ryder? Have you asked him?"

John lowered his gaze. "I haven't tried to find him. I came to you first. I would prefer to settle this before I have to confess to Sir Gawain that I allowed myself to be taken in by a treacherous schemer."

Caro nodded, understanding why John would want to keep his gullibility hidden. And if they could discover who had employed Danielle, then they could at least salvage some valuable leads from a potential disaster.

"We could use Santos's help," she said.

"I suppose you're right."

She knew why John gave her no argument. The Spaniard lived with his large family in town, near his tavern, which overlooked the harbor. He would likely be home asleep, but as a former smuggler, he would be invaluable if the Newhams attempted to escape by sea tonight. Santos knew all the tricks of sailing at night.

"Can they sail tonight?" John asked, as if reading her thoughts.

Caro glanced up at the moon that hung low on the horizon, judging that it would set in the next hour or so. "Possibly, if they are willing to risk crashing against the rocks at the harbor entrance. But they will likely have a skilled captain and crew in their pay." She pursed her lips. "We should check the harbor first.

If we don't find the Newhams there, we can seek them at their lodgings."

"That would be wisest." John shifted his gaze to Max. "Will you accompany us, sir?"

"Of course. But if you expect a fight, shouldn't we go armed?"

"I have two pistols with me," John said, patting his waist.

Caro added, "I have more weapons at home. And if we have to board a ship, I would do better to be rid of my skirts."

In silent agreement, John turned his horse, and the three of them made for Caro's stables.

Max felt himself frowning, the urge to shield Caro so strong, he wanted to forbid her participation. But he kept his reservations unvoiced, knowing better than to suggest she stay safely behind, out of danger. She looked totally determined and focused now. And when they reached her stable yard, she leapt lightly down and disappeared inside her house.

She returned after a brief time, wearing dark male garb like the guerrilla fighters Max had known in Spain. He eyed her sharply, having difficulty reconciling this Caro with the sensual lover who'd spent many of the past hours in his arms.

She was equipped with four pistols, two of which she handed to him.

"Are these loaded?" he asked, accepting the pouch of gunpowder and ammunition from her as well.

"Certainly." Grimly efficient now, she mounted her horse, saying to John as she led the way from the yard, "I have been thinking . . . we should fetch Captain Biddick in case we must sail after them."

When John nodded, Caro spurred her mount, leaving the two former cavalry officers to follow her swift pace.

They split up when they reached town—John heading for Captain Biddick's residence, Caro and Max for Santos Verra's.

They woke Verra from a sound sleep and quickly explained the situation. The Spaniard grinned, his teeth white in his swarthy face, and asked for only a moment to dress.

Shortly they met up with the others outside the tavern, where they dismounted and tethered their horses.

"Try to be quiet," Caro murmured for both Max and John's benefit. "Sounds carry easily over the water."

On foot they headed for the steep, cobbled road that led to the harbor and silently took shelter behind the last building in order to peer down the hill.

The dark water below shimmered in the moonlight. Verra pointed without speaking, and immediately Max understood his conclusion.

Among the myriad vessels lying at anchor, only a small, two-masted schooner had lantern lights on board. Lights that illuminated a glimpse of unfurling canvas.

"It seems as you suspected," Verra muttered grimly. "They are raising sail."

Chapter Eleven

Silently Max moved back into the concealing shadows, and the others followed.

"So to apprehend our spies," he murmured, "we must board and take control of that schooner."

"Without being seen," Caro added quietly.

"If we row a small skiff, we will likely not be detected," said Santos Verra.

"I can certainly row," John Yates volunteered, "even with my wooden leg. But I should be the one to confront Danielle."

Verra nodded. "The rest of us will make up a boarding party, while Yates remains with the skiff. Once we have control, he can come aboard."

"And then?" Max asked.

"Then we arrest the Newhams," Yates said grimly, "in the name of the Crown."

"Sir Gawain has that authority?"

"He has total authority over anything and anyone in these waters."

Caro spoke. "We should look for evidence against them—the list Danielle made, in particular. That would be sufficient proof to convince Sir Gawain of their guilt."

"Yes," Yates agreed. "Then we will take them to the castle, and Sir Gawain can determine how best to deal with them." Yates addressed Max. "Sir, you should take command and lead the boarding party."

Max raised an eyebrow, expecting debate, but the others agreed readily. "Very well. What kind of resistance should we expect to encounter?"

"I know the schooner's master," Captain Biddick said. "He won't put up much of a fight when challenged."

"But the Newhams likely will," Caro interjected.

Max looked at her. "Can you handle Danielle?"

"I should hope so." Her hushed tone was dry.

"Then I will take her brother, Peter. Biddick, you will have the ship's captain. Verra, you have the entire rest of the crew."

Verra grinned widely. "It will be my pleasure, señor."

"We should go now," Caro said, indicating the schooner.

The vessel had begun to move. There was only a faint breeze—which worked in their favor, since the schooner would have difficulty filling her sails. But she was already heading toward the narrow strait of the harbor entrance, preparing to negotiate the treacherous rocks on either side.

"Will you find us a skiff, Señor Verra?" Max asked.

One by one they crept down the steep hill that zigzagged to the harbor. Max allowed Verra to lead, watching as the smuggler searched the many boats tied up at the quay and located a skiff that would suit their purpose. Caro also seemed to know exactly what she was doing as she worked quietly and efficiently with Verra to cast off.

She took the tiller while the men manned the oars. John Yates put his back into the rhythm with grim determination, his teeth gritted in concentration, and soon the skiff was slicing through the dark water, the only sound the faint slapping of the paddles.

At Max's silent gesture, they slowed when they came abreast of their target. A grappling hook swung over the schooner's railing near the port-side stern provided their means of boarding.

Verra went first, climbing hand over hand up the rope, pausing to peer over the railing, then signaling all clear before easing over the edge out of sight.

Max went next, dropping onto the deck silently, then moving quickly forward to crouch behind some barrels that were lashed near the main mast. He could see no sign of the Newhams, merely a half-dozen crew members who were busy with sails and lines. The man at the wheel, barking orders in Spanish, was undoubtedly the schooner's master.

He wondered if Caro would have trouble managing the rope, but she appeared almost instantly, substantiating her claim that she'd had some unusual training for a woman.

She was soon followed by Captain Biddick. As planned, Yates stayed with the skiff until a rope ladder could be thrown down to him. The moment he boarded, Max gave the signal to begin.

Crossing the deck, Max pressed the barrel of his pistol against the base of the master's skull.

"Señor, you will surrender this vessel to me, if you please, and lower your sails. Sir Gawain Olwen would like to question your passengers."

Other than a startled grunt of surprise, the master made no protest as he swiftly complied. And his crew quickly followed suit, surrendering without a fight.

Max left Biddick to guard the Spanish captain and joined Caro where she waited at the hatchway that led belowdeck. Max preceding, they descended the ladder to search for the Newhams.

They found Danielle and her brother in the first cabin, seated at a small table, enjoying a glass of wine—probably in celebration, Max surmised. But her smug smile turned to stark alarm when she looked up to discover both of Caro's pistols trained on her.

Peter rose abruptly to his feet, as if he intended to flee, but seeing Max's pistol aimed at his chest evidently made him think better of moving. Raising his hands, Peter sank back into his chair.

"What is the meaning of this?" Danielle demanded shrilly.

"I think you know," Caro replied, her own voice biting.

Tucking one pistol in the waistband of her breeches, she began searching the cabin, starting with Danielle's reticule and cloak pockets.

"This is outrageous!" the woman protested just as John Yates entered.

He carried two lengths of rope, one of which he used to tie Danielle's hands, despite her vociferous protests. Max saw her wince as the knots were tightened. Yates seemed to be taking satisfaction at having her at his mercy, but as long as he restrained his anger and refrained from actually harming their prisoners, Max decided, Yates deserved the honor of questioning his treacherous former sweetheart.

Just then Caro opened a valise that had been stowed beneath the bunk and unearthed a leather pouch that contained a sheaf of papers. Danielle fell suspiciously silent as Caro perused her find.

She showed them to Yates, who nodded grimly and narrowed his eyes savagely at the auburn-haired beauty.

Danielle's chin rose with haughty defiance. "Of what are you accusing me? I have committed no crime."

"Not a crime perhaps, but you betrayed me all the same," John said, his tone bitter but controlled.

"I don't know what you mean."

He looked at her with scathing contempt. "You thought you could play me for a fool, my dear. But the journal you so eagerly examined was fabricated."

Her lovely mouth dropped open, but only for an instant. "So I was curious," she said, swiftly recovering.

"What were you seeking? A roster?"

Danielle remained stubbornly mute.

"Who employed you?"

"I have nothing to say to you."

"Then you will make your confessions to Sir Gawain. We'll see how comfortable you find his castle's dungeons. You will have a long incarceration there until you decide to give up your employer."

"You cannot hold me against my will!"

John smiled without humor. "I hesitate to contradict a lady, but we most certainly can."

"I will petition the lieutenant governor of the island."

"Petition away. You will find that Sir Gawain's rule is law here on Cyrene, and that the governor is very accommodating to his wishes. You should also know that if you choose to be uncooperative, Sir Gawain will have you shipped to the penal colonies of Australia. By the time you spend months locked together with other convicts, I suspect you will be eager to talk."

Danielle's eyes filled with dismay at that threat, and she averted her gaze.

Checking the knots one last time, John moved on to her brother, who had been sitting quietly all this time. But when he made to tie Peter's hands, the man leapt up, shoved John out of the way, and raced for the door.

Caro aimed her pistol at his right thigh and would have shot him had Max not caught her arm. "No need to shoot. Let him go."

She gave him a fierce look, clearly frustrated by his intervention.

"He can't get far."

Max proved to be right. When they ushered Danielle out of the cabin and above deck, they found Peter Newham sprawled facedown near the railing, a grinning Santos Verra standing over him with one booted foot pressed hard into the small of his back.

Captain Biddick's mood seemed just as jovial as he hauled Peter to his feet. "Caught ourselves a scurvy wharf rat, we did."

The captain took over, expertly trussing up Mr. Peter Newham. Then they lowered their unwilling prisoners into the skiff and rowed them to shore.

The moon had sunk below the horizon by then, so there was only starlight by which to see as they waited for Verra to round up a coach and team. They put the prisoners inside, with Yates and Biddick joining them in the role of guards, while Verra acted as coachman and drove to the castle.

Caro and Max fetched their saddle horses and rode after the coach.

Stars shone like diamonds in the black velvet sky as the night enveloped them. All was quiet but for the rattle of the coach wheels and the plod of horses' hooves ahead.

Caro felt a sweep of fatigue overtake her, yet it was accompanied by relief that they'd succeeded in stopping the Newhams' escape.

Her relief was short-lived, however, when Max began asking probing questions. "Will Sir Gawain detain them for long?"

"As long as it takes to discover what they were seeking and who hired them."

"Will they be sent to Australia?"

"Probably not, although Sir Gawain may likely use that as a threat."

"But they won't stand trial for espionage."

"No," Caro replied. "We don't want the publicity of a trial."

"You prefer secrecy."

Hearing the odd note in his tone, she shifted uncomfortably in the saddle. "I'm certain you understand why we prefer not to advertise our activities. And Sir Gawain may very well do nothing to punish Danielle and her brother. Instead he may choose to release them and let them return to England. If so, he will have them followed. But he will alert our agents in England first, and now that we're forewarned, we will be on our guard."

There was a long pause, before Max said softly, "Tell me, what exactly is a Guardian?"

Caro felt her heart falter. "It is just a name we give our division of the Foreign Office."

From the way Max was searching her face in the darkness, she wasn't certain he accepted her explanation. Nor did his next words comfort her.

"Your division seems to be extremely well organized. And Sir Gawain appears to have a vast degree of resources at his disposal. Are you even part of the Foreign Office?"

"Yes, of course." That wasn't a lie at least.

"I find it surprising that a branch of the Foreign Office would have been established on a small Mediterranean island."

"I thought I explained that. Our proximity to Europe is a benefit to government affairs, although our isolation can be a drawback at times."

"But there is more you aren't revealing?"

"You will have to ask Sir Gawain," Caro equivocated.

"Will he tell me if I ask?"

"He offered you a position with us. If you choose to accept, I'm certain he will tell you everything you want to know."

"But not before?"

"I doubt it."

She wished she could allay Max's suspicions, but she couldn't tell him about the Guardians on her own, not without Sir Gawain's permission. But that possibility was worth pursuing. Max's actions tonight had only confirmed her growing conviction that he was a born protector and would make a splendid Guardian.

If he were to learn the true history and purpose of the order, if he saw the gravity and importance of what they did, that might make him more amenable to joining.

"But I will certainly discuss it with Sir Gawain," Caro said. "He may make an exception in your case, considering how much you have already aided us."

It was nearly an hour later when Caro managed a private word with Sir Gawain. The Newhams had been delivered to his castle and interrogated at length, and afterward Caro took the baronet aside and put forth an earnest argument.

To her relief, Sir Gawain accompanied her to the drawing room, where Max waited.

"Mr. Leighton, I want to express my thanks for your generous service," he said as Max rose from the settee. "Miss Newham and her brother could have done serious harm to our organization. Operating our missions in secrecy is an essential advantage to our success, and exposing the identities of our membership would doubtless imperil our effectiveness, not to mention making our agents potential targets for retaliation."

"And did she give up the name of her employer?"

"She did indeed. An Englishman, she claims. It remains to be seen how truthful her confession is, but our agents in England will investigate, so we may take appropriate steps to protect ourselves. Until we know the Newhams present no further danger, however, they will remain here on Cyrene under house arrest."

Sir Gawain paused. "Caro has convinced me that you deserve a greater explanation than you have been given thus far. And that if we hope to persuade you to join us, it is time we showed you what we are about. Caro, will you assume the honors?"

"Yes, certainly," she said at once.

Max could detect more than a hint of elation in her voice, while Sir Gawain's tone remained solemn. "I trust you will understand why we must swear you to secrecy, Mr. Leighton. What you are about to see is a sacred trust. We will talk when you return."

Max nodded, puzzled by the baronet's cryptic statement but willing to play along.

He accompanied Caro from the room, restraining his curiosity as she led him deep within the castle, then down into the depths of the dungeons.

She used a massive key to unlock a sturdy oaken door and ushered him into a dark, musty storage room. After lighting a lamp, she unlocked an even more massive door and shut it firmly behind them before guiding him along a widish passage that sloped gently downward.

The air smelled damp and cool here, tinged with a tang of salt from the sea. Several minutes later, the passage ended in a cave whose floor was covered with dark, rippling water.

"An underground lake?" Max asked.

"Yes," Caro said, making for the first of three rowboats that were tied up at a short wooden dock. "There are intersecting tunnels here that connect a number of sea caves."

Glancing around him, Max studied this cave. In the lamplight that reflected off the rock, he could see strangely shaped deposits and growths that clung to the sides, glittering with minerals, while ghostly icicles dripped down from the ceiling. The result of springs and seepage of rainwater over countless centuries, he suspected, viewing the sliding liquid gleam of moisture in several places.

The black fissures in the walls were doubtless the tunnels Caro had mentioned—narrow passages that led off in different directions, linking a labyrinth of caves.

Caro secured the lamp in the prow of the rowboat, then waited for Max to settle in before joining him.

"I am sorry," she apologized, "but you will have to wear a blindfold."

"Is there really need for such secrecy?"

"You will understand in a short while, I promise. But Max, before we go, you must swear on your honor that you will never, ever reveal what you are about to see."

Her expression was as grave as he had ever seen it.

"I swear," he said solemnly, letting her bind his eyes with a kerchief.

She rowed for a long time while Max sat patiently, unseeing. Finally she stopped and stowed the oars. The air smelled fresher here and seemed to echo with a peculiar hollowness. He could hear water lapping gently at the rock walls, along with a faint whisper of distant waves washing against the island's shoreline.

"You may remove your blindfold now," Caro said quietly.

Max readily complied. They were floating on a vast lake, he saw, in the middle of a great, natural cavern. The flame of the oil lamp barely pierced the darkness of the vaulted chamber that was the size of a cathedral.

His pulse quickened with awe as he beheld the magnificence. Fantastic shapes and figures surrounded them. Enormous pillars and arches rose from the lake and melded with stalactites that vanished in the dimness of the high, curved ceiling.

Even in the diffused light, the incredible formations shimmered with color, from translucent to pure crystalline white, to gray mottled with delicate hues of red and yellow.

"Impressive," he murmured, hearing a hint of reverence in his voice.

"We aren't there yet."

Taking up the oars again, Caro rowed toward the far side of the cavern, which was seamed with shadowy clefts and recesses.

The water of the lake rippled like black satin, but Max's gaze riveted on the dramatic spectacle surrounding him as the golden lamplight shifted and skated around the cavern in an eerie dance.

After a while he realized that Caro was heading toward a particular crevice, for he detected a faint gleam of light ahead. The passage she found was barely wide enough for the little boat to slip through, and curved several times.

At the far end, the glow grew brighter, but when they emerged from the tunnel, the sudden dazzle caught Max by surprise. Torches blazed along the walls, brilliant as day.

This was a much smaller cave, more the size of Caro's grotto, but it held a hushed stillness, like that of a private chapel . . . or a temple.

And like a temple, it held what looked to be a shrine.

The water ended at a rock ledge. Some twenty feet back, a short flight of roughly hewn steps led up to an altar exquisitely fashioned of gold and silver. A massive sword was framed there—a magnificent weapon with a blade of steel and a golden hilt encrusted in jewels.

Max caught his breath as if he'd been struck in the throat. Light glittered off the precious stones, but it wasn't just the richness of the sword that rendered him spellbound. There was an aura about it that seemed remarkably powerful, perhaps even mystical.

"This was what Sir Gawain meant by a sacred trust," he said, his voice uneven.

"Yes."

She tied the rowboat up at the ledge and climbed out, then stood aside to allow Max to precede her. He slowly mounted the steps to get a closer look at the sword.

For a moment as the torch flames flickered and burned all around them, the world faded away. Max felt enveloped by a strange sensation. A sense of calm, of peace, yet filled with an unmistakable energy.

"My God," he murmured.

"You feel it, too," Caro said, not needing a reply.

"What is this place . . . this weapon?"

"It is legend in the flesh."

"Legend?"

"What do you know of King Arthur?"

"The mythical Arthur of Malory and Milton?"

"He was no myth, Max. He was very real. And this was his sword, Excalibur."

Stunned, fascinated, Max glanced around the cave, only to bring his gaze back to stare at the sword once more. "How did it come to be here?"

"It is rather a long story. Perhaps you would prefer to sit down."

On either side of the altar, slabs of granite formed natural rock benches. Caro led him to the one on the right, where Max could view the sword as she spoke.

"According to legend, Excalibur was forged by an elf smith on Avalon and given to King Arthur by the Lady of the Lake."

"In the versions I remember reading," Max commented, "the sword disappeared. As he lay dying, Arthur made his knight return it to the Lady."

"Yes. He bade Sir Bedivere throw it in the water."

"But the sword was spared?"

"Yes. And brought here by Arthur's exiled knights and followers, including the first Sir Gawain."

Frowning, Max studied Caro. She was entirely serious, he realized. "Sir Gawain was reputed to be Arthur's best and most loyal knight, but the narratives contend that he was killed."

"He was badly wounded, but he didn't die. Instead he came here to convalesce. Even then Cyrene was a haven for outcasts," Caro continued in a soft voice. "Sir Gawain and a score of other knights who had served at Arthur's Round Table settled here, but with a larger purpose in mind. Their own crusade, if you will."

Her voice dropped even lower. "They formed an order, Max. The Guardians of the Sword. Their intent was to carry on Arthur's noble ideals—championing right and using their might for good. They became a secret society of protectors."

Gooseflesh shivered along Max's skin at the vision Caro had painted for him. He hesitated a long moment before he responded. "If there is any truth at all to that tale, it would have been more than a thousand years ago. You're saying the sword has been here all that time?"

"It was hidden during the reign of the Moors and Cyrene's subsequent rule by Spain. But yes, it has been right here."

"And the Guardians?"

"During that dark period of our history, the order almost vanished from memory, but it was revived during England's civil wars."

"Why?"

"Initially to aid Royalists persecuted by Cromwell's rule. The Guardians helped countless victims escape to the New World, and gave shelter here on Cyrene to numerous other outcasts. But after the wars ended, they saw the necessity of continuing their cause. *Someone* had to defend the vulnerable, the helpless, the wrongfully oppressed. So they arranged to make Cyrene a permanent British possession. The Guardians were actually responsible for securing the island for Britain with the Treaty of Utrecht."

Max's brows drew together as he tried to absorb the enormity of what Caro was telling him. "And the connection to the Foreign Office?"

"That came years later. It was only a few decades ago that they formalized their status with the British government and became a secret arm of the Foreign Office. Since then, the Guardians have been used to meet any number of grave challenges, particularly those spawned by the French Revolution and the fight against Napoleon. They rescued countless *aristos* from the guillotine—in fact, my father was one of the main leaders then. He was killed several years ago during a mission, saving one of our agents from Napoleon's cutthroats."

Her voice fell to a whisper. "No one could know the truth about my father's death, or his life, for that matter."

"Why did it need to be kept such a secret?"

"Because our effectiveness would be severely impaired if our existence became common knowledge, so we've worked hard at keeping our activities clandestine."

"And Sir Gawain runs the order now? I gather he's a descendant of the original Sir Gawain?"

"Yes," Caro replied to both questions. "Leadership of the Guardians was passed down through the descendant families of the original knights. Our Sir Gawain is in charge of the current order—deciding what missions to accept and which of our agents to send out."

"How does he even know when a mission is warranted?"

"Sometimes a request for help comes from the British government. Sometimes from private citizens in numerous countries across Europe. Our members are constantly on the watch for ways to intervene. Sir Gawain weighs the merit of each case against the risks."

For the first time since he'd entered the cave, Max's lips curved in a smile. "Your friends don't strike me as being afraid to take risks. My initial impression was of a band of bold adventurers, of rebels."

"We don't mind danger, true. Certainly we value courage. And we don't always hold with rules. But we also want at least a chance of success. As Guardians, it is our sworn duty to shield and protect, but we've no desire to simply become martyrs. It would be foolish to champion every single cause, however just or worthy, if it only led to our deaths. Our order would shortly end if all of us were killed."

At that comment, Max found himself wondering just who belonged to the Guardians. "How large is the order now?"

"A dozen or so active members actually live on Cyrene, but more than fifty others are scattered all over England and Europe, positioned at the highest levels of society and government. We even have a few Americans. We also have two French officers who are double agents on Napoleon's staff—and who, by falsifying reports, have helped to keep the French navy from trying to invade Cyrene for the past two decades. Traditionally a son from each ruling family in each generation serves the order, but daughters can serve as well. And our members have various backgrounds—exiles, adventurers, former victims of persecution. . . . Sometimes prominent families send their disreputable sons here for redemption."

A sudden thought struck Max. "Such as Christopher Thorne?"

Caro smiled. "Such as Thorne. After one particularly infamous episode during Thorne's university days, his ducal father became so incensed that he begged Sir Gawain to take on the task of reforming Thorne."

"I gather it worked to some degree?"

"More or less. Thorne is one of our best agents."

"And Alex Ryder?"

"Ryder was a hired mercenary who proved himself

several years ago. No one is more effective at operating in the shadows than he."

"What about Santos Verra?"

"He was an unusually cunning smuggler who gave the Guardians some invaluable assistance, so he was invited to join."

Max shook his head in amazement. "You said daughters can serve as well as sons? That's how you came to be a Guardian?"

"Yes. I took my father's place after his death. I'm one of the few female members."

"I noticed you had no trouble boarding the schooner tonight."

"Because I trained for this role for much of my life. With no son to carry on his work, my father raised me to succeed him."

"It seems a vast undertaking, not to mention expensive."

"Missions indeed are often expensive. We need fast ships, horses, weapons, money for bribes and ransoms . . . occasionally we hire local guides and mercenaries. But we are very well financed. Our funds come from several sources. A treasure in gold recovered from a sunken Spanish galleon. The British government. Grateful beneficiaries of our services; those who can afford to pay usually offer a reward. And sometimes we receive private donations from wealthy citizens who simply hear tales of our feats and want to support our cause. In some places in Europe, the whispers about our secret organization have become legend."

Rising from the stone bench, Max moved over to inspect the sword once more. Perhaps the weapon wasn't actually enchanted, but it certainly was awe-inspiring. And unmistakably it possessed an otherworldly feel about it.

Moreover, Max mused, even if there was no truth to the tales of its mythical creation, a relic such as this would have served to unite Arthur's remaining knights, given them a cause to rally around.

Sir Gawain had called it a sacred trust. As a descendant of the original knights, he would have been charged with keeping Excalibur safe. Or perhaps the sword itself offered a measure of protection for its guardians. Max remembered Caro mentioning several strange events in the island's history.

"You told me once that a Moorish invasion of Cyrene was defeated by a great storm and a French assault by fog. Do your legends claim the sword had any influence?"

"We like to think so. Since Excalibur was brought here, Cyrene has been invincible."

Giving in to temptation, he reached out to run the tip of a finger over the jeweled pommel. The rubies caught the blazing reflection of torchlight but seemed to burn with their own fire as well.

"I suppose you don't show this sword to just anyone."

"No. Only to sworn members of the Guardians to complete our rites of initiation. But we knew you would be unlikely to join us unless you saw the import of what we do."

She had accomplished her goal, Max reflected, for he clearly saw the import. What he'd thought was simply an arm of the Foreign Office held a far greater meaning: a secret society of valiant men and women dedicated to an epic mission, bound by honor to protect noble ideals.

He had suspected that the island held secrets. But this was far more than he'd bargained for when he'd accompanied Caro here.

"Max . . ." Caro paused, then said with quiet conviction, "We want you to join us."

Turning away from the sword, he ran a hand roughly through his hair. No matter how special the order's purpose, he was far from certain he wanted to devote himself to a future that could lead to a repetition of his worst nightmare.

"I don't have to give you my answer now, do I?"

"No. We know this decision is not a simple or easy one."

His mouth curved wryly. "I should say not. You're asking me to wholly embrace your cause. To dedicate my life to the Guardians."

"Not your life. Only a few years. You should know there are conditions for noble newcomers settling on our island. Except for those granted asylum, any outsider of noble heart who wants to remain must commit to at least five years of service. The island charter requires it."

"And who enforces the charter? Sir Gawain?"

"Yes. He has the power of life and death over all of Cyrene's inhabitants. The charter confers that responsibility on him."

"Would he honestly sentence someone to death for choosing not to join?"

"No. But he can banish anyone he wishes from Cyrene, lock them away in chains, confiscate all property. . . ."

"So if I chose to stay here, I would be required to join your order?"

"Yes. But our members see service in the Guardians as a calling. And you said you wanted a greater purpose for your life."

"That was a long time ago. Before the war."

She remained silent.

"I am honored by your faith in me," Max said finally. "But I need time to decide something this momentous. Let me first get through this mission in Barbary."

"Of course."

With difficulty, Caro repressed the urge to argue further. At least Max hadn't refused outright, as she'd expected. Yet she didn't hold out much hope that he would accept. Knowing what she did about his past, she could fathom the effort it would take simply for him to participate in the rescue attempt.

Max was a lost warrior. An errant knight who had sentenced himself to emotional exile. She felt in her heart that he belonged here with the Guardians, but what she longed for and what he could bring himself to live with were two very separate things.

For Max to embrace the Guardian's cause, he would first have to come to terms with his demons. And Caro wasn't certain that would ever happen.

Either way, he had to decide his own future. She couldn't push him into it.

She could only hope that in the end he would choose to join of his own volition.

Chapter Twelve

Max drew rein before Olwen Castle two afternoons later, studying the massive stronghold with a fresh eye. Bathed in sunlight, the castle glowed golden, yet by some trick of light, it seemed almost ethereal.

His imagination, however, could be misleading him, Max admitted. After hearing the remarkable tale of the Guardians and viewing the legendary sword they protected, he was more open to the notion that the entire island possessed a special enchantment.

He was completely convinced, however, that Caro possessed a special enchantment.

He had admired her before, because of the odds she had fought, the challenges she had overcome, trying to enter the male field of medicine. Now that he knew about the Guardians, his admiration had only increased.

He hadn't seen Caro since that night. They had planned to meet at the grotto yesterday, but she'd sent word that Dr. Allenby had taken ill—suffering from chills and fever—and that she would have to assume his rounds over the island for the next few days.

Max expected her to attend this afternoon's conference, though, when they gathered to develop a preliminary plan of attack for rescuing Lady Isabella.

Caro was indeed already waiting in Sir Gawain's

study, along with John Yates and Alex Ryder. She looked a little weary, Max thought, as if caring for Dr. Allenby's patients had already taken a toll. But her soft smile suggested that she was glad to see him.

By the time the room filled with Guardians, her smile had faded and her expression was completely focused and intent. From the strain on her face, Max could see that her urgency hadn't diminished in the slightest.

Sir Gawain opened the meeting by making introductions. In addition to Santos Verra and Captain Biddick, a half-dozen other men were present. Max familiarized himself with their individual skills before taking control of the discussion.

"For the moment we will presume Lady Isabella is being held in the chieftain's fortress," he stated at the outset. "Our first objective is to find a way into the fortress. Our second is to extricate Lady Isabella safely and escape Barbary unscathed. There are three basic principles I like to follow when developing tactics," Max added. "Keep our plan as simple as possible. If our original plan goes awry, be prepared for a swift change in execution. And plan our retreat as carefully as we plan our entrance. Before we can even begin to plan, we need to understand the challenges we will be facing."

Drawing around a table, they poured over the map of the Kingdom of Algiers.

One of the men who knew the country well described the difficulty of the terrain southeast of Algiers. Two grueling days across an arid wasteland, then through several treacherous mountain passes before reaching the Berber chieftain's fortress. Additionally, their expedition would be even more complicated by the unfamiliar customs and culture of a strange country. And the Berbers were considered the fiercest fighters in Barbary.

"It would be suicidal to try and blast our way into the stronghold," Max said finally, "so we will need to rely on subterfuge to get inside."

"But wouldn't it be easier," Yates asked, "simply to offer to purchase Lady Isabella from her captor?"

Sir Gawain shook his head. "We cannot run the risk of tipping our hand. If the chieftain refuses to sell her, then rescuing her will be all the more dangerous, for they will be alerted to our goal and be on their guard." He turned his gaze on Max. "What do you suggest, Mr. Leighton?"

"That we bribe our way into the fortress."

"What could a Berber warlord want enough to lower his guard and allow us inside?" Caro asked.

"Weapons," Ryder said at once. "Rifles, specifically. There isn't a Berber warrior alive who wouldn't pay a small fortune to get his hands on the latest model carbine."

"So we send someone in with rifles to sell," Yates mused. "But who? Hawkhurst?"

Ryder responded to that question as well. "Not Hawk. He's too well known in Barbary, and there could be complications the next time he returns. We need someone unknown."

"I would be willing to volunteer," Max said.

"You will need a credible reason for approaching the chieftain, then."

"Perhaps a game hunter? I could pose as a sportsman eager to hunt the most dangerous quarry of all."

"Lions?"

The expert on Barbary nodded. "That mountainous area of Barbary is prime hunting territory for lions."

"What happens after you are admitted?" Yates asked. "As a man you would never have access to a sheik's harem."

"But I would," Caro said. "I should be the one to find Isabella and determine how best to smuggle her out."

Meeting her gaze, Max nodded reluctantly. He deplored the thought of Caro risking her life, but she was the only one of them capable of infiltrating a harem. "I suppose you could go as my slave."

Her eyebrows shot up. "Your *slave*?"

"It will be believable and explain your presence. Why else would a woman be in a party of sportsmen? Of course, you will need to undertake lessons in servility first."

Her gray eyes flared for a moment before her mouth curved with unwilling amusement. "Do you think anyone will believe such an obvious pretense?"

Max returned a crooked smile. "Perhaps if you practice very diligently."

"And what role do I play?" Ryder asked, breaking into their interchange.

Max shook himself. "You are the munitions expert," he replied. "We will need you to create a diversion so we can escape the fortress undetected. And possibly to rig some explosives to cover our retreat in the event we are pursued."

"If we must fight our way out, you mean?"

"Yes."

Sir Gawain winced. "I would much prefer that you accomplish your mission without having to kill or wound innocent bystanders. The chieftain's only crime was purchasing a slave. I would not like to see him lose his life over it."

"Nor would I," Max said with sincerity. "The fortress will likely be well guarded. If we could somehow incapacitate the guards . . ."

"Perhaps some kind of sleeping draught in their wine," Verra suggested.

"Berbers don't often drink wine," the expert chimed in, "although they like fig brandy. They aren't as religious as Arabs, but they still practice the Muslim faith, which forbids alcohol."

"A drug in their water or food, then."

Sir Gawain turned to Caro. "Can you concoct some kind of drug that can be used without causing permanent harm?"

"I'm certain I can."

"If we could debilitate the warlord's horses as well," Max said, "then they would be unable to give chase."

"Perhaps I can pose as your groom," Verra offered, "in order to gain access to the chieftain's stables."

"Yes," Ryder concurred. His brows narrowing thoughtfully, he gave a slow nod. "That plan could work. Leighton poses as a big game hunter in search of sport, while Caro and Verra accompany him as his servants."

Yates nodded as well. "I can have a message delivered to Thorne, requesting him to arrange for horses and tents and a proper retinue for a wealthy British gentleman on holiday."

"And I will take care of amassing the rifles and explosives," Ryder said.

"So we have a preliminary plan," Max said. "We can refine the details when we rendezvous with Thorne and Hawk in Algiers."

His pensive frown easing, Sir Gawain looked at Max with a smile of approval.

Max glanced around the table, seeing agreement, satisfaction, even a measure of eagerness. Hope shone in Caro's eyes.

"It is settled, then," Sir Gawain announced solemnly. "Now we must confirm Lady Isabella's location and you can sail for Barbary."

The setting sun made a bronze mirror of the lake's surface as Max waited for Caro to arrive several evenings later. Plucking a pebble from the bank, he tossed it toward the water's center, watching the flaming ripples spread.

A faint smile curved his lips when he realized he was throwing pebbles instead of knives. In fact, he hadn't thrown Philip's knife in some time.

The blissful moments of abandon he'd shared here with Caro had gone far in easing his dark restlessness, and the grotto itself seemed to be having a healing effect on him. Even without Caro's presence, Max had found himself frequently drawn here, as if lured by some intangible force. And each time his spirit grew a little lighter.

For the first time in a long, long while, he was able to notice the beauty surrounding him. Could feel sensations returning that had been numb during so many years of war. Feel the bleak ache inside him diminishing.

The nightmares had almost vanished as well. Only once recently had he awakened in a whimpering sweat, feeling the oppressive darkness closing in, but the intensity wasn't as severe as in the past. And when he closed his eyes, Caro had taken his hand and led him from the battlefield. . . .

He owed her a debt of gratitude for prodding him to confront his demons. Somehow she'd coaxed him to speak openly of things he'd tried to repress. To confess his dreaded secrets. Because of her, he was coming alive again. He felt more at peace now than he had in years. He was even allowing himself to remember the good times he'd shared with Philip.

He hadn't seen Caro since their conference at the castle. In the interim he'd refrained from thinking too closely about the Guardians and their invitation to join their order.

He didn't want to disappoint Caro, but he couldn't give her an answer just now. Couldn't make that kind of monumental commitment.

It was a noble ideal, fighting tyranny and saving lives. And he couldn't deny his instinctive need to slay dragons and battle evil for Caro's sake. But he might never be able to dedicate himself to the Guardians' cause, as she had done.

He'd seen the camaraderie among them, the close friendship they shared. It was the same fraternity he'd known with his fellow officers, with Philip. He wasn't certain he could open himself to that kind of pain again . . . If he could endure becoming part of a brotherhood again, letting himself grow close, only to risk watching his friends die.

He was having a hard enough time controlling his

concern for Caro, trying not to think about the danger she could face in their upcoming mission . . . in every mission she attempted.

That kind of apprehension could paralyze a soldier in battle, could paralyze *him*, Max knew.

He hadn't expected ever to be in this situation again. He'd simply tried to take one day at a time and had avoided contemplating his future beyond his sojourn on Cyrene or the mission to Barbary. But he would soon have to consider his answer . . . indeed, what he intended to do with the rest of his life.

For now, though, he just wanted get their mission over with and bring Lady Isabella safely home. He was beginning to feel the same urgency as Caro. They'd heard no word from Barbary since Thorne's last communication, but a storm had swept across the Mediterranean three days ago, no doubt delaying any ships. The storm had also drenched the island with much-needed rain and turned the waterfall at her grotto into a torrent, although the flow had almost returned to normal by now.

Shifting his gaze from the waterfall, Max glanced up at the sky, aware of the gathering dusk and his disappointment. Caro had expected to attend a lying-in all day. Her message had said she would try to join him at the grotto before nightfall but that it might be much later.

A low hoot sounded just then from the oak tree on the bank behind Max. He didn't flinch this time, for he'd grown accustomed to the brown ball of feathers interrupting his peace when he least expected it. In Caro's absence, the owl had kept him company.

Max glanced over his shoulder and nodded in sympathy. "You miss her, too, don't you, George?"

When the owl hooted again in response, Max scooped up another pebble and tossed it at the lake, watching the ripples spread out over the darkening surface.

When Caro arrived at nearly midnight, she looked exhausted but pleased.

"Mrs. Tompkins gave birth to a beautiful baby boy," she said as he helped her down from her horse.

Max felt desire knife through him as Caro slid down the length of his body, but he repressed his craving and unsaddled her horse before leading her inside the grotto.

She stopped short when she saw the welcome he had prepared for her. The candles he'd lit around the grotto gave off a golden glow, while the feast he'd laid out—roasted chicken and saffron-spiced rice and Spanish *truita*—filled the air with a mouthwatering aroma.

The lovely smile Caro gave him trapped his breath deep in his chest.

"Hungry?" he asked, drawing her close.

"Yes, but I think I am too weary to eat."

Max felt an immediate tenderness. He wanted to pull her beneath him and drive himself into her body until they were both mindless with pleasure, but he ruthlessly quelled the urge and merely kissed her gently. "Never fear, it is your turn to be cared for."

He settled her on the pallet among the pillows and fed her by hand until her hunger was sated. Then he undressed her, leaving only her shift, and took down her hair before stepping back to shed his own clothing.

When he joined her, to her surprise he lay down behind her, and pulled the blanket up to cover them both against the October night air.

When he began gently massaging the stiff, tired muscles of her shoulders and arms, she sighed in weary contentment.

"You are working too hard," Max murmured, his hands moving on to lightly rub her back.

Caro nearly groaned with pleasure and relief. "It can't be helped. Dr. Allenby still is too weak to leave his bed." She closed her eyes, letting Max's hands work their magic. "Perhaps it's selfish of me, but I hope he recovers soon, for more than his own sake. I cannot leave Cyrene as long as he is ill."

"You're concerned you won't be able to participate in Isabella's rescue."

"Yes. I don't want to abandon our islanders with no one to care for them."

"It seems to me that you need another doctor to take Allenby's place."

"I know." She was glad she no longer had to keep up the pretense with Max. He understood now why she couldn't become the island's full-time doctor—because it would leave her no time for missions, and she had no desire to give up her role as a Guardian. "Dr. Allenby is growing more frail with each passing year. Yet it will be difficult to lure another qualified doctor here to Cyrene."

"Why?"

"Because any surgeon with an ounce of ambition would far rather practice in London than our little backwater. I had hoped that someday we might build a real surgery and hospital on Cyrene, but that seems an impossible dream."

"Not so impossible, but you can worry about it tomorrow. For now you need to sleep."

Pressing his lips against her hair, he left off his ministrations and slipped his arm around her waist, drawing her back against him, cradling her in the curve of his body.

Caro silently savored the contact. She felt the heat of his arousal against her buttocks and knew Max wanted her, but evidently he intended just to hold her until she drifted peacefully to sleep.

With another sigh, she relaxed against him. She could feel his heartbeat, his heat, the strength of the arms that sheltered her.

She meant to draw from that strength, to take the comfort Max offered her. It had been so long since anyone had taken care of her, so long since she'd felt as if someone was guarding *her*, someone who would be strong when she was too weary to fight any longer.

His tenderness made her feel so cherished. The soft touch of his lips against her hair was so gentle, it made her throat tighten.

She wanted Max to keep holding her like this. She wanted to continue feeling this safe, this protected forever.

He was a protector at heart, she knew. Max possessed the same natural instincts to safeguard and defend that all the Guardians had. The same leadership skills she had seen in her father. That indefinable quality that would make men follow him into hell if need be. He would make a wonderful Guardian.

But it was foolish to hope he might become one of them. She doubted he would remain on Cyrene after their rescue mission was accomplished. Once he healed from his tormenting nightmares, there would be no reason for him to stay.

Even now the shadows in his eyes were lessening. He still wasn't completely healed, but he was growing less restless day by day. And when he was whole once more?

He would leave her like the last time.

Even if he remained, even if he became a Guardian, it didn't mean they would ever be anything more than lovers.

Caro squeezed her eyes shut as a wave of longing flooded her. She wanted more than to merely be Max's lover. Tonight when she had held Mrs. Tompkins's new baby in her arms, she had felt a fierce yearning in her heart. For a moment she had let herself wonder what it would be like to bear Max's child.

But she couldn't let herself think about such things. Max had told her clearly that he didn't want children, didn't want a wife.

She couldn't afford to dream such fantasies. Couldn't afford to let her emotions slip out of her control and leave her so utterly vulnerable.

It would be too easy to fall in love with Max then, and she would be left with only heartache and pain and regrets for the rest of her days.

Chapter Thirteen

Golden brightness flooded the grotto when Caro at last stirred awake.

This was no sensual dream, she thought languorously. She could feel Max's heat at her back, the soft stroke of his hand in the unruly mass of her hair, the thick, pulsing shaft that lay heavy and welcome against her bare buttocks where her shift had ridden up.

She opened her eyes slowly. Judging by the sunlight streaming through the crevice in the grotto roof, morning was half gone. Max must have awakened long before her but allowed her to sleep. He had already shaved in deference to her tender skin, she could tell from the fresh scent of his shaving soap and from the smoothness of his jaw when he nuzzled the column of her neck.

"Did I wake you?" His voice was low and husky and as caressing as his hand in her hair.

"Mmmm. I was dreaming about you."

"A pleasant dream, I trust?"

"Indeed, although not as lovely as the real thing."

As if reading her mind, Max slid his hand from her hair, around over her arm to cup her breast through the thin cambric of her shift.

Caro inhaled sharply. He could make her breathless with just a touch. Then he spread his hand flat against the quivering softness of her belly, moving lower between her thighs, feeling the heat and dampness and need of her.

She arched against him as unbidden, sensual images assaulted her, memories of everything his fingers had ever done to her . . . wildly wicked things that had left her gasping.

He gave a murmur of satisfaction when the liquid evidence of her arousal drenched his fingers, but to her surprise, Max only nipped at her earlobe before easing out from under the blanket and rising.

"Your bath awaits, milady," he said, a teasing note to his tone.

By the time Caro realized that he didn't intend to make love to her just yet, he had left the grotto.

Yet his absence gave her a moment of privacy to answer nature's call and to make use of the sponges. When she was done, she followed him out of the grotto, into the bright sunshine.

Max had already waded into the lake up to his thighs, Caro saw. At the sight of him, she paused, registering the sheer physical splendor of his nude body, his potent masculinity. And when he turned to face her, her attention was drawn to that masculine flesh that could give such wild pleasure, and her mouth went dry.

"What are you waiting for?" he asked, raising an amused eyebrow.

She felt color warm her cheeks as she realized he had caught her staring. Her flush rose even higher when she drew her shift off, for Max stared back, his eyes hot, touching her everywhere.

Her pulse beginning to race, Caro entered the water.

The lake was still moderately warm at this time of year after baking in the sun all summer, but the temperature of the falls was rather chilly, so she was surprised when Max swam toward them and stood up near the plunging cascade, where the swirling water was waist deep.

"The falls are a bit cool for my taste," Caro protested.

"Never fear, I will keep you warm."

He gave her that achingly familiar smile, and her pulse throbbed even harder.

Obediently she waded over to him. She could feel his gaze like a caress, drifting over her nudity as he scooped up water in one hand and let it run over her shoulders.

In his other hand he held a sliver of soap, and he began running it slowly over her neck, along her arms, down her belly, but not where she ached the most.

"Touch me," she whispered.

"I intend to. But you need patience."

He washed her bare breasts then, his hands moving against her pale skin, stroking possessively. His touch sent a pulse of pleasure shafting in her loins. The pale mounds were slick, her nipples dark and fully aroused, and Max's eyes were a heated, brilliant blue as he watched his own ministrations.

"Now for the rest of you." His knee came between hers and gently spread her feet apart, while his hand moved down between her legs, seeking and caressing, arousing.

Yet Caro didn't need arousing. She was already hot and aching for him. His touch burned her.

"Max, please . . ."

After another moment, he tossed the soap onto the

rock ledge behind her and rinsed off her body. Reaching up, he covered her breasts with his hands.

"Your nipples are such hard, delicious points." He bent down to her, his tongue circling the dusky crests, now pebbled and urgent. "They taste like ambrosia."

His devouring lips dragged across the taut peaks, pulling at the flesh, nipping softly, his tongue teasing and tormenting by turns while his lower body moved provocatively against hers, hardness against aching softness.

Her nipples hurt now, hard and pointed and chafed by the delicious arousal of his tongue and the sweet, hot suckling of his mouth.

Finally he left off and led her beneath the waterfall. Caro gasped as the water poured over them.

Unapologetically, Max smiled and dipped his head to drink a kiss from her lips. Then he drew back and put both hands on her waist, lifting her up to sit on the ledge so that her knees were nearly level with his chest.

The falls no longer spilled directly over them, but the sun barely reached her through the mist.

Caro shivered as gooseflesh rose along her wet skin. "Max, I thought you said—"

"Hush, you'll enjoy this, I promise," he murmured, holding her gaze with those astonishingly warm eyes.

She believed him when his hand splayed over her belly. His caress moved lower, his fingers encountering her thatch of fleecy curls. He teased her a moment, then parted her thighs, leaving her slim body open for his pleasure.

Ruthlessly his eyes devoured her; Caro felt she might melt from the blistering heat of his gaze. But then he moved between her legs, sending cold drops of moisture dripping off his wet hair onto her most sensitive feminine flesh.

An instant later, he bent to place his hot mouth on her. After the chill of the water, his touch was like fire, and she nearly moaned.

She did moan when he slid one finger inside her and his damp mouth found the nub of her sex. Her skin heated like a fever as a second finger joined the first.

His mouth gently suckled her then, his fingers buried deep inside her, dredging a groan from deep in her throat.

Caro shuddered helplessly, her flesh clamoring for release. She was trembling by now, her hips arched in desperation as she sought to press herself harder against his mouth.

But Max seemed to be in no hurry. Draping her legs over his shoulders, he slowly sucked and licked, bringing her dangerously near the peak, delving his fingers deep inside her while his tongue played over her . . . arousing her ruthlessly, then denying her for the apparent pleasure of hearing her moans grow wilder.

"Max, I can't bear any more. Please . . ."

"No, not yet," he answered.

He seemed to savor the breathy sounds she made as she thrashed feverishly beneath his caresses. Then suddenly she flowered for him. Her hands sank deep into his scalp as she gave one last keening cry.

"Easy." His voice was soothing, but she didn't need him to whisper gentle, calming words. She needed *him*. Desperately.

"*Now,* Max, please . . ."

He required no further encouragement. In one

smooth movement, he lifted himself onto the ledge, then repositioned Caro to lie beneath him.

Shifting his weight to cover her body, he eased between her thighs, stroking his velvet-sheathed hardness against her feminine folds. He slid into her while she was still pulsating with pleasure.

His face rigid with desire, he buried his hands in her hair. Caro saw his eyes, fierce with tenderness and intent as he sank into her, heavy and hard and deep.

She groaned to feel his rigid fullness inside her, filling her.

"God, I love being inside you." His voice was heated and devastatingly sensual. "Each time I slide into you I want more."

So did she, Caro thought, dazed. His possession brought her such bliss she thought she might faint with it.

"You feel so incredible, so warm and wet and tight."

His hips began to undulate while his voice murmured words of praise and pleasure in her ear.

He tortured her with exquisitely slow thrusts, each drugging stroke heaven. Whenever he drew back, Caro strained to hold the hot, sweet shaft buried inside her, whimpering with relief when he filled her again, but he kept moving, changing the rhythm, the pace, the depth. His hands and mouth caressed her body in unison, tantalizing her almost beyond endurance.

When at last he slid home to the hilt, plunging deep, Caro responded with equal fervor, trying to melt into him as he surged inside her.

He kissed her again, his mouth hard against hers, his tongue moving in the same demanding rhythm as he filled her again and again. Her hips met each plunge, her body straining for release, and she groaned, a pleading sound of need. This was desire, she felt it surging through her body. Felt herself shaking with it.

She could barely hear the rawly sexual things Max was saying to her over the rasping sound of her breaths, the frantic thudding of her heart, the rushing waterfall. She was writhing beneath him as he took her with urgent, deep strokes, her body soaring wildly out of her control.

A wave of stunning sensation hit her, colors and blinding light blurring before her eyes, yet Max never ceased his primitive possession. He seemed oblivious to her fingernails clawing his naked back as she surged and contracted, but when a raw cry ripped from her throat, he pressed her face against his water-slicked shoulder to bury her scream.

Long, long moments later Caro regained some of her fragmented senses.

Max was watching her, she realized, his eyes lustful as they lingered on her heaving breasts and jutting nipples.

And he was still hard and full inside her.

Without giving her time to protest, he bent to lave the aching peaks while he reached down to grasp her buttocks. He held a cheek in each hand, gently squeezing the soft flesh as he pushed into her again, deep and sure and powerful.

Reflexively Caro clenched him tightly within the depths of her body, even though she had no energy left.

He kept thrusting heavily into her and it happened again; she came in an explosive climax that was even more forceful than the one before, dredging more helpless cries of pleasure from her.

This time when she shattered, Max could no longer resist the delicious clasping and gripping of her inner muscles around him. Letting himself surrender, he drove into her, knowing a pure, raging joy as he unleashed the wildness in him. His own body ignited with a fiery urgency, and he came in his own fierce explosion as she wept soft, mindless sobs of rapture.

Afterward they lay tangled in each other's arms. The ripples of pleasure faded eventually, but the soft mating of their breath continued as Max's lips lingered on hers.

The mist was still cool on their overheated bodies, yet Caro knew the tremors that still shivered across their skin had less to do with the temperature than the searing passion that had claimed them both.

Caro shut her eyes, curling against him in sated contentment. She hadn't meant to respond with such raw unbridled need, but the racking pleasure had exhausted her. She had been twisting and straining with such ecstasy she'd been mindless with it.

"Oh, no, angel. You can't fall asleep now."

Wearily she forced her eyes open, to find Max gazing down at her with a lazy, breathtaking smile.

After the fierce demands he had made on her body, she'd thought herself beyond arousal, but his eyes were hot and held dark promise. Instantly she felt another fierce wave of longing sweep over her.

Wetting her dry lips with her tongue, she managed a smile. "Sleep," she said hoarsely, "is the last thing on my mind at the moment."

He pressed his hips closer, sending quivers of wanting shooting through her.

"Good," Max said with satisfaction, "for I still have any number of other ways to keep you warm."

"I want a word with you, sir."

Max raised an eyebrow at Dr. Allenby's brusque greeting. The elderly gentleman was sitting up in his bed, looking weak and pale but still full of vinegar.

Max had been surprised by the doctor's summons to visit that afternoon—yet judging by Allenby's surly reception, he didn't intend for this to be a social call.

"I hear you have been invited to join the Guardians," Allenby growled, narrowing his craggy brows. "Do you mean to accept?"

In the days since Caro's remarkable disclosure about the Guardians of the Sword, Max had thought of little else, but he had come no closer to making a decision. "I haven't yet made up my mind."

"If you don't intend to stay on Cyrene, it would be better if you left."

"I'm not certain I take your meaning," Max replied.

"My meaning? I wish to know your intentions toward Caro, sir! Are they honorable or not? Are you courting her, or merely trifling with her to pass the time?"

"I should think that is a matter between Caro and myself."

Allenby glared in a manner designed to intimidate. "I am making it my business, young fellow. I have stood in place of Caro's father since his death, and I have a responsibility toward her."

Max stifled the urge to retort. He understood why the crusty old doctor was protective of Caro.

"You have been spending an excessive amount of time in her company," Allenby charged.

That wasn't quite true. In the first place, Caro had been working too hard for him to spend much time with her. And in the second, he'd been very careful to continue socializing with his new acquaintances all over the island in order to keep his liaison with Caro from becoming common knowledge.

"I enjoy Miss Evers's friendship, Doctor. And she seems to enjoy mine."

"You claim you want nothing more from her than mere friendship? I was a young man myself once, and I know how this island can arouse a man's passions."

Max was not about to discuss his passions with the doctor, or reveal his intimate relationship with Caro, but he decided to offer an explanation Allenby was likely to accept. "Caro thinks of me as her patient," he prevaricated. "A soldier suffering from the stresses of war. If she has shown me inordinate attention, it's because she wants to patch me up like one of her other wounded creatures."

"Humph. Patient or not, I think she has become a bit too fond of you. No good can come of it."

"Why do you say so?"

"Because you can only hurt her. Unless you intend to stay on Cyrene, you have no future together. I won't permit you to lure her away from here. This is her home. She would be miserable anywhere else. She wouldn't fit in. Here she can fulfill her life's goals—to practice medicine and to continue her father's role in the Guardians. Have you thought of that, sir?"

No, he hadn't allowed himself to think that far ahead, Max acknowledged.

"And if your intentions are not honorable . . ." The elderly man on the bed pointed a gnarled finger at Max. "You will answer to me. Now go away and leave me to rest. I need to recover my health if I'm to ease Caro's mind at leaving Cyrene to go on her mission."

Abruptly dismissed, Max left Dr. Allenby's house and mounted his horse. He didn't know whether to be amused, indignant, or simply tolerant of the gruff old man's warning.

The interference was well meant, he had no doubt. And admittedly Dr. Allenby's interrogation had made Max more aware of his own selfishness. He *had* taken advantage of Caro—accepting the comfort she offered, using her to help heal his emotional wounds, not to mention slake his physical needs.

He had once thought that by sating his carnal desire for Caro, she would stop haunting his dreams. He'd expected that by the time he left Cyrene, he would have his craving for her under control. But their passionate encounters had had entirely the opposite effect.

He'd begun to want Caro beyond reason and logic, Max realized. He wondered if the urgency would ever lessen.

The doctor had raised another good question as well: What *were* his intentions toward Caro? Until now he hadn't even acknowledged the possibility of marriage to her. It said a great deal about the uniqueness of this situation that he didn't cringe at the mere notion. No other woman but Caro could make him contemplate taking a wife and risk losing someone he cared for.

And Caro herself? She had claimed she wasn't the

least interested in marriage, or in leaving the island. She would indeed be miserable living elsewhere, Max knew. He now understood why a woman as lovely as Caro would feel like a misfit in England. Why she had kept herself apart from her peers, her potential suitors, even lovers. She had created a fulfilling place for herself here as a member of the Guardians and had no wish to give that up.

He didn't, however, want to give Caro false hopes about his remaining. Certainly he didn't want to hurt her.

And if he declined to join the Guardians, what then? He would likely return to England, even though the prospect of settling into a mundane life in such tame surroundings now held little appeal.

But perhaps he was looking too far ahead, Max warned himself. His prime concern should be getting through this single upcoming mission without his demons returning to hinder his faculties.

The possibility of going into battle again troubled him. If he was required to fight, he hoped to God he wouldn't freeze or become paralyzed, as he'd seen so many young soldiers do. But it was the thought of what could befall Caro that made him break into a cold sweat. The closer their mission came, the more his dread grew.

Even so, perhaps the doctor had done him a favor by opening his eyes to the immediate danger. If he didn't take care, his obsession for Caro could spiral beyond his control. For her sake, it was only fair that he ease back from their relationship a measure.

At least until they completed their mission in Barbary and he decided what to do about his future.

* * *

The next time they met at the grotto, Caro sensed the change in Max. The easy rapport between them was missing.

They swam in the lake and afterward made love, but he seemed to be holding back. Even though he was the same tender and considerate lover, his passion was banked, and she sensed a reservation between them that had never been there before. And when Caro left him to return to her duties, Max didn't press her to name a time for their next meeting as he often did.

His apparent withdrawal disheartened her, for she suspected it meant he was planning to leave Cyrene once their mission was completed.

But then, she had always known there was little chance Max would join the Guardians' endeavors. It had been foolish to let her hopes grow too high.

Instead, Caro scolded herself, she should try to forget about Max and concentrate on the mission ahead.

Chapter Fourteen

At last the moment of Isabella's deliverance was at hand. The next ship to sail into Cyrene's harbor bore messengers from Barbary, confirming Lady Isabella's location: she was indeed being held by a Berber chieftain in his mountain stronghold southeast of Algiers.

Sir Gawain immediately summoned all the Guardians on Cyrene to the castle to hear the report from Algiers by two agents whom Max hadn't yet met.

In the end, their departure was set for the following day. A force of two dozen Guardians would sail for the Barbary Coast and land near a small seaport east of Algiers under cover of darkness. Viscount Thorne and the Earl of Hawkhurst—the Guardian known as Hawk—would await them with a caravan and guides to take them from the coast across the high desert plains into the Biban mountains.

By the time the council ended, they all shared a somber sense of purpose and a devout determination to succeed.

As they made their way to the stables, Max caught Caro's eye. "Tonight?" he murmured.

She nodded. Even though she had renewed her vow to distance herself from Max, she would not forgo this opportunity to be with him, knowing this could be their final night together. Once they left the island, they would have no privacy, for they would be living in close quarters with the rest of the rescue force, first on board ship and then in tents as they trekked across a ruthless land. And by the time they returned, Max might very well have decided he wanted no more part of their order.

He was waiting for her at the grotto when she arrived. Wordlessly he drew her into his arms, covering her mouth with a fierce kiss that was reminiscent of their former passion.

Their lovemaking this time was intense and feverish, yet held a poignancy that was new.

With effort afterward Caro refrained from repeating all the arguments why Max should join the Guardians. There was no point in imploring him. Max would have to weigh the consequences and choose for himself.

Instead, when he pulled her into the shelter of his body, she lay silently in his arms, feeling the solemn beat of his heart beneath her cheek while striving to subdue her longing.

The next morning when Caro boarded the ship, Max was there before her. She had promised herself that she would ignore him, but her efforts failed miserably from the very first.

It helped that Captain Biddick put her to work getting under way, and she threw herself headlong into her task, but she was aware of Max every moment. And regrettably, after they set sail there was little to do but wait. The next three days Caro spent listening to the creak of rigging, the slap of canvas sail, the quiet jests of the other Guardians as they whiled away the time playing cards or recounting stories of past exploits.

There were two other women in the party, both Spaniards, included mainly to give the proper appearance of a retinue of servants, but who would also cook and provide support for Caro and Isabella, once the lady was rescued.

The camaraderie on board was jovial as usual. Indeed, this mission was much like the countless others Caro had been on in past years—except for Max. The tension curling in her stomach was not just the healthy fear and anticipation of the dangerous challenges that lay ahead. She hadn't expected it would be so difficult to control her desire for Max, or to conceal it from all the observers on board. She felt somehow bereft, being unable to talk to him, to touch him.

He didn't feel the same way, Caro surmised. Whenever he met her glance, the burning fires she'd often seen in his eyes were now banked, to be replaced by a starkly emotionless expression.

It made her wonder if perhaps Max had retreated into himself, in order to build the defenses he would need if their mission turned violent.

They neared Barbary well before dawn, while the moon still shone. Standing at the ship's railing, Caro could just make out the high hills of the coastline silhouetted against the night sky, along with some faint pinpricks of light that the captain said came from the small seaport of Bougie.

Nearly an hour later, as the landmass loomed closer, she saw a series of brighter flashes in the darkness coming from the rocky shore—made by lantern light, she knew.

Just then Max moved to stand beside her. She felt her pulse quicken, for this was the first time since leaving Cyrene that he had come this close to her.

"I take it that is our signal to land?" Max said quietly.

"Yes. We have our own codes arranged. That signal means Hawk is waiting for us. We will row ashore, and afterward Captain Biddick will move his ship to safer waters to avoid being detected by pirates or the Algerian fleet. But he'll return five days from now and be ready to sail the moment we make it back to the coast with Isabella."

"Have you visited Barbary before this?"

"I was in Tripoli once, but never the Kingdom of Algiers. Hawk comes here regularly, though."

"To buy horses?"

"Yes, Arabians and Barbs for his racing stables. Which is why Sir Gawain chose him to be the prime agent to gather intelligence. Hawk speaks Arabic and a smattering of Berber, and he has numerous contacts here. He will have arranged for all the proper travel permits and papers for our caravan. And both Ryder and Thorne are familiar with the area as well, since they have been to Barbary several times. You would do better to direct whatever questions you have to them."

"I intend to," Max said cryptically before walking away.

Caro stared after him, trying to quell the disappointment that lay in her stomach like lead.

They dropped anchor in a small bay. Because of his familiarity with the coast, Alex Ryder led the first boat of the landing party. Caro and Max were in the second, Santos Verra in the third, along with crates of weapons and supplies.

Acting swiftly and silently, they went ashore on a rocky beach washed by gentle waves and quickly climbed a low cliff in the darkness, their presence camouflaged by shadows of cypress and myrtle that grew along the coast.

When they reached the meeting place, Caro could sense the gathering of men and horses even before she saw them. And Christopher Thorne was the first person she recognized.

Emerging from the darkness, he flashed her a smile of greeting and embraced her fondly, before quietly cuffing Max on the shoulder.

"I understand," Thorne murmured with an undertone of amusement, "that you found more than you bargained for on Cyrene."

Caro saw Max's wry grimace, heard his low, even dryer response. "You have a great deal to answer for, my friend. There were some rather pertinent details you failed to disclose."

"Because I was sworn to secrecy. But it is damned good to have you with us."

Thorne introduced Max to the Earl of Hawkhurst then. Caro watched the two men measuring each other as they shook hands. In the dark it was hard to tell them apart, for they were both tall, commanding men with raven hair. But she knew Hawk's chiseled features were more aquiline than Max's, and his eyes were piercing gray instead of striking blue.

"I've heard some very favorable reports about you,

Leighton," Hawk said, his brief words of greeting sounding genuine.

He then brought forward a shorter, swarthy-skinned man who was garbed in a long white robe and flowing head cloth.

"This is Faruq. He will be our guide to the mountains."

With a graceful salaam, Faruq tendered several flowery greetings in excellent English and offered his humble services. Their guide, Caro surmised, was one of the nomadic Bedouin Arabs of the plains, rather than the Moors of the cities or the fair-skinned Berbers who inhabited the rugged mountains.

Faruq's first task was to supply them all with proper garb as befitted the customs and climate. The men were given burnooses—hooded cloaks—to protect them from the blazing sun and sand that they would soon encounter. Caro and the two Spanish women from Cyrene were turned over to the three female Arabic servants and provided with robes and head cloths along with long scarves to cover their faces. Max kept his own British gentleman's attire, since he was posing as a wealthy sportsman eager to hunt the famed lions of Barbary, but he wore a burnoose as well.

"I suppose you'll do," Thorne quipped as he studied Max, "if you only will contrive to look a trifle more arrogant."

At their guide's direction, they mounted and struck out for the south—a caravan of horses and pack mules and camels. Caro rode at the rear with the servants and women, but she was glad to have a horse rather than a swaying camel, which she knew from past experience made her a trifle nauseated.

Faruq had said it would take three full days to reach their destination. They had avoided landing too close to civilization, but soon would be required to use the established trails, for there was no other safe way through the harsh terrain.

Caro settled in for the journey, the rhythmic sound of plodding hooves and the creak of saddle leather punctuated only by the quiet murmur of voices from the men up ahead.

Max, Caro saw, rode next to Hawk, and was no doubt being briefed on the specific intelligence Hawk had gathered over the past weeks that would aid in Isabella's recovery. They would also, she suspected, discuss the specific details of the rescue attempt based on the general plan Max had proposed.

Shortly, the sun rose over the high, hilly coastal region, and by mid-morning the sky glowed with the golden clarity particular to the Mediterranean. They crossed a broad and fertile valley where wild fig and olive trees grew in abundance, and then began to climb.

When they topped a rocky hillock, the landscape changed abruptly. Here the rainfall was obviously more abundant, for they rode through the cool shadows of a cedar forest. By afternoon, however, they had descended into another valley, this one flat and treeless, covered with rank shrubs and grass, with few signs of life other than the occasional nomads tending their grazing flocks of sheep and goats.

Just as suddenly the terrain turned barren and broken. The trail narrowed, flanked by chalk rock and red sandstone slopes. When they began weaving between steep precipices and wild ravines, their guide,

Faruq, rode to the rear of the caravan in order to address Caro.

"I beg you to take care, mademoiselle. There is much danger here."

Caro thanked him and promised to beware.

As well as being dangerous, it was also far hotter here. When they paused to rest the animals, she drank gratefully from the goatskin water bag that the women shared, and partook lightly of the barley cakes and goat cheese and figs that were offered for the midday meal.

By late afternoon she could see in the far distance the beginnings of a rugged mountain chain, but the sun burned red and gold on the horizon when their guide finally called a halt to the caravan.

The Arabs made camp swiftly, with the obvious ease of long practice, erecting nearly a dozen black tents made of goatskin while the women started the cooking fires and prepared the evening meal.

Caro saw to her horse and stretched her aching limbs by walking around the camp. Despite the harshness of the land, the evening was so peaceful, she realized she might have enjoyed the journey if the stakes were not so high—and if her relationship with Max weren't so strained.

He still seemed to be avoiding her, so she wasn't surprised that it was Thorne who came to fetch her for supper.

"So tell me," her friend probed as he took her arm to escort her back to the largest tent. "How has Max been acclimating?"

"Well enough," Caro prevaricated, not wanting to

share confidences Max had entrusted to her. "He seems to have enjoyed his time on the island."

"Will he join us, do you think?"

That was Thorne's real concern, she knew. From the first he had championed Max's membership in the Guardians, and he had instigated Max's visit to Cyrene chiefly for that purpose.

"I'm not certain," she replied honestly. "He has a number of unpleasant memories of war to overcome. I suspect a great deal depends on how he deals with this mission."

In the Arab culture, women dined separately from men, but since Caro was a special case, she shared supper with the other Guardians. Seated on a woven rush mat between Thorne and Ryder, Caro ate the simple but delicious meal: couscous with vegetables, olives, beans soaked in oil and vinegar, and golden ripe dates.

Afterward they drank small cups of thick black coffee while Hawk and Max reviewed the details of the plan they had agreed upon. They would try to prepare for every possible contingency, Caro knew, but if things went wrong, they would have to depend upon their wits and experience to get them out of trouble.

Hawk spoke as the others studied maps from his earlier reconnaissance.

"Tomorrow night we will make camp at the oasis of Akbou. The following morning, we'll leave the bulk of our caravan behind there while some twenty of us proceed into the mountains for the last leg of the journey."

"How long is the ride from Akbou?" Ryder asked.

"Nine or ten hours," Hawk answered, "so we

should reach Saful's mountain fortress by late afternoon, while it is still daylight. The chieftain's name is Saful il Taib. He leads one of the more powerful Berber tribes in Algeria, but I found him to be extremely hospitable when I visited last week under the pretext of searching for broodmares. He speaks a fair amount of French, so you should be able to communicate without an interpreter."

Max pointed to a place on one of Hawk's maps. "This northern mountain pass will be the approach we use?"

"Yes. The Berbers are essentially farmers, although their men are fierce warriors. And Saful's stronghold is actually a fortified town, built into the mountainside overlooking a narrow, fertile valley. There are only two safe routes in and out of his valley. The south trail doubles back to the west and eventually forks either toward Algiers or east to rejoin this route."

Hawk glanced around the tent at the two dozen Guardians who were giving him their undivided attention. "Leighton will lead a select party down from the northern mountain pass and cross the valley to the walled gates of the town."

"Not all of us will enter the town, surely?" Thorne said.

"No," Hawk replied. "Leighton will take only a handful of attendants into the fortress, including Caro, Verra, and Ryder. The rest of his entourage, including you, Thorne, will make camp outside the gates, in the valley, to ensure their escape when the time comes. And since I can't show my face again without raising suspicions, I will remain on this side of the north pass to cover your retreat."

"And once we are inside the stronghold?" Ryder asked.

"Leighton will be in charge and will determine your specific actions depending on the circumstances you find. But in general, the plan is this: When Saful receives him, he will ask for a guide to the interior mountains so that he may hunt the best game. As incentive, you'll offer him a dozen rifles in exchange."

"What if he wants to bargain?" was someone else's question.

"You can agree to increase the number of rifles—Ryder brought three dozen that we will leave for Saful as payment for violating his hospitality and taking his captive from under his nose. But I doubt you will need to barter significantly. Berbers are unlike Arabs, who make an art out of haggling for the best terms. I suspect Saful will consider your offer generous and fair."

"I should hope so," Ryder murmured dryly, "considering that these rifles have the longest range and accuracy of any gun ever made."

"And my role?" Caro asked.

Hawk glanced at her. "You will pose as Leighton's Portuguese slave, who speaks little English. You will undoubtedly be sent to sleep in the women's quarters, where you will find Lady Isabella and communicate our plan and the timing for her escape. It will be your responsibility to alert Leighton to any problems and to decide whether we must call off the rescue. If there are none, he will signal both Ryder and Verra that our plan can proceed."

Caro examined the map Hawk had drawn of the Berber chieftain's large dwelling. "How well guarded will the women's quarters be?"

"Possibly not at all. Berber women are not kept under lock and key like those in a Turkish harem. Stealing Isabella from there should not be difficult. As Leighton says, the problem will be afterward, getting her away from the stronghold without being detected. To that end, we will need to do everything possible to prevent pursuit—beginning with disguise. In your baggage, Caro, you will carry two black burnooses and turbans like the Berbers wear. You and Isabella will dress as men and carry weapons. From a distance you should be able to pass as warriors."

"There looks to be a wall all around Saful's home," she remarked.

"There is. But see the courtyard at the southeast corner? The wall there is easily scalable. Leighton will lead you and Isabella to the stables, where Verra will be waiting with your horses. Meanwhile . . ."

Hawk looked at Santos Verra. "You will act as both Leighton's manservant and groom, so you'll be responsible for incapacitating Saful's horses to make it difficult for him to follow. Caro, you have told Verra what to do?"

She nodded. "The herb I brought with me can be eaten or drunk and should do no lasting harm to a horse. It will only cause a great lethargy, which should dissipate after several hours."

"And how long before it takes effect?"

"An hour, perhaps two."

Ryder spoke up then. "Doubtless there will still be numerous other horses in the town that Saful can use to give chase."

Max was the one who answered. "Which is why you will create a diversion to lure Saful away from his home and keep him momentarily occupied. Without leadership, the other Berbers will be less likely to rally an immediate pursuit."

"By diversion, you mean an explosion?"

"Precisely—in a distant part of the fortress. As chieftain, Saful will be obliged to investigate. With any luck, he and his warriors will be engrossed in trying to determine where the threat came from long enough to allow us to escape through the gates without detection."

"And my goal?" Ryder asked. "Am I to remain 'undetected' after this explosion?"

"If you can. As soon as you light the charge, you will make for the town gates as swiftly as possible. But before that you will have arranged our escape route for us."

Hawk nodded. "The gates are barred at night but lightly guarded. I counted only two sentries when I was there before. Ryder, you will need to deal with the sentries and unbar the gates before you create your diversion."

Ryder grinned. "I will have a busy night, it seems."

Thorne broke in with a plaintive tone. "Don't I get a chance to play hero in all this action?"

There was general laughter around the tent from the other Guardians, who where well acquainted with Thorne's craving for danger.

Hawk smiled briefly, but then quickly grew serious again. "You will have plenty of opportunity for heroics, Thorne, for you will have disbanded your camp and be waiting directly outside the gates with a half-dozen men and a horse for Ryder. By then Leighton and Caro should already have made it through with

Isabella. Since you'll be well armed, you will be responsible for covering their escape and for returning fire if need be."

"It will be my pleasure." Beside her Caro saw Thorne's eyes dance wickedly in anticipation.

"But only if need be," Hawk interjected in warning. "Sir Gawain doesn't want us killing Saful or his people unless we have no choice, so we will shoot as a last resort."

"Of course."

"You will all then ride for the north pass," Hawk continued. "I will be waiting just beyond the pass with fresh horses. In the event you are followed, I will set off a charge of gunpowder, enough to start a landslide and block any pursuit though the pass."

Ryder nodded slowly, evidently satisfied.

"Now, what other questions does anyone have?" Max asked. "Any suggestions to improve our plan? Any thoughts on the precise timing and sequence of events?"

A reflective silence reigned for a time while the Guardians considered the merits and deficiencies of the plan and mulled ideas.

Feeling Max's gaze on her just then, Caro looked up from her map and glanced across at him.

He was frowning at her, she realized.

As his gaze locked with hers, she tried to read his expression, but his blue eyes were dark and unfathomable.

Yet she had the strongest feeling he wasn't entirely pleased with the plan, even though the major components were of his own devising.

* * *

. . . thunderous explosion . . . a horse's scream . . . agonizing pain . . . unable to rise . . .

Ahead, Caro wheeling her horse . . . returning for him . . .

Her hand reaching down to him . . . a sharp crack of rifle fire . . . her head . . . her face . . . the blood . . .

Caro sinking to her knees . . .

Dear God, no . . . please, God, no . . .

Max woke gasping for breath, his heart pounding.

He glanced wildly about him, feeling the knife edge of panic.

The dark tent was silent but for the quiet breathing of a half-dozen sleeping men. Guardians all. No sign of Caro, for she would be in the women's tent . . .

He lay back, still shaking from the nightmare.

This vision had been different, though, for instead of Philip, it was Caro who had returned to save him. Caro who was killed right before his eyes.

He had watched her die, watched her sacrifice her life for his sake.

Dear God, no . . .

They broke camp at dawn the next morning to take advantage of the coolest part of the day, but in only a few hours, the glaring sun beat down upon them. By midday, a desolate expanse of yellowish gray desert stretched before them, baking beneath a hot azure sky.

This was only the forerunner of the Sahara, Caro knew, and summer was long over, yet the cruel heat was almost unbearable. She was glad for the scarves that screened her face against the harsh sun and wind-blown grit.

The arid terrain, broken occasionally by a scraggly clump of broom or thorn, seemed pitiless and lifeless—until Caro's horse came upon a snake half buried beneath the sand.

Terrified, the mare reared with a shrill scream, then whirled in a panic, unseating her rider. Caro landed hard on her back, her senses jarred by the fall.

The snake was not large, but it was barely a foot away, staring at her with shining black eyes as it prepared to strike.

Fear heightened Caro's daze and kept her frozen, even as she heard the thunder of hooves and felt the earth jolting beneath her. Those same hooves flashed next to her head as strong hands reached down to grab the shoulder of her robe and pluck her up off the ground.

Caro found herself slung across the front of a saddle, the wind knocked out of her a second time in as many moments.

Gasping for breath, she struggled to sit up, yet she instinctively recognized her rescuer simply by the familiar feel of his hard body and his sheltering arms. *Max*.

Gratitude filled her as she sank back against his chest. He held her tightly, not speaking as the snake slithered off beneath a bush.

Several of the Guardians came galloping up then and halted beside them, barraging her with questions.

"What the devil happened?"

"Are you all right?"

"Were you hurt?"

"I am fine," Caro replied, relief and embarrassment

warring within her at their concern. "My horse shied at a snake, but I wasn't bitten."

Seeming reassured, Thorne turned to Max. "So that is the sort of fancy maneuver they teach you in the cavalry."

"Impressive," Ryder observed, his tone sardonically admiring.

Hawk nodded. "A Berber horseman could not have done better."

Max ignored their accolades and set Caro back on her skittish mare.

His expression remained grim as he turned his mount and rode off without another word, without even giving Caro a chance to thank him.

She stared after him, just as her friends were doing.

Max was angry at her for some reason, she realized, and she had no idea why.

It wasn't until late that evening that she had a chance to confront him.

When their caravan reached Akbou near dusk, Caro understood immediately why the oasis was a common stop for weary travelers. A cool green forest of feathery date palms towered over a profusion of oleanders, tamarinds, and pistachio trees and provided welcome respite from the barren wilderness.

All manner of people populated the bustling village, she saw, offering numerous services and produce for sale. Once their guides had made camp on the outskirts of the oasis, they were easily able to purchase fresh provisions and replenish their precious water supply.

The supper was more elaborate tonight as well, with lamb added to the couscous. As they had the previous night, the Guardians dined together in the same tent. The camaraderie was quieter this time, though, and they ate heartily, for the morrow would bring the real start of their mission.

After supper, as the gathering broke up so they could repair to their own tents to sleep, Caro approached Max and managed to ask for a private word with him.

When he left the tent, she followed a few moments later.

She found him a short distance from their camp, throwing his knife over and over again at some vague object in the sand.

He must have heard her approach, for he halted abruptly and slipped the knife into his pocket. When she moved to stand beside him, he stared out at the pale desert beyond the oasis.

It was a clear night, moonlit and almost chilly now that the blazing sun had gone down.

Max was the first to break the silence. "What did you wish to say to me?"

Taken aback by his gruff tone, Caro studied his profile in the darkness. "I merely wanted to thank you for saving me today. One of the Arab women told me about the species of snake that frightened my horse. Its venom is deadly."

"Very well. I consider myself thanked."

"Max, what is it?" She placed a hand on his arm, but he recoiled from her touch and stepped aside, out of reach, turning his back to her.

"Have I done something to offend you?" Caro asked in bewilderment.

His response was barely audible but sounded like a curse. "No."

"Then what is wrong?"

"You might say I'm having a difficult time accepting your participation in tomorrow's mission."

"But why?"

His hands closed into fists. "I had another nightmare last night, but this time . . . I saw you die instead of Philip."

She caught the note of grief in his tone, and her heart twisted. She wanted badly to reassure him, wanted to wrap her arms around him and press her cheek against his rigid spine, but she settled for saying softly, "Max, it was only a dream."

"Perhaps so. But what happened today was very real." His hands squeezed reflexively into fists, as if needing to crush something. "Seeing you on the ground so still and unmoving—"

He bit off the words, as if he couldn't bear to contemplate what might have happened had the snake struck her.

"You're worried about me," she said finally.

"Hell, yes, I am worried!" He glanced sharply over his shoulder at her. "I think I have good reason to be, considering the danger you will be putting yourself in."

"The danger is no greater for me than for anyone else—you included."

"And that is supposed to reassure me? I don't want to see you die, Caro! I watched Philip give his life for me, and that image will forever haunt me. I don't think I could live with the memory of your death."

Comprehending where his concern was likely headed, she felt herself stiffen. "You can't possibly be suggesting that I not go?"

Max ran a hand roughly through his hair. "That is exactly what I'm suggesting. I want you to remain behind with Hawk tomorrow where you'll be safe, and allow me to conduct the mission alone."

Caro stared at him in disbelief. "That would never work! You likely would never even be allowed near Isabella. You couldn't ascertain if she was well enough to travel, let alone arrange for her to escape. When Hawk visited the fortress last week, he never laid eyes on Isabella, only heard her name mentioned once. And he found no one who would discuss the rumors about the Spanish lady who had caught their chieftain's eye. I *must* go, Max. I am the only one who can enter the women's quarters."

He shot her a savage glance. "You seem to have little notion of the risks involved. You could be killed if you go."

"I am quite aware of the risks!" Caro retorted, feeling a smoldering knot of emotions crowd her chest.

Max comprehended better than most what they would be facing during their mission. He was a former soldier, a man intimately familiar with danger. She also knew why he felt responsible for her, why he didn't want her death or injury on his conscience. But she couldn't excuse him for demanding she forsake all her principles or abandon her closest friend so she could remain safely behind out of harm's way.

"Damn you, Max," she said in a furious, shaking undertone. "You of all people should understand. I have trained for this for *years*—this is my life's calling. My duty is to keep others safe, and that requires taking risks. Certainly I have no intention of putting my safety above the freedom of my dearest friend."

His angry gaze seared her, but he remained grimly silent.

She went on. "You would never put your safety first, either, I know it. If your positions had been reversed, you would have given your life for your friend Philip."

"That is entirely beside the point."

"That is exactly the point! Why is it acceptable for you to sacrifice for others, but they aren't allowed to make the same sacrifice?"

"I won't let you die, Caro!"

His fierce tone matched his blazing eyes as he spun around, reaching for her. His fingers clamped like bands of steel on her wrists, as if he could compel her to do his bidding with sheer physical power.

With a violent jerk, Caro pulled her arms free of his grasp and clenched her teeth. "Stop this! I won't listen to you!" She was trembling with rage. "You blame yourself for your friend's death, I know that. But I doubt he would have wanted you to punish yourself forever. More likely he would have told you to stop letting tragedy rule you and to move on with your life."

Max snapped his head as if she'd slapped him.

Ignoring the raw pain she saw fill his eyes, Caro continued, seething. "You can't control fate, Max! No one can. I love Isabella more than my own life. If I am killed trying to rescue her, then so be it. The risk is mine to take. *My* choice, not yours. You had best learn to accept that, because I am *not* remaining behind."

Simmering, she turned on her heel and stalked away, leaving Max to stare grimly after her, his angry, despairing gaze boring a hole in her back.

Chapter Fifteen

The dawn sky flushed rose and blue as a score of riders set out from the oasis the next morning.

Nursing her grievance, Caro avoided Max, who merely gave her attire a sharp glance from a distance. She had dressed carefully in a costume designed to fool the Berber chieftain, wearing rich robes and jewelry and cosmetics as befitted her role as slave and concubine to a wealthy lord.

But at Max's grim look, she felt his reservations even more strongly now that she understood the cause. She also realized, to her regret, that their argument last night had only increased the strain and tension between them.

Her heart felt raw and painful, even though her temper still simmered. As they traversed the arid, gloomy waste, however, Caro kept her eyes on the blue mountains that beckoned in the distance and tried to concentrate on the mission ahead.

By noon they reached the first jagged ridge of the Biban mountains. Gaunt masses of cliff rose steeply before them and dipped away to the south, and it was with great care that their little caravan negotiated the entrance.

The going became easier as the day wore on, and less arid as well. By mid-afternoon they were riding through an evergreen forest of holm oak. By the time they reached the treacherous pass that marked the lands of Saful il Taib's tribe, the sun had sunk low in the sky, blanketing the rugged mountains in a golden light.

Hawk remained behind there at the entrance with a half-dozen other Guardians and most of the extra horses, while Max led the rest of the party through the pass and began the descent to the Berber stronghold.

They paused at the last rocky slope to take in the view. The narrow valley below was just as Hawk had described—rich, fertile land terraced with fields of barley and wheat.

Beyond, a massive citadel perched precariously on the side of a mountain. The houses Caro could see appeared to be built on ledges, but the town could be easily defended. Not only did the stronghold have thick walls, but she counted three stone watchtowers as well as massive gates that even cannon would have difficulty penetrating.

Now that they had finally reached their destination, however, a fierce sense of purpose overtook Caro and calmed her nerves. She still felt a dire urgency, but also a renewed focus and intensity, even greater than for any other mission. Isabella was in that fortress, and she would never give up until her friend was safe.

She remembered Max once explaining why he had remained to fight in the war even after losing his close friend: because he intended to defeat the French or die trying. Well, Max would just have to understand that she felt the same way about this mission, Caro thought obdurately. She would succeed or die trying.

When he turned to glance over his shoulder at her,

she met his gaze without flinching. His look scorched her, but she refused to be cowed.

It was Thorne who broke the tension by grinning in anticipation. "Look hearty, me mates," he commanded in a rallying tone. "This is where we earn our paltry pay."

All the Guardians took a collective breath and rode forward, down into the valley.

They were barely halfway across when a horde of Berbers burst from the gates and raced toward them. Wearing black robes and turbans, they brandished swords and rifles as they surged around Max's party.

Caro felt her stomach knot and tried to remember what Hawk had said about the fierce warriors that populated the mountains. The Berbers had lived in Barbary for centuries before the conquering Arabs swept over the face of North Africa, and were known for their vast courage, honesty, hospitality, and good nature.

At the moment they didn't look at all hospitable or even civilized, she thought, eyeing the wicked blades of their long, curved swords. She could admire the way Max remained at ease in the face of their threatening display of athleticism.

Their leader broke from the pack then, and approached Max. Like his other warriors, he was tall, hard, and lean, with fair skin and hair and proud, almost noble features. Under less dangerous circumstances Caro would have even considered him handsome.

"Greetings, my lord Saful," Max said in French with a brief bow.

The Berber chieftain replied in the same language,

although not as fluently. "How is it that you know my name?"

"Your reputation is renowned in Barbary, *sidi*. You are Saful il Taib, leader of the Beni Abbes tribe. I have come a long way to seek you out."

"For what purpose?"

"I hoped you might be so kind as to entertain a request of mine."

Max introduced himself and his good friend Mr. Ryder as sportsmen in search of the famed lions of Barbary. "Perhaps you will permit us to make camp on your land for the night? We have had a long journey."

"Of course," Saful said graciously. "You will all be my guests."

"It will not be necessary," Max qualified, "to accommodate my entire party. I require only my personal servants with me."

He beckoned to Caro and Santos Verra, singling them out. "If someone would show the remainder of my people where to camp . . . ?"

When Saful gave orders to several of his men, Caro felt confident they had safely negotiated the first hurdle.

The Berber chieftain turned his horse then and led them to the stronghold. Max and Ryder rode bedside him, while Caro and Verra followed at a distance. As they passed through the massive gates, she felt the knots in her stomach ease a small measure. The second hurdle.

Being foreigners, they were the object of intense scrutiny in the gathering dusk as crowds of curious Berbers watched their progress through the town. Caro hid her own curiosity and surreptitiously tried to memorize the route they might possibly take for escape shortly before dawn tomorrow. Yet she couldn't help noticing the open, friendly smiles of the women. They were all dressed in colorful tunics, girdled at the waist, and adorned with numerous silver chains and bangles. Berber women didn't veil their faces as Arab and Turkish women did, Caro had been told, and she could clearly see the elaborate tattoos they sported.

Saful's house was built of baked clay and hewn rock, and was quite large, as befitted his position as chieftain. Verra was left at the entrance to see to the horses, while Max and Ryder and Caro followed Saful through an arched portal and into a room that was no doubt used for the chieftain's audiences. It was luxuriously furnished with thick carpets and cushions and several small low tables, lit with olive oil lamps, and warmed by a charcoal brazier.

Lord Saful handed his sword to a male attendant, but Caro noted that he still wore a curved dagger at his belt. When he invited his guests to sit, Caro silently settled on a cushion behind Max.

Shortly they were served small glasses of mint tea, which she found hot and sweet and delicious.

The conversation flowed politely for a time. At Saful's courteous inquiry, Max recounted a fabricated tale of his recent travels from the coast. When finally their host probed their reason for coming to this specific area, Max explained his desire for the best hunting and his wish for a guide to help locate lions that would provide sufficient challenge for their skills. Then Ryder described the new make of rifles they had brought as inducement.

Saful's attention was clearly caught.

"Would you care to examine a rifle?" Max asked.

"Yes, indeed."

"If you will permit me, *sidi,*" Ryder offered, "I will fetch one from my saddle scabbard to show you."

He left and returned a few moments later. Saful took the weapon with great interest.

After showing the rifle to several of his warriors, Saful looked up. "I should like to fire this rifle to see its accuracy for myself."

"Of course," Max said easily, "but night has fallen. Would you not prefer to wait until daylight when you can see your target?"

"That will not be necessary. Hitting a target in the darkness will be a good test."

To Caro's surprise, the men all exited the room, leaving her alone with merely the women servants.

The men were gone for the better part of half an hour, which began to raise her anxiety. When they returned, however, she could tell from the Berbers' expressions that the test of the rifle had proved a success. But then they began the negotiations for a guide.

In the ensuing interval, Caro could scarcely contain her impatience, for she was eager to find Isabella.

Max and his host finally settled on fifteen rifles, and Saful seemed well satisfied—enough to recall his duty to his guests.

"I think perhaps you would prefer to retire to your rooms to refresh yourselves before dining, yes?"

"It would be good to wash the dust off," Max replied. With his head, he indicated Caro behind him. "If you could find accommodations for my woman as well?"

Caro felt the speculative glance that Saful sent her,

but she kept her gaze lowered and avoided giving any indication that she had understood.

"She doesn't know much French," Max added. "Only Portuguese."

"My servants will see to her comfort in the women's quarters," Saful said, raising an imperious hand to summon one of the older Berber women.

Max kept his tone easy when he interjected, "I will want her to come to my rooms later, you understand."

This time Saful's perusal of Caro was purely masculine. "She has an uncommon beauty. I wonder if you would be interested in selling her?"

It was all Caro could do to keep her expression from showing her startlement. In her experience, few men had ever remarked on her beauty. Certainly none had ever offered to purchase her. She could only attribute her current appeal to the kohl she'd used to darken her eyes and the carmine that rouged her cheeks and lips.

She heard the amusement in Max's voice when he responded. "I doubt she would please you, *sidi*. She has yet to learn proper submissiveness, and has the stinging tongue of an adder."

"Then you would do well to sell her. I am fond of spirit in a woman and would appreciate those very qualities you decry."

When Max turned to look over his shoulder at Caro, his smug look made her want to hit him.

"Even so," he said regretfully, "she is not for sale. I expect you have women with whom you are loath to part."

Giving a brief smile, Saful nodded in agreement.

Max spoke a few words of Portuguese then, and

told Caro to follow the Berber woman. As she rose from the cushions, she heard Max's query:

"If I may be permitted to ask, my lord Saful, how is it that you speak such excellent French?"

She saw Saful flash a smile that was purely male and heard his answer as she left the room. "For many years I enjoyed the pleasurable services of a French concubine. . . ."

Caro shrugged off her exasperation with Max as she followed the servant through the house, her feeling of hope swelling with every step. With luck she would see Isabella shortly.

The women's quarters were located at the rear of the house, and Caro could hear the pleasant sound of feminine laughter as she entered the common living area.

She spied her friend at once—reclining on a divan, chatting in low, melodious French to a group of young Berber women who sat around her on cushions.

Isabella appeared to be holding court, which wasn't at all surprising, since she possessed an indefinable quality that drew people, especially men, to her like a magnet. Half Spanish, half English, Isabella was a sultry beauty with jet hair and sparkling black eyes, although well past her fortieth year. Her allure owed as much to her earthy vivacity and joie de vivre as her striking features and figure.

If the Berber chieftain liked spirit in a woman, Caro thought wryly, then he must be completely enamored of Isabella.

For an instant Caro paused, drinking in the sight of her beloved friend. It was all she could do not to rush across the room to embrace her, or to let her relief and jubilation show.

Just then Isabella looked up and gave a start as she spied Caro. But she covered it up well and went on with another tale that had the women laughing.

Caro forcibly tore her gaze away and followed the servant to a private chamber, where she washed and refreshed herself. With great discipline, she waited another endless few minutes before returning to the common room, where she was led to a corner and instructed by pantomime to sit.

Obeying, Caro settled upon a cushion and accepted a goblet of fruit juice, but she was so anxious to get on with her task, she could not have said what she tasted.

She sipped her drink slowly and pretended an interest in the trickling fountain in the center of the room. After a time, Isabella rose gracefully and crossed to her. Settling on an adjacent cushion, she offered Caro a wooden bowl of figs, oranges, and dates.

Accepting politely, Caro peeled an orange and tried to contain her joy as she waited for her friend to take the lead.

"It is safe to speak Spanish," Isabella said in a tone too low to be heard over the fountain's music and the women's chatter. "Some of them know a little French, for I have entertained myself teaching them."

"They won't be suspicious to see you talking to me?"

"No. They all know that I am eager for word of the outside world and won't think it strange that I would question you. We have a few moments together."

"You can't know how worried I have been," Caro said fervently. "Are you all right?"

Isabella smiled archly. "Indeed I do know, my love,

for I realize how I would feel if this had happened to you. Perhaps now you can understand the agonies I suffer each time you fly off on one of your missions."

Caro refrained from protesting that it was not the same thing. "You look well, Isabella. You weren't treated harshly?" she asked instead.

"Not at all. I have been treated like a princess, albeit a captive one. I am in excellent health and relatively good spirits—since I never doubted the Guardians would come for me. Indeed, I decided I might as well make the most of my captivity. It has been an . . . adventure."

"And your captor, Lord Saful?"

"Thankfully he is quite generous and kind." Her mouth formed a small, secretive smile. "To say nothing of a wonderful lover. That facet has been enjoyable, I must confess. Had we met under other circumstances, if our cultures were not so different, I even might consider taking him for my fourth husband."

At Caro's frown, Isabella's black eyes laughed wickedly. "Alas, Lord Saful has two wives already, and I am not inclined to share. Those ladies will doubtless be glad to see the last of me. I trust you are here to rescue me?"

It was Caro's turn to smile. "You don't believe we would come all this way simply for sport?"

Quickly then, she told Isabella about their plan. They had chosen four a.m. to slip stealthily out of the house, in order to avoid any early risers. They would wait in the stables, however, and delay the explosion until a half hour before dawn, when they would make their way through the stronghold to the gates. The visibility would still be poor then, but the sky would grow light enough by the time they reached the nearest mountain pass. It would be suicidal to flee through the treacherous terrain in the dark, Caro explained.

To Caro's relief, Isabella saw no impediments to the plan.

"What of Lord Saful?" Caro asked. "Is there any danger that you will be summoned to his rooms tonight?"

"No, not while my courses are flowing. And even if it should happen, I am not without persuasive skills of my own. I can arrange to return here in good time." She pursed her lips. "I do believe I will miss Saful. Perhaps I will write him a note to be discovered after I am gone, inviting him to come to Cyrene to visit me."

Caro shook her head in ironic amusement. Yet it wasn't impossible that the Berber chieftain would travel all the way to Cyrene to pursue his escaped captive. Her chief concern, however, was focused on the next twelve hours.

She went over a few more pertinent details with Isabella, laying out the exact schedule, finally adding, "It is important that my baggage be brought here so that we will have the proper disguises."

"I will see to it," Isabella said with total confidence. "I have a room all to myself, and I will demand that you be brought there to keep me company. And I will also ensure that we are well fed, so that we may endure a swift journey across the mountains. We cannot be certain when we will next have a decent meal, you know."

Caro even laughed this time. Considering how healthy Isabella's appetite was, it was a wonder she wasn't as plump as a roasting hen. Bella's next comment, however, nearly made Caro choke.

"So tell me about this Mr. Leighton, my love," she said without warning.

Caro felt her cheeks flush under her friend's perceptive gaze, and she quickly took a sip of her fruit juice to hide her dismay. Evidently her feelings for Max were too transparent.

"There is nothing much more to tell," she lied. "He is simply a close friend of Thorne's and has been invited to become a permanent member of the Guardians."

"Very well, I won't pry," Isabella said archly. "But I should very much like to meet this man if he can make you blush like a shy virgin."

This time Caro did choke as her juice slid down the wrong way.

The last three days had been hell, Max conceded as he sat drinking strong black coffee at the conclusion of the evening meal. Yet he tried to keep the scowl from his face so as not to offend their Berber host.

The dishes had been plentiful and delicious, starting with a rich lentil soup, followed by squabs, roasted chicken stuffed with olives, a savory meat pie, and as usual, couscous. Then barley bread and honey for dessert.

Thankfully Ryder had kept up a steady conversation with the Berber chieftain, for Max's own thoughts were all centered on the nether regions of the house, wondering if Caro had found Lady Isabella, and if the scheme they'd planned would succeed.

In truth, if he was honest, his thoughts had never strayed from Caro for a single waking moment during the entire journey from Cyrene. The torment of being near her but unable to touch made his body burn, but even more, he missed the sweetness of her smile.

Her withdrawal was understandable, of course. He had earned both her disappointment and her anger by allowing his dark fears for her to drive him.

He couldn't help himself, though. He'd suffered that same terrible nightmare about Caro last night, where she was killed right before his eyes, trying to save him. He'd gathered her bleeding body desperately against him, willing her to cling to life, to no avail. A primal grief welled inside him, and he felt shattered yet at the same time filled with a frenzied rage. He threw back his head and howled his agony even as scalding tears blinded him.

Remembering that dark vision now, Max felt a cold sweat break over him. He wanted only to protect Caro, to shield her from harm. He didn't doubt her courage or conviction or abilities in the least. She was the most capable, courageous woman he had ever met. But she had no control over fate.

Nor did he. He would do everything in his power to make their mission succeed, to ensure that his nightmare never came to pass. But no matter how he vowed to protect her, he couldn't guarantee her safety. She could be hurt or even killed, and the thought tore at his insides.

Even now his stomach was tight with nerves. Still, he had overstepped the bounds, Max knew. He had no right to ask her to abandon her closest friend.

He owed Caro an apology for asking her to remain behind, although he doubted she was in any mood to listen to him.

Max felt his jaw tighten. The worst of it was, he

knew she was right. There were times when taking risks was imperative, despite the possible cost.

But he would have to keep reminding himself of that truth until their mission had ended and she was safe.

Moreover, if they were to succeed tonight, he had to play his assumed role to the hilt.

Forcing himself to attend to the conversation with their Berber host, Max refrained from glancing at his pocket watch. Yet he counted the minutes until he could retire to his rooms and summon Caro to him.

Chapter Sixteen

The hour was late when the dinner broke up and a servant showed the guests to their rooms. As Max walked the dark, quiet corridors, he concluded that much of the household was already asleep, which should prove fortuitous when the time came to depart.

Santos Verra was already present in Max's room, pretending to perform the duties of a valet. Ryder, after examining his own nearby sleeping quarters, joined them.

"That door," Verra murmured as he pointed to the far wall, "leads to an outer courtyard."

Max and Ryder went outside on the pretext of smoking cigars, to judge the height and scalability of the walls, then returned to await Caro's arrival.

When she entered a half hour later, her eyes were shining. She didn't have to say a word for Max to know she had seen Isabella and that the news was good.

Verra broke into a broad grin. "The señora is well?"

"Yes," Caro replied, her relief evident in her smile. "But she is eager to be free."

Keeping her voice low to prevent being overheard by any curious ears, Caro related the details of her meeting and that Isabella foresaw no difficulty with the arrangements.

"Then we will proceed as planned," Max said. "Is everything ready in the stables?" he asked Verra.

"*Si.* The gunpowder is stored there, awaiting Ryder. And I will sleep there with the horses until it is time to drug them."

"I don't think Saful suspects us," Ryder added. "Leighton charmed our host well enough to put him in a congenial mood."

Max could have refuted that remark, since Ryder had carried the burden of disarming the Berber chieftain, but he said merely, "It helped that the rifles were such a new make." He glanced from Verra to Ryder. "You both know what to do?"

"Of course."

They all checked the time on their watches, and a short while later, Ryder and Verra left.

When the door closed behind them, Max focused on Caro, his gaze skimming her face. This was the first time they'd been alone together since their argument.

She must have had the same awareness, since her expression instantly grew cool.

"I am relieved you found Lady Isabella well," he said into the silence.

"So am I. Now I'm just anxious for this night to be over."

As if eager to be away from Max also, Caro moved toward the door. She had one hand on the latch when he spoke up.

"You cannot go just yet."

Caro halted in her tracks. "Why not?" The question was defiant.

"Because it would make Saful suspicious. In order to make our pretense look real, you must remain with me at least a few hours. He thinks I summoned you here to make love to you."

Her shoulders stiffening, she retorted in a tight voice. "Very well. I will stay for a while longer."

Not looking at Max, she turned and began fitfully circling the room. Occasionally he could hear the jangle of the elaborate gold and silver jewelry she wore at her throat and wrists.

Max went over to the low table in one corner and poured himself a cup of fig brandy. "I also want to keep you near me for your own protection," he added casually. "Saful was eyeing you covetously tonight, and I don't want to take the chance he might abuse his position as host by claiming you for his own."

Caro paused to cast him a sharp glance.

"Saful has excellent taste in women, I'll give him that," Max remarked.

"I don't need your empty flattery."

"It is hardly empty, my lovely witch. Those cosmetics you're wearing give you a mysterious allure that any healthy, warm-blooded man would appreciate. Trust me, Saful wants you for himself."

Caro shook her head scornfully and resumed her pacing, but Max remembered the lustful way the Berber chieftain had eyed her earlier. Possessiveness surged through him—the primal male instinct to fight for his woman, the wild need to mark her indelibly as his.

"I haven't had a chance to apologize for last night," he said finally.

Her glance skewered him. "Then you admit you were wrong to ask me to abandon my friend?"

"I hardly think it wrong to be concerned for you."

"It *is* wrong if it comes at the expense of one's principles!" Caro declared.

Max repressed a wry smile. "True. What will it take for you to forgive me?"

"Isabella going free," she snapped. "And true sincerity on your part. You don't seem in the least contrite."

He *was* contrite, but she seemed determined to maintain her fierce mood. He took a sip of brandy while he watched her restless movements, noting the graceful way her hips swayed beneath her robes.

He felt himself grow hard.

"Do you intend to pace the floor all night?"

"Yes. I couldn't possibly sleep."

"Who said anything about sleep? I know of a much more pleasurable way to pass the time."

He glanced pointedly at the bed. Typically Arabs slept on mats of painted rushes covered with carpets, but this bed was of Berber design—about two feet high, made from ropes and spread with quilts and cushions of colored silk.

"You cannot be serious," Caro said, her caustic tone unbelieving.

"Entirely serious. We have a long night ahead of us. And making love will take your mind off your fretting."

"I assure you, I don't need distracting."

"But perhaps I do."

"Your needs hardly concern me at the moment!"

Max offered her a slow smile designed to taunt. "But I am your lord and master, or have you forgotten? You were brought to my room to serve me. I think you should start by undressing me."

Caro sent him a scathing glance. "You are perfectly capable of undressing yourself."

"But it wouldn't be nearly as enjoyable."

When fire flashed in her eyes, Max recalled what Saful had said about preferring spirited women as lovers, and he found himself in perfect agreement.

Caro was certainly no meek-mannered, docile female. And the way she was appraising him—her eyes fairly shooting sparks—made desire curl, hot and intense, in his loins.

Refusing to respond to his provocation, however, Caro moved over to the window and opened the shutter to stare out at the dark courtyard beyond.

Her disdain was a blatant challenge that sent fierce need spiking through Max's body.

He wanted her. Wanted to lose himself in her wild sweetness, in the taste, the smell, the feel of her. He wanted to feel her shudder around his hardness, feel her shattering release when he exploded inside her.

Even more than carnal need, though, he wanted the physical closeness that passion could bring. Making love to Caro, being deep inside her, joined to her in the most intimate way possible, would reassure him that she was warm and alive and safe. Perhaps it might even help him forget the disquieting realization that this could be their last time together.

With deliberation, Max moved around the room, snuffing out all the oil lamps but one, leaving a muted, golden glow. He sat on the bed to draw off his boots, then stood to strip off his clothing. From Caro's sudden tenseness, he knew she was aware of what he was doing. Finally naked, he crossed to stand behind her.

She stood very still when he reached up to push the shutter closed, locking out the cool night air and giving them privacy once more. And when he pressed his lips against her hair, she went rigid.

Slipping his arms around her slim waist from behind, Max raised his hands to cup her breasts beneath her robes. As he found the tight buds of her nipples, his fingers brushed the precious metal of her jewelry—a half-dozen necklaces of Moorish design.

"It has been far too long, angel," he murmured, hearing his voice rough with need.

When she shuddered, he knew she felt the same fiery heat that was claiming him.

"Have you missed this as much as I have?"

"No . . . not at all," she replied, yet without great conviction.

"Then why is your breath so shallow? Why are your nipples so hard and eager?"

She didn't reply.

"I think you want this as much as I do."

"Max . . ."

"I know your body, Caro. I know how to make you wild."

Slowly he raised the hem of her robes to her hips, baring the soft curves of her buttocks, and pressed his swollen phallus against her, letting her feel his fierce arousal. Her sharp intake of breath was proof of her longing.

He kept his voice low, sensual, while resting the heavy ridge of his cock in the cleft of her bottom. "Let me make you wild, sweeting. Let me use my tongue, my hands, my heat. I'll kiss you all over your beautiful, silken skin. . . . I'll make you burn, flame at my touch."

A current of desire sizzled between them.

Max slid one hand around her middle then, to stroke the dusky curls crowning her thighs, making Caro arch instinctively against the suggestive pressure. She was trying to resist him, Max knew, but the soft moan she gave told him more than words that she was losing the battle with herself.

Keeping one hand between her thighs, he turned her so that her back was to the wall. Caro stared up at him, moistening her lips nervously with the tip of her tongue. It was an erotic gesture, for he could well remember those same luscious lips attending him, welcoming his cock into her open mouth, suckling and arousing him as he'd taught her.

Hunger, raw and primitive, streaked through him. But along with hunger, he felt the pounding need to pleasure her, to possess her, to please her. He wanted her writhing. He wanted her passionate, begging for what he burned to give.

Suddenly Max was so hot, he thought he might explode just touching her. Yet he forced himself to go slowly. When he was through arousing her, she would be pleading for him to fill her.

With his free hand, he captured one of the necklaces she wore—a string of embossed silver spheres—and drew it over her head, to her obvious surprise. Pushing her robes higher to bare her trembling white belly, he let the delicate strand of beads glide over her skin to dangle provocatively between her thighs. He heard Caro's strangled gasp.

When he went down on one knee before her, he caught her scent and felt his loins throb, yet he was more aroused by the erotic sight of her: the glinting silver balls nestling in the curls of her femininity, caressing the dewy pink lips of her sex.

His fingers lightly stroking between her pale thighs, he urged her legs to part for him. Ripe and perfect, her body opened to his heated gaze.

Then, slowly, he slid the beaded necklace over her silky female cleft, making her quiver.

"Stand perfectly still," he commanded, again drawing the strand over her heated flesh.

She jerked against the slithering kiss of the beads.

"I told you to remain still," Max admonished.

"I don't know . . . if I can."

"You must. I intend to pleasure you first. Then I mean to get deep inside you and listen to you moan."

His sensual warning sent a shaft of desire spreading through Caro's senses, echoing the throbbing between her legs.

She wanted to protest, yet to her dismay, she couldn't bring herself to push him away. Every nerve in her body was focused on the enchanting drift of silver balls that were taunting and arousing her. She could feel her own sexual need pulling with deep, warm contractions in the core of her feminine center.

When Max paused to twine one end of the necklace around his fingers, she couldn't imagine what he intended. She watched, puzzled, as he manipulated a large embossed bead between the moist lips of her sex.

She tried not to gasp at the searing jolt.

"What are you doing?" she breathlessly demanded.

"Appeasing your craving for carnal bliss." He pushed another silver sphere upward, past her slick, velvety folds.

"I have no craving," she lied.

"You will, I promise you."

Caro couldn't deny the truth of his prediction. Already the pulsing between her legs was intense, her senses inflamed. When Max methodically inserted more beads deep inside her, she shuddered with shocked delight.

"How does this feel?" he queried, his tone provocative.

She was too aroused to answer. She felt the cool metal warming within her body, felt her inner muscles clench helplessly around the silver balls suspended inside her. Then gently, ruthlessly, slowly, Max made her absorb several more inches of necklace, till he finally reached the end.

Caro tried to remain still, for the slightest motion stirred the lodged spheres, but she couldn't possibly manage it.

"What did I tell you?" Max warned when her hips squirmed. "You have to obey me, or I won't appease your craving."

Gritting her teeth, Caro leaned back against the wall, bracing herself with her palms.

It was fortunate she had a solid surface to support her, since Max started removing the nubby beads with deliberate slowness, withdrawing them one at a time.

The tantalizing vibrations strummed through her as each sphere slid free; every intimate caress was maddening.

"You're very hot, aren't you?" Max taunted. "But I can make you hotter."

She was already burning. An uncontrollable excitement possessed her body at the riveting pleasure, making her melt, making her weak limbs shake.

"You seem distraught, angel. I think you need soothing."

For a moment Caro thought he meant to take pity on her. But then Max leaned forward, the heat of his breath searing her. Caro trembled at his brazen intimacy, but she was incapable of defending against her longing.

With infinite delicacy, he ran his tongue over the bud of her sex as he pulled another sphere free.

It was sweet agony. The slow, deliberate drag of the necklace against her moist, sensitive flesh. The wet suction of his mouth. The languid strokes of his tongue.

The sensation was overwhelming.

At the next heated lick, reason fled. Too weak to support herself, Caro reached out helplessly to clutch Max's shoulders. She was wildly aware of his dark head between her spread thighs and the wanton way it made her feel.

His lips burned hot against her as another bead slid free. She whimpered at the blatant carnality of it. Unconsciously her fingers twisted in the waving thickness of his raven hair, while her pelvis surged forward to meet his feasting mouth.

His consummate skill was driving her mad. He knew exactly how to touch her, how to create an exquisite pressure that left her craving more, dying for more. His tongue played over her, rolling against the taut, erectile nub of her sex, while the beads continued to fall.

Half swooning from the staggering pleasure, Caro arched her back, seeking surcease.

"You're primed for climax, aren't you?"

She was whimpering now, unable to reply.

"Are you ready to come, sweeting?" He kissed her again, his lips suckling her swollen, plump flesh. "You *sound* ready."

She *was* ready. The stabbing pleasure was too much to bear. Fountains of fire leapt from his mouth into her flesh, making her cry out. She exploded an instant later, his scorching mouth forcing jolt after tormenting jolt from her.

Her body quaking with pulsating release, Caro sagged weakly against the wall.

Yet Max wasn't finished with her. He was still suckling her while she trembled with orgasmic fever, holding her body in thrall. He milked her senses for every last ounce of passion as he drew the final spheres of the necklace from their secret hiding place. . . .

The next moment another climax began, surging after the first, a spasm so savage and intense, so prolonged, she screamed.

The wild, turbulent seizure left her gasping.

It was a long, long moment before she even began to recover her dazed senses.

Panting softly, Caro gazed down at Max.

He was looking up at her, so she could see the fierce glitter in his eyes, the wetness of his mouth as it curled in a gratified smile.

He brushed one last kiss against her quivering flesh, then rose.

To her utter surprise, he turned and casually walked away, swinging the beaded necklace from one finger. Still dazed, Caro watched the muscles in his bare, tanned back coil and slide under satiny skin, his hard buttocks flexing.

Lowering himself to sit on the edge of the bed, Max

draped her silver necklace over his jutting manhood. Then he leaned back, bracing himself on his elbows, the length of him splendidly naked, utterly masculine, dangerously sensual.

"Now it's your turn to service me," he declared. "Take off your clothes. I want you naked."

Caro stiffened at his haughty tone. Even if he was deliberately provoking her with his lord-and-master affectation in order to distract her, she wouldn't suffer being his slave. "I have no intention of obeying you."

"I'm certain you will."

"How can you be so confident?"

"Because you want me inside you. You'll find my cock much more satisfying than your necklace."

That much was true, she had no doubt.

When she continued to defy him, his blue eyes ensnared her with a steady gaze. "I am waiting."

Caro felt herself weakening. It mattered not a whit that she was still angry with Max. Or that he was well aware of the potent sexual power he held over her, the devastating charm that could so easily breach her defenses. The way he was looking at her was enough to shake her resistance.

Just now his eyes were so intense, so hot, she felt the invading heat burn right through her clothing to the bare flesh underneath.

"Is this your notion of proper submissiveness?" he demanded. "You're my slave. It is your duty to cater to my sexual wishes."

His arrogant air of command aggravated her so intensely, Caro almost told him to go to the devil. But her blood was up and she was spoiling for a fight.

And the simple truth was, she didn't want to face the

dawn without knowing Max's passion once more. For a short while she wanted to pretend that danger didn't exist. She wanted to make him forget his nightmares—and her own: the fear that they might fail.

When slowly she reached up to remove her robes, his mouth curved in a sardonic smile at her capitulation. Caro gritted her teeth, resolving to have her revenge.

She made a show of undressing slowly, letting her robes drop to the floor. She left on her necklaces, though, aware of the sensuous feel of the gold and silver curling around her bare breasts.

Max's eyes sparked at her nudity, but his expression remained impassive. "Come here," he commanded.

Moving to stand before him, she pointedly gazed down at his naked arousal. His dark, pulsing shaft, exquisitely thick and long, thrust proudly out from his sleek loins. The sight was so rawly masculine that it made her stomach quiver. Even more erotic was his adornment: the contrast of the delicate silver spheres looped around his hard flesh only compounded the hunger surging through her.

"You want me, don't you." It wasn't a question, and his tone was faintly taunting.

Caro shivered with insatiable longing. "Yes."

"Yes, what, slave?"

"Yes . . . master."

"Very good. You're learning. Let's see now how skilled you are at pleasuring a man."

He sat up then and drew her between his spread thighs. He was all warm, taut muscle against her softness, and Caro inhaled sharply, feeling the rigid, heated length of his sex brand her like searing steel.

When he reached up to fondle her breasts, she could feel the peaks hardening and thrusting out to seek his touch, could feel her nipples throb against his palms.

Heat flared through Caro as she watched his dark hands play over her pale skin . . . but then she deliberately pushed him away.

"You said I was to service you, master." She kept her tone cool, making it sound more like a threat.

"So I did," he replied casually.

She knew, however, that Max was not quite as unaffected as he pretended. His eyes were like heated sapphires, and his gaze never left her as he lay back among the cushions, her beaded necklace still adorning his loins.

Joining him on the low bed, Caro knelt beside him, reaching out to caress the hard, velvety smooth flesh of his erection. His arousal was enormous, throbbing, burning hot, yet she knew from experience that Max could be aroused further. And she was determined to torment him the same way he had done to her.

With a sweetly taunting smile, she stroked his inner thighs slowly, then let her hand slide under his heavy testicles. She saw his phallus jerk hungrily, a tear of moisture weeping from the swollen tip. When she squeezed gently, Max drew in a sharp breath, but then she wrapped another loop of the silver necklace around him, and his breathing faltered altogether.

Her own hunger overwhelming, she bent over him, tasting the tip of his rigid phallus as she tightened the strand of silver around the base.

He sucked in a harsher breath. "Merciful God," he rasped, his voice heavy with desire.

She could imagine the vivid sensations he was

feeling—the friction of the beads rubbing along his entire length as she increased and loosened the pressure.

For long moments she went on attending him, until suddenly Max made a sound in his throat, a low growl. When he pushed her up, Caro narrowed her eyes at him in surprise.

"Not just your mouth. I want you as aroused as I am." At her puzzled look, Max glanced down at her loins. "Use your own wetness to make me harder," he ordered. "Stroke your fingers between your thighs."

When Caro obliged, she felt the dampness of her own need. She was dripping wet for him, aching for him. In fact, her whole body throbbed. Her pulse was reckless, her skin oversensitive, her breasts tight and feverish.

"Now touch me."

His raw-silk voice seemed to stroke her senses and played havoc with her desire for revenge. Fighting her yearning, she let her slick fingers glide up and down his magnificent member till his own flesh was glistening.

At her erotic caresses, Max arched his back involuntarily and groaned, his eyes bright with fire. As if unable to wait any longer, he pulled the beads off his arousal and tossed them to the floor.

"Now," he said, his voice ragged, "mount me."

Despite her resolve to torture him, she had no wish to refuse. The way he looked at her made her feel utterly desirable.

Caught by his brilliant, intent gaze, she eased one leg over his narrow hips and sank down on him, gasping in pleasure as the huge, hard shaft slid relentlessly between her silken walls. It was exquisite after such long torment to feel him so enormous and hard and fiery hot, filling her to bursting—yet she needed more.

She needed to feel pulses of life flowing between them.

Purposely giving no thought to sponges or any other barrier between them, Caro captured Max's wrists and pushed his arms over his head, pinning him down with her hands as she stretched out over him. The jewelry around her neck jangled faintly as it splayed over his chest.

She saw surprise darken his eyes as she slowly began to move her hips.

Max willingly let her have her way, surrendering to her evident need for control. It was several moments, though, before he became aware of the change that had come over Caro. She was no longer fighting him or herself, no longer taunting him.

Instead, her lovely face was set and intense, her eyes tormented.

With every rasp of her necklace-adorned breasts on his chest, every soft surge of her thighs, her passion became more feverish. Her hips began to move faster, with more urgency, her rhythm almost violent.

Bending, she kissed him wildly, and in a dazed corner of his mind, Max thought he understood her fierceness. The danger they faced had unleashed something dark and primal in her, and she was using their joining to express what she would never allow herself to say in words.

He found himself caught up in her savage intensity. When Caro shuddered convulsively, each tremor burned through him.

She was sobbing by the time she pushed herself up

and threw her head back. And when she shattered, her cry stabbed into his soul.

Swept up in her storm, Max clutched desperately at her as a matching cry tore from him, a deep, raw sound that echoed the tumult pounding through his body.

In the end Caro collapsed upon him, her hair a cloud of waves around them. Max lay there, stunned, feeling her shivers, the aftershocks of passion and craving and release mingled with something deeper. Fear.

She might be unwilling or unable to admit it, but she feared losing him, possibly as much as he feared losing her.

When Caro finally moved again, she only wrapped her arms more tightly around him and buried her face in the curve of his neck, seeking comfort in a wordless plea.

His heart heavy, Max felt the same foreboding. And the same longing. To cling to the night, to deny the dawn. To somehow escape the danger that tomorrow would bring, yet still hold to the merciless commitment that duty and honor demanded.

Chapter Seventeen

At half-past three, in the deepest hours of night, Caro left Max to return to the women's quarters. They had made love twice more before resting. Not sleeping. Merely holding each other, tangled together, breaths mingling, drawing strength from each other.

No doubt it had been shameful for her to seek pleasure with Max under such dire circumstances, Caro reflected, but she felt no sense of guilt. She had needed his passion, needed the courage she derived from simply being with him, in order to face what lay ahead.

On the way through the dark house, she met only one guard, which encouraged her. The women's quarters were silent, for all its occupants seemed to be slumbering.

All but Isabella. Her friend was wide-awake when Caro stealthily entered her room.

Wordlessly they dressed in black robes and turbans and girded their waists with daggers and primed pistols, before slipping into the corridor where Max awaited them.

He was just bending over the body of the guard, Caro saw.

Behind her, Isabella faltered, lifting shocked eyes to Max.

"He isn't dead," he murmured. "Merely unconscious."

He propped the guard up in a sitting position so he appeared to have fallen asleep.

"This way, my lady," Max added quietly.

Isabella showed no further hesitation as she followed Max through the corridors to his rooms. Caro remained behind her, protecting her back, until they reached the courtyard outside.

The sunken moon had nearly disappeared, and in the cool night, pale light illuminated the stone wall at the rear.

Max led them directly to an apricot tree that grew near the wall and hoisted Caro into the limbs first.

She crawled out along the sturdiest branch, then swung down to drop lightly to the ground. She found herself in a narrow alleyway. Turning, she stretched her arms up to assist Isabella, grasping her friend's waist and lowering her carefully.

When Max followed the next moment, Caro released the pent-up breath she'd been holding.

Max gestured to his right, indicating the direction they were to take. Then he moved swiftly, unerringly along the dim alleyway, the two women close on his heels.

Upon attaining their rendezvous point, he held up a hand, silently ordering them to wait while he slipped through the door. Several taut seconds passed before Max returned to usher them into the dark stables.

Caro's heart jumped when a shadow appeared in front of her, and her hand reflexively went to her dagger. But it was only Santos Verra, she saw in the faint moonlight that filtered in through a window.

Pressing one finger to his lips, the Spaniard pointed to a near corner. There were two figures lying on pallets—Berber grooms, evidently sleeping soundly.

When Caro raised an eyebrow in query, Verra nodded, acknowledging that he had managed to drug the grooms. Then, his white teeth flashing in the dim light, he turned to Isabella and took her slender hands in his strong ones.

With a bow, he kissed her fingers gallantly. The lady acknowledged his joy with a regal smile before pressing her palm against his swarthy cheek as an admission of her fervent gratitude.

"Now we wait," Max murmured with barely a breath of sound.

The Spaniard showed them to a stall near the center, where they would remain hidden until it was time to leave. It came as no surprise to Caro that Saful's stables were as magnificent as his house. Berbers reportedly prized their horses and pampered them far more than their own children.

All but a few of the horses were lying down, pleasantly snoozing, she saw. Four that had not been drugged were already saddled in preparation for a swift departure.

Caro settled in a comfortable pile of straw next to Isabella and took her hand, but she knew it was as much for her own reassurance as for her friend's. She could hear the quiet snuffling of the horses and the snores of the Berber grooms above the beating of her heart.

They waited for over an hour before Verra began bridling their horses. He had wrapped the animals' hooves with cloths to muffle the sound, so when they mounted and crept out of the stables, they made little noise that would alert the Berbers to their escape. Bracing for a confrontation, however, Max had drawn his saber.

Both Verra and Caro were also armed with sabers, since a blade was more useful in close quarters and could be wielded repeatedly, unlike a pistol or rifle that had to be reloaded after a single shot. A blade was less lethal than a gun as well, and they didn't intend to kill their Berber hosts unless given no other choice.

Caro held her breath as they rode through the dark, silent streets, but there were no sudden cries of alarm to indicate they had been spied. When Max halted a hundred yards from the gates, she saw no sentries on the walls. Ryder most likely had disabled the guards as planned. And the huge wooden beam that should have barred the gate had been removed so that the massive doors hung open a mere crack.

Caro silently blessed Ryder for his proficiency, and blessed him again a few minutes later when the explosion came.

Their horses all startled at the powerful boom, and Isabella had difficulty controlling her mount, who clearly wanted to bolt back to his stable. Fortunately Caro caught the panicked animal's rein as it tried to flee past her.

"Keep close," Max ordered as he rode for the gate.

Willingly obeying, Caro spurred her mount to follow him, pulling Isabella's along in her wake.

Max had already opened the gate when she reached it. He went first, his saber raised in anticipation of trouble.

Swiftly glancing behind her, Caro saw that flames

had lit up the southern sky. And she saw movement in the streets as the Berbers were rudely roused from their beds.

Verra, at the rear of their little party, turned to defend the gate while the ladies escaped. By now Isabella had regained command of her horse, and she rode through, with Caro immediately following.

A group of mounted horsemen awaited them outside the stronghold in the shadows of the wall.

Thorne, leading a spare horse, was the first to greet them. "Welcome, my lady Isabella. A great pleasure to see you, as always."

Hearing the high-spirited humor in his voice, Caro could tell that Thorne was enjoying himself. But his attention quickly shifted to Max, as if waiting for orders.

"We will ride ahead with Lady Isabella," Max confirmed, "while you wait here for Ryder."

"Very well." Thorne's tone turned deadly serious. "But keep her ladyship safe, will you?"

Max glanced at Caro, locking gazes with her. He was responsible for escorting Isabella from here, since with his experience he could best protect her if it came to a real battle. But he would far rather keep Caro safe.

"He will," was all Caro said, yet he read her unspoken plea as clearly as if she had said every word aloud: *I trust you with Isabella's life. Upon your honor, keep her safe as you would me.*

Her silent entreaty made Max renew his vow to succeed. Nodding brusquely, he edged his horse closer to Isabella's.

At just that moment a black-robed figure burst through the gate. When he ran straight for the spare horse, Max realized the man was Ryder.

And that he had been followed.

Several Berbers rushed through the gates after Ryder, swords raised in an attempt to prevent his escape. They wore no turbans or boots, yet even in their nightclothes, they seemed prepared to fight to the death.

In the dim light of the gathering dawn, Max thought he recognized Saful in the lead. Evidently the warlord hadn't been fooled by the diversion for long.

When the Berbers charged the group of rescuers, Max responded to the danger out of sheer reflex. Keeping Isabella safely behind him, he wielded his saber expertly, holding off the assault with grim determination.

The familiar sounds of clashing blades sent blood surging hotly in his veins, and in a small part of his mind, he realized that at least one concern had been unfounded: When the time came to fight, his training and his instincts took over, his long years as a cavalry officer standing him in good stead.

Caro had less training in hand-to-hand combat, though. Out of the corner of his eye, Max saw that she had insinuated her horse between Ryder and the attackers, trying to give her colleague time to mount as she wielded her own saber against the fierce Berbers.

Fresh fear coursing through him, Max started to wheel his mount toward Caro before he heard her cry.

"Max, for God's sake, *go*!"

"To me!" he shouted at his men.

Energized by his command, the Guardians closed ranks around him and Isabella like a swarm of locusts, surrounding them, protecting them. As one unit, they spurred their horses toward the mountains.

Max rode furiously with the exodus, shoulder to shoulder with Isabella. After a few strides, he threw a glance behind him. It vastly relieved him to see Caro and Verra were close. And bringing up the rear were Thorne and Ryder, bending low over their horses' necks.

They set a swift pace across the valley, the hooves of their mounts pounding in Max's ears. How many times had he played out this same scenario in battle? His heart pumping to the violent rhythm of churning hooves, the explosive report of muskets and rifles reverberating like cracks of lightning . . .

Hearing the unmistakable sound of gunshots behind him, Max glanced back again to see a dozen Berbers galloping after them in hot pursuit. Evidently they had found mounts elsewhere in the stronghold, and Saful looked to be one of the leaders. Worse, the eastern sky was beginning to lighten, which would make the Guardians easy targets for the Berbers' rifles.

Thorne and Ryder must have understood the danger as well, for suddenly they both swerved to their left, heading west, no doubt in an attempt to draw off the pursuers.

A moment later another sharp crack from a rifle sounded and Ryder's horse went down; the man was thrown head over heels, while his horse somersaulted over him.

The animal instantly began flailing, trying to rise, but Ryder lay still.

Max felt his heart falter, yet it alarmed him even more when he saw Caro abruptly draw rein. Her mount reared for a brief moment, but she held on, then spun to her left, chasing after her fallen colleague.

Max's heart stopped altogether as he recognized her purpose. She would never leave her fellow Guardians behind, any more than he would have abandoned one of his soldiers in battle.

But it was his worst nightmare come to life—that she would sacrifice her own life for her friend.

Unconsciously he started to slow his mount, but Verra shouted at him, "Leave them! Your duty is to Isabella!"

Please. I trust you. Upon your honor, keep her safe.

Caro's plea ripped at his conscience, at his very soul.

It was the hardest thing Max had ever done, but he gritted his teeth and kept his horse racing beside Isabella's.

The group of pursuing Berbers split up then, a few breaking off to the left after Caro, while the main body continued north.

Max saw the distress and fright on Isabella's face when she realized the implication of this disastrous turn of events, and knew his features showed the same anxiety. With sheer force of will, he tried to divorce his mind from all emotion, to concentrate only on the task of bringing Isabella to safety.

By now they had reached the far edge of the valley and begun the upward climb to the mountain pass. Their horses were already laboring before they had gone two hundred yards up the rocky slope.

These were not the magnificent Barbs that the Berbers prized so highly. These were fleet-footed Arabians, but without the strength and stamina necessary to outdistance the other, more powerful breed for long. The strides of the Guardians' horses slowed almost to a crawl as the incline grew steeper.

Dawn broke in full-fledged glory just then, lighting the sky with rose and gold. Another backward glance showed Max that Saful's warriors were gaining on them.

In the part of his mind that still functioned logically, Max knew they would be fortunate to make the pass before being overtaken. They'd been wise to keep fresh horses ready. And Hawk would be standing by with gunpowder to blow up the pass and halt the Berbers' pursuit. . . .

His whole body went cold with fear as he recognized the new danger. If Hawk's explosion succeeded, Caro and her compatriots would be trapped on this side of the barrier, at the mercy of the Berbers. Already Ryder could be injured or even dead, which would make escape nearly impossible.

Gut-wrenching panic seized Max. He clenched the reins, his fiercest instincts warring inside him.

What decision to make? They were about to enter a canyon that would force them to ride single file, and his retreat would be blocked.

But it would be foolish to try to return for Caro now; not only was he too late to help her, he would only jeopardize their mission.

With sickening fear knotting his gut, Max bent grimly forward, helping his struggling horse lunge up a boulder-strewn bank. A moment later the cold shadows of the pass closed in around them.

When the trail leveled out, he glanced up at the rugged rock above. At first he saw nothing, but then some hundred yards ahead, he spied several figures poised above the narrowest part of the pass.

Desperation ran through him like a sword as he rode closer. But he maintained formation and urged his mount after Isabella's. When they had gone beyond the point where Hawk was positioned, Max braced himself for the imminent explosion.

Yet even though he was mentally prepared, when it came seconds later, he felt the reverberating force like a cannon shot directly through his heart.

And then an avalanche of rock and dust thundered down the side of the canyon, making the earth tremble when it hit, muffling the agonized cry that welled up inside Max when he acknowledged the terrible fact that Caro was cut off from him completely, trapped behind a wall of rubble with the enemy.

Chapter Eighteen

In the aftermath the silence seemed as thunderous as the explosion. The acrid smoke of gunpowder hung in the air, reminding Max of other battles he had fought—of his helplessness, his powerlessness to change a tragic outcome. The dry dust choked his throat, making it a struggle to breathe.

He squeezed his eyes shut, striving for the strength to carry on.

When he looked back again, he was forced to face reality. This was no nightmare. The immense pile of rubble blocked the pass, isolating Caro and her friends from all the other Guardians.

He was grateful for the sheer numbness that overtook him. He watched Hawk scramble down from the ledge to the canyon floor. Saw the earl's expression grow grim as Santos Verra reported to him what had happened.

But then Hawk nodded and mounted his horse, turning toward the north end of the canyon, evidently intending to proceed with the original plan and spirit Isabella away as swiftly as possible.

Max abruptly shook off his lethargy and spurred his mount through the crowd of horses and men until he reached Hawk.

"Where the hell are you going?" he demanded in a hoarse voice. "We can't leave them behind."

Hawk's gaze held sympathy but remained unyielding. "Our duty is to our mission. And they may manage to escape."

"*How?*" Max rejoined.

"By way of the southern route from the valley."

"Even if they reach it, the Berbers will follow and hunt them down."

"Perhaps not."

"And if they do reach it, how will they survive? They will need water, food, fresh horses."

"If anyone can find a way, it will be those three." Hawk's penetrating gaze probed Max's own. "Don't underestimate our resourcefulness, my friend, or our strength of will."

The muscles in Max's jaw worked, but he forced himself to contain his frustration and fury. "So we intend to wait at the oasis for them to join us?"

"No. Once the rock is cleared, the oasis is the first place Saful will look. We will ride for the coast as planned. We'll wait there for three days. If they haven't made it out in that time, we will assume they have been captured."

"And then?" Max asked dangerously.

"We will send Isabella back to Cyrene while we regroup and form a new plan."

"That isn't good enough!"

Hawk's mouth tightened. "It will have to be, Leighton. Our first duty is to Lady Isabella."

Santos Verra interrupted then, saying quietly, "It is what they would have wanted."

Max bit off a sharp retort, knowing he couldn't refute that truth.

"We will not abandon them," Hawk promised. "I swear to you. Right now we need to get away from here in the event our Berber friends try to climb the wall of rubble we just created and target us with the rifles we gave them."

Max had to be satisfied with that, even though every instinct in his body was screaming at him in denial and protest.

With Hawk in the lead, they wound their way carefully and quickly through the treacherous pass to the camp where the remainder of their party awaited.

The rescuers exchanged their weary mounts for fresh ones and then they rode north in earnest. By midafternoon they left the mountains behind and pressed on across the desert flats at a relentless speed.

They deliberately bypassed the oasis of Akbou, not wanting to leave any trace of their trail. At nightfall they made camp, more to rest the exhausted horses than for their own comfort. When they shared a meal, everyone remained silent, intent, watchful.

Too restless to sleep afterward, Max found himself pacing a stretch of arid earth some distance from the tents, staring out at the desolate moonlit desert, his fingers clenching Philip's knife. He couldn't bring himself to throw it, though, for it reminded him too much of Caro.

It was perhaps ten minutes later when Verra's quiet voice broke into the turmoil of his thoughts. "You must have faith, my friend."

Anger and despair clawed at Max's chest, struggling to break free of his rigid control. "Do you have faith?"

Even in the dim light, he saw uncertainty flicker across Verra's swarthy features. But his reply held a hearty confidence. "We have been in worse situations. And every one of us is prepared to die for our cause. Caro knew the danger. Thorne and Ryder did as well."

"You realize Ryder may already be dead."

"If so, then we must make certain he has not sacrificed his life in vain. Our mission must come first—but as Hawk promised, we will never abandon them. Sir Gawain would have our heads if we were simply to exchange their freedom for Isabella's."

Max gave a grim nod. "Yet if Caro has been captured, it will be a hundred times more difficult to rescue her now that Saful knows our game. Worse, he may be set on vengeance because we stole his prize possession directly from under his nose. He may very well take his anger out on Caro."

"But you know her wishes in this matter," was all Verra replied.

"Yes. Hell and damnation," Max said quietly, "I do."

"You should get some rest, my friend," Verra added as he turned to go. "You may need all your stamina in the coming days. And if you know any good prayers, now would be an excellent time to voice them."

The soft laugh that escaped Max held bitterness. There had been so many times when prayer had had no influence whatsoever on the outcome he wished for. And yet all he could do was pray desperately that Caro and her friends would survive.

They reached the coast by noon of the third day and set up camp a few miles distant from the seaport of

Bougie, in the shelter of a grove of wild olives. But the atmosphere among the Guardians remained tense and uncertain, with little of their usual jovial camaraderie to break up the long, monotonous hours.

Max especially felt the strain. Even with all his experience of waiting for battles to begin, he found it impossible to summon any patience, or to hold his tormenting thoughts at bay. And his nightmare returned with a vengeance . . . Caro returning to save him, her blood and life draining away right before his eyes.

Had his worst fear come to pass? Caro could be dead. And he hadn't even tried to help her.

He had dreaded facing this possibility. Over the years he'd lost countless fellow soldiers and friends to death. But what he felt for Caro went far deeper than the brotherly or fatherly sentiments he'd felt for his men, deeper even than the kinship he'd felt for Philip. Caro was his lover, his solace, his guardian angel. With their passion they had formed a bond more intimate than Max had known with any other human being.

What if he truly had lost her? The very thought made him want to rail at the fates. Made him want to do violence. If she had been killed, Max vowed, he would tear Saful's stronghold apart with his bare hands.

But no vow of vengeance could mitigate the sickening dread roiling in his gut as he waited for news, or ease the terrible apprehension that tore at his insides. He'd thought that when the war had ended, he would be finished with uncertainty, with fear, with grief, with loss. But until he knew without a shadow of a doubt that Caro was safe, he would be haunted by the nightmare of losing her.

And even then he might still never again know another moment's peace.

Two mornings later still had brought no signs of the missing Guardians. Breakfast consisted of couscous with milk and honey, liberally sprinkled with dates and almonds, but it might have been sawdust for all the pleasure Max took in eating.

Needing to work off some of his fractious energy, he saddled his horse. He would have liked to ride a great distance until he was too exhausted to feel, but he had no wish to rouse the suspicions of the local inhabitants, so he settled for riding the perimeter of the camp numerous times.

He felt like a caged animal, though, forced to keep to the boundaries of his confinement. Upon his return, when he caught sight of Lady Isabella entering her tent, it struck him that this was possibly how she had felt the past two months as a captive.

He had nearly finished untacking his horse when he was surprised to see Lady Isabella approaching him, as if he'd conjured her appearance with his mere thoughts.

She had donned Arab dress, with scarves covering every part of her face except for her dark eyes.

"I wished to thank you for rescuing me, Mr. Leighton," she began, those lustrous eyes probing his.

Max felt his jaw hardening. This was the first time he'd spoken privately to Isabella. He had subconsciously avoided her—or perhaps she had avoided him. Either way, he had no desire to accept thanks for a rescue that he considered a disastrous failure.

"Think nothing of it, my lady," he replied tersely, offering her a brief bow only because he professed to be a gentleman.

When he would have walked away, Isabella touched his arm lightly. "I can understand if you hold me to blame."

Strangely disturbed by her searching appraisal, Max hesitated to reply. He wanted to refute her, but in some uncharitable, angry part of his mind, he did blame this woman. Her rescue had put Caro in danger.

Yet his view was hardly fair. Isabella hadn't arranged her capture by Algerian pirates, any more than he himself was responsible for Boney's rapacious assaults across Europe.

Max blew out his breath in a slow exhalation. "You are not to blame, my lady. Caro made her own choices. And she could never have left you imprisoned—not and be able to live with herself."

"Even so, I pray she is unharmed. I love Caro like a daughter, and I could not bear to live with the guilt if something terrible befell her because she acted for my sake."

Max remained silent, although he could fully sympathize; he knew a great deal about guilt. But he was under no obligation to bare his personal demons to a perfect stranger.

Isabella, however, hardly seemed a stranger to him, Max admitted, aware of the unsettling way she was looking at him, as if trying to understand his character.

As he stood suffering her scrutiny, he wondered what had driven her to seek him out—whether it was her need for absolution for herself, or her desire to offer absolution to him. Both, perhaps, he thought, recognizing the shrewd perceptiveness in her dark gaze.

When some unspoken communication passed between them, it occurred to him that Lady Isabella Wilde was a formidable woman. He could suddenly understand why the Guardians thought so highly of her.

A brief smile curving her lips, she nodded, as if coming to a similar positive conclusion about him. But her smile disappeared just as suddenly.

"I do not wish to leave on the morrow," Isabella said earnestly. "Perhaps you could convince Hawk to permit me to stay."

Max shook his head, knowing Hawk was right. "You must leave. Otherwise this entire mission will have been in vain."

Before he could say another word, he heard a low shout from one of the sentries who were posted at the south edge of the camp. A dozen Guardians sprinted from their tents to investigate.

Max immediately followed with Isabella and found them watching a glittering flash of light that seemed to come from a distant hill.

The sentry responded with haste, Max saw, using a mirror and the sun's rays to send a code, the same way naval ships communicated.

When a coded reply came, an excited murmur broke out among the Guardians.

"It is Thorne," Hawk said with satisfaction. "But one of them is injured."

Max felt his heart leap, then settle into an uneven rhythm. When he met Isabella's worried eyes, he knew her relief and dismay were reflected in his expression.

But then Hawk was issuing orders for the next communication to Thorne: *Remain where you are and we will come fetch you.*

"How will we find them?" Max asked Hawk as the sentry flashed out the code.

"I know their location. Thorne and I discovered a place when we scouted the terrain. I expect you want to accompany us, Leighton?"

"Yes, of course."

"As do I," Isabella interjected.

"No, my lady," Hawk said firmly. "You will remain here in the safety of the camp. We will bring them back as soon as possible, I promise."

Isabella pressed her sensuous lips together, her black eyes snapping, but she didn't argue. Max suspected the lady's unaccustomed meekness was due more to her professed guilt than any desire to be obedient.

In a very short time a half-dozen Guardians armed themselves and rode out to meet their prodigal compatriots.

The three had taken shelter from the sun beneath a carob tree, beside a trickling stream that flowed from an underground spring. Caro and Thorne were sitting with their backs to the tree trunk, obviously resting, fatigue and grime lining their faces. Ryder lay fully prone, apparently asleep, a blood-soaked, makeshift bandage wrapping his left thigh.

All three looked the worse for wear, fugitives on the run for their lives. Both men sported rough stubble on their jaws that lent them the disreputable air of pirates, while Caro seemed more a refugee from a shipwreck, with wisps of hair straggling free from the scarf she'd used to tie back her untidy mane.

There were only two horses sharing the shade, heads drooping as if at any moment they would drop from exhaustion.

Upon the Guardians' arrival, Thorne struggled to his feet and helped Caro up, but after the first moment, Max only had eyes for Caro. Despite her ragged appearance, he thought she had never looked more beautiful.

When Hawk swung down from his horse and embraced her, it sent a fierce stab of jealousy through Max and made him yearn for the same right to take her in his arms. Yet even jealousy couldn't dampen the profound relief surging through him.

His throat was so tight, he could barely speak. "Are you all right?"

Over Hawk's shoulder, Caro locked gazes with Max, returning his intense stare with a weary smile. "Yes. I'm fine."

Max wished the other Guardians would vanish so he could hold her and kiss her and reassure himself that she was truly unharmed.

Not unsurprisingly, though, Caro's first concern was for her friend. "What of Isabella?" she asked Hawk.

"She's safe and waiting impatiently for you to return so we can leave Barbary."

"Thank God."

"Yes," Hawk added fervently, giving Thorne a friendly cuff on the shoulder. "And thank the devil you three survived. What happened?"

"Ryder was shot in the thigh when his horse went down," Thorne answered. "But it wasn't too serious."

As if hearing his name spoken, Ryder roused enough to push himself up on one elbow, his eyes a trifle glazed and feverish. "It's still bloody damned painful."

Thorne grinned at him. "Cease your bleating, you codling. You have so many scars on your body, what is one more?"

He turned back to Hawk. "When we returned fire, Saful's lackeys gave up the chase to follow Leighton's group. And once we made it out of the valley, we were never in any real danger—except for the possibility of Ryder's wound turning putrid. But Caro found a plant that she used to poultice his leg and make him almost as good as new. The trouble was, we only had two horses for the three of us, and not much water or food. And we couldn't afford the time to rest in case Saful was on our trail. So we're utterly exhausted and starved. I, for one, could eat a horse."

"Not these valiant beasts!" Caro protested emphatically, gesturing at the weary animals that had carried them to safety. "They've earned a year's worth of oats for their yeoman service these past few days."

"Very well, then. A camel."

"That I could possibly manage," she agreed with a weary laugh. "And I would give my soul for a hot bath. I swear I could soak for a year."

At her glib reply, Max felt a different turmoil of emotion flood him. How could she jest at a time like this? He'd been a soldier, so he well understood the value of using humor to relieve tension. And Thorne's levity was habitual, Max knew. But he couldn't accept it from Caro. Didn't she have any notion of the agony he had suffered the past four days, not knowing if she was alive or dead?

Max was torn between wanting to hold her close and wanting to throttle her for putting him through such anguish and then joking about it.

But there was no time to do either.

"We will feed you shortly," Hawk said. "But a bath must wait until we reach the ship. Saful could still be pursuing you."

His warning made even Thorne grow sober again and ended all hint of laughter from any of the Guardians.

Four hours later found them welcomed by Captain Biddick on board the waiting schooner. They used a sling to hoist the wounded Ryder from the row boat onto the deck and then helped him below to one of the small cabins. As the schooner got under way, Caro tended to Ryder's wound with supplies from the ship's medical stores.

For her promised bath, she appropriated one of the other cabins. Isabella personally supervised filling a copper tub with hot, fresh water and then remained to assist.

After washing her hair, Caro leaned her head back against the tub's rim and soaked to the rhythmic sway of the ship while her friend talked. Isabella's yearning for female companionship was obvious, for she had not spoken English or Spanish in months.

She also apparently felt the need to express her great remorse for the twentieth time.

"You cannot know how I regret the dangers you endured in order to rescue me."

Grimacing, Caro shook her head. "You would have

done the same for me, Isabella, I have absolutely no doubt."

"But of course I would have. That goes without saying."

"Then there is nothing more to discuss. I don't want to hear another word of apology."

"But you must allow me to—"

"Enough!" Caro snapped, glaring with mock fierceness.

"Oh, very well."

Isabella's musical laughter soothed Caro down to her very soul. She lay her head back again and sighed.

In that moment she felt a tremendous wave of fatigue swamp her, possibly because she had let down her guard for the first time in days.

When Caro's eyes fell shut, Isabella made a soft sound of self-deprecation. "Here I am chattering like a magpie, when I can see you are exhausted. I will leave you to rest."

Caro made no protest, for she felt as if she could sleep for a year. Indeed, she barely had the energy to dry herself off. And her hair was still damp when she crawled into bed.

When she woke late in the middle of the night, she discovered that Isabella had brought a supper tray of bread and cheese and fruit juice. Caro ate hungrily and then promptly went back to sleep. When she woke in the morning, sunlight was shining brightly through the porthole.

She dressed, then went to check on her patient.

She found a dozen Guardians, including Max, crammed into Ryder's small cabin, laughing at one of Thorne's jests.

Her eyes briefly met Max's searching gaze before she caught herself and shooed them all out so that she could rebandage Ryder's injured leg.

She was pleased with his wound's rate of healing and with the rapidness of his recovery. His fever was gone after a good night's sleep, and he looked his usual handsome self, having bathed and shaved. But he had already grown restless and bored—not surprising for so active and intensely vital a man.

Relenting to his cajolery, she gave Ryder permission to go above deck if the captain would make a pallet for him. But she ordered him to keep his leg immobile until they reached Cyrene on the morrow. Then returning to her own cabin, Caro crawled back into her bunk.

It was late afternoon before she felt halfway human again. At the captain's invitation, she joined the Guardians on deck at sunset.

They all gathered around Ryder, who was propped up on the cushions of his pallet like some sort of Eastern potentate, and celebrated with generous glasses of Madeira. After several toasts to victory, Isabella gave a heartwarming speech in which she thanked her dear friends and Mr. Leighton for orchestrating her rescue.

During the speeches, Caro found Max watching her with that same, quietly smoldering expression he'd shown during the early days of their journey—as if he was forcibly quelling his emotions.

It was all she could do to tear her gaze away, for she had her own turmoil of emotions to deal with. Namely, what choice Max intended to make for his future. The dangerous trials they'd endured when their rescue plan went awry would hardly have endeared him to the prospect of joining the Guardians.

She was grateful to be distracted moments later when Isabella linked an arm with hers and led her over to the port railing.

Golden-red rays of sunlight slanted across the Mediterranean, turning the surface to shimmering copper. It was a scene of breathtaking beauty, a symbol of life and hope and infinite freedom.

Isabella inhaled deeply, drinking in the view, then gave a shudder that Caro knew was heartfelt.

"I know I agreed," Isabella murmured in a voice suddenly husky with tears, "not to regale you with further expressions of gratitude, but this view brings home so vividly to me all that I could have lost. I feared I might never see the sea again, or any of the loved ones I hold so dear."

Caro slid her arm around her friend's waist and hugged tightly. "It is over now, Bella. You must try and put it out of your mind. You are back among your loved ones now, and that is what really matters."

Swallowing hard, Isabella responded with a watery smile. It was a moment, though, before she had her tears fully under control. "Your Mr. Leighton was quite concerned for you during the time you were missing."

Caro hesitated before nodding. "That doesn't surprise me. Max tends to assume a burden of responsibility for anyone he cares for."

"I would say he cares for you a great deal."

Averting her gaze, Caro stared out at the shining sea. She knew Max cared for her, but the question was, how much? Enough to remain on Cyrene now that their mission was accomplished? Enough to become a valued member of the Guardians? Enough to understand that this was her life's calling, and to make it his own?

She was trying desperately not to think about the future. For days she'd been too exhausted to concentrate on anything more than survival. And certainly the Guardians' cause was far more important than her own personal feelings. But now, when she should be elated by their success, she couldn't shake her depression, knowing that her relationship with Max could soon come to an end. His goal of rescuing her friend had been met, so he had no further reason to stay on Cyrene.

Perhaps that was why he seemed to be avoiding her again. After his initial greeting, he hadn't made a single attempt to speak to her. And Caro had the terrible suspicion it was because he'd decided he couldn't bear to do as she wished and was reluctant to disappoint her.

Max had been a soldier, tempered by the forge of war. The scars on his soul were enough to make any man think twice about dedicating his life to a cause where danger was common and death might even result. A cause where you could so easily lose people who were dear to you.

He cares for you a great deal.

Was that true? Caro wondered. Had Max allowed her to become dear to him, perhaps even against his will? Was she a factor in his decision whether to join the Guardians?

She could very easily have died during their escape.

Most assuredly, Max wouldn't want to see her risk her life again. But would he rather end their relationship now and return to England so he would never have to face possibly seeing her be killed?

She felt her stomach clench. She knew she cared deeply for him. She'd been so certain Max would make an ideal Guardian because of his natural proclivity to cherish and protect others. And if he decided against joining, she would be bitterly disappointed. Yet she would be devastated if he left Cyrene for good and disappeared from her life.

At the pain that ripped through her, Caro inhaled a sharp breath. She would likely have to prepare herself for that eventuality.

Until now she had been glad that Max was avoiding her. True, it had been a torment not being able to touch him, or even to speak a word to him in private. But she hadn't wanted to risk learning what his choice would be.

Perhaps, though, she would do better to question him about his intentions sooner rather than later. To confront him now, since waiting would only prolong the torture. In any event, she hadn't properly thanked him for saving Isabella. If not for Max they might never have succeeded.

Even so, Caro couldn't bring herself to face such devastation just yet. It might be cowardly, but she preferred to postpone the moment of truth as long as possible.

When she shivered, Isabella fell back into her motherly role. "Are you cold, dearest?"

The temperature was indeed dropping as the sun melted into the glittering sea, Caro realized, and the

October salt-wind was cool enough to raise goose bumps on her skin.

Eager to get away from her friend's penetrating gaze, she latched on to that excuse. "A bit. Will you forgive me if I go below to fetch a shawl?"

"Of course I will. And perhaps you should go back to bed. You do look rather pale."

Without waiting for further permission, Caro made her way to her cabin, where she wrapped a shawl around her shoulders. Instead of returning above deck, though, she sank listlessly onto the bunk, her thoughts still in turmoil as she debated what course she should take.

The quiet rap on the door surprised her. Expecting Isabella, she bid entrance, only to give a start when Max appeared.

She felt a jolt like lightning spear through her body at his unexpected presence.

When he stepped into the cabin and shut the door behind him, his powerful form seemed to take up the small space. And his intense blue eyes swept over her face in a way that made her pulse falter. She couldn't look away.

"What . . . do you want?" Caro asked, her voice uneven.

"What do you think?"

He stood there as if drinking in the sight of her. After a moment, he moved across the cabin and drew her into his arms.

Caro's heart lodged in her throat at the expression in his eyes—despair, anger, tenderness, all warring in the blue depths.

He stared at her another long moment, clenching his jaw as if striving for control. Finally he cursed and bent his head, as if he couldn't help himself.

His kiss was fierce. Scalding. His mouth on hers, hard and hot and compelling.

Her breath fled at the raw surge of longing that tore though her. The thrust of his tongue was so deep, so urgent, she forgot all her questions, all her uncertainty, all her torment. The well of hunger she'd suppressed for days returned in full force, excitement replacing lethargy. She throbbed with the need to taste Max, to feel his heat, and she knew he felt the same way.

Her fingers clenched in his hair, trying to draw his mouth closer, but Max required no encouragement. His tongue plunged and stroked while his hands moved to cover her breasts. Desire instantly engorged her nipples, and she arched against his touch. She was gasping when he broke off his kiss and his mouth moved lower, to her throat.

"I've been dying to hold you like this," he rasped against her throat. "To touch you like this."

She had been dying, too. She needed his passion. Needed to celebrate the sweetness of life, the triumph of victory over danger.

His lips set her aflame, even as she felt cool air rush over her sensitized skin. When she realized he was undressing her, Caro murmured his name and pushed at the lapels of his coat, trying to aid him.

Her shawl had long ago slid off her arms. Now he tugged the neckline of her gown over her shoulders, then the bodice of her shift. Her bare breasts tumbled forward, begging for the touch of his teeth and tongue.

When his wet mouth seared her nipple, Caro half

moaned, her body on fire. Responding to the sound, Max nudged her backward till her knees touched the bunk. Her limbs were so weak, she helplessly sank down upon the mattress.

Max followed, spreading her thighs with his knee as he sprawled over her, his hot mouth returning to capture hers, drinking feverishly.

Lost in the depths of his heated, intimate kiss, Caro scarcely heard the knock on the door. She moaned again as Max's wonderful hands tormented her bare, aching nipples—

Suddenly she felt Max stiffen, even before she heard the low curse that came from across the cabin.

"Damn you, Leighton."

She recognized Thorne's hard voice with a sense of shock.

A brittle silence followed. Max sat up slowly, using his body to hide her disheveled state.

Her breasts were fully exposed, Caro realized with horror. She hastily fumbled to replace her shift and bodice and cover her indecency as she struggled to regain her dazed senses.

When she sat up, she ventured a glance at Thorne, who stood planted in the doorway.

His face had darkened to a thundercloud, but she might not have existed for all the attention he paid her. His angry gaze was riveted on Max.

"How long?" he demanded, his sharp tone slicing like a knife. "How long have you been taking advantage of her?"

Max didn't reply at once. His jaw merely set in a rigid line.

Thorne's jaw tightened just as rigidly as he crossed

his arms over his chest. "I have no doubt you intend to do the honorable thing. You will wed her, of course."

A mask fell down over Max's expression. He cast a brief glance at Caro, then looked away.

"Of course," he agreed, his voice holding scarcely any inflection at all.

Chapter Nineteen

"Thorne, that is perfectly absurd!" Caro protested. "In the first place, Max did not take advantage of me—I was a willing participant. And in the second, it is none of your business whom I choose to kiss."

"Stolen kisses are one thing," Thorne retorted. "Ruining you is something else entirely."

"He didn't ruin me—"

"It's close enough. You're like a sister to me, love, and I won't stand by while some bounder seduces you, even if he is a friend of mine."

"What rubbish! Do you hear yourself, Thorne? How many women have you seduced in your rakehell career?"

"Which is precisely what makes me an expert. And the cases aren't at all alike. I've always been astute enough to keep well away from complete innocents."

Caro bristled at his characterization of her. "I am hardly an innocent. A woman of my age and experience is permitted more license than a girl just out of the schoolroom."

"Not in my book. When a man dishonors a genteel female, marriage is the only possible course."

"Oh, go to blazes!" Caro spat.

"I have no objections to wedding her," Max interjected into their argument.

"Well, I have objections!" she exclaimed. "The entire notion is ludicrous."

Max winced at her fierceness, then sent Thorne a wry smile. "I think this discussion would be better continued in private. I'll thank you to make yourself scarce, friend, and allow me to make my own proposals."

"You will do the honorable thing?"

"You may trust me, I assure you."

Stifling an oath, Caro rolled her eyes in frustration.

When Thorne had left, shutting the door behind him, silence fell over the small cabin. Caro ventured a glance at Max and found his unsettling blue gaze locked on her.

With another heated exhalation of disgust, she scurried off the bunk and turned away to smooth the bodice of her gown, determined to eliminate the evidence of their aborted lovemaking.

"You shouldn't listen to the ravings of a madman," she muttered. "The difficulties of the past few days evidently affected Thorne's senses."

"He seemed of sound mind to me."

"He clearly is not! And there is no reason whatsoever for you to propose to me."

"I think there is."

She turned to stare at Max. "You can't possibly wish to wed me. You haven't spoken even two words to me since I returned."

His mouth twisting in a crooked smile, Max leaned back, bracing himself on his elbows. "If you care to know, I was trying to act the gentleman and give you time to recover from your ordeal. But I've had the devil of a time staying away from you. Witness what happened between us a few moments ago. I nearly ravished you. And I'm still as hard as granite."

A swift appraisal of his breeches suggested to Caro that he was telling the truth. She could clearly see the swollen bulge of his arousal beneath the fabric.

She felt color rise in her cheeks. "You know that is purely a physical response of male lust. Perfectly understandable after a separation. It's also quite normal for a man to feel a certain fervor after a victory. Now that the danger has passed, your desire has returned in full force."

"Thank you for your expert medical opinion, Madame Physician. But permit me to be the judge of my own motives."

Her hands went to her hips. "Just because Thorne found us together is certainly no reason for us to marry."

"My proposal has little to do with Thorne's finding us."

"Perhaps not, but you are obviously trying to be noble. You believe that honor dictates you make amends, but in this instance, there are no amends to make, Max. You certainly haven't ruined me. Nor did you seduce me. I went into our affair with my eyes wide open, fully understanding the consequences. I won't have you offering for me out of duty or honor. And I absolutely won't accept."

"So you are refusing my proposal?"

"Of course I am refusing! We wouldn't suit in the least. Marriage between us would be impossible."

"Why?"

Her eyebrows shot up. "Have you even considered what our union would mean? Just begin with the simple matter of where we would make our home. Would you expect me to return to England with you? I would hate living there, Max. With all the stifling strictures they have for feminine behavior, it would be difficult for me to continue working as a Guardian. And it would be impossible to continue my medical vocation. I couldn't willingly relinquish either."

A shadow seemed to fall over his expression. "I would never ask you to."

"So we would live on Cyrene? Do you mean to join our order, then? If you stay, you will have to, you know."

When he hesitated, Caro searched his face. The graveness of his features spoke volumes.

Her heart contracted painfully in her chest, while her lungs felt suddenly tight, making it difficult to breathe.

She had been wrong, she realized that now. She'd been totally selfish, pressing Max to deny his most fundamental instincts of survival. She had no right to demand that he become a Guardian. No right to condemn him to such an uncertain future, where he might never be free of his nightmares.

A sickening sense of inevitability flooded Caro. Despite the hollowness in the pit of her stomach, however, despite the ache in her throat, she knew she had to brazen out her response to Max, pretending she didn't care that her heart was bleeding.

Regrettably, when she finally allowed herself to speak, her voice sounded hoarse and uneven. "You have more than proved yourself worthy, Max, but you don't belong as a Guardian."

Pushing himself up, Max rose slowly to his feet. "Why do you say so?"

"Because it would make you continually relive your nightmares, for one thing. And if we were to wed, I would be the chief cause of them. I won't let you make such a sacrifice, Max."

He moved across the cabin toward her, holding her gaze. "It wouldn't be a sacrifice."

"Yes, it would. If your heart isn't truly committed to our cause, then you would be damning yourself to a life of misery."

He didn't refute her, Caro noted. She took a slow, deep breath, trying to quell the relentless ache inside her. "I couldn't bear for you to remain simply for my sake."

A long moment passed before he spoke. "I want you as much now as I ever did, probably more so."

She tried to smile. "I understand. I feel the same need. But it is simply the island's influence."

Max shook his head. "That isn't true, and you know it. We are still a hundred miles from Cyrene. And our night together at Saful's stronghold demonstrated clearly that your island legend has nothing to do with my desire for you."

"You want my body, I have no doubt. But I am not the kind of woman you would want for your wife. Even if I were, you are forgetting that I don't want a husband. I don't want any man commanding me, controlling my life, telling me what I should or shouldn't do."

His blue eyes held hers. "What about children? What about companionship?"

"I don't need those things," Caro replied, her tone insistent.

"Liar," he said softly.

Her eyes shut. She was indeed lying. She didn't want to contemplate a future without Max. The emptiness. The long, lonely years ahead . . .

She tried to turn away, but he forestalled her, his fingers a gentle band of steel around her wrist.

"Don't, Max," she rasped. "Please believe me. We agreed to a few weeks of pleasure, only that. I have no interest in anything more."

"Pleasure is not a bad basis for marriage."

"But it would never be enough when there are other more overwhelming problems to consider."

When his grasp tightened, Caro roughly pulled her arm away. "I won't marry you, Max!"

"So you just want to end it now?"

"Yes! That is exactly what I want. As soon as we reach Cyrene, I think you should return to England. Now that Isabella is safe, there is no reason for you to stay."

A dark, stormy expression fell over his features, making the intensity of his blue eyes even bluer. He intended to argue with her, Caro knew.

"And what about us?" he demanded stonily. Drawing close again, he captured her face in his hands, his thumbs stroking her lower lip. "You can't claim you are eager for our lovemaking to cease, for I will never believe you."

"Our lovemaking has nothing to do with the matter."

"Nothing? Should I remind you what you will be giving up?"

This time instead of just slipping her bodice off her

shoulders, he reached around to unfasten the hooks at the back of her gown.

"Max . . ."

As she began to protest, he captured her mouth, kissing her with a hard assurance that beguiled even as it claimed.

To Caro's dismay, her surrender was just as swift as before. She would never be able to deny Max anything he wanted—and just now he wanted *her*.

In only moments he had bared her breasts again to his caresses. His tongue dueled with hers, mating fiercely, while his fingers rubbed her nipples to hard little points of fire.

Her heart was thundering when his hands slipped under her aching breasts and thrust them provocatively upward, leaving the mounds high and jutting. Bending, he fastened his lips around one peak and began to suck hard.

Caro let out a helpless gasp. Desire knifed through her, sharp and insistent. Feeling the searing heat of Max's loins through their clothing, she knew she wouldn't stop him.

She wanted one last time with Max. Wanted it desperately. She needed to know his passion once more to sustain her in the barren years to come.

He must have sensed her capitulation, for suddenly he broke off his kiss and drew back. His expression was hard and sensual as he swiftly unfastened the front placket of his breeches, almost tearing at the fabric. His male length rose thick and full from his groin as he stepped toward her again. Reaching down, he tossed up her skirts, as if he couldn't wait to have her.

She couldn't wait, either. The blazing heat had become a hurting, painful need. She made a small mewling sound when his hand slid between her legs to cup her sex, his fingers gliding over her already sleek wetness, finding her ready. Instantly his hard thighs pressed between hers, parting her legs as he clasped her buttocks to lift her against his erection. Caro helped him, needing the hot slide of his flesh into hers.

He took her without further preliminaries, impaling her on his rigid shaft.

She let out the soft, shocked cry of the surrendering female. The carnality of it was staggering. Reflexively she arched against him, but his arms were shackles, holding her to him, keeping her breasts crushed against his chest.

She was trembling violently now, her sheath clenching rhythmically around him. Twisting his hand in her hair, Max claimed her mouth again, his tongue penetrating possessively.

The taste of him was wild and heady, making passion, hungry craving, erupt between them. Caro made a soft, ragged sound that was matched by Max's low groan. He was setting her aflame, and her fire only fed his own.

She was only dimly aware of Max moving over to the bunk. Still joined to her, he laid her roughly down on the mattress and covered her. Keeping her shaking thighs spread wide by the weight of his body, he surged into her with hard, fierce urgency.

With a hoarse whimper, Caro twisted beneath him, frantic with heat and desire and a deep empty ache that only he could fill. Her nails clutched at his shoulders while her heels dug into the backs of his muscled thighs, drawing him even closer. She wanted him with a blind, ferocious need.

She heard herself moan again, heard herself pleading for him to take her harder, the words smothered between their starving mouths. And Max complied, plunging into her.

They were both shaking violently now at their frenzied mating. It was a raw, powerful bonding, her hips straining and reaching as he drove into her, ruthless and deep, the force of his thrusts almost savage. Writhing, Caro arched in a powerful bow, lifting Max with her as flames of explosive sensation overtook her.

She felt him bucking heavily against her, felt his rhythm breaking as the first cataclysmic waves began.

Her keening cry became a scream of ecstasy, while a harsh groan tore from his chest. His head thrown back in mindless abandon, he shook and convulsed and spurted his seed into her.

The spasms of painfully intense pleasure faded slowly. Her flesh still quivering from the impact of his thrusts, Caro buried her face in Max's shoulder, holding him close, cherishing the fierce intimacy of his body locked with hers, the feel of his vital weight crushing her into the mattress.

She had wanted their final union to be this way: raw and forceful, both of them helpless in the wild grip of passion, their coupling shatteringly intense.

A dozen heartbeats later, Max eased away from her and fell limply back against the pillows, his chest rising and falling swiftly as he gulped in air.

When at last he could speak, his voice was low and hoarse. "You will never convince me that you won't miss that."

Caro shut her eyes, deliberately swallowing the ache in her throat. "I know I will miss it. But I won't marry you, Max."

The following morning Max stood braced at the ship's railing, watching as Cyrene's rugged, picturesque coastline grew ever closer. A brisk breeze had set whitecaps jumping in the blue waters and waves surging against the bow, yet he scarcely noticed.

He'd spent a sleepless night, tossing and turning on his pallet. For once, however, his restlessness had nothing to do with nightmares. Instead, it was his offer of marriage and Caro's adamant refusal that had kept his thoughts in turmoil.

He had indeed proposed to her in part because it was the honorable course. He fully understood his obligations as a gentleman. He'd been caught in a flagrant act of seduction. Thorne had walked in on them as he was about to claim Caro's body. Yet no matter how good a friend, Thorne could not have forced him to propose, Max reminded himself.

He had chosen to do it willingly.

Caro, however, had spurned his proposal out of hand, in no uncertain terms. He couldn't deny that many of her reasons for rejecting his suit were valid. And her first was the most important.

The bald truth was, he wasn't certain he wanted to become a Guardian. They needed his special expertise in military tactics, perhaps. And he had a talent for the kind of skirmishes the Guardians often engaged in during their missions. But did he have an obligation to use his skills on their behalf?

Admittedly, their goals were laudable, as was their

determination to serve a greater purpose. This was not war. Their intent was not to kill people or to battle armies for superiority. Rather, they were set on righting wrongs and championing noble ideals. But did their high-minded aspirations really make a difference to his own circumstances?

Unseeingly, Max gazed across the bright expanse of azure sea. For him it all boiled down to one issue: He didn't know if he could live with the terror of losing Caro at any moment, never knowing whether she would return from a mission alive.

The trouble was, he would be required to face that hell regularly, whether or not he joined their cause. If he left, he wouldn't have to watch a tragedy happen, yet no matter where he went, he wouldn't be able to escape the knowledge that she could die. At least if he became a Guardian, he could try to protect her. But even then he couldn't control fate.

With a muttered oath, Max ran a hand roughly though his hair. The damnable dilemma was, as long as Caro remained a Guardian, he would never be free of his fear.

And Caro saw the Guardians as her life's calling. How could he persuade her to give it up? He didn't have that right, nor was he certain he wanted it.

Yet what was his alternative? Returning to England, to a tame, safe, boring existence? What meaning would his life have then? Could he bear to live the rest of his life without Caro?

He didn't want an empty, meaningless existence. He wanted a purpose to his life, a future that made him look forward to each and every day. He wanted friends, love, family. He wanted joy.

For so long he had felt no joy. Until Caro. She was his joy.

He couldn't imagine ever wanting another woman the way he did her. No one else had ever made him ache, made him shudder at a simple caress the way Caro did. If he chose to leave Cyrene, he would be giving her up for good. And without a doubt, it would be like a light going out of his life.

Perhaps it might be possible for him to visit the island occasionally. But he wanted more than just a few stolen hours with Caro now and then. He truly wanted her for his wife. He wanted her as his lover, his companion, his life's mate. Forever.

And if he were to overcome her objections and convince her to wed him? He would first have to accept who and what Caro was. He would have to come to terms with his fears about her possible death. Acknowledge the fact that no matter how much he might want to protect her and keep her safe, he couldn't wrap her in cotton wool.

If he was honest with himself, though, he would never want to dim her special fire—her courageous, determined spirit that made up her very essence. Her willingness to risk her life for others was part of what made her special. Her courage was one of the things he loved most about her—

Max felt his heart skip a hard beat. *Love.* Was that what he felt for Caro? Having never before experienced the emotion, he had no basis for comparison. Yet he suddenly had no doubt. He loved her.

Turning abruptly, Max stared fixedly across the schooner, searching out Caro from among the women who were gathered on the quarterdeck. She was there, pacing restlessly, avoiding his gaze as she'd done all morning.

His mind reeling, Max leaned weakly back against the railing. It stunned him to comprehend his feelings. He truly loved Caro. Not only because of the fierce desire that he had always felt for her, but because of her courage and honor and strength and inner beauty.

She had possessed him.

And he wanted to possess her in return. He wanted to bind her to him any way possible.

His thoughts went back to their night together at the Berber stronghold, to the soul-shattering passion they'd shared then—and again last evening. He'd held nothing back either time. He had been driven by the desperate need to bury himself so deeply inside her that their union fused them together into one being. So tightly, so profoundly, that neither of them could break free.

Was that why he had failed to withdraw from her body during climax as he should have? Had he subconsciously wanted to plant his seed in her? Because getting her with child was a way to bind Caro to him? Had he surrendered to man's most primal instincts to procreate? Or was it that making Caro part of him had become so vitally important to him?

He hadn't wanted children. Never wanted to risk losing anyone who could become so precious to him. But the image of Caro swollen with his child seared him with a rush of tenderness.

Would she want to bear his children? Did she even want children? She had claimed not to—

Fiercely Max shook his head. The questions were coming too swiftly for his dazed mind to fathom, and none of them mattered in the least if Caro refused to wed him. He would first have to convince her that he wasn't making a noble sacrifice for her. He would have to prove his love to her. And even before that, he would have to face his own demons.

He turned back to stare out at the sea.

It was a long while later before Max realized they had rounded the southernmost tip of the island and were approaching the harbor. They were near enough that he could glimpse the dazzling white walls of the town above, glittering in the sun.

He remembered the last time he'd made this journey, only a few short weeks ago. Even then his interest in Caro had been more than physical. But he'd never expected to lose his heart and soul to her.

Max glanced back over his shoulder, wondering if he should confess his shocking revelation to her. He doubted she would believe him. Caro had little faith in her own attractions. She still believed it was the island's enchantment that was influencing him. But the time away from Cyrene had shown him beyond doubt that the island's legendary spell had nothing to do with his desire for her. His craving for her had been just as great, no matter how distant.

She was the passionate lover who set him aflame.

It made no difference to him that Caro exhibited few of the feminine qualities expected of genteel females. That in the eyes of society, she didn't quite fit in. That she was utterly out of place for the times. She was wholly unique, and he loved her for it.

In centuries past, Caro would have been a warrior princess. She was still a warrior.

Drawing in an aching breath, Max shut his eyes, remembering the dismaying image of Caro wielding her saber against a horde of fierce Berbers. And worse, when she had ridden after her fallen compatriot, prepared to sacrifice her own life for her friend.

Max felt himself shudder. Could he bear to deal with that fear for the rest of his life?

Could he bear not to?

Chapter Twenty

Perhaps she truly *was* a coward, Caro reflected as the skiff carried her from the schooner to the docks. She'd made certain she was among the first to debark, scurrying down the rope ladder without so much as a glance at Max, focusing her sole attention on getting Isabella home.

She saw no reason to prolong their farewells. She wanted no sad, pathetic good-byes with Max or repeats of last evening's arguments. Yet if she was honest, she would admit the true reason she was fleeing: she feared that if she had to face him once more, she might create a scene by retracting all her adamant refusals and begging him to stay.

Even now she felt Max's gaze boring into her back. But she wouldn't let herself dwell on him at the moment. Her only goal—the only thing that mattered now—was helping Isabella resettle into island life after her ordeal.

Pretending an enthusiasm she didn't feel, Caro told Isabella about various changes that had occurred during her long absence.

When the skiff reached the quay, Sir Gawain was waiting there to greet them. Caro wasn't surprised to see him. Lookouts posted in the towers of Olwen Castle would have watched for their arrival and informed him the moment the schooner neared the island's southern point.

On the quay, Sir Gawain bowed low over Isabella's hand like a gallant courtier, his expression grave but pleased. "Welcome home, my lady. You have been sorely missed."

Isabella responded with a musical laugh, resembling something of her usual flirtatious self. "You cannot have missed me as much as I missed you, I promise you, my dearest sir. You have my undying gratitude."

Rising up on her toes, she embraced him fondly and kissed his lined cheek. In return, Sir Gawain stiffened, his face coloring the slightest degree.

Caro had sometimes wondered if the two of them had once been lovers. If so, they had been totally discreet, for she'd never heard any rumors to that effect. But the stark flash of admiration and awareness in the baronet's eyes clearly showed his attraction to the beautiful widow. But then, that was true of nearly any man who came near Isabella.

He seemed relieved to turn to Caro. "I gather your mission went well?"

"We encountered a few problems, but nothing we couldn't handle. Ryder was injured, but he should recover fully."

"And Mr. Leighton? Did he comport himself well?"

Caro felt her own face flush. "Very well. You would have been pleased with him."

Sir Gawain nodded solemnly. "I expected nothing less." To Lady Isabella, he added, "I doubt there will be much awkwardness over your return to Cyrene. Few people know of your capture. They believe you have been traveling abroad all this time. But I would appreciate your discretion regarding our involvement in your rescue."

"You may count on me," Isabella assured him.

"To account for your lack of baggage, I suggest you claim that your trunks were swept overboard during a storm."

"A great pity," she said with a smile. "All those marvelous Paris fashions sunk to the bottom of the sea."

Sir Gawain had arranged for a carriage to take the ladies to Isabella's estate in the southwest interior of the island, so shortly she and Caro were ensconced in a landau, driving across Cyrene. The October breeze was a bit brisk, but Isabella had insisted that both sides of the double hood be folded back. For much of the journey she sat silently drinking in the view as they passed acres of olive groves and vineyards and prosperous farms basking in the golden sunlight.

"I never knew how much I loved this island until it was nearly lost to me," she finally said.

Caro well understood the sentiment. She loved Cyrene deeply, but unlike her friend, she'd always known she belonged here. The island was *part* of her. And she suspected it would be much like severing a limb if she were to leave it to live anywhere else.

When they turned through the iron gates of her estate and drove up to the great hacienda, Isabella's eyes filled with tears. Her third husband had been a wealthy member of Spain's minor nobility, and his will had deeded the vast property to her, against all custom and the protests of his conventional relatives, who had severely disapproved of his choice of wives.

"I vow I will never take this for granted ever again,"

Isabella said with a fervency that left no doubt of her sincerity.

It brought tears to Caro's own eyes to watch Isabella's joyous reunion with her servants, and then again when she wandered through her magnificent home, touching various objects, staring at portraits, as if recalling cherished memories. Once more Caro was reminded how special home and hearth was, how precious it was to be among loved ones.

But then in typical Isabella fashion, the lady shook off her dark mood with a laugh and rang for her butler, declaring she was sick to death of coffee and the Berbers' mint concoction and longed for a cup of genuine British tea.

She also ordered a roast of beef for dinner—another British dish she hadn't tasted in months—and begged Caro to stay to share it with her.

"Of course I will stay, for as long as you need me," Caro responded. "Would you like for me to sleep here tonight as well?"

"No, my dear. I will be perfectly all right, once I am properly fortified with familiar food. But you must come and visit me tomorrow, if you can tear yourself away from Dr. Allenby. I am sure you are eager to return to his clinic and bury yourself in work. But you must promise me an hour or two of your time every day, for at least a short while, until I am more myself again. Nothing will help me recover more quickly than your delightful company."

Caro smiled. "I promise, since I consider you my most important patient."

It was only late that evening, when Caro returned to her own home, that the despairing emotions she'd held at bay returned to haunt her. Even though she tried to sleep, searing memories of Max kept intruding—dozens of them, one bleeding into the other mercilessly.

The ache inside her swelled until it was a painful clawing in her chest. Max hadn't even left the island yet, and already she felt bereft.

Her throat tight with the pressure of tears, Caro buried her face in her pillow, fighting back sobs. She couldn't allow herself to dwell on what might have been. She and Max had no future together, and there was no point in wishing otherwise.

Directly after breakfast the next morning, she drove to Dr. Allenby's clinic. He took one look at her dark-shadowed eyes rimmed with fatigue and ordered her back to bed.

"There is no need, I assure you," Caro protested. "I am perfectly fine."

"You don't look fine to me," Allenby retorted. "That mission clearly took more out of you than you are willing to admit."

"It was difficult, but I suffered no ill effects. At least nothing that food and rest cannot cure."

The doctor grunted. "I heard all about it. Nearly got yourself killed."

"What about you?" Caro asked, trying to change the subject. "Have you fully recovered from your illness?"

"More or less."

"You look weary yourself."

"My only trouble is that I am getting old."

Caro couldn't disagree. Dr. Allenby might have recovered his health, but he no longer had the same vitality he once had. He needed her now more than ever.

"Well, I am ready to resume my duties as your assistant. I intend to help you, whether you wish me to or not."

"Suit yourself," Allenby grumbled. "If you insist on defying my wisdom, I suppose you might as well make yourself useful."

From that moment on, Caro threw herself into her work in an effort to forget the man who was the cause of her sleeplessness.

She saw Isabella every day, for she was determined to help her friend reclaim her former life. Not that Isabella truly needed her support. The vivacious widow's popularity was greater than ever after her long absence, and she was welcomed back eagerly into the social fold, with several impromptu dinners and evening parties immediately held in her honor.

Caro turned down those invitations, however, secluding herself away, for fear of encountering Max. She couldn't bear to see him again, for it would only intensify the raw wound that breaking off with him had opened up.

She evaded her friends for that reason as well. She ceased treating Ryder's wound, since he could rely on a real doctor now. And she refused to see Thorne altogether, since as far as she knew, Max was still his houseguest.

Thus, for the next week she saw nothing of Max, and heard nothing about him, either, although any day, she expected to learn that he had departed for England.

She told herself that she couldn't wait for him to

leave Cyrene, for then she could attempt to move on with her life. Perhaps then her misery could begin to diminish. As it was now, merely rising each morning proved to be an exhausting exercise in sheer willpower.

Even the island's beauty no longer had the power to soothe her. She avoided the grotto and the Roman ruins entirely, and anywhere else that reminded her of Max, including Sir Gawain's castle.

When she failed to appear at the castle, John Yates paid her a visit to report on the Newhams. He seemed to have recovered from his wounded heart, Caro was glad to see.

"I cannot believe what a witless fool I was to be taken in so easily," John told her with a rueful smile. "I suppose I was just susceptible to a beautiful face. But I intend to find the Englishman who employed Danielle to discover the Guardians' membership. And now that Isabella is returned safely, we will have ample agents to devote to a full investigation. Sir Gawain has decided to allow the Newhams to go free in a few weeks, but he will have them followed to see where they lead."

Caro was pleased that John hadn't suffered too deeply except for his pride. But she had difficulty summoning interest in the Newhams or their machinations.

When Dr. Allenby didn't need her services, she was left with too much time on her hands, so she took her aging mare on long, slow treks across the island, wandering the wild hills to the north, amid swaths of bracken tangled with juniper and laurel and myrtle. At this season, the maquis was richly hued and heavily scented, and the strawberry trees, which flowered in autumn rather than spring, provided even more vibrant color, appearing almost ablaze.

Frequently when she returned, Caro found herself remaining in the horse's stall, more for companionship than anything else. The mare was the only one she could safely share her secrets with—and it did seem as if the animal was willing to lend a sympathetic, nonjudgmental ear.

Mostly Caro argued with herself in muttered undertones, repeating all the reasons why she had been right to refuse Max's grudging offer of marriage.

"I would make him a dreadful wife," she insisted as she groomed the dozing mare. "Can you just imagine? I would always be haring off in the middle of the night, seeing to a patient. Or I would be called away from Cyrene on a mission and be gone for days or even weeks, while he suffered terrible nightmares about me. . . . No, it is far better this way. Max should count himself fortunate that I gave him a reprieve before it was too late."

At other times, she wound up stubbornly railing against the fates and Max himself, and wishing she had never known him.

He was to blame for her current anguish, she had no doubt. He made her want things she couldn't have. Worse, he had made her realize all that she was missing, just as he'd threatened to do.

Until now she'd always been satisfied with her choices. She had made a good life for herself, independent of any man. Before Max she had never minded her solitary existence, never minded the loneliness.

Yet now she felt truly alone—so completely alone, it was a raw ache inside her. Merely thinking about the empty future without Max ripped open a longing so deep and wide that she nearly wept.

Early one afternoon upon returning from a ride, Caro did weep. Surrendering to her desolation, she leaned against the mare's neck and sobbed out her heartache. When she finally regained control of herself, she felt drained to the point of numbness, yet even then, the relentless ache still clawed at her.

Was it possible to die from a hollow feeling, Caro wondered as she pushed herself wearily away from the mare and left the stall.

To her dismay, when she entered her house, she was told that Lady Isabella was waiting for her in the blue parlor. Swiftly Caro scrubbed at her face, but she couldn't hide the evidence of her tears from her dearest friend.

"My heavens, have you been *crying*?" Isabella exclaimed, tossing aside her book and rising abruptly from her position on the settee.

"Not at all," Caro lied. "I merely have something lodged in my eye."

Not believing her, Isabella took Caro's hands and drew her down to sit with her on the settee. "You must tell me what is troubling you, my dear. You have been moping around for the past week, ever since we returned from Barbary."

"Surely not," she murmured, her protest sounding lame even to her own ears.

"I suppose it is your Mr. Leighton."

When Caro winced, Isabella's sensual mouth turned down in a frown. "You will forget him in time. It is never easy to get over a charismatic man like that."

She paused, shrewdly eyeing Caro. "Perhaps you

should endeavor to speed up the process. Turn your attention immediately to someone else. There are several gentlemen on the island who would vie for your favors, if you would only permit them. Of course, any liaison would need to be handled discreetly."

It was Caro's turn to be taken aback. She couldn't believe that the woman who had been like a second mother to her was advising her to engage in an affair. "You are suggesting that I take a lover?"

"Exactly."

"Isabella!"

"Don't act so shocked, dearest. You are grown up now, and a woman of your age and vitality has needs, no matter how you might try to deny them. I fully understand, trust me on this. I know what it is like to live without a man in your bed, how utterly lonely it can be. I am only surprised you never permitted yourself to indulge before now."

Giving a brief shake of her head, Caro looked away. She wanted no other man. Max had spoiled her for anyone else. And she knew in her heart that she would never take any other lover.

Isabella must have sensed her feelings, for she continued in a speculative tone. "Mr. Leighton was deeply disturbed at having to leave you behind during my rescue. And he was like a caged lion until you reappeared safely. I think that shows how much he cares for you."

"More likely it shows merely that he felt responsible for me. He was in command of the mission at that point, and he failed to save me. After what he experienced in war, he cannot stomach the thought of having any more blood on his hands."

"Yet on the ship, when I caught him gazing at you,

his eyes fairly smoldered with passion. He is quite enamored of you, Caro, I have no doubt. Indeed, his desire seemed so ardent, I found myself hoping it would lead to something more than an illicit affair. Marriage, perhaps."

"He did propose," Caro said in a low voice. "But I refused."

Isabella's eyebrow rose, but she waited patiently.

"He was merely trying to be noble," Caro insisted. "He only offered because he believed he had compromised me."

"That does not explain why you refused," Isabella prodded gently.

"Because I couldn't bear for him to be forced to wed me. Nor did I want him to feel compelled to join the Guardians. I once hoped he would. I was certain that if he accompanied us on our mission, he would see the good we do and would choose to become one of us. But after what happened in Barbary, I no longer believe that is the right choice for him. I don't want him to be trapped here, in a life that would only bring him pain."

"So what is to prevent you from settling with him in England? I know Cyrene is your home . . . how much you love it here. But would you refuse to leave if it meant losing your cherished lover?"

No, Caro thought silently, her throat constricting with the ache of tears. She wouldn't refuse if it meant losing Max. She had only recently come to that realization.

Max was more important to her than her beloved island. More important than her medical vocation. More important even than her remaining a Guardian.

She would live anywhere with him—if he wished her to. But would he ever wish her to?

"What *do* you feel for your Max?" Isabella asked. "Is it possible you love him?"

It was indeed possible, Caro thought despairingly. She loved Max with an intensity that frightened her.

For weeks now she had denied her feelings, refusing to admit the staggering truth to herself: she had lost her heart to Max long ago. During their first magical night together, in fact.

Perhaps it had even been inevitable. How could she help loving so extraordinary a man? His tenderness, his caring, his passion had all torn away her defenses. And she had permitted it to happen.

Burying her face in her hands, Caro gave an anguished moan. How could she have made the dire mistake of falling in love with Max? She couldn't believe he felt the same way toward her. He had never once mentioned love during his proposal, never in all their heated exchanges that evening. Surely if he loved her, he would have told her so?

Or perhaps he considered it immaterial, given his profound reluctance to become a Guardian . . . because he knew how much she wanted to remain here on Cyrene. Was it possible he was being noble again?

An odd mixture of hope and fear curled in Caro's stomach. Was it conceivable Max did love her even a little?

She forced herself to drop her hands. "I do love him, Isabella. So much that it hurts. But I don't know if he could ever return my love."

"Then you will simply have to make him do so,"

Isabella declared with the supreme confidence of a woman who always got her way with men.

Looking up, Caro fixed her friend with a skeptical stare. "Surely one cannot just make a man fall in love."

Isabella smiled. "Pah, it is not so difficult. Particularly a man who is more than halfway there already, as I'm certain your Mr. Leighton is. I can easily advise you how to go about it."

"So you think I should pursue him? But Max has always loathed being chased. It is one of the reasons he came here to Cyrene—to evade all the females who were after him."

"What I think," Isabella replied, "is that if you truly love him, you would be foolish to let him get away. True love is far too fleeting to let slip through your fingers, Caro. You want to win his heart, do you not?"

The terrible yearning that swept over Caro answered that question for her. She wanted desperately for Max to love her.

"Yes, I want to win his heart." She looked at Isabella. "But what if he has already left Cyrene? I've been afraid to inquire, but he might have returned to England by now."

"Then you must follow him, of course."

Yes, of course. If Max had left, then she would follow him. If he couldn't bear to be a Guardian, if he couldn't bear to live here on Cyrene with her, then she would go with him, for she couldn't bear to live without him. It was that simple. She was willing to do whatever it took to win his love.

Just then a servant appeared at the parlor door, bearing a silver salver. "A message for you, Miss Evers, from Lord Thorne."

Wondering why Thorne would be writing to her, Caro broke the seal and quickly scanned the message.

Her heart plunged to her stomach before she was halfway done. *"Dear God . . ."*

"What is it?" Isabella asked in alarm. "You have turned white as a ghost."

"Max . . ." Caro rasped, her voice no more than a hoarse croak. "He has contracted some kind of grave illness. Thorne says for me to come at once."

She glanced up blindly at her friend. "Max is on his deathbed."

Chapter Twenty-one

Isabella ordered her carriage brought around immediately, for Caro was too distraught to drive herself. Her stomach churned with turmoil, while her heart pounded with fear. Was Max truly *dying*?

Even though Isabella tried to soothe her during the endless journey to Thorne's villa, Caro couldn't control her trembling. The moment the carriage drew to a halt, she leapt out and ran up the front steps.

Without waiting for admittance, she burst through the door and startled a footman who was polishing a bronze statue in the entryway. When Caro demanded, "Where is he?" the astonished servant gaped at her as if she were a madwoman.

The next instant, Thorne emerged from his study down the hall, as if he'd been expecting her.

"Max—*where is he?*" Caro pleaded again, her voice shaking.

Thorne's gaze narrowing on her thoughtfully, he pointed to the grand staircase. "Upstairs, third bedchamber on the right. But Caro—"

Whether Thorne intended to reassure her or warn her further about Max's condition, she didn't remain to find out, for she had to see for herself.

She ran up the stairs, nearly tripping in her haste, and hurried along the corridor, before her years of training made her recall the need to approach an invalid quietly. Struggling for a semblance of control, Caro pushed open the third door on her right.

She had expected the worst, but when she took in the scene, she came to a sudden halt. Max was indeed lying on the canopied bed, reclining against the pillows. Yet he was resting *on top* of the counterpane rather than beneath it, with one knee drawn up casually, propping up the book he was reading. And he was fully dressed in breeches and boots and a superbly tailored burgundy coat, like any gentleman of leisure. Nothing like any invalid she had ever attended.

When he looked up from his book, his blue eyes connected with hers, giving her a jolt.

He appeared the perfect picture of health, her confused mind registered. Her hand went to her breastbone, where her heart was still galloping in a violent rhythm.

As she stood staring, his mouth curved with the ghost of a smile. "I confess I am flattered by your haste."

"I . . . don't understand. Thorne's message said your condition was critical."

"It is. But Dr. Allenby claims he can do nothing for me. You are the only one who can cure me, Caro."

"So you are *not* on your deathbed?" she breathed, taking a bewildered step into the room.

"Not exactly." He set his book aside. "You refused my offer of marriage, and I need to know why."

It took a dozen more seconds for his words to sink in . . . for her to realize how thoroughly she had been duped. Despite her overwhelming relief, her temper ignited.

Caro shoved the door shut behind her, her gaze narrowing with outrage. "You . . . you bastard. You *terrified* me! You made me think you were dying!"

"At least now I know you care."

She wanted to strike him. Her hands curling into fists, Caro marched over to the bed. When she aimed a punch at his shoulder, though, Max caught her wrist and hauled her down before she could do any real damage, covering her body with his, pinning her arms above her head.

Caro struggled beneath him, practically sputtering in her fury at his deception. "I swear I could shoot you for what you put me through!"

The glint in his eyes turned sober as Max gazed down at her. "Perhaps now you understand how I felt in Barbary when I thought you might have been killed."

She jerked her hands from his grasp. "Is *that* what this conniving subterfuge is all about?" Fighting free of his weight, Caro leapt up from the bed, whirling to glare at him, while planting her hands on her hips. "You mean to punish me for what you endured in Barbary?"

"Not at all. I wanted you to give me a chance to plead my case."

"What case?"

"Sit down, and I will tell you." Max gestured toward a wing chair that had been drawn near the bed.

He had planned this encounter, Caro realized, still seething, and she doubted he would rest until she had heard him out.

"I prefer to stand," she muttered, crossing her arms over her chest and waiting. "*Well?*"

Max studied her belligerent stance for a long moment before raking a hand through his hair. "First let me say that I didn't entirely deceive you. The truth is, Caro, I am in terrible pain, and I desperately need you to heal me."

"What is wrong with you?" she demanded, baldly skeptical.

He tapped his chest, directly over his heart. "I've been bleeding inside, ever since you ordered me out of your life."

"You are *not* bleeding, you . . . cad!" Returning a glance filled with withering scorn, she spun around, intending to storm out, but he forestalled her with a simple statement:

"I have joined the Guardians."

Her sharp intake of breath was loud in the quiet room. Caro stood frozen for a moment before slowly turning back to face him. She gazed at him in shock, her brow furrowed with mingled hope and wariness. "Do you really mean it? You wouldn't jest about something so momentous, would you?"

"You know me well enough to realize I would never jest about this, angel."

Caro did sit down then; she sank into the chair, her limbs too weak to hold her, all the while searching his face earnestly. If it was true, if Max had actually joined the Guardians, it would take her a moment to absorb the enormity of his commitment.

"Why?" she finally said.

Shifting his position, Max swung his legs over the edge of the bed so he could face her.

"After we returned from Barbary, I did a great deal of soul-searching." Bracing his hands on his thighs, he leaned closer, focusing all his attention on her. "You were right, Caro. I need a purpose in my life. Something with meaning. I could return to England, of course. Someday I will inherit my uncle's title and wealth—which fairly guarantees me a life of pleasure and ease, with no worries or danger to contend with. But I suspect the shallowness of it all would drive me mad within a few short months."

Her involuntary smile implied agreement. "I rather suspect it would."

His mouth curved but his intense gaze never faltered as he continued. "So I concluded I would do better to acquire an occupation of some sort. I think I would make a fairly good Guardian. I have expertise that could prove valuable on a number of your missions."

Caro nodded solemnly. "Few people have the skills and the dedication to be part of our order, Max, and you are one of them. But . . . what about your nightmares?"

His eyes grew hooded. "I haven't conquered those yet. And I may never. But this past interminable week, I finally began to understand."

"Understand what?"

"That I've been so afraid to risk losing anyone else that I lost the capacity to live."

Caro remained silent, hardly daring to trust the gladness filling her.

"I may not be able to control fate," Max admitted in a low voice. "I can't guarantee victory. And I may still lose people I care for. But striving and failing is better than living as a numb shell of a man, with no loved ones to bring me joy."

He reached out to grasp her hands. "You are my joy, Caro."

"Oh, Max," she said hoarsely, her throat suddenly tight with tears.

His gaze softened, but his grip remained forceful. "It took me a while to understand it. For so long I had dreamed about you. You were my guardian angel, the loving spirit who watched over me and sustained me through that final hellish year of war. But even afterward, you haunted me. I knew I'd become obsessed with the bewitching woman who had offered me solace. Then I saw you again in London and . . . I felt the same bond between us, Caro."

Releasing one of her hands, Max reached up to touch her cheek. "I returned to Cyrene because I needed to know if what I felt was real. If our bond was just a fantasy I had conjured in my feverish soldier's dreams. If the enchantment that night was simply a spell cast by the island's magic. If the passion we shared was as soul-shattering as I remembered. I discovered the answers, Caro. I'm even more bewitched by you now than I was then."

For a moment Caro shut her eyes, buffeted by the wild pendulum of her emotions, aching with the desperate longing that surged in her heart.

Rising, Max drew her to her feet. "I know you think I was only offering for you out of honor, but you were wrong. I want you for my wife, Caro." He captured her face, framing it in his hands. "I meant it when I said I was bleeding inside. You wanted to send me away, but I could no more leave you than I could cut out my own heart. I love you, Caro."

He saw wonder and doubt in her gaze, and it was

a long moment before she spoke. "You . . . truly love me?"

"So much that it frightens me."

Her tears spilled over, wrenching at Max. "Good God, there is no reason to cry, sweetheart."

"Yes, yes there is. I never thought you would actually love me."

"Come here."

When his arms went around her, she buried her face in his shoulder, trying to stem her tears.

Max pressed his lips against her hair. "I don't know if I could survive the terror of losing you, but I am absolutely certain about one thing: I can't live without you. You make me glad to be alive. You give meaning to my life, Caro. You *are* my life. I only existed before you."

Caro gave another helpless sob. She was crying from happiness, she realized.

"I think," he said softly, "that I've loved you since our first night together at the ruins."

"It was the same with me, Max. I fell hopelessly in love with you that night."

He drew back to stare at her, his gaze sweeping over her, wild and intense. "Is that true?"

"Yes. Oh, Max, I love you so much." She loved him down to the deepest corners of her soul.

The ragged sound that came from his throat was part triumph, part prayer of thanks. Without warning, Max lifted Caro off her feet and whirled her around and around, embracing her so fiercely, her ribs hurt.

She was dizzy and breathless and laughing through her tears when he finally set her down again.

But his arms remained tightly around her, his gaze keen as he demanded, "If you love me, then why the devil did you refuse my proposal?"

Caro sniffed, giving him a shaky smile. "I wanted you to be free to choose your fate, not be forced to wed me or to join our order out of a sense of obligation. I couldn't bear to see you suffer for my sake, Max. I knew it would only cause you more nightmares if you couldn't accept my being a Guardian."

"I've come to terms with your being a Guardian." His mouth pursed in a frown. "I can't say that I won't worry about you whenever you're on a mission, but I will endeavor to control my protective urges at least."

"Even if there are times when I must go without you?"

"Even then."

She exhaled all the shaking air in her lungs and pressed her face again into his shoulder. "I still find it hard to believe that you have become a Guardian."

"I think Philip would have wanted this for me," he said quietly.

Her heart twisted at the wistfulness in his voice. "I'm certain he would have. But I had given up hope."

"Sir Gawain hadn't yet given up," Max recounted, "but he seemed vastly relieved when I accepted his invitation to join. I don't think he wanted to press the issue of banishing me from your island."

"I was prepared to live in England with you," Caro admitted, "if that was the only way I could have you."

Max went still. "You would have made that sacrifice for me?"

"Yes. But now you will be the one making the sacrifice."

"It won't be any sort of sacrifice, Caro. Cyrene is a paradise, as you well know. And if I have you, I can be happy living anywhere. At any event, I couldn't ask you to give up your medical career when I know how vital it is to you. But I fully intend to bring a surgeon to Cyrene to take over Allenby's role, so you won't work yourself into the ground caring for his patients. You will have to forgive me if I'm selfish enough to want you for myself part of the time."

Caro raised her gaze to him, a smile in her eyes. "Do you really think you could persuade a surgeon to practice on Cyrene?"

"I'm certain of it. I know several excellent army doctors who are currently unemployed and who could fulfill Allenby's role here. I promise you I will persuade at least one of them to settle here."

She kissed him lightly, then shook her head in disbelief. "Max, do you really want to marry me? I will no doubt make you a terrible wife. If I remain Dr. Allenby's assistant, I will sometimes be called away from home, day or night, for long hours at a time."

"I don't give a damn," Max said. "I intend to marry you, love, and I assure you, I won't take no for an answer. If you won't agree, I will simply plague you until you give in."

Her watery laugh expressed her capitulation. "Then I suppose I will just have to give in."

When a slow, devastating smile crept across his lips, Caro shut her eyes again, wanting to pinch herself to make certain she wasn't dreaming.

Max seemed to be wondering the same thing. "Say it again, angel. Tell me that you love me."

"I love you, Max Leighton. I will love you now and forever and always." She raised her hands to his raven hair. "But I think I would rather show you instead."

She kissed him again, letting her lips brush his slowly, fervently, this time.

Raw need bolted through Max, and he wrapped his arms around her tightly, drinking her in, absorbing her. After all the apprehension and uncertainty of the past weeks, he was like a parched desert, craving the life-giving rain that was Caro.

And like rain, she brought all his body to vivid life; he suddenly felt white-hot with desire.

Max heard himself groan, heard the soft whimper Caro made as she responded to his impassioned kiss. Yet with a herculean effort, he wrenched his mouth from hers.

Breathing hard, he gazed at her in frustration, clenching his teeth in an effort to ignore the burning in his loins. "Enough!" His voice held an unmistakable hoarseness. "If you keep that up, I'll wind up taking you here and now. As much as I want you, angel, I don't intend to make love to you until we are well and truly wed."

Escaping her embrace, Max flung himself on the bed and pushed back against the bed's mahogany headboard, creating a safer distance between them.

Caro stared at him, obviously bewildered.

"I'm told," Max said with a pained grin, "that I can petition the bishop at Gibraltar for a special license to wed, so we won't have to wait three weeks to call the banns, but it will still take the better part of a week."

Her confusion easing into a smile, Caro climbed

onto the bed beside him. "If we were at sea, Captain Biddick could marry us."

"But I want a proper wedding. I want the whole world to know that you are mine."

Shifting onto her knees, she leaned closer to Max. "Must we really wait that long?" She reached out to run a provocative finger down his chest, lingering on a button of his waistcoat.

Flinching, Max caught her hand and held it away. "I'll thank you to behave yourself, witch. Thorne would carve out my liver if I made love to you again without the benefit of matrimony. It was all I could do to convince him to write that note to summon you here."

Caro frowned suddenly. "Thorne was in on your ruse? Devil take him! I will carve out *his* liver for terrifying me so."

"You can't blame him. He only wanted to be certain that I proposed to you again. In fact, he'll be waiting below to learn if I succeeded."

Caro pressed her lips together, not at all mollified. "I suppose I should inform Isabella as well. And I should let her know that you aren't on your deathbed after all. She came here with me because she feared for your life, as I did."

"By now Thorne will have told her why I resorted to subterfuge." Max regarded Caro thoughtfully. "How will she take the news of our marriage?"

"She will be delighted, no doubt." Caro gave him a sugary smile. "*Despite* the fact that only an hour ago she was encouraging me to take another lover so I could get over you sooner."

Max's gaze narrowed. "Was she, now?"

"Only because she saw how miserable I was when I thought I had lost you."

"I can see I will need to have a serious discussion with Lady Isabella. I warn you, as long as I have a breath left in my body, you won't be taking any other lovers."

Caro's smile softened. "You needn't worry, Max. I would never, ever want anyone but you."

"And I only want you, my bewitching angel." His voice was rich and husky, while a hard and beautiful vibrancy shimmered deep in his eyes. Caro glimpsed such love there that it rocked her soul.

Her fingers rose to caress his cheek. Her aching heart was too full of joy, yet she wanted to give him one last opportunity before he sealed his fate.

"Max, are you *truly* certain you want to wed me?" she asked. "I would be content to just be your lover."

Max turned his face to press a kiss against her palm. "But I couldn't be. I want you for my wife, Caro. I want to be your husband, the companion who grows old and gray with you, as well as your only lover."

Her smile was tremulous. She still couldn't accept how desirable she was, Max knew.

Despite the danger of losing control, he gathered Caro fully against him. Resting his cheek on her hair, he simply held her, letting his embrace communicate how much he desired her. He could feel the shaky breath vibrate through her body, and a fierceness took him.

He wanted Caro as his lover for all time. Yet while he would claim her body, he knew it would never be enough. Even her love would not be enough. He wanted to possess her soul, the way she possessed his.

He wanted every part of her, for the rest of his days. And he would take great pleasure in convincing his lovely bride of that unalterable fact.

Epilogue

Torches blazed on the walls of the rock chamber, casting a brilliant glow over the small private ceremony where Max was being knighted as a Guardian.

The initiation rites to welcome him into the order were simple but solemn. He stood before the altar, with Sir Gawain presiding, and solemnly swore an oath to protect and defend the ideals that the Guardians held so dear. Then, commanding Max to kneel, Sir Gawain raised the magnificent sword Excalibur.

Light flashed and glittered on the jeweled hilt, infusing Max with the same sense of awe and wonder he'd felt when he first spied the legendary weapon. And when the heavy steel blade touched his shoulder as he was dubbed, he could swear that a sizzling current of energy leapt from the metal into his flesh, almost burning him. At the same time he was filled with a powerful feeling of calm, of peace, of rightness.

"You are now a Guardian of the Sword," Sir Gawain pronounced gravely.

When Max rose, his bride of four hours moved forward, her joyous smile bright enough to rival the torch flames.

Caro intended merely to embrace him, Max knew, but he drew her into his arms and captured her mouth with a fierce kiss. She tensed in startlement at first, then returned his caress with obvious fervor, her hunger matching his, revealing how difficult it had been for them both to endure their abstinence.

Their kiss went on for such a long moment that eventually Sir Gawain cleared his throat. When Caro emerged from Max's embrace, her face flushed with embarrassment, the jovial sound of male laughter rang out from their sparse audience.

Behind the baronet, Thorne looked on like a benevolent older brother. John Yates beamed, while Santos Verra grinned ear to ear. Ryder, much recovered from his thigh wound, was there, as was the Earl of Hawkhurst.

"Evidently, Leighton," Hawk drawled wryly, "no one informed you that kissing is not part of the customary initiation."

Max grinned but kept one arm possessively around his bride, feeling no remorse. This was the first time he'd been able to do more than touch Caro since their espousal hours earlier.

They'd been married in the great hall shortly before noon. It seemed fitting that Sir Gawain had acted in place of Caro's father, to bestow her hand on Max.

The wedding breakfast that followed was a splendid feast that had gone on all afternoon. The guests were still merrily celebrating when a handful of Caro's closest friends and fellow Guardians had slipped away, into the depths of the castle, and rowed across the underground lake to the chamber where the legendary sword was kept secreted.

Now Sir Gawain carefully restored the sword to the altar. Then one by one, the Guardians heartily shook Max's hand and embraced his new bride.

Sir Gawain was last, and his eyes had grown misty when he kissed Caro's cheek. "I wish you a long and happy life together."

Her smile was radiant as she slipped her arm through Max's. "I have high hopes that it will be."

"Well then," the baronet murmured, "we should return to the wedding celebration before we are missed."

Max gave the resplendent sword one final look before descending the stone steps after Caro. The Guardians separated into two boats, with Thorne rowing the newlyweds.

Taking the lead, his boat retraced their earlier route, entering the giant cavern with its fantastic shapes and hues and crossing the dark, shimmering lake, both of which still held Max spellbound. After docking in the sea cave, they climbed up from the dungeons and negotiated several castle corridors and storerooms to emerge in the great hall.

The sound of musicians tuning up greeted them. There would be a supper soon and a ball afterward, which would continue long into the night.

"You must promise me a dance later, love," Thorne murmured wickedly to Caro. No doubt, she surmised, because he knew how much she had once despised dancing. Yet that was before Max had taught her to waltz.

Before she could reply, Max shook his head. "Sorry, old fellow, but you will have to claim my wife's hand some other time. We won't be remaining long enough for her to dance."

"Spoilsport," Thorne gibed.

"Go find your own bride if you're so keen for a partner."

Laughing, Thorne held up his hands as if to ward off the very thought. "Pray, don't wish such an appalling fate on me just because you found the one woman in the world who is worth a kingdom."

"Much more than a kingdom," Max said softly, gazing at Caro.

His intimate, loving glance warmed her down to her toes. And when he drew her to his side, she was intently aware of the strength of the arm that lay draped so casually over her shoulders, and the heat of his body.

Just then Dr. Allenby broke from the crowd and came toward them. The doctor had not been part of the ceremony, for he was not officially a Guardian, but he knew enough about their order to guess what had just happened.

He clasped Max's hand, offering his congratulations, before kissing Caro's cheek fondly. "You look positively radiant, my dear. And I retract all the derogatory remarks I made about this chap of yours. He isn't as bad as I feared."

"No," she agreed, laughing, "he isn't bad at all. You might even say we are extremely fortunate to have him here."

Dr. Allenby gave a reluctant grunt.

Max broke into their musings. "Doctor, pray excuse us."

Without waiting for a reply, he drew Caro to one side of the hall. When he bent to whisper in her ear, the brush of his warm lips made her shiver. "I think it's time for us to take our leave, don't you?"

The sensual heat in his eyes began to work on her

pulse, and she had no trouble reading his unspoken message: He badly wanted to make love to her.

"I must say good-bye to Isabella first," Caro replied, an aching need for Max welling up in her.

"Very well, but do it quickly. I can't vouch for my control much longer. I'm likely to throw you over my shoulder and carry you off so I can ravish you."

They found Isabella holding court among a half-dozen male admirers, but she soon spied them and excused herself.

With a loving smile, she embraced Caro in her soft, perfumed arms. "It does my heart good to see you so happy, my dearest girl."

"I *am* happy, Isabella. Deliriously so. But will you forgive us if we take our leave now? It is our wedding night after all."

"Go," Isabella said with a laugh. "I still remember what it was like to have a handsome rogue for a husband."

They were mostly silent when they stole from the hall and walked hand in hand to the stables, where Max had already made preparations for their escape, including horses and supplies to last several days.

He helped Caro up, then mounted behind her and wrapped his arms around her. The waning November afternoon was bright with sunshine, so there was no need to warm her, yet Max was driven by the compelling need to hold her.

They turned north as they rode away from the castle, for they intended to visit their secret grotto before consummating their marriage at the Roman ruins. By the time the horses began the climb through the tangle of myrtle and pine, perhaps a half hour of daylight was left, and the setting sun cast a golden hue over the wild terrain.

A feeling of great contentment settled over Max. He was home now. He belonged on Cyrene. Yet he would always be home as long as he held Caro in his arms.

This island was a haven, but it was Caro who had sheltered him, who had healed him. Who had made him see the beauty in life again.

This island was a sensual paradise, with an uncanny ability to arouse the senses, but the soul-deep pleasure he felt was due wholly to this remarkable woman.

When she leaned back against him and sighed, desire, heavy and urgent, began tightening his body.

Wincing against the relentless ache, Max shut his eyes. He was grateful the waiting was almost at an end so he could make her his wife in truth. In his mind he was already inside her, tasting her, feeling her, giving her pleasure. . . . Loving her.

He had become a Guardian in more ways than one when he'd sworn the oath to protect and defend the order.

He was Caro's protector now, the guardian of her heart. And she was his.

He pressed his lips against her hair, telling her wordlessly of his love.

"What are you thinking?" she murmured.

"How fortunate I am to have you."

She gave another dreamy sigh and laid her head back on his shoulder.

The sun was setting majestically when they arrived at their secret hideaway, the brilliant, rose-gold rays casting a radiant light that set the jeweled lake ablaze and turned the misting waterfall to molten lava.

Struck by the spellbinding sight, they paused to take in the view of their own special paradise. Then driven by a more corporeal desire, they spurred their mount forward.

Caro saw to the packhorse while Max made brief forays into the grotto to carry supplies and to light the brazier for when they returned later that night. When he joined Caro outside, he found her standing at the entrance, gazing at the incredible sunset.

"This is so beautiful," she whispered almost reverently.

Max couldn't refute her. The splendor had the power to make his breath catch. But he shook his head as he wrapped his arms around her from behind. "Not as beautiful as my lovely wife."

She gave a soft laugh. "Max, you don't need to shower me with flattery any longer. I know you desire me."

"But you aren't yet sufficiently convinced." He gave her a hard squeeze. "Repeat after me. 'I am the most alluring woman a man could ever want. Desired and cherished and adored by my wonderful husband.' "

Her laughter rang out, disturbing the quiet hush of their hideaway, but she obeyed, repeating his declaration word for word.

"Not good enough, my sweet temptress," Max declared. "I still hear a measure of doubt in your tone." He turned her to face him. "You really *are* extraordinary, you know."

Smiling, Caro reached up to loop her arms around his neck. "Whether I am or not, I am glad you believe it."

"I do. And I believe our children will be extraordinary as well."

She went still, searching his face. "Do you truly want children, Max? I know you couldn't possibly be anything other than a devoted, caring father, but you will be risking your heart."

"I realize that, my love. But I am ready for it. I want a family of our own."

She was mesmerized by the emotions playing in his eyes. "Then give me a child, Max."

His smile held a quiet brilliance that touched her deep inside. Taking her hand, he led her to their waiting horse.

Night had fallen by the time they reached the Roman ruins, but the moon rose silently above the dark horizon to light their way. They halted at the foot of the baths, drinking in this new scene of spectacular beauty: the calm, shimmering Mediterranean beyond the cliff's edge. The silver, terraced pools rippling luminously in the night shadows.

To Caro the ruins seemed just as enchanted now as they had over a year ago. More so, since Max was now her husband as well as her lover. But this time the serenity of the ruins matched the serenity she felt in her heart.

Max escorted her up the terraced steps and made a bed of blankets beside the center pool, where they had first known passion together. With the steamy warmth given off by the waters, the night air was pleasantly temperate, but they undressed each other without lingering, eager to be together at last.

While he shed the last of his clothing, Caro slipped beneath the blankets, waiting in an agony of anticipation for his touch. Max roused a wild yearning in her blood, and only he could assuage it. She drank in the raw power of his beautiful, moonlit body before he joined her beneath the covers, and relished his heat as he lay close beside her.

There was a rich, welcoming glow in his eyes as he eased his weight over her. He cupped her breasts in his palms, running his thumbs lightly over her nipples, then bent to kiss the taut peaks.

When she arched against him, he set about exciting her with all the sensual skill he possessed, using his hands, his mouth, his hard body. In only moments her flesh was hot enough to burn.

"Please, Max . . . now," she pleaded with him.

"Yes, love, now. I want you sheathing me. . . ."

Willingly she opened to him, wrapping her limbs around him to bring him closer. His hot, tender look held her enthralled as he entered her, while joy whispered through her with heavy urgency.

Max felt the same joy. For a moment he was content to watch the lush sensuality suffuse Caro's lovely face, but then sensations began to shimmer outward, taking control.

He seized her hips with feverish hands, desperately wanting more of her. His roughly muttered words of love and lust and need were harsh against her lips as they cleaved to each other, shattered together.

It was a long while later before the wondrous ecstasy ebbed away. Max could still feel the ripples caressing him, feel the tremors that flowed through her body as she lay replete beneath him.

Finally easing his weight from her, he lay back and gathered Caro against him, her cheek on his shoulder, her hair a wild tangle across the breadth of his chest.

His heart was still beating painfully as he stared up

at the moonlit sky. It had been their deepest bonding, sweeter than anything he had known before. He wondered if they had made a child together.

He pulled her close.

It didn't matter if it had happened tonight. It would, Max had no doubt. They would build a new life together. Their own family. Showering the love and devotion on their offspring that they had denied for themselves for so long. They would be guardians of their children and of each other.

"You were wrong, love," he murmured, his lips caressing her damp temple. "There is no island spell. But the enchantment is very, very real."

He felt Caro smile against his throat, while her contented murmur told him of her complete agreement.

Please read on for a sneak peek
at the next sizzling romance from Nicole Jordan

Lord of Seduction

Coming in December 2004

Prologue

London, March 1814

The passion in her kiss caught him off guard. Christopher, Viscount Thorne, braced himself as his mistress clung tightly to him, her fingers twining sensuously in his hair, her mouth trying to devour his.

Moments before, he'd been admitted by a servant to the elegant little house in St. John's Wood and shown upstairs to the parlor that he'd recently refurbished for Rosamond at great expense. But he barely had time to shed his greatcoat before she threw herself at him with a breathy little sigh.

"At last," she'd exclaimed, pressing her rosebud lips hotly against his.

Thorne couldn't quite understand her lust. As kisses

went, this one was hungry and eager, tasting of urgent need, almost desperation. He had significant expertise arousing a woman's body, but he'd done nothing yet to elicit such a fervent response.

Gingerly pulling her hands from his hair, Thorne drew back to study his mistress of two months. She was a creature of remarkable beauty, with translucent skin, large blue eyes, and a petite but magnificently shaped figure. Her blond tresses, several shades lighter than his own golden hue, spilled over her shoulders in sensual disarray, as if she'd just risen from her bed and intended to return there as soon as she could lure him to join her.

"Your eagerness is flattering, darling," Thorne admonished, "but there is no need for such haste. We have the entire night."

"I know, but I don't want to waste a moment of it. Come, my lord, please. . . ."

Eagerly Rosamond took his hand and led him into the adjacent perfumed bedchamber. Candlelight filled the room with a golden glow, while a fire blazed in the hearth, illuminating the pale silken sheets of the enormous bed.

Thorne permitted Rosamond to guide him to the bed and press him back so that he was half sitting, half leaning against the high mattress. With a graceful shrug then, she slid her dressing gown off her shoulders and down her hips, so that the garment pooled on the carpet, baring her voluptuous body to his heated gaze.

Thorne felt his loins throb.

When she knelt before him, he concluded that she meant to attend him while he was still fully clothed.

But he let Rosamond have her way with him, watching indulgently as she unfastened the front placket of his satin evening breeches.

His hand moving to her fair hair, he shut his eyes at the burgeoning carnal pleasure and gave himself up to her expert ministrations and the ravishing delight she offered.

It was several moments more before he realized that the soft sounds coming from Rosamond's own throat were not moans but quiet little sobs.

She was weeping—and not with passion.

Bewildered, Thorne opened his eyes to stare down at the beauty kneeling between his spread thighs. His lovemaking frequently made women sob with ecstasy, but something else was the matter here.

Catching Rosamond's wrists to stop her, he drew her to her feet. Her pale cheeks were streaked with tears, while her huge blue eyes shimmered with a disturbing sadness.

"Tell me what is wrong, sweetheart," he said gently.

"Forgive me, my lord. I am overwrought." She brushed at her streaming eyes. "The thought of never kissing you again, never making love to you again, makes me weep."

"I beg your pardon?" Thorne murmured, not certain he had heard correctly.

"This will be our last night together," she said sorrowfully.

He felt the heat of passion start to drain away. "Pray tell me why you think so."

"Your father says you mean to offer for a bride any day now."

Mention of his illustrious father definitely cooled

Thorne's ardor. The Duke of Redcliffe had long tried to rule his life, and in recent years had schemed and plotted to get him respectably married. Indeed, avoiding his father's machinations had become something of a game between them.

"You never told me you planned to wed," Rosamond added with a pout of her lush lips.

Thorne felt the hardness of his erection fade altogether. "Possibly," he replied, releasing her wrists, "because I have no intention of shackling myself with chains of matrimony."

"Your father says differently."

"I'm certain he does," Thorne said drily, torn between amusement and exasperation at his noble father.

"I do understand the ways of the quality," Rosamond assured him. "You are a duke's only son and heir, and Redcliffe craves seeing you settled with a proper wife and a son of your own to carry on the title. Furthermore, he wants no impediments to your securing a distinguished bride, and the wealthy young lady he has chosen for you has grave objections to you flaunting your mistresses. At least, that is what his grace told me."

"I assure you," Thorne vowed in clipped tones, "I will never marry my father's choice of a bride."

"Even so, this must be farewell between us. . . ." Tears welled in Rosamond's eyes again. "I have agreed to your father's terms."

"Terms?"

"Redcliffe offered me his patronage," she confessed. "He promised to secure me a leading role in the opera if I break off my liaison with you."

"My father *bribed* you?" Thorne's eyebrows shot

up as he debated whether to laugh or curse. His father had never gone so far as to interfere directly in his amorous affairs before, but this was a devilish intrusion—bribing his mistress to leave his protection in order to clear the way for his marriage to a wealthy, well-born debutante.

Thorne bit off an oath, promising to deliver a few select words to his sire when next they met.

"It is not precisely a bribe," Rosamond objected. "And it is for your own sake more than mine."

"You may spare me your concern, love," Thorne replied, his drawl languid.

She bit her lip, evidently realizing the hollowness of her argument. "Truly, I will miss you dreadfully, my lord. No one is as magnificent a lover as you."

"I am gratified you think so."

Rosamond peered up at him through her kohl-darkened lashes. "Are you very angry with me?"

Thorne fastened his breeches while he pondered what he felt. Admittedly his pride smarted to have his mistress choose her opera career over him. And unquestionably it stung to be outmaneuvered by his father.

He could offer Rosamond a higher bribe, no doubt, but he didn't want a mistress so disloyal that her allegiance could be bought— The thought brought a sardonic grin to Thorne's mouth. Rosamond's delectable charms had always been for sale to the highest bidder.

But his father had won this round of their game, he conceded, amused in spite of himself. He would regret losing Rosamond, naturally, for her amorous skills could satisfy even a man of his jaded and discriminating tastes. But he could bear the disappointment.

Summoning a smile, he ran his thumb tenderly over

her lower lip. "No, I am not angry with you, love. My heart is wounded, of course, but I understand why you would favor your career over me."

"Thank you for being so understanding, my lord. . . . But please, won't you stay the night? I had intended to make this an occasion you would long remember."

With a reluctant glance at her luscious nude body, Thorne shook his head. "I think not, sweetheart."

Reaching for him again, Rosamond gave him one last, clinging kiss, until he gently pried her hands away.

Leaving her sobbing anew, Thorne made his way downstairs and collected his greatcoat, then let himself out the rear door, heading toward the mews behind the house.

Since he'd planned to stay the evening, his horses had already been stabled, and he had to rouse his coachman from a pleasant game of draughts in order to ready his carriage.

Waiting in the frigid night air, Thorne stamped his feet against the cold. This was the harshest winter in memory, and he found himself longing for the golden warmth of Cyrene—the small island in the western Mediterranean where he spent several months of each year. He would have made his home there permanently had not many of his missions required his presence in England.

Oddly enough, he had his father to thank for the drastic change in his fate. Years ago his outrageous behavior had so provoked his illustrious sire that Thorne was banished to Cyrene, where he was given the chance to redeem himself. He'd joined the secret society of protectors headquartered there—the Guardians of the Sword. The order had been formed centuries ago with the purpose of rooting out evil and tyranny across Europe, its members sworn to uphold the ancient ideals once championed by a legendary leader.

Thorne had not only developed a passion for the golden island, but his recklessness and his love of danger had proved assets in his new career, and he'd become a highly effective Guardian. He had continued, however, to be at odds with his father, despite the affection they bore for each other. Redcliffe continued to deplore his wild ways, Thorne was well aware.

If he ever did marry, it sure as the devil wouldn't be to a milquetoast miss his father chose for him, but to a woman who was brave and spirited and worthy of being a Guardian's life mate.

He would never settle for less.

Meanwhile, he fully intended to enjoy his bachelorhood along with his rakehell friends, while continuing his frequently dangerous role as a Guardian.

Just then his groom held open the door to his town coach for him.

"Home, my lord?" his coachman queried.

The question reminded Thorne that he had just been rejected by his mistress. Rejection was a novel experience for him. Usually he could have any woman he wanted.

"No, not home. Take me to Madame Venus's club."

Climbing inside, he sank back against the velvet squabs. Venus's sin club on Mount Street was part gaming hell, part high-class brothel. There he could find delectable female companionship if it suited his mood, or a high-stakes game of faro or hazard amid excellent company.

Thorne settled in for the half-hour drive, focusing primarily on cooling the savage ache in his loins that the lovely Rosamond had intentionally aroused, curse her.

By the time his carriage came to a halt, Thorne had himself well under control. Soft lights shone from the windows of the large mansion as he mounted the front steps, and he could hear the convivial chatter of contented guests as he was admitted by a hulking brute of a footman.

Venus's nightly soirees were famous for their superb wines, exhilarating games of chance, and titillating carnal indulgences. The large, elegant drawing room was the center of the club's activity. One end boasted a low stage for erotic performances and an orchestra for patrons who enjoyed dancing. The remainder of the room was decorated with plush brocade sofas and card tables.

Thorne stood a moment surveying the company. Hearing his name hailed, he made his way toward one of the card tables.

"Hah! You owe me twenty guineas, Hastings!" a seated gentleman proclaimed. "I told you he would show."

"My dear Boothe," Lord Hastings drawled. "The wager was whether Thorne would concede victory to his illustrious papa. So tell us, Kit, did La Rose refuse you her favors?"

Technically Rosamond had done just the opposite tonight, but Thorne didn't intend to mince words. Instead he flashed a self-mocking grin, admitting his defeat. "Sadly lowering, isn't it?"

"And you did nothing to fight back?"

Evidently word had already gotten around about his father's latest attempt to force his hand.

"I fear not," Thorne replied. "It would have required too much effort."

Drawing up a chair, he joined the table, even though he had no particular desire for cards at present. For the next round, he pretended an interest in the play while the conversation flowed around him:

"His grace won't win in the end. Thorne has slipped out of more marriage traps than an eel out of nets."

"Never knew a gentleman so wary of getting leg-shackled as you, Thorne. The married state ain't so bad."

"Might as well give in gracefully. Redcliffe has deep enough pockets to buy off all your mistresses from now to eternity."

"Know what you should do, old trout? Take refuge on your island. Foil your sire's damnable plots. He cannot reach you there."

"I might consider that," Thorne murmured with all sincerity.

Chapter One

The Isle of Cyrene, March 1815

She wished she could paint him. His nude body was beautiful, set against the backdrop of a turquoise sea.

Feeling her pulse leap, Diana Sheridan stared transfixed at the breathtaking sight as Christopher Thorne rose from the gently foaming waves.

The sun-drenched cove below the bluffs was one of many small bays and inlets secreted along the island's rugged, picturesque shoreline. The scene would make a magnificent landscape on canvas, Diana well knew. The golden line of sand dotted with palms, the white, rocky promontory stretching to meet the sparkling, endless Mediterranean beyond . . . Both of these dazzled in the sunlight. But it was the man's virile form glistening with seawater that most captured her attention.

She wet her dry lips.

She had only seen Lord Thorne once from afar, several years ago. If she'd thought him a beautiful man then, she was even more captivated by his physical attributes now. Unable to help herself, Diana studied his body, admiring him from both artistic and feminine perspectives.

She had never seen a completely nude man, nor had she ever painted one. She'd trained in human anatomy and the techniques of oils by duplicating sketchings and paintings by prominent artists and by studying plaster casts of ancient statues. But canvas was still inanimate, and statues had no color, no life.

Not like this man did.

Even the great masters would have relished so vital a subject.

Admittedly she had a measure of talent, yet she wasn't certain that she could do Christopher Thorne justice; that she could capture the vivid feeling of life in his lean, lithe body.

He looked almost leonine. His streaming wet hair was dark gold in color, while a sprinkling of hair on his powerful chest arrowed down to his groin to widen in more dark gold curls. He moved with the grace of a lion as well, as he climbed up the narrow beach and flung himself down on a linen towel spread on the sand.

Diana stood riveted, fascinated by his body—his broad shoulders, strong back, slim hips and tight buttocks, athletic flanks. . . .

Her heart was beating far too rapidly, she realized, and her skin had suddenly flushed. Worse, she felt an unmistakable warmth pool between her thighs at the primal sight of him.

"Don't be a fool," she suddenly muttered, scolding herself beneath her breath. "You should know better than to allow an attractive man to affect you."

Perhaps she could blame her flush on the unfamiliar climate. It was only mid-March but the golden afternoon was warmer than many summer days in England. And her unsteadiness was no doubt due to the solid surface beneath her feet. She'd arrived on Cyrene with her younger cousin Amy merely two hours ago, and after spending a lengthy voyage on the swaying deck of a ship, she still hadn't properly regained her balance.

They'd traveled a great distance in search of Thorne—from London through the cold Atlantic, past the peninsula of Portugal and Spain, around Gibraltar, and another day's sail beyond the Balearic Islands of Ibiza and Mallorca and Menorca.

When she'd hired a carriage and sought out Thorne's estates, they were taken to a splendid villa perched on the eastern shore of the island. His servants suggested he might be found in the cove beneath the bluffs, at the rear of the villa, so Diana left Amy to enjoy a refreshing tea while she investigated. Upon seeing a man swimming below, Diana had carefully negotiated the steps carved into the rock. But when she reached the beach, she was taken aback to discover him nude.

No doubt she should have expected something so scandalous from Thorne. This was the charmingly wicked nobleman she had heard so much about over the years—both from her cousin Nathaniel and from the scandal sheets. By all reports Thorne was a rebel, wild and reckless and totally unconventional.

It was no surprise that he was one of England's most eligible and unattainable catches. He bore the title of viscount, and was heir to a dukedom. And his fortune was said to be substantial, even without the prospect of one day inheriting his father's vast estates.

After seeing him now, however, she could understand better why he was considered a devil with women: because he was so sinfully beautiful. But she'd made that disastrous mistake before, falling in love with a beautiful face.

"Confound him, don't you dare allow his looks to addle your wits," Diana chastised herself.

Trying to regain control of her senses, she remained in the shadow of the bluff as she debated whether to leave or to make herself known to Thorne.

She needed to speak to him alone, the sooner the better. He might have been awarded guardianship of Nathaniel's younger sister Amy, but Diana still felt responsible for the girl. At nineteen Amy was now an heiress and, as such, was the target for numerous fortune hunters and rakes bent on seduction.

Since Nathaniel's shocking death last year, they'd both spent the interval in mourning for him, quietly living in the country. But such a tranquil life had made Amy highly susceptible to male attention and flattery, and now she fancied herself in love with the handsome fortune hunter who'd begun to pursue her during the Christmas season.

Diana was determined to prevent the girl from making the same ruinous choice she had once made—to stop Amy from being so badly hurt, the way Diana had been.

If it meant dealing with the devilish Lord Thorne, she would do it.

Diana squared her shoulders. She didn't intend to let any man, wicked or not, beautiful or not, naked or not, sway her from her purpose.

Summoning her courage, she took a deep breath, raised her muslin skirts to keep them from dragging in the sand, and stepped forward into the sunlight.

* * *

He knew he was being watched.

His sixth sense alerting him to danger, Thorne glanced covertly at his pile of clothing, assuring himself that the dagger he always carried was close to hand.

Pretending to keep his eyes shut, he stretched languidly and rolled over onto his back, so that he could glimpse the intruder who was now moving toward him.

The watcher wore skirts.

What the devil was a woman doing down here in his private cove? And a lady, by the looks of her attire.

Irritation was Thorne's automatic response. The last genteel female to unexpectedly see him in the buff had tried to trap him into wedlock.

In fact, that lamentable incident was what had driven him to take refuge on Cyrene for the past two months. At a house party in the English countryside in January, a calculating young debutante had sneaked into his bedchamber while he slept and was caught naked with him by her avaricious mother.

Feigning shock, Mama had immediately petitioned his ducal father, insisting that Thorne be forced to marry the girl. Redcliffe contended he should do the honorable thing and accept his fate, but innocent of seducing the little schemer, Thorne had refused to be dishonorably trapped in marriage. As soon as he'd concluded his current assignment for the Guardians, he'd sailed for Cyrene to escape their connivances and his father's hounding.

Highly suspicious now, Thorne peered through his lowered eyelids at the interloper. She had stopped a short distance away—the moment he'd rolled over, in fact—and was staring at him as if fascinated.

If she was a blasted husband-hunter, he would send her packing. And if not . . .

He couldn't deny she was a beauty, with her delicate fine-boned face, flawless ivory skin, and nicely curved body. Her high-waisted muslin gown of dark blue flattered her slender, shapely figure and firm, high breasts, and sent an immediate shaft of awareness down to his loins.

She looked, however, to be a bit older than the usual debs who pursued him, perhaps in her mid-twenties. She wore her rich dark hair pinned up in a simple knot, Thorne noted, and her eyes, which were just as dark and lustrous, held awe and curiosity as she surveyed him.

Deliberately he opened his own eyes and locked gazes with her.

The impact made him feel an instantaneous heat—an involuntary physical response that came as a sweet if unwelcome shock.

She felt the same sweet shock, he was certain. She had stiffened, looking wary and unsettled now, as if all her feminine instincts were on keen alert. Just as all his male instincts had suddenly roared to vibrant life.

To Thorne's further irritation, he could feel himself hardening. It was difficult to remain unmoved, though, when a lovely young woman was contemplating his body so intently.

Cursing his swelling erection, Thorne pushed himself up on one elbow. "Do you realize you are trespassing on private land?"

"Your servants said I might find you here."

Her low, husky voice sent a further charge of heat along his nerve endings. "Did my father send you?" he demanded. "If so, then pray let me inform you that I have no intention of wedding you."

She blinked at that. "I beg your pardon?"

"The last young lady to see me nude claimed I compromised her and insisted that I wed her. If that is your aim, sweeting, you can turn around at once and take yourself away."

He watched as her sensual mouth thinned in a wry smile. "I promise you, my lord, you are safe with me. I have no interest in marriage whatsoever."

Her claim reassured him to a degree, yet Thorne couldn't let himself relax. "You obviously have an interest in my body."

Color rose in her cheeks, and she looked flustered to be caught ogling him. "Forgive me. I was contemplating you with an artist's eye . . . trying to determine how I would paint you."

Thorne's lips curved in a sardonic grin. "Now *that* is a tactic no one has ever used on me before."

Her chin lifted with a trace of defiance. "I am perfectly serious. I am an artist."

He regarded her for a long moment. "If that's true, then I suppose I should be flattered by your attention."

"It *is* true. You would make an admirable subject for a portrait."

"Is that all? You see me as one of your subjects?" He arched a taunting eyebrow. "You don't feel the slightest urges beyond the artistic?"

"I regret to disappoint you, but no, my interest in your male anatomy is purely objective."

"How lowering. I am mortally wounded."

Her wry smile held genuine humor this time. "I

should think you would be pleased. By all reports you have an army of eager females fawning all over you."

"A regiment, at the very least," Thorne drawled, feigning a shudder. "And all with matrimony in mind. But I have no desire whatsoever to be leg-shackled."

She took a step toward him. "Well, you can rest easy, my lord. I have no intention of wedding anyone, most certainly not a man of your rakish reputation."

"I am hardly a rake."

"If you were a gentleman"—she gave his lower body a pointed glance—"you would cover yourself."

Realizing his manhood was fully erect now, Thorne reached for his shirt. "I confess that a beautiful woman staring at my loins has an arousing effect."

The flush in her cheeks fascinated him. In truth, *she* fascinated him. From her bold appraisal, he had to conclude that she was no meek-mannered miss. Nothing like the chaste, featherheaded young innocents who often pursued him. If he hadn't sent her scurrying away in fright by now, she had to have some measure of experience. An enticing thought, Thorne reflected.

Draping the shirt around his hips, he tied the sleeves together and rose to his feet. "Better?"

"Yes . . . I think so."

"I *am* a gentleman, you know—although my father would sometimes dispute it. What of you?" His gaze raked down her body. "Most ladies would think twice before coming to a secluded cove where a strange man was sea-bathing in the nude."

Her eyes kindled a little at that. "Of course I am a lady."

"Yet you come here alone, and you don't shy from the sight of me."

"I wished to speak to you in private. And I must warn you, attempts to intimidate me usually have precisely the opposite effect. You won't frighten me away."

He was beginning to enjoy himself, Thorne realized. Certainly he no longer wanted to drive her away. Instead he wondered if he could persuade her to stay. "In that case you are welcome to join me. But you have on far too many clothes. You would be far more comfortable without your gown."

Her eyes widened at his brazen suggestion.

He'd often been accused of having a wicked sense of humor, yet suddenly she was no longer amused. She lifted her chin again, eyeing him coolly.

The directness in her gaze, in her stance, was challenge incarnate.

And he could never resist a challenge. Especially not from a woman so alluring as this one.

He took the final step toward her, so their bodies almost touched. It startled him, how badly he wanted her. He couldn't remember ever being this aroused this swiftly. . . .